Midnight Revenge

A Fighter. A Survivor.
Rebuilt Through Strength...

Kathryn Marie

MIDNIGHT Duology Book Two

For information contact :

Kathryn Namenyi

55 Spencer St

PO Box 342

Lynn, MA 01905

authorkathrynmarie.com

Cover design by Celin Graphics

Chapter Header Design by Silver Wheel Press Designs

Developmental Edits by Cassidy Clarke

Copy Edits by Renee Dugan

ISBN: 9781734832327

First Edition: May 2021

10 9 8 7 6 5 4 3 2 1

Disclaimer:

This book has talk and conversations about abuse, sexual assault, and PTSD. Please be advised.

Dedication

To Nathaniel

For showing me what the word love truly means and

encouraging me to follow my dreams.

Always & Forever.

Chapter One

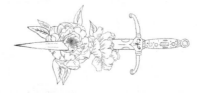

THE HUMID SUMMER AIR CLUNG TO Christiana's cheeks as she stumbled down the moonlit forest path, searching for a way back to the Palace. Her silk burgundy dress was caked with mud and ripped along the skirt from twigs biting her skin like feral animals attempting to capture their prey.

Yet she didn't let that stop her. She pushed forward, back to where she belonged, back to her best friend's birthday ball, to the event that would change her life forever.

"I need to get back!" she yelled into the emptiness ahead, her fingertips raw and chafed from pushing through the thicket of leaves and branches that blocked her way. "I need to tell Zander I love him!"

Her heart flooded, pressing against her chest as she saw the first glimmering outline of the palace turret along the horizon above the treeline. She pushed onward, forgetting the sweat melting her cosmetics and her mud-crusted hair half pinned back. All she could think about was getting back to the palace, to where she belonged.

To Zander.

"Don't worry, My Lady, I'll be kind..."

Christiana froze, her spine crawling, skin numb. Her eyes darted, squinting into the darkness to find the man who spoke, his venom-filled words shaking her to her soul. She knew that voice all too well, that phrase whispered into her ear on a night just like this.

The words repeated, over and over, filtering through the trees with the summer breeze. They pressed in all around her, smothering her screams down her throat before they could escape. She wanted to find him, to fight, to kill, but the coils of roots burrowing up from the ground trapped her feet and ankles, keeping her in that spot.

Her gaze lowered slowly, her breath shallow. Her hands were no longer her own, but bound together with a cord of rope, the rough, taupe bindings snaking around her wrists and rendering her useless. She struggled against them, twisting and tugging, desperate to get free, but it was useless. She wasn't in control anymore.

He was.

He emerged from the thicket of trees, his black doublet and pants ripped and burned in spots. His usually pale, smooth skin now mottled with angry red blisters and charred black skin. His injuries didn't stop him though, it only strengthened him. He stalked toward her, each movement full of purpose, until he was directly in front of her, his sour breath filling the inches between them, his body flushed against her own.

She wanted to run, to escape, but it was no use. She was at his mercy.

"You belong to me now." Julian laughed in her face, his twisted, diabolic grin and bright icy-blue eyes filled with glee as he rushed her, ready to devour every part of her: body, mind, and soul...

Christiana woke with a scream still lodged in her chest, her throat scratchy, body covered in a thin layer of sweat that stuck her nightgown and sheets to every inch of her flushed skin. Her blood pumped loudly in her ears, deafening as she looked around, disoriented and panicked for the few seconds it took to realize where she actually was.

She was not in the forest or back with Julian. She was safe in the palace walls, where she belonged.

The nightmare had been plaguing her for months, ever since she returned home for the fall season to pack up her belongings and prepare for her official move back to the palace. The sleepless nights and panic attacks over that time were almost unbearable, but she fortified herself to fight through them. She had hoped when she returned to the palace last night—the place she was so desperate to get back to in the dream—the images would subside. Yet it seemed her subconscious, and her Battled Brain, had different plans for her.

She stretched her tired, aching muscles, peeling herself out of bed, the seasonal winter chill still biting in the air as she waited for her stone fireplace to heat the space. She wrapped the comforting fabric of her wool robe around herself, her fingers still shaking as she tied it around her waist. The vise in her chest eased a bit when she gazed at her bedside table, a steaming cup of cinnamon black tea waiting for her to wake.

Her bare feet padded against the plush carpet, her fingers warming against her teacup as she moved to stare out the window. Her guest room was nothing more than an oversized bedroom, with a giant bed, a two-person table for eating, and a corner of elegant, sage green chairs placed by the window. Christiana pulled in a deep breath, the spicy steam infiltrating her senses, a rush of peace flooding her body as she watched leaves dance in the wind across the garden lawn.

She was home.

A rapid knock disrupted her newfound calm. She dropped her cup on the table, securing her robe tighter around her thin nightgown before pulling the door open. Dorina waited on the other side, beaming as she jumped into Christiana's arms. The Princess squealed, her curly brown hair tickling Christiana's cheek as they embraced each other.

"I'm so happy you're back!" Dorina pulled away, letting herself into the bedroom.

"I can tell," Christiana teased. She went to close the door and almost slammed it into a shy servant girl, a tray full of steaming pumpkin chocolate chip scones and chilled fresh fruit in her hands. She yanked the door back toward her. "I am so sorry!"

"It's quite alright, My Lady," the ginger-haired girl squeaked, eyes downcast as she scurried to place the tray on the dining table.

"I figured you would be hungry," Dorina said, grabbing a grape from Christiana's breakfast before sitting down. The princess was already dressed for the day, her delicate green dress flowing over the side of the chair.

"Thank you." Christiana sat down in the opposite chair, ripping off a piece of scone and savoring the spicy flavors dancing on her tongue. The heavy pastry filled her, helping to give back some of the strength her dreams had sapped overnight. "Although I'm surprised Natalia didn't bring it to me."

"Probably because she's too busy. She's been overseeing your room setup since early this morning. I think she wanted to get as much done as possible before you woke up."

"But why?" Christiana took a sip of her tea, trying her best not to eat too quickly and look like an uncultured child. "I could have helped."

"You're going to be a royal, Christiana," Dorina laughed, her fingers tracing the woodgrain pattern. "You need to get used to giving up control over a lot of things."

Christiana forced a laugh, her shoulders tense. Although she had grown up with a life of privilege, the majority of her childhood was spent under her abusive father's thumb; it was difficult at best to give up control of anything. "Well, even so, I would like to see where I am going to be living. Would you like to show me?"

She wanted to forget about the dream and the lingering terror.

Today was her first day back, and she wanted to savor every moment. She wouldn't let the darkness of her mind ruin this for her.

She was not broken. She was a survivor.

Dorina nodded enthusiastically, jumping from her chair and over to Christiana's travel trunk. Her hands rummaged through its contents, retrieving a steel blue dress, the light skirts and simple design perfect for a full day of unpacking. She dressed as quickly as possible, allowing Dorina to help only after changing into her underthings and pulling the dress over her head. She didn't need her friend to question the mangled mess of scars on her back, a gift left behind by her father. She quickly combed through her hair to make it silky smooth, the dark strands hanging softly down her back.

Then they rushed from the room, arms linked as they walked through the winding palace hallways. When they reached the Royal Wing, two guards stood at attention and saluted as they walked past. Most of the rooms in the hallways remained empty, only in use when other members of the extended Royal Family visited. Currently, only the King, Queen, Prince, and Princess lived there full-time. It was easy to tell which apartment would be hers, the door wide open as servants scurried in and out. Christiana walked in, her breath catching in her throat as she looked around her expansive new living quarters.

The setup was similar to her old apartment, with a large common area and multiple doors leading to adjacent rooms; but unlike her last place, this common area was meant for entertaining. The sitting area was twice as large, with overstuffed navy blue and silver couches and chairs crowded around the slate fireplace. The dining area consisted of a rectangular, mahogany table with eight chairs around it and a fully-stocked liquor cabinet standing proudly behind it.

She walked through the common area to her new bedroom, where Natalia, her Lady's Maid, directed people to unpack all of her belongings. Her four-poster bed already had her favorite smoke-gray-

and-burgundy quilt draped over it, the matching decorative pillows meticulously placed against the dark headboard. Her favorite cosmetics and hairpins were displayed on her three-paned mirror dressing table, and a stack of her favorite books was neatly arranged on the table next to a navy chaise lounge looking out the window and across the gardens. A pair of servants pulled each of her dresses and outfits out from her trunks, hanging them in the walk-in closet, rows of fabric arranged in color-coded order.

"What do you think?" came the deep voice she craved so much. She turned to find Zander leaning in the threshold of her bedroom, a gleam of amusement in his sapphire eyes.

Her pulse raced against her wrists. Her fiancé had welcomed her when she arrived late last night, yet that rush of heat still crawled up her collarbone and her heart strained with the need to be closer to him. She hoped this feeling never disappeared when she looked at the man she loved.

She joined him, her fingers tugging on each other. "Zander, this is too much."

"Of course it isn't." He pulled her hands to him, gently placing a kiss on each one. "It's exactly like all of ours."

"I just feel like I don't deserve it."

"Well, I feel the same way about you sometimes, so I guess we're even," he teased, pulling her into a hug. "Don't get too used to it, though. We'll be moving into our apartment in only a few months."

"Now, that, I'm excited for," she smiled, placing a small kiss on his cheek.

"Why are the two of you so cute together?" Dorina whined from the common area, a smile teasing her lips.

"You better get used to it, little sister. It's only going to get worse from here." Zander laughed and took Christiana's hand, bringing them both to join Dorina. The princess had helped herself to the glasses and a bottle of sparkling wine from Christiana's liquor cabinet, which she poured in three generous servings.

She handed glasses to Christiana and Zander. "To great friends finally becoming family."

"Thank you," Christiana smiled, taking a sip of her favorite bubbly drink. She silently sighed as the chilled liquid fizzled down her throat, not even bothered that it was still a bit early to be enjoying an alcoholic beverage.

"Did Zander tell you the exciting news?" Dorina asked, dropping herself onto one of the plush velvet chairs and curling her legs onto the seat.

"Not yet." Zander frowned, sitting on the matching couch opposite it, Christiana curling up next to him.

Her brow furrowed. "What is it?"

"Mother and Father invited you to have breakfast with us tomorrow morning," he explained, his fingers playing with hers. "We have it three mornings a week together in their apartment."

"Only the family is ever invited," Dorina beamed. "Not even Julian was allowed to attend."

"How nice," Christiana said, her stomach twisting.

She couldn't stop thinking about Julian's admission at the end of the summer, moments before Christiana ended his life, that the King had known about her father's constant beatings and punishments. Seeing King Lucian again was a cause of dread for Christiana the past few months. She didn't have any proof that Julian's words were valid, but her nerves still itched at the thought of reuniting with a ruler who potentially approved of abuse—or at least allowed it to avoid messy conversations. She hadn't even told Zander; she wasn't ready to say it out loud and break the wonderful image he held of his father—especially since she had no proof the allegations were true, only her twisting gut and shadowy thoughts.

"I was going to tell you tonight," Zander explained.

"It's going to be wonderful. I'm just a little nervous is all," she lied.

"Don't worry! We will both be there next to you." Dorina winked as she took another sip of her sparkling wine.

"She's right. You won't have to be alone for even a moment during it. That's a promise." Zander brushed a gentle kiss against her hair. "Now, I hate that I have to, but I must leave. Meetings for the rest of the day. Come to my apartment for dinner?"

"Of course," she agreed, squeezing his hand one last time before he departed.

"So," Dorina plunked down next to her, the cushions bouncing underneath them. "Need help organizing everything?"

"Of course." Christiana leaned her head against her shoulder, allowing Dorina to refill her glass in hopes that she would forget tomorrow morning's plans.

Chapter Two

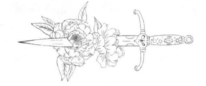

CHRISTIANA WANTED TO AVOID BREAKFAST WITH her future in-laws at all costs, but it didn't matter if she was able to evade it for a day or a week or even a month. Eventually, she would have to face the Royal Family.

Eventually, she would have to face the King.

She wasn't sure what her reaction would be or how she would handle it, but whenever she thought about Lucian, her heart flooded with anger, bubbling along every inch of skin and flushing her with heat. Anger that she had held back for so long, assuming it was just her father's inability to control himself that had allowed him to beat her for so long. She could only wonder what other nobles and commoners had pleaded for their safety just to be laughed away by King Lucian. The idea made her shoulders ache with deep-knitted tension.

The rap of knuckles against her front door pulled Christiana out of her angry trance. Placing one last pearl pin in Christiana's hair,

Natalia walked into the other room to open the door.

"My Lady," she called from the common room. "Prince Alekzander is here to escort you to breakfast."

Christiana shot up instantly, cheeks slightly flushed through her cosmetics, and hurried into the common room to greet Zander. He looked incredibly handsome, dressed in a simple black-and-silver doublet paired with gray pants and black boots. His dirty blond hair was tamed down with style cream, well-coiffed out of his face. It wouldn't stay tidy for long, as his favorite nervous tick was to run his fingers through it in frustration.

"You look beautiful, love," he remarked, taking in her simple pewter-and-lavender dress, its full skirt and long sleeves keeping her warm in the chilly morning.

"Thank you," she greeted, pushing herself up on her toes to steal a kiss.

"Are you ready?" he smiled, taking her hand in his arm.

"As I'll ever be," she sighed, following him from her apartment and down the hall toward the King and Queen's suite.

"It's just breakfast, it's an hour at most." He turned toward her, taking her hands in his to give them a reassuring kiss. "It will be quick and painless."

Taking a deep breath in, trying to believe Zander's words, she nodded. Knocking on the large double doors, they waited for them to swing open, revealing the King and Queen's grand apartment.

They were the first to arrive, Dorina nowhere in sight. Lucian and Penelope were already sitting down to enjoy their meal, Lucian reading over some reports while Penelope enjoyed a leatherbound poetry book.

"Hello, Son." Lucian looked up from the parchment in his hand. "Christiana." He gave her a quick nod, a warm smile spread across his lips.

"Your Majesties." Christiana curtsied, her knees knocking together beneath her skirts.

"Oh, please, dear, you can call us Lucian and Penelope from now on. We're going to be family, after all." Penelope smiled, glee dazzling her face.

"Thank you...Penelope," she replied, the taste of the Queen's first name foreign on her tongue. Her skin prickled, gaining intensity along her limbs with each step she walked inside. She took the seat Zander graciously pulled out for her, and servants placed plates of steaming food in front of them instantly. Zander indulged almost immediately in the fresh griddle cakes topped with stewed apples and cinnamon compote.

"Did you read this yet?" Lucian handed a piece of parchment over to his son.

Zander swallowed his bite before taking it from his father's outstretched hand. "What is it?"

"The budget for the military base repairs in Astary." Lucian leaned back in his chair, his eyes never leaving Zander's face as he scanned the page. "Seems there was a military exercise gone wrong and one of the barracks was damaged in the process."

"Sorry I'm late!" Dorina interrupted as she entered the room. Christiana wished she could be that perky in the morning; Dorina looked absolutely radiant in her hunter-green dress, every inch of her perfectly placed for the day.

"Good morning, darling," Penelope greeted her daughter, finally putting her book down next to her. Dorina greeted her family with quick pecks on their cheeks before settling into the free seat across from Christiana with a wink.

Zander barely moved when Dorina leaned down to kiss his cheek, his brow creased, tapping the end of his fork gently against his lips. "Seems a bit high, though. Was the whole building destroyed?"

"Not to my knowledge." Lucian leaned forward, elbow braced on the table between him and Zander. "However, I haven't sent a Council Member out yet to assess the issues."

"Did I miss something?" Dorina's eyes darted between her brother and father as she smoothed her crème cloth napkin across her lap.

"Not too much," Penelope answered. "Just their typical work talk they can never seem to keep away from family time."

Dorina shook her head, lifting her steaming teacup to her lips. "They'll never learn."

"Can I see the report?" Christiana inquired, leaning over Zander's shoulder to get a peek at the words and numbers scribbled across it in onyx ink. She had received reports like this in the past, specifically from tenants requesting funds to rebuild dilapidated buildings that they needed for the harvest. Although it was ultimately up to Christiana if she wanted to renovate her properties, she always tried her best to find the funds to make her businesses profitable. However, she had come across some bad reports over the years claiming more damage than there actually was so the farmers and workers could line their own pockets.

"Of course," Lucian said, his voice light and kind as he smiled at her. Zander placed the parchment in between them. "Although, the numbers might not make complete sense since you haven't attended one of our budget meetings recently."

"It cannot hurt to begin getting used to the reports," she challenged, her eyes never leaving Lucian's face. "I will be a part of reading and reviewing them one day, after all."

Lucian's smile held, but his fingers tightened ever-so-slightly around his fork.

"Maybe Ana should join us for the Council meeting tomorrow when we go over this," Zander suggested. "It might be good for her to start sitting in on them."

"We'll have to see if we can work that in," he took the parchment back. "She may not have time, depending on what Penelope has scheduled for her."

Christiana's fork hovered a few inches from her open mouth. "Excuse me?"

"Oh, that reminds me!" Penelope perked up. "Now that Dorina's here, we can discuss the schedule for the day."

"Yes!" Dorina's face lit up and she practically bounced out of her chair.

"Here you go." Penelope handed her daughter a square piece of parchment, then offered another. "Christiana?"

"Oh, I'm sorry." She dropped her fork so she didn't have to let go of Zander's hand to grab the parchment. She wasn't about to let go of the only thing anchoring her through the excruciatingly slow meal. "I didn't realize we had any events today."

"Not events...meetings," Penelope explained. "To plan out the wedding."

"Oh." Christiana fought to keep a tight smile plastered across her face. "I didn't realize we would be starting that so soon."

Penelope beamed. "Of course. We don't have a lot of time before the first day of spring arrives and we need to make use of every second we have."

"What makes the first day of spring so important?"

"That's your wedding day!" Penelope exclaimed.

"Is it?" Christiana's stomach churned, the few bites of her breakfast threatening to escape as she turned to Zander. "Were you aware of this?"

"Can't say I was." He peeked over her shoulder, scanning the scrawl of words scratched across the parchment card. "Why didn't you tell me?"

"Oh, you've been so busy with Council meetings and whatnot, I figured I would just tell you both together." Penelope waved her hand, her smile never fading as she jotted notes down on a length of parchment next to her.

"I see," Christiana peered at her new schedule for the day. It was packed full, starting right after breakfast and not ending until dinner.

Planning the wedding was something she had barely thought about the entire time she prepared to move here. She was looking forward to her marriage to Zander, to their future and the plans they were preparing for the betterment of Viri, but the actual wedding eluded her thoughts.

"Did you have something more pressing to work on?" Lucian asked, peeking up from the forms in front of him.

"No, not technically." Christiana's voice faltered, her throat constricting. "I just wanted to start getting my new normal in order for running my business in a different province."

"Oh, of course." Lucian nodded. "Just make sure you carve out plenty of time for Penelope's meetings for the next few months. It's the first royal wedding in decades, we want to make sure it's perfect for the two of you."

Her mood fell, stomach twisting at that responsibility. Although she adored attending events, she never relished the thought of actually planning an opulent ball. She wasn't the type to get excited over picking out the perfect place setting or arguing about what flowers were in season. She didn't care about shades of white or if the décor on the pastries matched the lace patterns of the linens. She cared about plenty of things, but event details were not on that list, and she had little desire to add them to it.

Tension squeezed her body in a vise-grip, every inch of her speckled with numbness. She pulled in deep breaths as nonchalantly as possible while anxiety tried to sneak to the surface. She had to force it down; she couldn't let them see her this way, her weaknesses on display.

Christiana's eyes fell to the table, her discarded fork and barely-touched plate. She wouldn't be able to eat anymore. "Of course, Lucian."

Still holding Zander's hand in a deathgrip, Christiana refused to let go for the rest of breakfast.

***

Christiana was right: she hated wedding planning. Each of the meetings bled into the next, with one professional after another coming in to talk about the honor of being considered for the royal wedding. After hours and hours of sitting in a chair pretending to be interested in different types of linens and plate designs, Christiana just wanted to relax in her apartment, away from all the scrutiny.

Growing up a victim of abuse meant staying out of the light was a part of daily survival; risking yourself by being in the middle of social chaos was a gamble not worth taking. Once her father died, she'd continued living out of society's light, but by her own choice. She had spent her entire adult life as an assassin, keeping out of the public eye for her own safety, taught to be one with the shadows and to never step out of them. She had been comforted by them for so long; when she was enveloped in them, it felt like being hugged by darkness that understood the stains on her soul. It protected her from the pain, and she wore it like armor. But now she was marrying the future King of Viri and was about to become its future Queen.

She wasn't allowed to hide anymore.

Wrapped up in her own thoughts, she barely paid attention to where she was going as she meandered through the hallways back to her apartment. She didn't even look up until she collided headfirst with someone's broad chest.

"Ow," Christiana winced, startled she could be so oblivious to her surroundings.

"Are you alright?" asked a strained, familiar voice.

Looking up, she met Rowan's guarded green eyes. Her breath hitched, and she fiddled with the bodice of her gown. "I'm fine, are you?"

"Yes." He took a step back, his posture rigid and his hands set behind his back. His face was made of stone, giving no emotions away at seeing Christiana for the first time since she left. Her fingertips went numb, desperate to reach out to him, to hug him like the friend she saw him as, even though he was treating her like a stranger.

They were all in an awkward position right now, and Rowan got the short end of the stick. He'd wanted to court her, he did all the right things and said all the right words, he was everything she had thought she wanted. Then Zander also made his intentions known, scrambling Christiana's mind and heart. The two men hadn't made it easy for her, showing her the two completely different lives they offered. In the end, she realized being in love and having passion in her future marriage meant more to her than a stable life, which was something only Zander could provide.

"How are you?" Her whisper filled the tense silence that settled between them.

"Fine. I heard you arrived a few days ago."

"Yes, I'm all moved into my new apartment." She swayed, her feet tingling, begging her to move so she could work off the energy building in her core. "I didn't realize you would be here."

"I live here," he replied flatly.

"I know, I just thought..."

"That I would move out?"

Her words tripped out of her lips. "N-no, I just meant..."

"I felt no need to leave the place that has been my home for the past three years." He shrugged, his throat quivering as he looked down at her. "No matter how hard it might be on all of us at the beginning."

Although she didn't want to marry Rowan, she always felt a deep friendship with him. It had been the part of their connection that made him such a good courtship option to begin with. They were never afraid to be comfortable around each other, and she missed that terribly. She missed the goofy, almost boyish grin he always wore. She missed the spark of joy that used to radiate from his forest-green eyes. But most of all, she missed talking to him.

She tugged at her fingers. "Would you like to have dinner with us one night this week? Or maybe we can all play a few rounds of cards together? I'm sure Dorina and Zander..."

"I haven't spent much time with Zee since you left." His gaze avoided hers, his shoulders hunched as he took a few steps past her.

She kept on his heels, following him down the marbled-floor hallway. "He mentioned that a few times in his letters." The heartbreak over losing his best friend's companionship had radiated off those letters whenever Zander mentioned it. It had shattered her heart every time. "But that doesn't mean we can't try and fix things!"

"Just because you are ready to repair friendships, doesn't mean I am." He halted, turning back to face her. "I can't just forget what happened this summer."

"I know it isn't easy..." His face flashed with pain, his cheeks flushing. "I just want you to be happy, and I will do anything to help make it so."

The whisper of a smile appeared at the corner of his lips before disappearing back into a frown. "I know you've always been there for your friends, but your companionship isn't what I need right now to be happy. What I need is space from you and Zander while I try and figure out what comes next."

"Alright, if that's what you want." She swallowed a lump in her throat, staring down at her feet to conceal the shame creasing her face. Her pulse raced painfully against her neck, her vision beginning to tunnel.

Not again, she thought as panic crept from her mind like a poison.

He sighed, lifting her chin to look up at him. "If you need me for an emergency, a real emergency, you can call for me. But otherwise, please, just leave me alone for a bit. I can't do this every day of my life."

"Of course," she agreed. He began to walk away, but something compelled her to say one more thing. "At least ...tell me you're staying occupied with things that make you happy?"

He halted his steps, rubbing the back of his neck before turning back around. "I'm doing everything I can to move on from this summer."

With a nod, he hurried away, leaving her and her breaking heart alone in the quiet hallway.

Chapter Three

"DON'T MAKE ME GO BACK!" CHRISTIANA teased as Zander led her back inside the palace after a brisk morning ride through the frost-coated forest, the sunrise filtering through the trees as they cantered along the paths surrounding the palace grounds. They had been busy for the past few days, Zander always pulled into a meeting with his father and Christiana forced into more wedding planning; it was nothing short of a dream to steal some time alone to just be Zander and Ana again.

"It cannot be that bad." He placed a gentle kiss on her temple as he tucked her hand in the crook of his arm, leading them down the marble-floor hall of the main entrance.

"We spent *two hours* debating between a damask rose and a peace rose and which one would look better in the arrangements." Christiana's feet dragged with each step up the carpeted staircase that led to the Royal Wing. "I personally didn't see much difference between the two."

"Roses?" His brows creased, his wind-blown hair still hanging partially in his eyes. "I thought peonies were your favorite flower?"

She bit her bottom lip. "You remember that?"

He leaned down, lips grazing her earlobe. "It's easy to remember when you concoct your perfume with them."

"Fair," she giggled, her head bowed to hide her flaming cheeks from him. "Doesn't matter, though. When I suggested them as the main flower, your mother informed me that roses are the traditional choice and have been the main flower in the past five Royal Weddings."

He squeezed her hand, stopping her in front of her apartment door. "I'm sorry."

"Don't be." She shook her head as she entered her rooms, Zander right behind her. A pot of tea was already set out on the dining table, two steaming cups poured for them to enjoy. "They're just flowers."

"I just hate that Mother isn't listening to your ideas." He pulled the smooth mahogany chair out for her, her black winter riding jacket spilling over the sides. "It is your wedding, after all. Would you like me to talk to her?"

Christiana almost choked on her first sip of tea, her chest burning as she forced it down. "No, I don't, because I highly doubt that will make any of this better. I think I just have to get through all of this planning. It's just a party...what really matters to me is the marriage."

"I agree. A ball is a ball and it will certainly be enjoyable." He leaned forward in his chair, his eyes sparkling, grasping her hand in his across the table. "However, getting to spend the rest of my life with you sounds like a much more pleasurable adventure I cannot wait for."

She rolled her eyes, but couldn't stop the laugh that escaped her lips or the droplets of sweat that beaded along the base of her neck. How he still affected her as if it were still the first day of their courtship was beyond her understanding, but she didn't care at all.

A hard punch against the front door stole her attention, her tingling nerves settling a bit at the distraction. Natalia came scurrying from Christiana's bedroom to open the door; Jay, Zander's valet, panted as he stumbled over the threshold.

"Jay? What's wrong?" Zander stood, his shoulders pulled back as he approached the man.

"Your Highness, My Lady," he bowed quickly, his breaths still labored. "The King and Queen have sent me. They need to see you right away. There seems to be an emergency they need your assistance with."

"What kind of emergency?"

"I'm not sure." Jay shook his head. "They just asked me to fetch you and bring you to them."

"Alright, then. Christiana, are you coming?" Zander turned to her, his hand outstretched. Her stomach lurched as she grasped it, the two of them rushing out the door on Jay's heels.

***

"Mother, Father, what is going on?" Zander asked, as they came upon the King and Queen standing rigid in one of the narrow servant hallways. People were milling around, trying to get their morning chores done, but a small cluster of bodies blocked their way, crowding around something in the middle of the claustrophobic area.

"We need to discuss something with you," the King started, his sharp, sideways glance trailing Christiana as she approached.

"What is it?"

Lucian's arms crossed tightly against his chest. "A month ago, a young servant died in the hallways late at night."

"What?" Zander balked. Christiana's stomach dropped, her jaw slack as she stared at Zander's parents.

"The physicians ruled it an illness. However, two weeks later, another young servant died mysteriously in the night." Penelope

23

twisted a handkerchief between her hands as she looked up at her son. "We have been trying to figure out the cause."

"Did you find another body?" Christiana asked, frost snaking through her veins as she tried to peer around the huddling of men crouched a few feet ahead, their faces tense and pensive. Sunlight streamed through the single window, casting their shadows against the stone wall.

"Yes." Lucian nodded tightly, grimness settling across his pale face. "The third one in the past four weeks. We're trying our best to get the poor girl's body out of here before too many people catch a glimpse of it and rumors start to fly like birds in the rafters, but the physicians insisted on examining it before we move her."

"Why are you just telling me about this now?" Anger laced Zander's voice. Christiana grabbed his hand, rubbing her thumb in gentle circles against his palm. "Don't you think I deserved to know the moment it started?"

"We didn't want to trouble you," Lucian explained. "I was already keeping you busy with so many other things, and your mother felt it was best to wait until we had more details to trouble you with it."

"Did you now?" Zander said, looking down at his mother, eyes dull.

"You were already burying yourself in work to keep your mind busy while Christiana was away," Penelope said, and a blush spread across Zander's cheeks. "I didn't want you to become obsessive about this, too. I just wanted to protect you."

"I get it, but you can't keep protecting me. If you want me to be prepared to take the crown soon, you need to prepare me for everything. It's time for complete transparency here."

"He's right," Lucian nodded, his arm snaking around his wife's shoulders, pulling her to his side.

"Fine," Penelope sighed. "From now on, you'll receive all the information along with us. First thing we have to do is figure out what's killed them."

"You don't know yet?" Christiana pressed, a lump in her throat making it difficult to force the words from her lips.

"Unfortunately, no," Lucian admitted. "As I said, it was originally ruled an illness with how it affected the skin and body."

"Did the physicians rule that out already?" Zander leaned against the wall, gently stroking his chin.

"I'm assuming it ruled itself out," Christiana muttered under her breath.

"And why would you say that, my dear?" Lucian's gaze burned into her like flame trying to consume a scrap of parchment.

"Diseases are erratic." She took a step forward, shoulders pulled back to make herself as tall as possible when she stared into Lucian's eyes. "If it was one that spread from person to person, we wouldn't see such perfect timing in the killings. Which means the deaths are happening on purpose and the exact moment someone wants it to happen."

"Very perceptive." The King smirked, his eyebrows perked upwards.

"Alright," Zander interjected, his hand wrapping around Christiana's arm, gently tugging her backwards. "Since disease is ruled out, what is killing them?"

"Poison." Christiana's cheeks went numb as the physicians cleared away, the young woman's body finally coming into her view. Her insides twisted when she looked at the poor victim, her golden-flecked green eyes still frozen open from her last moments of pure pain and terror.

"That's what we were thinking as well," Penelope confirmed.

"May I take a closer look?" Christiana didn't wait for a response, her feet taking her toward the body sprawled on the floor.

Lucian sighed. "Just don't touch her."

The King's words barely registered with Christiana, who used every bit of her self-control not to touch the victim's tender skin. She had seen this before, every symptom and marking. She knew exactly what killed this young girl, and the other victims.

But it was impossible.

"What is it, love?" Zander asked, circling around her to stand on the opposite side of the body.

"Nothing," she lied through her teeth. "It's just horrific is all." She looked up at Zander, locking their gazes, pleading silently with him to understand. His face softened with a gentle nod.

Looking down again, she took in every inch of the affected skin: the dark red coloring that enveloped the body, the dozens of fiery blisters, and the scent of burned flesh mixed with old sweat. She had seen this poison used just a handful of times, because only two people had ever killed with it—herself being one of them, to kill Julian all those months ago. She had learned to brew the special poison, Crimson Fire, from the person who created it.

The only other person who knew how to brew it: her Mentor, Marek, the Crimson Knight.

Chapter Four

ILENCE FILLED THE AIR, THE TENSION between them hanging heavy as Christiana and Zander walked back to her apartment. Her brain wouldn't calm down, conjectures and conspiracies swirling as she tried to make sense of what she just saw.

There was no doubt Crimson Fire was the cause of that poor girl's death; she knew that poison and the symptoms that came with it all too well. Yet she had no idea how that could even be. Marek was the one to create it almost fifteen years ago and he'd kept the recipe a secret for almost as long. The only other person he ever taught it to was Christiana herself, after years of training with him. So how did it end up in the castle?

"Are you going to explain?" Zander finally asked when they entered Christiana's quiet apartment.

Robert, her Head Guard and assistant in all her assassin duties, had arrived for the day, his fingers nervously twirling one of his daggers as he sat at Christiana's table. "Is everything alright? Natalia told me you both rushed off about an hour ago."

"No, it's not." Christiana fell into the comforts of her couch, muscles and mind laced with exhaustion. Although she had only been awake for a few hours, the day had already flown by, wearying her with all its confusing thoughts and concerns. She buried her face in her hands, pulling in deep breaths through her nose to push herself through the fog clouding her mind.

"My parents just informed us that there seems to be a serial killer in the castle. Three young girls have died over the past six weeks and they have no idea how it's happening," Zander related, sitting down next to Christiana, his fingers gently stroking her back, waves of calm spreading down her spine and through her limbs.

"That's terrible!" Robert exclaimed, sheathing his dagger as he stood, his long stride bringing him to sit across from them.

"Did you recognize something?" Zander asked her.

"Yes," Christiana admitted. Her training as an assassin pleaded with her to keep the secret locked safely in her mind, but that wasn't the right thing to do. People's lives were at stake—young women who couldn't defend themselves. This was her duty as a noble, and future Queen, of Viri. "I was right, the girl *was* poisoned."

Zander's brow creased. "How could you know without the physicians diagnosing her?"

"Because I recognized the poison. It has a few distinct aftereffects." She sighed and shook her head as she stood up on tingling legs, walking like an entranced person to her bedroom—curious if her stash was still safely untouched. She knew deep down that no one could have found the false top of her trunk, but her tightened heart pushed her to make sure it was safely secure.

To most people, the trunk's contents were underwhelming, just spare clothing and other unnecessary items for Christiana's daily life, but to her, this was more important. Her fingers ran along the top of the trunk, finding the hidden tab and pulling it downward, revealing the compartment for the essential contents of her alter ego. Her small pouch of poisons fell out, tangled in the soft confines of her long coat. She picked it up, the leather supple against her palm as she walked back into her common area. She rifled through the contents for a few seconds before encountering the long vial, a blood-colored liquid swirling against the sides as she handed it to Zander.

"Crimson Fire?" He read aloud the hand-written label.

"Yes, it is a strong and painful poison. I have only used it maybe a half a dozen times." She sighed, dropping her poison pouch onto the mahogany table and settling back into the warmth of her velvet couch. "It's a cruel punishment, but sometimes my clients want that for their abusers. So I always make sure to have a stash on hand just in case."

"What does it do?" Zander asked, gingerly handing the vial back to Christiana, as if holding it would kill him instantly.

She rolled the vial in between her fingers, the glass cool against her flushed skin. "It simmers the blood, practically boiling the victim alive from the inside out."

"That's horrific." Zander's sapphire eyes widened as he stared at the dark liquid.

"The killing doesn't take too long, but it's effective. It's what I used on Julian when I had to change my plan. He suffered, just like Eliza wanted him to."

"Alright...so it's a poison that assassins use. Do you know how many other assassins know how to make it? Or at least an idea?"

"Well..." Christiana stalled, feeling Robert's gaze bearing into her. Her shoulders squirming under the pressure, a bead of sweat rolling down the back of her neck as she avoided his eyes. Christiana had told Robert about her mentor a few years into their partnership, once they had finally become friends. He knew Marek's assassin identity and the poison he used in most of his killings. She could only imagine the questions he had for her now.

"Christiana..." Zander coaxed.

"I know the person who created it," she admitted, her eyes downcast. "The last I heard, he hadn't told anyone else besides me how to make it."

"Who is it?" Zander demanded, his fingers wrapping around her wrist as she looked up at him.

"My mentor," she whispered.

Zander blinked rapidly. "Are you sure?"

"I would know it anywhere. No one else has made a poison quite like it." Her body began to vibrate, every inch of her desperate to move. She pulled away from Zander's grasp, grabbing her poison pouch and safely storing her Crimson Fire back inside. "Other assassins have tried copying it, but never seem to get the recipe right."

"So are you saying he's the one behind this?"

"Of course not!" Christiana snapped, glaring at Zander.

Marek was a talented assassin, but one of the things Christiana knew for sure was that he was not a murderer. He saw it as a job and nothing more, something that she learned from him and took to heart every time she chose to take on her clients.

"But you're saying the two of you are the only ones who know about it." Zander crossed his arms tightly. "And I know you aren't the one behind it."

"Do you think he could have taught someone else without telling you?" Robert mused, his shoulders hunched as he leaned his elbows on his legs.

"Absolutely not."

"He did teach you," Zander argued. "Maybe he enjoyed teaching and wanted to pass on his knowledge to more people."

Christiana stepped furiously toward him. "What are you accusing him of?"

"Nothing! But obviously he's good at teaching with the way your skills turned out. Maybe he wanted to keep going."

"Absolutely not." Christiana shook her head as she paced circles around the room, the two men's gazes following her every footstep. "Even if he had, he would have told me."

"Are you sure about that?" Robert asked.

"Yes." She leaned against the slate fireplace, her fingers tracing patterns against the rough texture of the stone. "He barely leaves his house now that he's retired, and prefers to be alone. Unless someone approached him about it, I don't see him actively searching for people to teach."

"Even so, he is the originator of the poison." Zander slowly stood, his footsteps muffled against the thick carpet as he approached her. "Which means he is the best lead we have right now."

"I know," Christiana admitted, her head hanging as Zander grasped her shoulders, the touch almost searing her anxious body. She dug her fingernails into the jagged fireplace stone, pulling deep breaths in through her nose, counting to four before releasing them from her body again. She logically knew there was a chance Marek could be tied to this somehow, since she never shared information about it with anyone, but it didn't stop the pang of guilt that settled in her gut.

She was very protective of the Crimson Fire recipe, almost as much as she was protective of the recipe for her own Midnight poison. Marek taught it to her as a graduation of sorts, a way of admitting how much he trusted and cared for her after years of training together. She held onto that information and that memory with such care, she never wanted to betray it.

"I can arrange a meeting with him," she said, her spinning head finally coming back to equilibrium. She needed a clear mind to exonerate Marek's name from this mess. "But I'll need to travel to him."

"He can't come here?" Zander asked.

"No, he avoids Cittadina when he can." Though Marek's reasons for avoiding the capitol were extremely valid, they were not her secrets to tell. "Like I said, he lives near my estate. I can travel back home soon with the excuse that I needed to see my family for something."

"Let me come with you," Zander offered.

"I don't think that's a good idea."

"I figured, but I still want to come."

"Zander..." She was at a loss for words, not exactly sure how to explain why she was hesitating. It wasn't just the fact that Marek wouldn't like having a royal poking into his business, but the faint voice in the back of Christiana's mind told her that she could take advantage of the situation. Her dreams about Julian were more vivid and terror-inducing as ever, her nights restless and exhausting each time she laid her head on a pillow. She needed to figure out a way to get her Battled Brain under control again, and in the past, Marek always seemed to have answers for her. This could be the perfect opportunity to bring it up.

However, she had yet to let Zander know about her condition. Guilt always twisted her stomach when she thought about it, but she still kept the secret locked away. She wasn't ready to show him how dark her mind really was, how tainted she felt some days or how weak her condition tried to convince her she'd become.

She was not broken. She was a survivor.

He raked a lock of hair behind her ear, breaking her from her trance. "This isn't just about you, it's about the safety of the people in this castle. My people. I need to be a part of figuring out who is trying to hurt them."

Christiana grazed his cheek with her fingertips, her heart melting.

"How about this: I'll write a letter to him saying I have to meet him about an important state issue and you want to come along. If he agrees, then you can join me. But only if he gives permission."

She pointed sharply at him, the tip of her finger barely grazing the tip of his nose. His boyish grin spread across his face, his lips pressed together tightly as if he was trying to stifle a laugh—which he most likely was. "Deal." He leaned down and kissed her on the cheek. "As long as you promise to make a decent case to him as to why I should be allowed to."

She rolled her eyes. "I've been told I can be quite convincing."

He shook his head. "I hate to leave, but I have a meeting in twenty minutes and I have to grab a few things from my room before I go to the council chamber. Will you be alright?"

"I'll be fine." She kissed his knuckles. "I've seen dead bodies before."

"Oh, of course, it slipped my mind." He kissed hers back before pulling away, turning toward Robert with a nod. "Take care of her, Lieutenant."

Robert straightened, gripping the pommel of the sword swinging from his hip and beaming with pride at his recently-reinstated military status. "Always, Your Highness."

Zander let himself out, Christiana's shoulders falling the minute he left the room.

"Are you alright?" Robert strode over to her, his hand resting on her knotted shoulder. "You look a bit pale."

"I'm fine." She shook her head, walking over to her desk opposite the dining table, different reports and parchments already strewn across it. "This is all just a bit more complicated than I anticipated."

Robert retrieved his satchel from the dining table, offering her a palm-sized envelope. "Then maybe this isn't the best time to be handing this over to you."

She fell into her chair, arms flopping over the rests. "What is it?"

He strode over to place the envelope on her outstretched hand. "It's a letter from Ellie." It had been a while since she heard from her Tagri informant. "You told me to wait for the perfect job to come in. I think this might be a good one for you."

She tore it open, the seal already broken from when Robert read it. After Julian, she had decided to go on a hiatus for the past few months; that physically and mentally exhausting job, along with the fact that she had only a few months to completely uproot her life, had made the break from Maiden jobs a necessity. However, a few weeks ago, her fingers began itching for her assassin life again. She had spent countless hours at her little hidden cottage back home, sharpening her weapons and brewing as many poisons as possible. She had asked Robert to filter through all the requests sent into her to find the perfect job: one that was simple, yet would bring the sizzle of adrenaline to her blood that always came when she was hunting.

She scanned the letter, the muscles in her cheek twitching. "Actually, I think this is perfect timing."

It seemed simple enough: a young man needed her to take out his mother, who had been molesting him for about a year. The details of her routines and physical descriptions were well-written in the client's letter. He didn't even want to meet her, he just wanted his mother's life to end. Christiana's heart ached, her limbs tingling.

She was ready for her next job, to remember the strength she carried inside her. No matter what her body and mind tried to convince her every day.

Chapter Five

THE AFTERNOON CAME TOO QUICKLY FOR
Christiana, her mind already clouding over as she stared
at the dozens of color swatches meticulously arranged
across Dorina's dining table. After the first few meetings talking about
all the different details that needed to be planned out, it was time to
start actually making decisions—which apparently started with
choosing the color palette of the wedding.

Christiana wished she didn't have to focus on this now, not when
hours ago she had learned innocent lives were being taken in the castle.
She wanted to help, the urge to assist those in need churning inside
her, begging to do everything and anything necessary to capture the
person behind the cruel attacks. Yet she also knew there was nothing
she *could* do until she heard back from Marek.

It was going to be a long week waiting for his response.

Christiana walked around the table, a teacup in one hand as she
scanned the color-coded swatches, the rainbow of shades ranging from

the purest white to the brightest greens and the deepest blacks. She pulled out a few pieces, a smile gently pressing against her lips as she held them up for Dorina and Penelope.

"These are my favorite colors." She rubbed her thumb over the silky fabric, the deep burgundy, midnight blue, and pewter gray complimenting each other in their mysterious allure.

Penelope fiddled with the edge of her own teacup. "Well, they are lovely, dear..."

Christiana sighed. "But?"

"They are too dark." Penelope put her teacup down on the table, picking up a few of her own choices: a girlish blush pink, a soft lilac purple, and bone ivory with flecks of gold running throughout. "Royal weddings are meant to evoke hope and joy within the guests, to represent the prosperous future of the next King and Queen. I think these colors would be best."

Christiana tried not to balk at the pieces of fabric Penelope handed her. They were bright, festive for spring, and the complete opposite of what Christiana found soothing. They reminded her of the past, of the poofy dresses her father made her wear when she was a child. When he wanted her to be someone she was not; to hide the truth of their dark, dangerous secrets. Those colors were not who she was, and they were not Zander, either. They were the expectation, but not the reality.

"They are...very suitable for a spring wedding." Christiana nodded. "But I think I would be more comfortable if it wasn't so...bright."

Dorina pulled the fabrics from her mother's hands, then from Christiana's. "I think there is an easy solution to this; we just need to get creative."

She fiddled with the swatches, eyes zipping between them as she rearranged them into a few different combinations, even snatching a few other fabrics that hadn't been chosen yet. Christiana's heart warmed; leave it to Dorina to make sure everyone was pleased.

"There." She stood back proudly, her chest puffing out as she gestured to the three pieces of fabric on display. "Midnight blue, blush, and oyster ivory. One color from each of your piles with one that combines both. See? It's an ivory like you want, Mother, but with a grayish undertone for Ana's preferences. What do you think?"

Christiana stepped forward, wrapping her arm around Dorina's shoulders and tapping their temples together. "I love it. Thank you."

Penelope sighed, her shoulders sagging. "I suppose it will do. We just have to make sure to balance everything properly so it doesn't look too dark during the event."

Dorina squeezed Christiana's arm, the two of them giving a sideways glance at each other. They silently agreed: that was the best response they were going to get.

***

Two more hours of debate passed before Penelope had to leave for a meeting with one of her charity councils, leaving Christiana and Dorina alone. Dorina made the best of it, yanking Christiana into her bedroom where a row of new gowns and dresses were lined up and ready for her to try on.

"Sit down!" Dorina practically shoved Christiana into the mountain of gold pillows strewn across her bed. "I need your opinions."

Christiana welcomed the excuse to relax, graciously removing her flat shoes and placing them at the foot of the bed before curling up into the soft, down-feathered bedding. Dorina disappeared for a few moments, leaving Christiana's eyes to catch on something particularly alluring on the bedside table: a lovely bouquet of ivory calla lilies, pink roses, and blue hydrangeas. Christiana ran her fingers over the soft petals, her brow creasing. Dorina didn't typically leave a floral arrangement on her bedside table.

Unless...

Dorina came bustling back in with a bottle of red wine and two glasses, pouring both of them generous servings before handing a glass over to Christiana. "I think you deserve this." Dorina clanked the rim of her glass against Christiana's and they took their first sip. "I'm so sorry Mother isn't receptive to the type of wedding you want."

Christiana leaned back, enjoying another generous sip. "Do I really seem like the type that would have dreamed about her perfect, royal wedding since she was a little girl?"

Dorina choked on her wine, suppressing a giggle. "No, I can't say I imagine you spending hours thinking of the perfect opulent decor or appetizer to serve during your first dance."

"Exactly," Christiana laughed as Dorina put her glass down so her lady's maid could begin unlacing her dress. "I should be giving you the appreciation, though. I have a feeling you'll have to be our mediator for the rest of this planning."

Once her corset was loosened, Dorina shimmied out of her sage day dress, the fabric pooling at her feet as she stepped out of it, her underskirts simple in comparison. "I'm used to my mother's opinions. You'll learn how to work them to your benefit soon enough."

"It is quite amusing to think about," Christiana arranged herself to face the opposite side of the bed so she could watch Dorina try on each dress. "That I have to learn not only Zander's ticks and personality traits, but your parents' as well."

"Trust me, it's a skill you'll want to acquire if you are going to live here somewhat peacefully." Christiana raised her eyebrows at the princess's sagging shoulders. "Look, my parents are wonderful people, I love them with all of my heart. But I'm sure you can already tell they are a bit...judgmental of other people's opinions."

Christiana twirled the stem of her glass between her fingers. "I supposed it comes with ruling a country."

Dorina shrugged, pulling in a deep breath while the maid laced the ribbon corset up her back. "I suppose, although my parents don't seem to take it well when people try to suggest anything outside what they deem comfortable and proper. It just seems a bit odd to me, but what do I know?"

"Better than most, probably. They did raise you."

"Fair." She smoothed her hands down the skirt. "It's just something you'll have to get used to over time. You'll learn to let their comments roll off your back. Oh, and make sure to keep their judgementalism a secret from everyone. Wouldn't want that dark secret about our King and Queen to get out."

Christiana's stomach lurched. If only Dorina knew the true depths of the King and Queen's secrets. That is, if what Julian said last summer was true.

"So, what do you think?" Dorina asked, twirling lightly in a deep magenta-and-gold dress.

"It looks gorgeous!" Christiana helped herself to a second glass of wine, melting back into the Princess's plush bedding.

"But is it...?" she trailed off.

Christiana swallowed. "Is it what?"

"Alluring enough?" Dorina giggled, her lips twisting into a bashful smirk, a blush crawling up the back of her neck.

"And who are you trying to allure, exactly?" Christiana couldn't help but tease. "Maybe the person who sent you this particularly stunning bouquet of flowers?"

Christiana knew her best friend wanted to one day have a loving marriage, just as she and Zander were lucky enough to find. But it would never happen if her parents had a say. She was lucky, as it was the reigning King's decision of who and when a Princess married, and that Zander promised Dorina he would give her complete control over her decision. The two were trying their best to distract their parents, particularly with Zander's own wedding, before they realized they would lose control over Dorina's future husband. So far, their plan was working.

Yet even with that in mind, Christiana had never heard Dorina talk about the different men in Court. Intrigue crept through her, a list of men forming in her mind as she tried to figure out which special one had captured her best friend's attention.

"Would you excuse us for a moment?" Dorina asked her lady's maid, who left with a short curtsy. Once the door closed, Dorina hopped on her bed next to Christiana, the velvet plumes of her skirt flying around her as she landed, a few gold embroidered pillows falling off the side of the bed at the impact. "If you must know, it seems that there is a particular man interested in me."

"I'm sorry, what?" Christiana exclaimed, eyes widening as she sat herself up, leaning in closer to her friend to hear every detail.

"Yes!" Dorina squealed, reaching across Christiana to pull open the drawer in her bedside table and emerging with a stack of envelopes wrapped in a steel-blue ribbon. "He started writing me letters about a month ago. He sent me those flowers last week with the latest one."

"Who is it?" Christiana asked, nudging Dorina's shoulder with a few pokes.

Dorina laughed, pushing Christiana's fingers away. "See, now that is where things get complicated. I don't know who it is. He just signs all of them from Your Loving Secret Admirer."

"Oh, my goodness." Christiana laughed. "It's almost as nauseating as a romance book."

"I happen to like romance books!" Dorina shoved Christiana, lucky that her wine glass wasn't full enough to spill over the edge. "Which is why I happen to find this incredibly romantic."

"I guess there is something romantic about letters." Christiana blushed, remembering the wildly poetic letter Zander had written her last summer. She still kept it in the wooden box that housed the silver-and-sapphire dagger he had gifted her as well. "Did he give you any indication on who he might be?"

"No." Dorina pouted, her cheeks burning red. "Which is why I wanted to show these to you. You've corresponded with more nobles than I have, maybe you'll recognize something."

Dorina handed her the stack of letters, and Christiana unwrapped the ribbon and pulled out a few pieces of parchment to read over. She took in every detail, trying her best to piece together some kind of clue that would bring his identity to her mind, but nothing seemed to spark an idea.

"The handwriting doesn't look familiar." She looked over the simple-styled words, her fingers tracing a few of the letters. "I'm sorry."

"Nothing about his words or dialect brings anyone to mind?"

Christiana gave Dorina a sympathetic smile, handing her back the letters. "I'm sorry. Most of the correspondence I have with these men are completely business-related and get right to the point. I can't say any of them spoke so...melodiously in the letters they sent to me."

Dorina's shoulders sagged, her hands shaking as she wrapped the letters back in their ribbon. "That's unfortunate. You were my best hope of figuring out who this is."

"Who said we were giving up?" Christiana nudged her again, and a smile spread on Dorina's lips.

"You want to help me figure it out?"

Christiana wrapped Dorina in a hug. "What are best friends for if not this?"

Chapter Six

CHRISTIANA COULD BARELY CONTAIN HER anxiety by the time Marek's reply arrived a week later. It was waiting for her on her desk when she returned from a wedding meeting, covered by a note from Robert saying it had arrived earlier that day. She turned the envelope in her hand, rubbing her thumb along the partially-weathered parchment from the journey here. If anyone else saw it, they would just assume it was yet another correspondence from a tenant or noble looking to conduct business.

No one would really know it was a letter from one of the most important people in her life.

She tore into the envelope, the black wax seal pressed down with nothing but the back of a spoon to keep the contents safe. Her eyes consumed his words, fingers already numb and shaking as she read:

Dearest Maiden,

I was almost concerned that you had forgotten about me with so many new changes to your life ahead.

I am shocked and disheartened to hear that my own creation is being used for a purpose that I would never accept. The person who has taken this deadly secret from me must be caught as soon as possible. With that, I would be honored to see you again, to discuss how such a heinous act could have been committed over the past few weeks.

As for your other request, to allow your fiancé to accompany you, there is a part of me that wants to say no. You know I am weary of him and his family and you know why it makes me nervous. However, I cannot help but be curious about the man, since it has been quite some time since I have laid eyes on him myself. I think it is best if I meet him and make sure that he is good enough for someone I hold dear. He is welcome to come, as long as he understands my limits, which I trust you will relay to him before the meeting.

Finally, I anxiously await to see you again, to make sure that you are safe, since you are only now telling me that your condition plagues you again. I would be lying if I said I wasn't concerned about this happening after your previous letter, recalling the events of your last job. I think it is best if we talk about it, to see what is best for you and your health.

Meet me in ten days' time, in the clearing southwest of my homestead at two past midnight. I look forward to seeing you again and meeting the man you find worthy to bind yourself to.

Sincerely,

Your Dearest Knight

Christiana sank deeper into her couch, her breath shaking, her hands falling into her lap with the letter still clutched between them. She hadn't realized how scared she was about Marek's reactions to all of her requests until the tension in her spine started to unravel a bit, crawling down each vertebra.

He was going to meet with them. Both of them.

She wasn't sure if she was pleased or not, if she was being honest with herself. She was looking forward to telling Zander that he could come, even if it was a bit nerve-wracking. However, she needed to talk to Marek in private, and Zander coming along just made having a necessary conversation that much more complicated.

Christiana's Battled Brain was not a new discovery for her—she had known about this part of herself for five years. But she had conquered it years ago; she had control of herself. So why was it all of a sudden taking control again? She didn't want to think about it, because she knew the answer, she knew what was causing this, but she wasn't ready to face it. She didn't want to admit defeat. She didn't want to go back to being the broken girl she once was.

She was not broken. She was a survivor.

"My Lady?" Natalia touched her shoulder, the muscles tensing under her hand.

Christiana looked up, her head propped on the armrest. "Yes?"

"Is there anything I can do to help?" Her jade eyes were soft as she lowered herself onto the couch, concern creasing her face. "You look so tired. Let me draw you a bath or get you some treats from the kitchen."

"No, Natalia, I'm fine," Christiana sighed, biting the inside of her cheek. She didn't need special treatment, she didn't need to be treated like a porcelain doll about to break.

She was not broken.

"Are you sure?" Natalia stood. "I know all of this wedding planning has been stressful on you, and I just want to help."

"I'm fine." Every inch of her body tightened, her fists curled into the chiffon of her skirt. She forced the anger away, the unkind words

44

trying to crawl up her throat and escape in a fit. She hated that part of her. She hated the outbursts that lashed out on people she cared about. "I do need to go and talk to the Prince, though, so I'll be back in a little while. Make sure my dinner is here in an hour?"

Christiana rose, slipping the letter into the pocket of her skirt. Natalia blinked rapidly. "Of course, My Lady."

"Thank you," Christiana nodded, quickly escaping through the door.

Each step away from her room brought a fresh, cooling relief to her heavy chest. She wandered away from the Royal Wing, down to the main level to try and catch Zander after his last land-tax meeting of the day. She needed to tell him right away, so she would have time to plan the trip and have Robert send word to Ellie that she was going to take that Tagri job in eight days. She was going to go back to the life that made her who she was, the part of herself that made her feel whole.

And she needed to feel strong again. She needed to remind herself she was still useful, that she was still helping those who depended on her. She was going to be there for this young boy and make sure his mother never touched him again. This was what she was made for: helping people.

She felt bodies brush past her, her glassy eyes refusing to take them in, everything fading away into a fuzzy haze as she started to make mental lists and notes about what she needed to pack and the logistics of this whole trip.

"You know, if you keep looking this tired, people are going to start spreading rumors."

Christiana looked up at the snide, unexpected voice, her eyes trying to focus on the raven-haired girl striding toward her. She frowned as she realized who it was. "Hello, Elaine. I didn't realize you were still in the castle."

"My father is on the King's Council," she sneered, arms crossed against her curvy chest. "I live here most of the year."

Christiana's brow rose at that new tidbit of information. Elaine was the Royal Family's original choice for Zander, even though he wasn't too keen on the pompous girl. She wasn't surprised that it was a council member's daughter who was considered 'good enough' for the future king. "Well, isn't that just splendid."

She technically had no reason to dislike Elaine, except for their joint interest in Zander. Yet there was just something about her snobby personality and constant need to seem important that rubbed Christiana the wrong way.

"It would have made being a Princess easier." Elaine raised a perfectly-manicured eyebrow. "I already know this castle like it's my own."

"Well, good thing I'm a quick study." Christiana pushed past Elaine, desperate to move away.

Elaine followed closely, keeping pace. "What did you have that I didn't? What could he have possibly seen in you that I didn't have?"

"I will not have this conversation with you."

"Just tell me!" she burst out, her cheeks mottled with red splotches.

Christiana halted, her pulse racing against the side of her tender throat. She didn't want to have this conversation, but it needed to be said.

She turned around, looking over Elaine. Her cheeks had become a bit hollowed out and her usually-lustrous hair dulled in the candlelight surrounding them. "You would have to ask him that."

"I'm not desperate enough to ask a man why he didn't choose me."

"But you're desperate enough to ask the girl he chose over you?"

Elaine's cheek twitched, her fingernails tapping against her upper arms. "You will never be the Queen this country expects."

Christiana couldn't help laughing at the stiff retort, the conservative drawl of the council's influence obvious with each close-minded word. She didn't have to deal with this, especially since there was no getting through to someone who assumed they were always right.

"True," Christiana shrugged, ready to put this unnecessary encounter to an end. "But I am going to be the Queen this country needs, even if they don't know it yet."

"Always on your high horse, Christiana," Elaine shook her head, her eyes cold. "You may think you understand everyone around you, but one day you'll come to learn things aren't always as they seem."

"Funny," Christiana smirked, her spine straightening as she took a step closer to Elaine, their noses nearly touching, "I was going to tell you the same thing. Now, if you'll excuse me, I have more important matters to attend to."

Christiana pushed herself forward, her shoulder knocking with Elaine's as she left her standing alone in the middle of the hallway. She turned the corner, pulling in a cleansing breath with each step, the council chamber doors now visible at the end of the hall. She collapsed on the bench just outside, her head leaning against the cool stone wall.

She waited for the next hour, focusing her breathing and her mind, clearing the angry fog until the doors finally pushed open, a dozen men filing out with grumbling voices and tired faces. Then she stood, rubbing her sweaty palms down the front of her dress, her heart racing as she waited for Zander to come out.

His face lit up the moment he spotted her. "Hello, love." He placed a gentle kiss on her lips, his hand rubbing lightly on her upper arm. "This is a nice surprise."

"I thought I could walk back to your apartment with you." She laced her arm with his, but he didn't move. "What's wrong?"

Zander sighed, "My day isn't actually over. Father and I need to have dinner with the Treasury Keeper tonight."

"And we can't keep him waiting," Lucian drawled as he came up behind Zander, clapping his son on the back.

"Oh, of course," Christiana kept her smile wide, the tight edges screaming against her cheekbones. "I just wanted to let you know that my mother invited us to come and visit her and Isabelle next week."

Zander's shoulders perked up. "She did? Both of us?"

"Of course."

"We are very busy," Lucian interjected. "I'm not sure if you'll have the time."

"That's unfortunate," Christiana let her spine fall, as if defeated, although she knew this was far from over. "Zander's never seen my childhood home and I was looking forward to a little time away with him."

"Duty comes before desire most of the time." Lucian crossed his arms. "That's something you'll have to come to terms with when you become Queen."

"Of course." Christiana wrinkled her nose at him. "A lesson I'm eager to learn."

"Father," Zander sighed, inserting himself between them and facing Lucian. "Last I remember, we have one meeting next weekend, and it is one you could easily do without me."

"Doesn't mean I should."

"You're also the one that has been scolding me for days to try and get my mind refocused. Ever consider that some time away with the fiancée you've been keeping me from might do just that?"

Christiana stifled a laugh, rubbing her fingertips across her lips. She wasn't used to seeing Zander so candid with his father; she couldn't help but be amused by it.

A few silent beats passed, Lucian's stern face twisting and

hardening as he stared down his son. Finally, he uncrossed his arms. "Fine, you have four days to travel together."

"That's all we need," Christiana assured.

"Alright." Lucian turned back to the council room. "Are you coming?"

"I'll be right there." Zander just shook his head, facing Christiana. Lucian strode away, mumbling under his breath, but Christiana forgot all about it when Zander wrapped his arms around her waist. "Sorry about him, long days and unbalanced numbers tend to disagree with his moods."

Christiana sank into his touch, ignoring a painful pang caught in her chest. "It's fine."

"Begin planning everything and we can discuss the details over breakfast tomorrow, alright?"

"Of course." She stood on her toes to brush a kiss across his lips. With a tired sigh, he pulled away and walked back into the council chamber, sending her one more weary smile before shutting the door behind him.

Chapter Seven

THE WEEK FLEW BY, CONSUMED WITH PLANNING last-minute trip and preparations for the busy few days in Tagri. It was all such a whirlwind, swirled together with adrenaline-filled nerves for her next job and anxiety over Zander and Marek finally meeting. With just one night to go before they left, she needed peace. She needed an escape, and she knew exactly where she wanted to find it. She walked down the hall, her muscles tense with weariness. Her knuckles rapped against Zander's door, her fist so tight they turned white.

The door swung open, a raven-haired man answering with a kind smile. "Good evening, My Lady."

"Hello, Jay." Christiana smiled at Zander's valet. "Is the Prince available?"

"For you, always," Zander declared, his smile peeking over Jay's shoulder.

Jay pushed the door open all the way, moving to the side with a straight spine to allow her entrance. She moved swiftly, her feet light as she fell into Zander's open embrace. She didn't care that there was an audience, she just needed to have his arms around her, a breath of peace finally escaping her lips.

"I'm all set for the next few hours, Jay," Zander smiled over her head, and Christiana peeked at the valet.

"Of course, Your Highness. Ring for me when you are ready to prepare for bed." He gave a quick bow before closing the front door behind him. Her stomach fluttered as she leaned into Zander's touch, calm rushing through her.

"I've missed it here," she grinned, raising herself up on her tiptoes to plant a kiss on his mouth. She'd missed the comfort of his lips, too, fire igniting and burning down to her toes. For so long, she felt uncomfortable with her body's reaction to Zander, confused by the foreign sense of wildness. But once she deciphered her complex feelings for him, she embraced the out-of-control feeling, basking in the flood rushing through her body at his touch.

He wrapped his arm around her waist and they walked in tandem toward his sitting area. The plush hunter-green-and-gold couch welcomed her as she collapsed into its velvet embrace, the soft fabric smooth against the back of her neck. She stared into the dancing flames of the onyx fireplace before her, her fingers mindlessly tracing the royal crest stitched into the cushions as Zander fiddled behind her, the clinking of crystal glasses ringing in the room. A few seconds passed before he joined her, offering a large serving of whiskey.

"How did you know I needed this?" she teased.

"I can see it in your eyes." He sat next to her, brushing a light kiss against her temple before they settled. They each savored a sip, honey-soaked apples and sweet butterscotch dancing on Christiana's tongue as she rolled the delectable liquid around her palette. "What's wrong, Ana?"

She stared down into her glass. "What makes you think something is wrong?"

"I know you well enough to see you're tense." He rubbed her shoulder. "Would you like to talk about it?"

She squirmed in her seat for a few moments, her eyes roaming the room. She could barely decipher the mess of emotions and feelings raging inside her on a daily basis. Learning how to speak them out loud, to make them coherent thoughts, was another matter entirely, and she couldn't stop a dark thought from creeping into her mind: what if she never could?

"There is just...so much about this weekend that needs to go right." She shook her head, her stomach clenching. "I want answers, I want to make this castle safe again, yet we have no idea if this trip will even bring us closer to that goal."

"It's a lead," he consoled her. "The only way to start investigating is to follow every one and see if it goes somewhere, so it can't hurt."

"That's fair." She nodded, taking another sip of whiskey.

"Besides," he said, "even if this doesn't help the investigation, at least it is a reprieve from wedding planning for a few days."

Christiana groaned, remembering all the uncomfortable moments between her and Zander's mother throughout the process. She wanted to enjoy planning her future, but the longer the meetings droned on and the more frivolous, inconsequential questions they asked her, the more her head pounded. She was missing the hours of paperwork she was used to. "I wish it was, but your mother gave me an assignment to handle while we are away."

Zander laughed. "You're kidding?"

Christiana shook her head. "Oh, it's not just me, it's both of us this time. We need to make a list of our favorite fruits, pastries, and sweets. Apparently, the pastry chef is ready to start working on the menu but needs our preferences."

"Well," Zander leaned forward, placing his glass on the table in front of them. "At least we will have something to keep us preoccupied for the ride to your house."

"I was hoping to use it to catch up on my own work, actually." The muscles snaking up Christiana's shoulders knotted tighter, spreading down through her shoulder blades. "I am so behind on letters and requests from my tenants and this is such a busy time of year for them with winter coming."

"Alright. How about I start the list for Mother and you do your own work? You can check it on our way back and make sure I didn't miss anything."

"Really?" She perked up.

"Yes," he nodded. "I think if I make sure there are plenty of chocolate desserts on there, you'll be fine."

She laughed, dropping herself against his chest, his warmth pressed against her cheek.

"Let's not talk about it anymore." His fingers trailed down her jawline. "How about a distraction?"

"What did you have in mind?" She bit her lip, glancing up and finding the answer glimmering in his eyes.

His head dipped low, trailing kisses down her jaw before gently tugging her cheek toward him, his lips enveloping hers. Their past kisses, rushed and in anxious moments, would stoke flames of passion within her, but this time was different. Their lips explored each other delicately, Christiana taking her time to remember the softness and curves of his with each miniscule movement as they pressed against hers. The fire started slowly, deep in the pits of her stomach, before branching out, wrapping around her heart and down her limbs until she was completely consumed by the man tucked against her.

They continued to play with each other, their lips never losing contact. He pressed her backwards, her back leaning against the armrest once again, as his body moved next to her, half of his weight pressed against her side. She giggled, his lips roaming away, allowing her to catch her breath. His tender kisses moved upward, his teeth gently nipping her earlobe, freeing a squeal of delight from her as a shiver ran down to her toes. She let her hands explore, slowly moving downward to feel the defined muscles in his back through his silk cream shirt.

Christiana pulled back, her head cushioned by a pillow, biting at the edge of her swollen lips. "Now, that was a perfect distraction."

"It also reminded me of a part of wedding planning that is just for us to decide." He winked at her, his forearms propped up on either side of her head to keep him above her.

She frowned. "And that is?"

"Our wedding night." Desire laced his voice, flirtation glistening in his eyes illuminated by the candlelight around them.

Christiana's stomach twisted a bit, her body flushing with heat. She turned her face away, attempting to hide her blushing cheeks in the folds of her hair that spread out around her. "Yes, that is certainly something we need to talk about."

She had never been this intimate with a man before, but she had also never been in love before. She had never felt the stirring, the craving, of another person's touch the way she did with Zander. She wasn't scared to begin creating intimacy between them; she wanted to experience everything with him and take her time doing so. She didn't want to forget a single moment.

However, it didn't stop her nerves from tangling. She preferred to be an expert on things before sharing them with others, but it seemed this was going to be a moment she wouldn't get that chance. The only way to learn was with someone else...someone she loved. All Christiana could do was hope she and Zander learned with each other and for each other. The rest would develop naturally.

"I'm nervous, too," he whispered in her ear, his warm breath against the tender skin sending a shiver down her spine.

"You are?"

"Yes, but I cannot wait to share every part of myself with you, Ana." He ran his fingers through the tangles of her hair, his eyes soft as he stared down at her. "I cannot wait to experience all of you."

His words washed over her, a frost-bitten chill running through her veins, breaking the trance of the moment and stiffening her muscles. He wanted to experience all of her. Which meant he was going to see all of her, every inch of her body, every scar that covered her back. The once creamy, perfect skin, ruined and violated by her father and his many forms of punishments ranging from whips to floggers to canes. Her entire back was a mangled mess of lines, branded into her as a constant reminder of what he did.

She may have taken her life back, but he had owned her for many years, and he made sure she would never forget it, even after his death.

"Christiana?" Zander's face creased and he pulled away slightly.

She knew she should answer him, say she was alright, but all she could do was stare blankly at his perfect, handsome face and what she could only assume was a perfectly seductive body underneath that thick layer of clothes. She longed to see it, to touch it, to be with him in a way no woman ever had. She wished she could give him the same in return, but how could a man desire a woman who was as disgusting as her underneath the façade of her expensive dresses?

"I'm sorry," he stuttered, leaning back on his haunches, fingers running through his already-tousled curls. "I didn't mean to overstep."

"You didn't!" She shifted herself to sit upright. "I think I'm just much more nervous about the whole idea than I anticipated I would be."

He tentatively stroked her cheek. "Are you sure?"

"Of course." She smiled at him, leaning into his touch, twisting her fingers into the folds of her skirts to hide the uncontrollable tremors spreading through them—the symptoms of her dreaded Battled Brain reawakening from the depths of her mind.

Chapter Eight

THE NEXT DAY WAS FILLED WITH DREARY, overcast skies and chilled sprinkles of rain hitting against the side of the carriage as Christiana and Zander travelled back to Tagri for the weekend.

Christiana had slept restlessly after her time with Zander the night before, her mind racing over all the different reactions Zander might have to seeing her back for the first time. Would he accept her? Would he cower away from her? Would he sneer at her in disgust and regret choosing her as his wife? She knew logically that so many of the possibilities that she came up with were far from the truth, but it didn't stop her mind from feeding her more dark, twisted ideas.

But her misplaced fears were not the priority at the moment. The priority was the job that she had to complete and the answers she needed to get. She had people to protect, which meant putting them before herself, like she had been doing for many years. There was no need to get anxious about something that was months away.

Christiana's gaze drifted out the window, Zander snuggled up next to her on the bench as they watched her manor house come into view from the road. His arm snaked around her, pulling her close, his lips brushing against her ear. "Are you happy to be back home?"

Christiana wasn't sure if she was ready to go back. No matter how much she wanted to show off the place she grew up, she had been looking forward to putting it behind her, too. It may have held some beautiful childhood memories, but they were all tainted by the horrors of her teenage years, her father's cruelty still haunting the halls some days.

"I'm happy that you are finally seeing where I grew up." She turned to him, their faces inches apart, the warmth of their fur-lined cloaks encircling them.

He kissed her forehead as the carriage jostled up the long drive. "I can't wait."

A few more moments passed before they stopped at the front door, Robert pulling the carriage door open for them. He held out an umbrella for her to grab onto as she stepped out, clutching it as she and Zander ran to the front door. They pushed inside, where her mother, Maria, and little sister Isabelle waited in the entryway to greet them.

"Ana!" Isabelle launched herself into Christiana's arms, her blonde curls secured in a high ponytail, twists of hair pulled back to frame the sides of her head. "I missed you!"

"It's only been a few weeks, Belle." Christiana looked down at her sister, although she didn't have to crane her neck as much as she remembered. "Although it does seem you've gotten taller."

"I'm already fitting into some of the dresses you left behind!" Isabelle twirled, the ruby dress flowing around her. "Although they are quite dark. I never understood why you only wear dreary colors."

Christiana laughed. "Matches my personality I guess."

"Plus, she looks beautiful in darker tones," Zander teased.

Isabelle stopped her dancing immediately. "Hello, Your Highness." She curtsied, dropping her gaze to her feet.

Maria followed suit, then stepped forward. "It's an honor to have you in our house this weekend, Your Highness."

"Please, call me Zander." He unhooked his cloak, handing it off to Jay as he came inside with Zander's trunk, Natalia close behind toting Christiana's travel things as well. "There's no need to be so formal in your own house."

Isabelle didn't need to be told twice, her effervescent steps bringing her forward to stand in front of him. "Have you ever been here before, Zander?"

"I've never had the honor until today." He smiled down at her. "But I look forward to getting to know where you and Christiana grew up."

"I had your room all cleaned and set for you, Ana." Maria pulled Christiana into a hug.

She tensed at the touch before wrapping her arms around her mother, placing a demur kiss on her weathered cheek. "Thank you, Mother. Which room did you have set for Zander?"

"The Jade room," she said, pulling away and smoothing her skirt as she turned to Zander. "One of the servants will show you."

"No!" Isabelle interjected. "I can show him! It's this way, Zander!"

She looped her arm through his and pulled him forward, laughter erupting from his lips as he let her drag him away. He turned to Christiana with an amused look. "I'll see you soon, I guess."

"Have her show you my room once you're settled!" she yelled back before he disappeared around the corner. "Robert, can you help Natalia with my trunk? My room is this way."

Christiana made her way to her bedroom, Robert close on her heels, the steps so instinctual she barely remembered the walk there.

She pushed the door open, the sound of pelting rain echoing off the walls as it smacked against the windows. So much of the room looked the same—the large, imposing bed, the carved mahogany wardrobe, and the three-mirror dressing table—but gone were all of the personal touches. A nondescript claret quilt sat on the bed and the dressing table was completely empty, no longer cluttered with her jewelry and cosmetics.

"Does it feel odd?" Robert placed her trunk at the edge of the bed, leaning against the post to look at her.

"A bit," she shrugged, pulling her gloves and cloak off and tossing them over the dressing table before taking a seat on the bench in front of it. "It's just an adjustment."

He nodded with that peaceful, all-understanding look he gave her often, and calm settled over her muscles as she relaxed into the plush seat. One of the many new perks about having him as her head guard was that it required him to follow her everywhere. She needed his soothing presence more often than she realized.

"Your sister is a whirlwind of energy," Zander laughed as he leaned against the open door frame of Christiana's room.

"She has been like that for years." She waved him inside, his steps dulled by the carpet as he closed the door behind him. "I just wanted to let you know I'm going out tonight to start tracking my next case."

Christiana had told Zander the basics about it when they first planned the trip a week ago. They had agreed last summer that the dirty details of her clandestine jobs were best kept to herself, but she also didn't feel right sneaking out and hiding it from him. The best solution was to always let him know when she had a case, without giving away the actual specifics of it.

Zander's jaw tensed a bit, his body relaxing against the wall. "Alright. We're meeting your mentor the day after tomorrow and we leave soon after that. Are you sure you'll be able to handle this case?"

"Yes. I had Robert do some research into the mark, it's straightforward and simple."

The information Robert found had settled Christiana's mind. This woman worked in a laundry house fairly late into the night. It made for the perfect first mark back into Maiden work—easy, straightforward, and instinctual. Christiana had no worries that this abuser would be gone from the world by tomorrow evening.

"Certainly a unique aspect of your job," Zander smirked at Robert.

"It was an adjustment, that's for sure, but I'm used to it." Robert shrugged. "If it is alright with you, My Lady, I am going to find my quarters for the evening."

"Of course." She craned her neck to look at him. "Natalia can show you where it is."

"Then I'm on the hunt for Miss Natalia. Excuse me." He bowed quickly before scurrying out the door, closing it firmly behind him.

Christiana took Zander's hand and walked them to her bed, perching them both on the end. His foot tapped against the carpet, rattling the bedframe underneath them.

"Zander?" Christiana leaned forward, running her fingers through his curls to push them out of his eyes. "What's wrong?"

"Nothing." He looked at her sheepishly. "Just a bit nervous to meet your mentor."

Christiana's chest tightened, her mouth dry as a desert. She knew all the reasons Zander was nervous, and they did not match up to the real reasons why he should be. "It's going to be fine." She rubbed his cheek with her thumb. "Just..."

"Just what?"

She nipped at the edge of her lips. "Just...don't say anything when we meet with him. Let me do the talking."

His brow creased, his body wincing away from her touch. "I have questions, too, that I need answers for."

"And we will." She didn't want to hurt him, but this would be a delicate situation. One wrong move with Marek, and he would disappear. "I'll make sure we do, but Zander, you are a Royal and he is in an illegal profession. He has reasons to be wary of you."

"Then why did he agree to meet with me there, if you don't mind me asking?"

She sighed, rubbing circles against her temples. "Honestly? He's not as much interested in meeting Alekzander, the Prince of Viri, as he is in meeting Zander, my fiancé."

His face dropped, eyes blank. "Come again?"

"He knows we're engaged." Christiana struggled for words, trying her best to find ones that would gloss over what she actually expected to happen at this meeting. "I guess that it would just make sense that he would want to make sure you are...well-matched with me."

His gaze narrowed at her. "Ana, when you say he's your mentor, what does that mean, exactly?"

Her lips pressed together. "You know, the man who taught me my skillset...and developed into being a...paternal-like figure in my life."

"Like a father?" His eyes went wide, jaw slack.

Christiana slowly nodded. "Yes, that's one way of describing it."

"So basically, the day after tomorrow, I'm going to be meeting my surrogate future father-in-law?" She nodded again, smiling. He sighed. "Any advice?"

She wrapped her arms around his waist. "He knows how to kill, so don't get too close?"

"Why didn't you tell me this sooner?"

"I didn't want you to get nervous! I knew there was already a lot of pressure on this meeting to get answers, I didn't want to make it worse on you."

"Wonderful," Zander groaned, rubbing his hands across his face, his back hunching forward. "Now I'm even more nervous."

Christiana rubbed his back. "It will be fine as long as we handle it gently. Just remember, assassins are very private, we don't like people poking into our lives unless they have to."

"You let me poke into yours." He tilted his head, his face still half-covered by his hands, his eyes glimmering in the candlelight.

"Call it a unique case," she teased. "I don't think many other assassins would find themselves falling in love with a royal."

"Fair." He exhaled loudly, pulling himself up from the bed. She let out a deep breath as well, but it did not relieve any of the stress stitching deep into her muscles.

Chapter Nine

THE FRESH WINTER CHILL BIT AT CHRISTIANA'S cheeks as she hid in the alleyway around the corner from a laundress shop. Only her second night in Tagri and she was ready to take out her client after one evening of surveillance.

The tiny village was quiet, the harsh winter breeze the only noise as it pushed itself against windowpanes and creaking roofs. The minutes ticked by agonizingly slow; it was impossible to know how many had gone by without a clocktower to tell her the time. She fought not to bang her head against the stone wall next to her as she waited, her impatient fingers tugging at the ends of the detachable sleeves she wore with her assassin outfit during the winter months.

After what felt like hours, she perked up at the grumbling goodbyes through the window above her head, her mark's voice wafting down toward her before she stomped out the front door.

Christiana smirked as she straightened and took a few steps back farther into the alley to set herself up for the perfect ambush. She gripped the dart between her fingers, a fresh dip of Midnight glistening around the needle's sharp tip. Heels clicked on the pavement as a shadow entered the alley, the clacking getting closer and closer.

The moment the lithe, middle-aged woman was in reach, Christiana wrapped her hands around her waist and slammed her into the wall, her forearm pressed against her chest so she could smother the terrified woman's screams with her hand. Panic spread across her slightly wrinkled face, her bright green eyes wide as she stared at Christiana.

"It seems you've been a bad mother, Nicoletta," she said in the deep, tenor voice she used as the Maiden, the vibrations on her vocal cords soothing the nerves zipping along her arms as she fell back into the steps of her assassin life.

"Wha—What are you talking about?" she stuttered, her voice muffled through the cracks between Christiana's clenched fingers. "Who are you?"

"I'm the one your son sent to punish you for the treacherous things you do to him when you get home at night," Christiana rumbled, her body clenching against Nicoletta's. This woman was a monster, and she would do what she had to: she would take down the monster.

Her body hummed to life, her fingers raised and ready to stab the dart against Nicoletta's neck and wait for the poison to snake its way through her body and slam a heart attack into her system. When her eyes caught Nicoletta's, a light ignited behind her green irises, a smirk pushing against Christiana's hand with what Christiana would only explain as desire. Disgusting, unwarranted desire for the toxic acts Christiana was here to kill her for.

Nicoletta whispered through Christiana's fingers. "I'm always kind to my son."

In an instant, Christiana's mind flooded with flashes of scenes from that night: the scratch of tree bark against her back as her weapon went flying from her hand, the tears streaming down her face, the feeling of Julian's lips forced against hers.

"Don't worry, My Lady, I'll be kind..."

She could still feel the warmth of his breath on her cheek as he whispered those putrid words against her ear.

Christiana unraveled. Her fingertips began to pulsate with vibrations, the paralyzing shakes snaking down her fingers until they controlled her hand and forearms. Her mind spiraled, her thoughts pulling her in different directions as she tried to focus on her surroundings when all her brain wanted to do was pull her back to the past.

She bit back a scream as the dart fell from her hand, her grip loosening on the writhing abuser. That was all it took for the desperate Nicoletta to push against Christiana's weakened palm and free her mouth from her grip. She let out a piercing screech, the sound echoing off the walls around them and up into the air.

Christiana's heart dropped, her hands desperate to contain Nicoletta's screams, but it was fruitless; her hand was too weak to keep control over the thrashing woman. Grumbling drifted down from the open streets, most likely wondering what the commotion was about. She didn't have much time; she had to get away as quickly as possible.

She moved as fast as she could, picking up the abandoned dart, her rattling fingers barely able to keep hold of it. She used every ounce of strength to keep her fingers around it as she plunged it into the back of Nicoletta's hand, the only exposed flesh Christiana's trembling fingers could find. She pulled the dart out almost as quickly as she plunged it in, giving it just enough time to let the drops of poison invade her body.

Steps and voices were gaining on them. She had seconds to disappear and hide before someone saw her. She wanted to wait and make sure the poison was properly administered, but she didn't have time. Not here. She looked around frantically, running down the opposite end of the alley, weaving through different narrow passages and streets. She clung to the side of the buildings, keeping her black ensemble hidden within the safety of the shadows.

After far too long of weaving and evading groups of people, she stepped into an alley between two abandoned buildings, their walls crumbling just like Christiana was. She braced her hands against the wall, her forehead resting against the cold stone, trying to ground herself back into reality, to stop the tremors and panic from spreading even further. She forced herself to think positive thoughts, reminding herself where she was: she was safe, she was out of danger, and she was alive.

She took in deep breaths through her nose, the frosty air biting her nostrils as she pulled it in and let it swirl in her system before she pushed it out through her mouth. Her heart began to calm after a few minutes, her fingers scratching at the wall as her chest settled. She flipped herself around, her back leaning against the wall as she gripped her hands against her bent knees. She repeated the words that would make her feel better in her head, the mantra she had been taught many years ago on a loop to remind herself who she was.

She was not broken. She was a survivor.

Chapter Ten

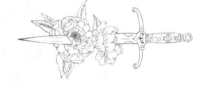

*T*HE NEXT DAY PASSED IN A BLUR, AND Christiana was thankful for it. Her mind still struggled to clear from the fog of her mission gone almost wrong. After waiting another hour to make sure the coast was clear, she had looped back to the kill spot, leaping from roof to roof in hopes of getting a bird's eye view of a scene. She hadn't been disappointed. Soldiers crowded around the dank space, surrounding Nicoletta's body, her eyes frozen open in fear, her face twisted and sweaty from the convulsions of the heart attack. Christiana had finally been able to let out a breath after seeing the body. She had never failed on a case. She always refused to let her clients down and so far, she never had.

Yet.

She focused on what was ahead of her, their meeting with Marek only a few hours away. She focused on getting answers about the Crimson Fire and trying to piece together theories about the serial killer; but mostly, she focused on seeing Marek again and being back in his soothing presence. After last night, she needed that. She needed him to remind her of her strength and banish the darkness. He had been the one to help her so many years ago; hopefully he was that key again.

Isabelle was the perfect distraction during the midmorning, Christiana surprising her with a trip to their favorite dress shop to pick out a few new gowns to wear to the different events for the wedding, including her bridesmaid dress.

"I still don't understand why you picked such a dreary color for us to wear." Isabelle stuck her tongue out at Christiana as two servants helped them remove their cloaks in the manor's entryway.

"It's one of my favorites, little one," Christiana shook her head.

"It's barely a color!" Isabelle linked her arm with Christiana's as they walked deeper into the house.

"So, are you saying you want me to return that stunning gown I just purchased for you?" Christiana smirked. Isabelle's shoulders slumped at the question. "That's what I thought."

"Can you help me pick out what dress I should wear to the engagement ball?" Isabelle bounced on the balls of her feet, shaking Christiana's arm.

Christiana laughed. "Of course, but only for a little while. Zander and I are going to go riding this afternoon."

"Aw," Isabelle crooned. "How romantic!"

Christiana had spent the time before leaving for her job yesterday with Zander, taking the carriage around to some of her tenants to check in on them. She hated that she had been so distracted with wedding planning that her response time to their letters and requests was delayed. Visiting a few of them had put her mind and heart at ease, seeing their smiling faces and hearing their welcoming words. Since they had spent the whole day basically working, she had promised Zander a riding trip to some of her favorite wilderness spots as a way for the two of them to relax with some of the alone time they didn't always get back home at the palace. After last night, Christiana needed the relaxing distraction.

She nudged her shoulder against Isabelle's. "Let me just grab a book from the library. I'll come up to your room in a moment."

"Alright!" Isabelle placed a kiss on her sister's cheek before skipping up the stairs toward her bedroom. Christiana went right to the library, in search of one of her favorite fiction books she enjoyed growing up. The last few hours of the night would be the hardest before she had to leave, but reading might be at least somewhat of a distraction until then.

She pushed the double doors open, the fireplace already lit and casting a warm glow into the room, the rows of leather-bound books on display. Maria sat in her favorite corner, a cup of tea next to her and a book in her hands.

Christiana smiled at first, walking to greet her mother, but her feet faltered the moment her eyes cast toward the mantle, her heart dropping at the sight of her father's imposing portrait hanging proudly over it. Her fists balled at her sides, her knuckles white. "Mother, what is that doing back up there?"

Christiana had removed any portrait of Francis the moment she took control of her title and the household. She didn't need the constant reminder of her father, her abuser, still watching her from the walls of her manor; he did enough of that in her memories.

"I figured since you were not living here anymore, you wouldn't care if I took it out of storage." Maria shut her book, dropping it on the side table. She stood up, smoothing her mussed gray skirt before strolling over to stand next to Christiana.

Christiana's legs shook as she stared up at it. Even in the portrait, she saw the similarities that others saw in her; the same dark, reddish-brown hair, steel blue eyes, and porcelain skin. She hated how much she looked like him, almost as much as she hated this portrait. He smiled, eyes bright, standing tall and proud. To the untrained eye, he looked innocent of cruelty, full of life and hope, ready to lead his family into the future.

Unfortunately, Christiana knew the truth behind the pretty picture.

"Well, I do mind." Christiana's insides quaked, the pressure on her chest building with his gray-blue eyes still staring down at her. "He doesn't deserve to be up there."

"Well, you never wanted a portrait of yourself up there," Maria pointed out. "It is very improper not to have some type of head of household portrait on the walls, so I figured having the man who taught you everything would be a good replacement."

Christiana sputtered, at a loss for words for a few seconds before she could regain her composure. "Improper? That is your defense? When are we going to stop playing this game, Mother?"

Maria's cheeks flushed, her eyes darting around the room, and she edged toward the door. "Game? I have no idea what you're talking about."

"Yes, you do," Christiana blocked Maria's path, stopping her from escaping. "We keep dancing around the subject without actually talking about it. When are we going to stop pretending that what is depicted in that portrait is nothing more than a lovely, fictitious picture? When will you give up the charade you are so desperate to hold on to even though he has been gone five years?"

"Have manners, Christiana!" Maria took a step forward, her finger grazing Christiana's chest as if to scold a young child. "I am still your mother, and that man was your father—the man who taught you everything! Who prepared you to be the woman you are!"

Christiana's skin prickled, crawling up her arms and devouring her chest. Of all the emotions that could pull her out of her fog, anger won. This had to stop. She had enough stress and problems to work through, she didn't need her mother being a part of them.

"That man has no claim on me and who I've become!" Christiana's fist slammed into the long research table in the center of the room, the impact shuddering a dull pain through her fist and up her forearm. The anger bubbled over, stirring in her gut and snaking its way through her system. "I promise you, Mother, I am the woman I am *despite* his cruelty and your lack of courage."

Christiana wished she *wanted* to take the venomous words back as her mother's eyes went wide, mouth gaping...but Christiana didn't regret them. It had been a long time coming, years of festering wounds and unspoken words building up until finally they escaped.

"You have no idea what you are saying." Maria's eyes were glassy. "You have no idea what happened between your Father and I."

"I know that you married a treacherous man who beat you, and when he got bored with that, he moved on to me." Christiana straightened, fists on the table as she leaned over toward her mother. "I know that you sat back for six years, *six years*, and let him take his anger out on us. You let him whip and hit and mark every inch of me that he could."

"I didn't let him..." Maria choked on her words. "I didn't want him to!"

"But you stayed. You kept us here." Christiana's words rumbled from deep in her chest. "That's as good as accepting the issue."

"Christiana...you just don't understand the whole story." Maria's hand snaked across the table to touch Christiana's.

She flinched away. "Then tell me. Tell me the truth of what happened."

Silence fell, Maria staring at Christiana with tear-stained cheeks and silent sobs. Christiana willed the words, the apparent truth, out of her mother's lips, but they stayed shut in a straight line across her face.

She wanted to know what excuses Maria had for the situation, but it seemed her mother wasn't willing to give them up.

Christiana wished she was surprised, but she wasn't even a bit shocked.

"Until you tell me the whole story, his portraits stay off the walls of *my* manor." She pushed away from the table, her heavy feet walking toward the door. "I'll send a servant in to remove it at once."

"Ana..." was the last thing Christiana heard before she slammed the door behind her.

Chapter Eleven

*N*IGHT CAME, THE STARS THE ONLY LIGHT illuminating the chilled winter eve as a new moon hung in the deep blue sky. Christiana was more than ready to see Marek for the first time in months; dressed in her full Maiden outfit, adding an overcoat that covered just her arms and exposed chest and neck, she led the way on her mare, Willow, with Zander and his horse close behind.

They entered silently into the thicket of trees, the bite of a chilled winter night brushing against their cheeks, traveling in silence for forty-five minutes with the anticipation of meeting Marek driving them forward. Finally, Christiana slowed their horses, bringing them to a stop a half-mile away from the meeting point. "We should walk the rest of the way."

Dismounting, they secured their horses to a nearby tree and continued on foot, the crunching of dead leaves and the whistling of bare branches in the wind the only sound filling the voided silence between them.

"Are you alright?" Zander asked at last.

"Yes," she nodded, keeping her gaze ahead as she pushed a handful of tree branches out of the way. "Just ready to see him again."

She was ready for so much more than that, though; she was ready for answers, both professional and personal ones. Her back muscles tightened, her mind spinning with hope that something productive would come from this conversation.

After a few minutes of hiking, they came to a large, circular clearing, the starlight twinkling against the pine needles and underbrush littering the forest floor. A thump brought them to attention as a large figure dropped from one of the half-dozen trees surrounding them, landing gracefully on his feet. His face was mostly concealed by his broad hood and mask. Just like Christiana, the only part of his face showing was his eyes, the gaze bearing into both of them. He was dressed completely as the Crimson Knight, but unlike the graceful, soft features of Christiana's outfit, Marek was in a steel-gray ensemble, the thick fabric encasing his body in what looked like armor. He crossed his arms, a menacing air surrounding them, and Zander winced slightly. His face did not betray him, but beads of sweat formed along his hairline even in the dark winter night.

"Thank you so much for meeting with us tonight." Christiana pulled her hood off, her long ponytail freed, the wind whipping it behind her.

"For you, of course," Marek said.

"Yes, thank you so much for this," Zander agreed, a tight smile on his lips.

Marek's gaze flicked to him before turning back to Christiana. "So, you mentioned an imposter?"

"Yes, we have a serial killer in the palace," she explained. "All three victims have been killed with Crimson Fire."

"Are you positive?" His posture was rigid, his fingers curling tightly against his biceps. "You checked all of the symptoms to confirm?"

Christiana nodded. "I confirmed them myself. There is no other poison out there that it could be."

"Well then, this is a mystery. Did you lose any recently?" Marek looked her up and down, his eyes filled with cold detachment. The sting of his straightforwardness ran through her, piercing her chest with needles.

"No, of course not!" She took a few steps forward, her hands falling limp at her sides. "The vial I carry is safe and sound, I confirmed it right after we learned of the killings."

"Hm." Marek contemplated for a moment. "Do you have any other details that could be useful, Your Highness?"

Zander blinked rapidly, leaning over to whisper to Christiana. "Should I answer?"

Christiana's grip tightened around his arm. Why was Marek doing this? "Probably for the best."

Zander cleared his throat as he stood tall, facing Marek. "As of right now, all we know is three young women were killed overnight with your poison, one every two weeks. Their bodies were found the next morning deposited in the middle of the servants halls."

"Not much to go on," Marek mumbled, pacing forward a few steps. "This is deeply disturbing news. That poison is vicious, I don't like that it is in the hands of someone I don't even know."

"So, you really aren't sure how your poison got out into the world?" Christiana asked.

"Of course not. It took a long time for me to trust you with it in the first place, I wasn't about to go around giving it to just anybody."

"You know, I wouldn't judge you if you had decided to train someone else." She peered up at his face, which gave absolutely nothing away. "I know you loved it, even if you refuse to admit it."

"Suffice to say, I didn't hate it as much as I expected to when you first hired me." He shook his head, a deep chuckle escaping his lips. "I'm sure you are not shocked to hear, Prince, that your fiancée was a force to be reckoned with even back then. Made me think twice about getting another student."

Zander let out a stiff laugh, staring warily at Marek, who was only a few feet away from them now. Christiana rolled her eyes at the glittering amusement in Marek's. He was getting too much joy out of Zander's nervousness. She raked through the roots of her contained hair, a painful pulse pounding against her tender temple. "Would you consider helping us with this?"

"How could I do that?"

Christiana traced a pattern on the hilt of her dagger hanging on her hip. "Maybe you could come back to Cittadina for a bit? You might recognize someone."

"Christiana," Marek groaned, shaking his head, his veil billowing in front of his face. "You know I can't do that."

"Please." She took a step forward, Zander's hand still clutched in hers. "You're the only link we have to the killer. We need you."

Zander cleared his throat. "If safety is an issue, I will do whatever I can to assure your comfort."

"It's not that. I just have a complicated history in that city."

"Oh," Zander mumbled. Christiana knew his history, his own ghosts that lay within the city and palace walls. What she was asking wasn't easy, but she was desperate. She needed his help.

Christiana pushed forward. "Please, consider it."

"I'm sorry." Marek sighed. "You know you can always reach me by letter."

Christiana's heart ached, but there was nothing else she could say on this matter to convince him. It was time for her to try and get answers on the other important subject.

Christiana tugged on Zander's arm. "Zander, can you leave us alone for a few minutes?"

He looked down at her. "Is everything alright?"

"Of course, I just want a moment alone with him." Christiana grazed her fingers against his knuckles. "Go check the horses. I'll be back soon."

"Fine," he sighed, kissing her lightly on the cheek and shooting Marek a sharp stare before disappearing into the thicket of trees.

She waited for Zander's footsteps to disappear before walking quickly to her mentor's side, allowing him to envelope her in a tight hug against his chest. She breathed in his familiar scent of musk and spice, the comfort that his protective arms had given her over the years. He pulled away, finally removing his mask, revealing his tanned, chiseled face and square jawline. His mouth quirked up in a half-smirk, the biggest smile Christiana had ever seen him give.

"I really appreciate you meeting with us," she smiled back.

"He's a stiff young man, dear one." Marek pulled his hood down to let his curly chestnut hair free. "Are you sure he's a good match for you?"

She rolled her eyes, punching him in the shoulder. "Oh, shut it! You make him nervous."

"Good, he should be wary of me." He winked, lightly shoving her backward. They began a slow walk, meandering through the trees. "Now, can we talk about the truly concerning subject mentioned in your letter?"

"I wasn't sure if tonight was the right time to bring it up, but I don't really have anyone else to go to about this." She rubbed the back of her neck, unsure if she was ready to do this, but she had no other option. She needed answers. "You're the only one who has ever been able to help."

Shallow lines around his eyes creased inward. "What is it?"

She leaned against a nearby tree, the bark scratching the damask fabric of her corset coat. "I've started having this new...nightmare..."

She told him every detail, down to her bound hands and legs and Julian's menacing grin. Marek stood in front of her, his hands heavy on her shoulders. "I knew that last job was more dangerous than you originally told me."

"I knew I shouldn't have said anything to you," Christiana grumbled. She had written Marek soon after she returned home to begin her transition to the palace. The idea of Julian had been haunting her, and she wanted to talk everything out with the one man who would understand. He had commended her for her quick thinking and even said she had made the right decision. But now, a few months past Julian's death, his haunting presence was only becoming worse.

"Is that all that's changed?" Marek asked, concern bright in his forest-green eyes.

She swallowed a lump in her throat, remembering last night. "No."

"Tell me, Ana." He leaned next to her, his hand above her head.

"Marek..." Christiana whined, her head falling back against the tree, the ends of her hair tangling in a low-hanging branch.

"I can't help you if you don't tell me the truth."

"*Fine*. The nightmares make my anxiety worse. I'm constantly terrified that some new catalyst is going to appear at the worst time possible, my mind is constantly in a fog." She banged her fist against the tree trunk. "My hand tremors have also returned."

"I think the attack affected you more than you would like to admit." He squeezed her hand, moving back in front of her. "It makes sense, Ana. Most people wouldn't be able to come out of that experience completely themselves, and you were already susceptible to Battled Brain."

"This is different." Her eyes burned, a combination of the

79

whistling wind against them and forcing herself not to shed a tear. "I can't just...lock myself in seclusion like I did before. I'm expected to constantly be ready for people to surround me. How can...I can't...."

"What does the Prince have to say about it?" Christiana avoided his gaze, staring down as her boots dug into the frozen earth. "Ana...have you not told him?"

She shook her head. She knew she shouldn't be keeping this secret from the man who was to be her husband; she trusted him, yet she still couldn't seem to sit him down and tell him the truth. She didn't want to watch the disappointment in his face when he realized she wasn't as strong as he thought she was.

Marek let out a deep breath, puffs of air escaping his nostrils. "Well, I certainly have an opinion on that decision, but that isn't a conversation for now. I'll need more time for that."

"I can't even hold a weapon, Marek!" Christiana fumed, punching the tree behind her with the pent-up aggression that sat in her fingertips. "What kind of assassin can't even hold her daggers without them falling out of her shaking hands?"

"One who had something horrible happen to her. This doesn't make you any less of a fit assassin," Marek lifted her face until they locked gazes. He took deep breaths in, forcing her to mimic his action until her breathing evened out, the fog of her mind slightly dissipating. "What can I do?"

"Please, come back and help us," she begged. "Not just with the case...but with my healing. You helped me last time I got out of control, you can help me again."

"You know my aversion to that place."

"Marek, I need you. Please, help me."

They stared at each other for a few moments, the starlight reflecting in Marek's eyes. His face softened as he finally pulled her into a comforting hug. "Alright, I will come and help."

She dropped her head on his shoulder, wrapping her arms around him. "Thank you."

"Of course." He kissed the top of her head, his fatherly embrace easing the tightness enveloping her whole body. "Besides, it will probably be good for me to get to know this Prince of yours more personally."

"Be nice to him," Christiana warned, poking Marek's chest.

"I'm always nice, dear one."

Christiana laughed, breaking the tension that had settled deep within her chest.

Chapter Twelve

CHRISTIANA STARED OUT THE WINDOW AS THE streets of Cittadina came into view, the carriage quaking with swift travel. They left early in the morning at her request, her aching heart and twisting stomach not ready to face her mother after their fight. She left a note behind with plenty of excuses as to why they had to leave, but it did nothing to settle her soul. She tried her best not to think about it; she didn't want to give her father's legacy any more control over her thoughts.

A few more minutes passed before the carriage slowed, the palace turrets looming in front of them, the slate gray stone blending into the wispy gray clouds that dotted the sky. The moment they stopped, servants rushed to their caravan, pulling their belongings out and carrying them back to their room. Robert opened the carriage door for them, his arm outstretched to help Christiana down.

"Welcome back, Son." Lucian was the first to greet them, approaching the carriage with a determined stride. Zander was barely out of the enclosed space before Lucian grasped his forearm. He turned to her, giving her a slight smile. "Christiana."

"What's wrong now, Father?" Zander sighed, his journey-tousled hair falling into his eyes as he shook his head.

"Yet another report from the Astary Military Base." He dragged Zander toward the front door, Christiana hurrying on their heels. "Apparently they need even more money than before. We have to go over these reports with a fine-toothed comb, and if that doesn't work, I'm sending you out there to make sure what they are claiming is true."

Christiana almost fumbled on her own feet. Zander might have to leave? So soon after returning? She didn't like that at all.

He shot her a weary gaze over his shoulder, scanning her up and down. "Maybe Christiana can come to the meeting with us. That way she can be up to speed when we travel to Astary."

Lucian stopped in his tracks, slowly pivoting to face his son. "Travel with you?"

"It only makes sense." Zander stood a bit taller, his spine straight as he stared into his father's icy-blue eyes. "If, as the future King, I am sent around the country, then it seems smart to send the future Queen as well."

"That is an excellent point." Lucian's gaze slowly moved between them. "However, Penelope already scheduled at least a dozen meetings for the wedding, so I don't think Christiana will be able to make it this time. You understand, right, dear?"

Christiana bit the inside of her cheek. "Of course, Lucian."

"Don't worry, there will be plenty of time for you to learn once the wedding is over." He patted her shoulder, squeezing gently, and a shiver ran up her throat. "Now, let's go, we have hours of work ahead of us."

Zander shot her a sorrowful glance over his shoulder as his father dragged him away, his lips forming a parting *I love you* before the King pulled him around a corner and out of sight. Christiana sighed as she watched the flurry of servants part around her, some carrying items inside, others preparing to bring the horse and carriage back down to the stables.

"No need to let my father bother you anyway." Dorina flitted out the front door, bouncing to meet her. "I need you on a much more important matter."

Christiana chuckled as she linked arms with her friend. "Oh, do you now?"

"Well, it's the matter of holding on to my own sanity." She dragged Christiana toward the entrance. "So, I thought you may be interested in helping."

"Seems I couldn't have come soon enough." Christiana removed her gloves and cloak, handing them off to Natalia. "Can you take these for me, please? I'll be back to the apartment soon."

"Of course, My Lady," she curtsied. "I'll have some tea and cookies waiting for you when you return."

Dorina steered them away from the commotion of the servants. "I received yet another letter while you were away."

"And?"

"Still no closer to figuring out who it is. I need to send my reply as soon as possible."

Christiana halted them in an unfamiliar tapestry-lined hall. "Wait, if you don't know who he is, how are you sending letters in return?"

"Well, I don't technically *send* them anywhere." She fiddled with her fingers, twisting her ruby ring counterclockwise. "When he sent me the first letter, he instructed me to a place where I could drop them, and he promised that they would find their way to him."

Christiana tried not to laugh. "So, he gave you a drop location?"

"Is that what that's called?"

"Yes." She had plenty of her own drop locations around Viri set up for her and her network to continue with business. "Where is it?"

"He has me place them in a filigree vase that sits on a pedestal in the nobility residence wing."

"So, this mystery man could be living in the palace?" Anxiety crept through Christiana's veins.

"I suppose." Dorina shrugged. "Although there aren't many men close to our age that are available for marriage."

"Age and wedding vows haven't stopped men in the past from writing love letters to beautiful young ladies."

Dorina frowned. "Must you always assume the worst of people?"

"Yes," Christiana said matter-of-factly. "Especially when there is a serial killer running around and you are writing to a mystery man."

Dorina laughed. "Oh, Ana, you're the one who told me the killer is only targeting servants before you left, how are these two events even connected?"

Christiana's pulse raced, her mind coming up with about a half a dozen over exaggerated ideas of how they could be. She took a deep breath, attempting to remind herself that her thoughts tended to never occur. She had to trust Dorina. If this is what she wanted, she would support her as best she could.

Christiana rubbed her forehead, releasing a bit of tension. "Have you ever dropped a letter and then hidden yourself to see who would come by?"

"No," Dorina blushed. "It didn't seem right."

"Why not?"

"I don't have a natural talent for subterfuge. Unlike you, apparently."

A blush crawled up her chest, and she ducked her chin low to conceal it. "It just seems like the natural thing to do. Can you show me where this drop location is?"

"Of course." Dorina grasped her hand, the two taking off through a winding of halls and up staircases Christiana didn't recognize, sparking the idea that she certainly needed to explore more of the palace. "Here we are!"

Dorina stopped them in an entryway similar to the one of the Royal Wing; but instead of guards standing post out front, there were just a few pedestals with different sculptures and seasonal floral arrangements to make things more inviting. Christiana peered down the hall at a line of doors creeping backward before disappearing around a corner. She assumed it led to more apartments for the different council members and other nobility who had full time residences.

The vase in question was a worn-out cream with gold leaf patterns delicately crafted around the edges, circling to the center to frame a gold silhouette of a dancing couple, the woman's dress flourished outward as the gentleman held her waist.

"How romantic." Christiana leaned over to take a closer look, scanning not only the delicately-crafted piece but everything that surrounded it: the pedestal, the wall behind it, the floor surrounding it. Anything that could give away a spark of a clue of who this mystery person could be. "Is there a place to hide around here?"

"Right behind this tapestry, actually." Dorina pulled one that covered the hall's end, a two-person alcove hidden behind it.

"Perfect!" Christiana peeked inside. "When you send a new letter, you and I can hide out in here and wait for someone to pick it up. Then we can ask them a few questions."

Dorina fiddled with the tapestry's thick edges. "That seems just so...improper."

"Well, I don't think many would find this whole flirtation of yours is being handled properly to begin with," Christiana teased. "We can push a few boundaries. Don't you want to know who it is?"

Dorina nodded sheepishly. "But that doesn't mean—"

"Shh." Christiana cut her off, listening closely to a mumble of voices that grew louder with each second, echoing down the hallway. Christiana perked up, her throat tightening.

"You'd better start explaining yourself," a deep tenor tone crept closer to them. Christiana shoved Dorina into the hidden alcove, dropping the fabric in front of them.

"What are you doing?" Dorina seethed through her teeth.

"I don't want anyone to see us," she whispered back. Dorina just looked at her quizzically, nose scrunched, but she didn't have time to reply before someone else spoke up.

"I told you, Father, it was nothing."

Christiana's spine straightened as she recognized the piercing soprano.

Elaine. Her companion, her father.

Christiana leaned slightly forward, her ear closer to the thick tapestry.

"I'll be the judge of that," her father snapped. "You have been impertinent for weeks now, and I am sick of your behavior."

"I don't understand the problem." Their voices didn't move, and Christiana's heart beat heavily against her chest. They were right in front of the tapestry. "I'm available for every dinner and event where you demand my presence. You've never had an issue with me spending time with others around the palace before."

Christiana leaned back, squinting to see through the crack where the tapestry met the wall. She couldn't spot both of them, but Elaine stood with her back to them, her dull raven curls hanging limply down her back, contrasting against the evergreen velvet of her dress.

"Yes, when you *tell me* where you are going," her father grumbled. "You've been out late almost every night for weeks now. You don't tell me or your mother anything about how you spend your time. Even worse, your Lady's Maid brought me one of your gowns last week and it was covered in *blood*!"

Silence fell, and Christiana sat frozen. So many questions filled her brain, all of them blending together as she tried to figure out what exactly was happening. What were they talking about? Blood? Staying out too late? Her stomach rolled, her throat dry as her mind fed her the terrible thought of what Elaine could be doing. It was moments like this that Christiana wished she had Dorina's optimism to see the best in people, because all of Christiana's notions went dark when she heard such ominous words.

Elaine yanked her velvet sleeves down so far, they covered half her palms. "I'm an adult now, Father, I shouldn't have to tell you everything." Her voice was shallow and weak, barely above a whisper, as if she were hiding something. Christiana's arms crawled with gooseflesh.

Her father lunged at her, grabbing her upper arm and yanking her toward him, "You live under my roof until we find you a husband, so be grateful for what I give you."

"Let me go!" Elaine shrieked, before a smack echoed off the walls around them. Christiana stiffened, her hand covering her mouth to smother her gasp as a mottled red spot appeared on Elaine's father's face.

"F-F-Father, I—" Elaine shook as she backed up a step, but it was too late.

Her father's eyes darkened, his posture rigid as he stalked after her. "We are going back to our apartment, and you will stay there until you explain what you have been doing these past weeks." He grabbed her arm and yanked her out of sight. Their footsteps drifted away, but Christiana held Dorina in place until she heard the slam of a door. Then she pulled the tapestry away, freeing them from the claustrophobic confines.

"What do you think that was about?" Dorina's face was flushed red, a bead of sweat breaking up the cosmetics around her hairline.

"No idea." Christiana mumbled, her eyes trailing down the hallway, mouth gaping.

"Well, I hope Elaine is alright." Dorina brushed off her dress. "She may not have been my favorite choice for Zander's wife, but she shouldn't be forced into seclusion because she wants to have a life."

Christiana tried to smile at Dorina's remark, but the heavy weight bearing down on her shoulders was far from funny. Her pulse picked up, her mind jumping to a dangerous conclusion about why Elaine had come home with blood on her dress.

Chapter Thirteen

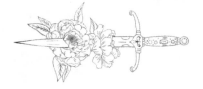

ANOTHER WEEK PASSED BEFORE MAREK finally arrived in Cittadina, and another life was lost in that time. The rumors Lucian had feared were now openly whispered around the castle, both with the servants and the nobility. The Royal Family was trying their best to put on a brave face, to show everyone in the castle that the Crown was investigating vigerously, but inside, Christiana's soul shook at the reminder of the lives lost.

She hadn't slept the night of the last killing, her stomach rolling with nausea and her mind filled with darkened, helpless thoughts. She kept imagining that she heard the poor woman's screams, the hallucination taunting her until the morning when Robert had come and delivered the grave news that a body had been found.

She tried to look ahead, knowing that she could finally do something to help since Marek had arrived. Christiana and Zander, accompanied by Robert, sped through the forest, hoofbeats echoing around them across the frozen earth. Christiana's insides buzzed, the hairs on the back of her neck standing at attention, but she didn't care. She was ready to see Marek again and start the investigation.

Although he would technically have residence in the palace itself, Christiana knew he wouldn't feel comfortable living there every day. She wanted to make sure he had a sanctuary by offering up her cottage for him to live in while he was in town, a sanctuary secluded in the depths of the forests surrounding Cittadina. Marek would feel right at home in the peaceful, quiet area.

They slowed their pace when they broke through the trees into the quaint clearing that housed her private property. Smoke already billowed from the stone chimney, an orange glow emanating from the few windows that speckled the walls. She jumped off Willow, Robert taking the reins from her and whispering something before she shot for the door. Marek already waited in her common room, his kind half-smile welcoming her as he stood from the threadbare couch.

"I'm so happy you made it!" She wrapped herself into his arms, not caring that she was smearing his clean tunic with the dirt and grime from her steel-gray velvet riding jacket.

"Thank you." He squeezed her back in return, rubbing a soothing circle against her back as his chin rested on top of her head.

Once they pulled apart, Christiana turned to see Zander hovering in the entryway, shifting his feet as if he didn't know if he was welcome or not. Christiana rolled her eyes. "You can come in Zander, he knew you and Robert were coming."

"Yes, Prince," Marek stood tall, his menacing steps gaining on Zander as he looked him up and down. "We are planning to work together over the next few weeks, so I think it's only fitting that you see my face."

Zander winced. "Of course, Sir."

"*Sir?*" Marek shook his head, a low, deep laugh erupting from his chest. "Haven't heard that in a while."

"I'm—I'm sorry," Zander rubbed the back of his neck, his shoulders caving downward. "Did I offend you?"

"Yes, you did." A frown settled on Marek's lips.

Christiana shoved in between them, grasping Zander's hand. "No, you didn't. Marek's just using you for his own amusement."

"Oh," Zander gave a tense chuckle, following Christiana into the common area. The two of them sat on the couch, Marek in a chair across from them.

"So," Christiana started, rubbing her hands together to ignite warmth into her cold-bitten fingers. "You start working tomorrow. You'll have to show your papers...you have all of those, right?"

"Of course," he said, pointing to a stack of scrolls on the two-person dining table near the kitchen. Proof of citizenship, including his birth record, a tradesman record, and his proof of residency from Tagri were needed to make a move from one part of the country to another. It helped potential employers keep track of the men they chose to work for them. With years of military espionage under his belt before being forced into assassin work, Marek had assured them he would be able to secure the proper paperwork to make up his new identity as a servant. Zander had told his parents when they arrived back home that he had decided to move one of Christiana's favorite stablehands to the palace for a work posting.

"Perfect." Christiana let out a deep breath. "Take your time integrating yourself. There is no rush if it makes you uncomfortable..."

"There is plenty of rush, dear one." He side-eyed her. "We need to figure out what is going on and we will get more information from me integrating quickly into the staff."

"I know," she sighed, giving up trying to convince Marek to be careful.

Zander's eyes darted between them. "Is there a reason we should be concerned about your presence?"

"You didn't tell him?" Marek asked Christiana.

She stiffened. "I wasn't sure if you wanted him to know!"

"You should have her tell you," Marek jutted his chin at Zander. "My past is quite the tale to enjoy."

Christiana shook her head. "Actually, it is complicated and disheartening."

"How so?" Zander asked.

"Let's just say, assassination isn't the only thing I'm technically wanted for." Marek peeked up at Zander through his eyelashes.

Zander's eyes widened. "Excuse me?"

Before Christiana could scold Marek for twisting the situation for his amusement yet again, the door opened, ushering in Robert with his riding bag slung over his shoulder and his cheeks still red from the nip of cold air. Marek stood to meet him. "Welcome, I'm Marek."

"Robert Donoghue. It is a pleasure to finally meet you." Robert offered his hand to Marek. Without hesitation, Marek grasped it and shook it.

"Ah yes," he nodded with a grin. "Christiana's informant in this area. She's told me a lot about you and your days as a soldier. How you went back in the military to be her guard. Thank you for keeping my favorite girl safe."

Christiana rubbed her forehead, trying to hide her reddened face behind her palm. "Marek...stop it."

"I should be thanking *you*, actually," Robert laughed, pulling Christiana to him in a side hug. "It's because of you that she and I even met."

Zander's brows creased down. "What are you talking about?"

"It's nothing, Zander," Christiana shook her head. "Marek just helped me connect with Robert is all."

She had never told Zander how she and Robert came to be friends;

it never felt like her place to let him know Robert had hired her to take out his abusive older brother. In the beginning, Robert hadn't reached out to Christiana, he had reached out to Marek for help. Ready to finally be done with jobs, Marek had offered the kill to Christiana, marking her first job on her own. Without his assistance, Christiana never would have met the only man she ever considered to be a brother.

"So, is this everyone on our little investigative team?" Marek offered his seat to Robert before pulling a second chair from the kitchen table over.

"Yes, Marek," Christiana sighed.

"Perfect, then here is the plan I've come up with so far." Marek clasped his hands. "I will be spending the next few days listening and learning as much as I can about the first few victims. Maybe if we dig deeper into their lives we can figure out a pattern this person has for choosing victims."

"Smart," Robert nodded. "If we can figure out that pattern, we can try and find his intended targets before he gets to them."

"Exactly. Speaking of, I was bored last night, so I decided to sneak into the palace to search those hallways you've been finding the bodies in."

Christiana gaped at him. "So much for being careful!"

"It was easy enough, and I just wanted to drop in to see what it was like at night." He waved his hand, dismissing her necessary concern. "Anyway, I already deduced something that I wonder if you are aware of."

"Alright," Christiana sighed. "What is it?"

"First, you tell me what you know about Crimson Fire." Marek leaned back in his chair, arms crossed.

"Marek," Christiana groaned, banging her head gently against the back of the couch. "I don't need a teaching moment right now."

"Apparently you do, if you didn't figure this out weeks ago." He shook his head. "So?"

"It is a poison that infects the blood and boils it from the inside out." Christiana rattled off as if she was once again a child back in a tutoring session. "It is violent, extremely painful, and causes burns and blisters to form along the skin, mutilating the body until it finally gives out. How does that help?"

"Think about it for a moment."

Zander sat up straight. "He isn't killing them in the halls, that's just where he dumps the bodies."

Marek nodded in approval. "Exactly. One point for the Prince."

"How did you deduce that?" Christiana looked over at Zander, pride radiating off of him.

"Well, if it's as painful as you say, the victims must scream and fight a lot while it's ravaging their body." He shrugged. "Those halls are so narrow, that type of struggle would echo and catch someone's attention. Especially now that my father has increased the number of guards that patrol there on the nights he is expected to kill."

"I'm impressed." Christiana leaned over and kissed his cheek. His eyes cast downward as a blush spread up his cheeks.

"So am I," Marek smirked at Zander, who relaxed at the approval. "Now, it isn't too much to go on, but I will hopefully have more in a few days' time."

"It's more than we knew before today." Christiana hoped that this was only the beginning of the new details they would learn, preferably before another body appeared in the halls.

Chapter Fourteen

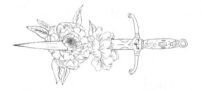

FEW DAYS WENT BY, EVERYONE KEEPING quiet as they continued on with their daily lives. Christiana attempted to look enthused during wedding planning, wanting to make sure her relationship with Penelope didn't become strained under the constant pressure. It was also a distraction from Zander, who was constantly busy with work, or her and Dorina's lack of results trying to figure out who the secret admirer was.

"Here you go, My Lady." Natalia placed a cup of tea in front of Christiana as she read a letter, the gingery steam wafting against her cheeks.

Christiana wrinkled her brow. "Thank you, but I didn't ask for this."

"I know," Natalia smiled down at her, rosy lips tight, her hands twisting in her apron. "I just wanted to make sure you had everything you needed before I left for the laundry room."

"Thank you." Christiana tilted her head, looking Natalia up and down. "As always, I am perfect when in your care. Take your time with the laundry, no need to rush since Zander will be here soon with dinner."

"Yes, My Lady." Natalia lowered her eyes as she dropped into a curtsy, skirts ruffling as her legs trembled. She gave one more weary smile before gathering the sack of soiled clothing from the corner and hurrying from the room.

Christiana watched her leave, frowning. Natalia had been her Lady's Maid since she was eighteen and took over her title. She had always been accommodating and seemed to know what Christiana needed at any moment. Yet, something about her actions recently seemed a touch more intense, as if she needed to be on her best behavior. Not that Christiana minded, but the change in conduct was odd. Concern wrapped around her heart as she wondered what might be going on with Natalia. Christiana couldn't help but wonder if Natalia was more nervous about the killer and was attempting to put on a brave face. Her chest ached at that idea, knowing she would need to have a conversation with Natalia soon about it.

Christiana shook her head, her fingertips tracing the edges of the teacup as she went back to reading her correspondence. The tea soothed her, the gentle bite of ginger root at the back of her throat freeing a slight sigh from her lips. Maybe she did need this tea more than she realized, the tension in her spine loosening ever so slightly with each sip.

A knock soon interrupted her reading. Christiana dropped her papers to rush to the door and open it, revealing Zander's handsome face.

"Hello, love," he greeted with a small peck on her cheek. A handful of servants entered the room behind him with trays of food for dinner. "Sorry if I'm a bit early. "

"Your early arrival is never a problem." She walked back inside, watching the servants quickly drop the trays of food and dismiss themselves.

"Good," he smirked, settling into the chair next to her, opening the silver satin napkin and settling it on his lap before picking up his utensils.

Christiana stacked her papers quickly and set them aside, pulling her food closer to enjoy the roasted pheasant and purple potato puree with leeks and braised carrots. "How were the budget meetings?"

Zander's face creased as he vigorously cut a piece of meat off the bone. "A bore as usual, but I think we're starting to make some progress."

"Well, what kind of struggles were you dealing with? Maybe I can help," Christiana said slowly, her fork twisting in her fingers as it scraped against her food without actually picking any up. Zander's fork hovered above his meal, his whole body frozen as he stared at the table. "Zander?"

"I'm sorry, love, but I can't discuss any details with you right now." He glanced up at her, gnawing at his lower lip as he tapped his fork against his porcelain plate.

Her fingertips began to tingle, a lump forming in her throat. "Why not?"

"My father asked me not to," he whispered, his head falling back against the chair. "I'm sorry."

"But *why*?" Christiana pinched the bridge of her nose and rubbed soothing circles into the skin.

"He keeps saying that he doesn't want to distract you from your current responsibilities."

"You can't actually believe that excuse by now." Christiana dropped her hand back on the table.

Zander rubbed his forehead. "He's...traditional. He's not used to it yet."

"Well, that's not a good enough reason!" Christiana's voice rose slightly, echoing off the dark stone walls. "When we get married, I'm going to be the future Queen. I need to learn about matters of state sooner rather than later."

"I know," he agreed, leaning his elbow on the corner separating them. "And you will learn. I'll teach you once we take the throne. Then you'll have as much access and say in Viri as I do."

Christiana shook her head and dropped her fork, sending droplets of jus splattering against the table. "We have plans to help this country...changes that we need to start implementing the moment we take the throne. We can't be worried about my tutoring the first few years when we have plenty of time for me to learn now."

"I know, and I promise we will keep trying to get you into those meetings." He grazed his fingers against her cheek. "But just think, I'll be a much kinder tutor than my father ever will," he teased, leaning forward, his lips pursed to kiss her.

"Shhh. Don't worry, My Lady, I'll be kind."

It was only a second, but that was all it took for the darkness to settle into her, the flash of icy blue eyes and a wicked grin brushing against her tear-stained cheek overtaking her memory.

"Don't touch me!" The words burst from her mouth before her mind could even process them, her body seizing at the feeling of his breath against her cheek.

He jerked away, his brow furrowed. "What's going on with you?"

"Nothing," she mumbled, pushing herself away from the table to get some distance, her insides quivering with each step. She pulled in deep breaths, her jagged fingernails scratching against her velvet sleeves.

"Don't lie to me." His chair scraped backward against the stone floor, his footsteps light as he approached her. "I know you too well.

Just talk to me, you know I'm here for you."

She pulled in one more deep breath before turning to find him standing a few feet away. "I know, but it really is nothing, I just didn't want to be touched. Is that so wrong?"

His face creased, lips blending into a thin line. "You're really not going to tell me?"

"I'm sorry." Her gaze fell, her mind desperately trying to think of anything else besides that night in the woods. She wasn't ready to show Zander that part of her, the weakness that brewed inside her every day. She loved the way he looked at her like she was flawless...she didn't want to let that look go.

But the weight of this secret kept her heart in unrest. It would be so easy to tell him right now, to open up and tell him the truth of her condition. The logical, reasonable part of her mind knew he would listen intently, and love her no matter what. Yet her mouth stayed shut, the words never passing her lips. When it came to trauma, when it came to her Battled Brain, logic rarely won an argument. The darkness was always the victor. Zander would never know about her Battled Brain and the symptoms that came with it. She wanted to be that strong woman he fell in love with. She could handle this without him.

"Look, back to the matter at hand..."

"Ana! Why are you changing the subject?"

"Because this is more important than my personal space! We have so much that we want to do for this country, and I don't want to delay it any more than it already is."

He shook his head, taking a tentative step forward. "Maybe we should put together some of the plans that we want to accomplish for Viri. If we go to him with clear reasons why this is so important to us, he may not be able to ignore our requests."

"A lot of good that would do us," she mumbled under her breath.

Zander's spine straightened. "Excuse me?"

"I know how much you care about your father." She rubbed the back of her neck, accidently pulling a few strands of hair free from her updo. "But I don't think he would be as helpful as you believe."

"That's not true. If he knew the truth..."

"He has been King for twenty-five years. If he hasn't accepted the truth by now and helped his own people, I don't think he ever will."

He walked around the navy-and-silver chaise. "I understand you're upset with him for not helping you and your mother. I would be, too. But I swear, if he had known..."

"But he did know!" The words spilled out like hot oil, burning Zander as he heard them, his face twisting in pain.

"Excuse me?" His voice quivered.

She tried her best to keep her tone even and calm, but her insides shook with each word of truth. "I found out a few months back that my mother did tell someone about what was happening to us. *Your mother.*"

He shook his head. "Wh—what? How—what are you talking about?"

"Remember how part of my plan involved Julian discovering my identity? So I could get him close enough to poison?" Zander nodded. Christiana's fingers ached, the tremor setting in. She had told him that part of the plan because she had to warn him that she might be exposed if something went wrong. Zander just didn't know how close Julian actually got to her that night. "Well, he told me that your mother tried to help us by writing a letter to your father while he was away at war delegation talks." Christiana pushed herself off the mantle, her fingers laced behind her back to keep them hidden. "But your father refused to take down a man as powerful as my father. He thought it was more of a burden then a benefit."

Zander collapsed into her chaise, his face falling into his hands, fingers curling into his hairline and tugging the strands forward. She knelt before him, her hands resting on his knees.

"Julian is a liar," Zander rumbled, his head wagging back and forth. "You have no proof."

"I know, but—"

"This can't be happening..." His body rocked slowly.

"Zander..."

"My father is a good man." His voice cracked, "At least...I thought..."

"I'm so sorry," she whispered. "I didn't want you finding out this way."

"You've known this for months." He looked up at her, his eyes flashing with hurt. "Why are you only telling me now?"

"Because you're right, I don't have any proof to back up the claim, except my own gut telling me it's true." She stared down at the floor, biting her lip. "I know what it feels like to lose the perfect image a father weaves for his children. I didn't want to be the one to ruin it for you until I could prove its validity."

Zander clutched his fingers at the roots of his hair. "But you think it *is* true?"

Christiana took a deep breath. "Yes, I do. Maybe I just want to believe that my mother did something to try and protect me, but when Julian told me, it just felt...honest."

Christiana wished she could fix this, to take the pain away from him, but there was nothing she could do except sit there helplessly. Zander just stared at the ground, his fingers so tightly wound in his hair that she was scared he would rip it out by the roots. This wasn't how tonight was supposed to go.

"I'm sorry, love, but I'm not hungry anymore," he stood abruptly, his eyes still frosted over with disorientation. "I think...I'm going to take a walk."

Christiana grasped his hand. "Do you want some company?"

"No." He shook his head, lifting her hand with a squeeze, placing a kiss on her knuckles. "I just need to be alone right now."

He walked from the room, his movements sluggish and dragging as if he had just woken up from a terrible nightmare. Christiana's heart ached as the door clicked shut behind him, wondering how what was supposed to be a relaxing evening together could take such a terrible turn.

Chapter Fifteen

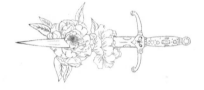

THE NEXT DAY, CHRISTIANA TOOK THE morning alone in her room to enjoy a peaceful breakfast. Her emotions were exhausted, her body heavy like her bloodstream was filled with lead, every inch of her dragging. Her heart ached for Zander, wishing she could do something, anything, to bring him peace, but she wasn't the one who could bring that to him.

"Is everything alright, My Lady?" Natalia asked her as she placed the final few sapphire-crusted pins into Christiana's dark hair. Her hands moved delicately, never pulling or hurting Christiana's head as she sculpted her long locks. She had been lucky to find Natalia all those years ago. She was looking forward to formally offering her the position as First Lady's Maid to the Queen. She would be in charge of Christiana's entire household and slew of maids. Natalia had done so much for Christiana over the years, she deserved the honor more than anyone else.

"Yes. Just a bit tired, I guess."

"We should really get you a sleep draught of some kind." Concern filled Natalia's voice as she leaned over, her fingers fiddling with a few items strewn across the long dressing table. "It worries me how much sleep you lose every night. I feel like you always tell me you're tired or didn't sleep well."

Christiana played with one of her pearl necklaces sitting in front of her, her vision fuzzy. "I appreciate it, but I don't really like using medicine to sleep."

"If that's what you would like, My Lady." A hint of doubt still laced her melodic voice.

"Thank you." Christiana patted Natalia's hand gently before she walked to the closet, Christiana's black lace nightgown in her hand.

She pulled her tired muscles up, trudging to her full-length mirror to take one more appraising look at herself. She had dressed in a simple gown, the deep plum-and-black pattern flattering her pale complexion. The long sleeves had little frill, and the tight bodice flared out at the hips into a more modest-sized skirt. It was the perfect amount of formality and comfort for the long wedding meeting Christiana was about to enter. With one last goodbye to Natalia, Christiana left her apartment and headed down the corridor to the King and Queen's suite.

The walk felt longer than usual, her chest tightening as she passed Zander's door. She hesitated a moment in front of it, scanning it up and down as if just her eyes could push it open. She could knock and see if he was still inside, just to see his handsome face once before she had to go, to give him a kiss, to remind him he wasn't alone in this struggle.

But if it was her in his position, she would want time alone to decipher everything in her own mind and heart.

Taking a deep breath, she continued on, her eyes straight ahead to her intended destination. Knocking quietly, she entered through the open door. To her surprise, she found Penelope sitting at the dining table; but it wasn't Dorina with her this time, it was Zander.

"What are you doing here?" she couldn't stop herself from asking.

His sapphire-blue eyes stared up at her, tired and rimmed with purplish bruises from a sleepless night. "I wanted to talk to my mother about what we discussed last night." He came to stand in front of her, his hands resting gently on her shoulders as he leaned forward to whisper in her ear. "I knew you probably wouldn't be comfortable with me going to my father about it directly, but I thought maybe you would let me talk to my mother about it."

Christiana crossed her arms, shoulders hunching. "I see."

"Love, I know that you hate talking about this. You know I wouldn't ask you to reveal this secret if it wasn't important." He sighed, his forehead resting against hers, his warmth seeping into her. "I need to know what kind of man is teaching me to lead this country, and the only way I can find that out is if we verify the claims set against him. This was the only way I could think of doing that."

Christiana stared back at him, her stomach squirming, threatening to release her breakfast back up her throat. She wanted to know the truth as well, even though deep in her soul she believed Julian's confession. There had been a gnawing in her gut for months that something was off, a tiny pang of doubt sitting in her mind.

If the Queen really didn't know, if her mother never went to her, then she was about to tell the Queen and her future mother-in-law that she spent the majority of her life being beaten by her own father. She wasn't sure if she was ready to see the pity in Penelope's eyes every time they saw each other. Yet, if Zander learned that his father was aware of the country's problems and chose to ignore them, then maybe he would start fighting back on the decision to keep her from learning matters of rulership.

With a deep breath she said, "Alright, let's tell her."

He let out a deep breath before taking her hand and leading her into the room, pulling a chair out for her to settle in before sitting next to her.

"You two are certainly keeping me in full suspense," Penelope said flatly, her fingers playing with her snow-white feather quill.

Zander adjusted himself, turning to face his mother. "I know you and Father have worked hard to rule Viri. And you would do anything to protect our people."

"Of course." Penelope's face crinkled as she leaned closer to Zander.

"But I have come to learn that there are a few other...problems that I'm not sure you've been made aware of in the past." He gently took Penelope's hand.

"Hm," Christiana grunted, hoping it wasn't as loud as she heard it.

"What kind of problems?" Penelope inquired.

"Well, Christiana was recently made aware that her mother may have told you a secret many years ago. About her father and the household he chose to raise her in." He danced around with his words, as if it was impossible to say the dreaded truth out loud.

Abuse. Beating. Whipping.

Penelope sat silent in front of them, her stern face softening, her breath ragged as she squirmed in her seat to sit up straight. Her eyes turned glassy, as if tears were trying to escape. Zander continued, "But that can't be true. Can it?"

Penelope dropped her chin to her chest, the back of her fingers delicately touching her flushed cheek. Christiana stared at her, hoping she would answer, hoping she would say she never knew. She wanted to have hope that the Queen would have helped her friend and her children.

Yet as the moments passed with the Queen still in silence, the hope of that answer coming from her mouth dwindled.

"So, it's true. You did know." Christiana's words added to the tension settling around them in the expansive room.

"I'm so sorry, dear. To think of what you went through for so many years..." Penelope leaned over the table, her arm sliding across like she wanted to touch Christiana. Christiana kept her hands in her lap, her spine straight against the chair as Penelope continued, "My heart broke every single time you and your family left the palace at the end of summer. It made me want to be sick just thinking about what he did to you and poor Maria."

Zander rocked back and forth in his chair, his fingers twisted in his hair. "Mother, you couldn't have known because you would have done something. I know you would have."

"She did, Zander. Didn't you?" Christiana asked, turning to Penelope, who nodded.

"Soon after Maria told me the truth, I knew I had to get her out of that house. But the only way to do it, and do it properly, was to have your father arrest Francis. He was out of the country on political business, so I had to write him." A tear escaped her eyes, trailing a streak of her cosmetics down with it. "I planned to have him send an official warrant of arrest, so I could dispatch soldiers to your house immediately to take all of you to safety and Francis to jail. I was going to have the three of you move in here for a bit. To help you relax and feel safe."

"The warrant didn't come, though," Christiana finished.

She looked over at Zander, his mouth agape, head shaking slowly. She desperately wanted to wrap her arms around him and stroke his hair, but she was frozen, her body stitched to the seat below her as she waited for the rest of the story to unfold.

"It took weeks for the letter to make it back to me, and it wasn't what I was expecting. Lucian was livid at me, appalled that I would even suggest arresting his most powerful noble in Tagri." She wiped a few tears away, her lips tight. "He said it was up to Francis how he wanted to run his household, and we had no right to interfere with his choices."

"He had every right if it meant saving innocent people!" Zander seethed, pounding his fist on the table, shaking the cups of tea and strewing papers across it. He kicked his chair behind him as he stood, pacing a circle around the table.

To hear the confirmation of Julian's taunts spoken out loud, Christiana's heart felt as if it had been shattered by a forge-hammer. She kept her face straight ahead, never taking her eyes off the Queen. She wanted to remember every moment of this.

She wanted to remember when she lost complete hope in Zander's parents.

"Why didn't you try to talk about it with him once he returned? Why didn't you fight for your friend's safety?" Zander shouted, flushed with anger.

"Your father asked me to never speak of it again, for the safety of our marriage," she swallowed, her cheeks twitching. "I wasn't going to do anything to lose my husband or to lose you and Dorina. I chose my family, and I kept silent."

Zander grabbed an empty teacup from the table and threw it across the room, the clash ringing through the room as it made contact with the stone wall and shattered into dozens of sharp pieces. Christiana winced, her hands once again trembling as she hid them under her skirts. She didn't know how much longer she would last in this room before she broke down.

"I can't...I don't..." Zander stammered, his hands flexing in and out of fists. "I can't even be in the same room as you right now!"

"Zander, please..." Penelope stood to pull him toward her. He jerked away at her touch as if it burned him.

"Do not touch me. Do not even look at me right now. I can't

believe you could be such a heartless woman!"

"Do not talk to me that way!" Penelope hit her fist on the table. "I raised you to be a better man than that."

"And I thought I had been raised by kind, moral people." Zander shook his head. "I guess we were both wrong, *Stepmother.*"

Penelope's cheeks flared the deep red of fresh rose petals. More tears flooded from her eyes, slowly dripping down her dark skin. "You never call me that."

He scoffed. "Well, for the first time in my life, it's fitting."

Christiana looked between them, skin prickled with numbness. She'd always known Queen Penelope was actually Zander's stepmother, apparent just in the way her dark ebony skin contrasting to his pale complexion. Zander's birth mother, Queen Evette, had died in childbirth, depriving him of the chance to know her. Penelope had raised him from the time he was two years old, and Christiana knew that he loved her as if she had given birth to him, but his anger had gotten the best of him. He would regret those words in a few hours when he had the time to calm down.

"Zander..." Christiana stood and reached for him, halting him next to her.

He turned back to her, his eyes softening as he took her in. "I love you, and I am so sorry that we could have done something to help you. My parents should have done something. I just need time alone right now. Alright?"

She touched his wet cheek, a shiny layer of sweat coating his face. "Of course."

Zander nodded, walking out of the room without a second glance to his stepmother. Penelope sobbed, and Christiana's insides crawled from the tense silence between them. Slowly, she approached the Queen. "Penelope..."

"I'm so sorry Christiana. I am so sorry that I never helped you," she wept, grabbing Christiana swiftly to pull her into a hug. The Queen's tears fell onto her shoulder, soaking into her dress. Her body went rigid at the touch, her skin crawling. She bit down on the desire to pull away, slowly wrapping her arms around the Queen, patting her back in comfort. "I betrayed you and Maria all of those years ago and I have been carrying that guilt for so long. I felt so much relief when we received the news that your father had passed because I knew you were all finally safe."

"Penelope...you don't have to apologize..." Christiana stumbled over her words, wishing she could run away from the uncomfortable moment she was forced into.

"Yes, I do." Penelope pulled back to come face to face with Christiana. "And even that isn't enough. You deserved so much more growing up, and I am so happy to see that you were able to find joy. That you have found freedom."

Christiana looked away. Penelope was only trying to be encouraging, but she never felt free from her father. Not as long as she was forced to live with her condition. All she could do was nod.

"Maybe today isn't the best time for us to talk about the wedding," Penelope said. "Why don't we take the day off? I'll send a servant to let Dorina know she isn't needed."

With one more slight nod, Christiana left the room in silence, Penelope's weeping drowned out as the door shut behind her.

Chapter Sixteen

CHRISTIANA REFUSED TO LEAVE HER APARTMENT
the rest of the day. After hearing the truth from Penelope,
her soul and mind had refused to settle down. They
churned and filled with the smoky darkness consuming every inch of
her body. She spent most of the day lying on her couch with a blanket
wrapped around her and a never-ending cup of tea at her side,
desperate for a distraction. Yet her mind kept wandering to the man
she loved and the pain that had swept across his face all morning.

Just after finishing her quiet, light dinner, her entire self itched to
see him again. She straightened her appearance, making sure her hair
and tear-stained cheeks looked acceptable before she left, her feet soft
against the carpet leading to Zander's room. She knocked a few times,
louder and louder with each rap against the hard wood. Yet no one
came to answer the door.

Her stomach rolled, bile rising in her throat. Zander was always
back at his room by this time at night. She looked up and down the

hall to make sure she was alone before she wrapped her hands around the doorknob, the shining brass giving way as she twisted.

She walked in and closed the door quietly, her entire body aching as she took in the scene before her. Zander was huddled on his couch, curled on his side as he stared into the dancing fireplace embers. Her gaze lingered on the half-consumed decanter of whiskey on the table, a crystal glass already refilled. Then she knelt at his head, her fingers raking his sweaty, unruly curls from his brow.

"I'm so sorry, love," he whispered, his shaking hand reaching out to cup her cheek. "I am so sorry for what my family did to you."

"It isn't you who needs to apologize," she said. "If it was your decision back then, you would have done anything in your power to help us."

"I would have come right to your house and arrested your father myself, then brought all of you to safety." His voice hardened, his head shaking against the couch. "I just wish I could have done *something*. It was hard enough to accept that you were forced into that life when you told me over the summer, but to learn that you could have received help and we did nothing..."

"There is no point in wishing for the things we could have done in the past. Trust me, I've done it plenty and it only makes it worse."

"You were right," he mumbled, his lips half-pressed into the evergreen cushion. "I didn't want to believe it, but damn it, you were right."

Fresh tears pricked at Christiana's eyes, every inch of her desperate to help him, to stop the silent tears flowing from his eyes. "I didn't want to be." She brushed her thumb across his cheek, gathering drops falling down his flushed skin. "I wanted your mother to prove me wrong."

"Stepmother."

"Alekzander Vlastino," Christiana cupped his face, forcing his glassy eyes to focus on her. "Don't you dare say those words again. The more you say them, the more you'll regret them in a few days."

"How can I look at her the same again?"

"Honestly, I'm not sure." Christiana lifted his head gently, slipping onto the couch and placing it back in her lap. "But she raised you. She is your mother through and through, no matter your bloodline."

His cheek rubbed against her dress, the pressure slight as he sat up, wiping his face clean. "I know. I know you're right, but I just...each time I try and wrap my head around this, more questions keep forming."

Christiana leaned back, propping her arm on the back of the couch to run her fingers through his hair, fingertips massaging his scalp in soothing circles. "Moments like this are never easy to accept." She was trying to say something encouraging, but words seemed flat compared to what he was going through. "It takes time to accept the truth."

His head leaned into her touch. "But what if..."

Her fingers stopped. "What if what?"

"What if I'm not as ready to be King as I thought?"

"Zander. That is not true."

"How can it not be?" he demanded. "How can I be ready when the man who taught me how to lead isn't the leader I thought he was? I looked up to that man, I studied and learned just to make him proud, to be the leader he wanted me to be. I know it doesn't make sense, since I have what he would consider radical ideas for change, but still, I thought...I hoped...I just wanted..."

He stared at her, his sapphire eyes wide and glistening. The truth was coming to him all at once, like a tidal wave ready to destroy anything in its path and flood it with pain. Christiana wished she could take that pain away, that she could absorb it into herself and remove it from his heart and body. She was used to pain, she could deal with it.

For Zander, she could live with it.

She placed a soft kiss on his forehead. "You are not your father. Just because you are learning about his true character doesn't mean it changes yours."

"He is a hypocrite. I've tried to emulate the leadership skills of a hypocrite my whole life. How can I not question myself?" Zander leaned forward, his elbows resting on his knees. "He acts peaceful, yet sits back and allows turmoil to happen within his borders between his own people. He turns a blind eye to issues that don't affect him directly. If it doesn't hurt him, then it isn't worth fighting for. That's no way to lead."

"I agree," she nodded, her other hand tracing mindless patterns down his back and arm. His muscles slowly relaxed under her touch. "Which is why *we* can't lead that way."

"We won't." Zander peeked up to her, his jaw set firmly. "We will never let people think we are that careless of their safety."

"This is why I fell in love with you," she whispered, and a tiny smile finally broke onto his lips. "One of the many reasons. You're going to be a spectacular King, Zander. I just know you are."

"I don't know how," Zander sighed, his eyes wandering to stare aimlessly at the ceiling. "How can I be a worthy King when the one who taught me wasn't?"

"Don't look at it that way. Look at this as your final test before taking the crown. You could let it break you or you could let it strengthen your resolve. You know what you want to do for this country, you have for a long time. Don't let your father's mistakes dictate your future. What do you think would have happened to me if I had given that power to *my* father?"

He chuckled. "That is not something I want to think about."

"Neither do I." She nudged his shoulder. "It's going to take time, but you will get through this. You will accept your father for who he is and you will decide what kind of man you want to be despite what he tried to teach you. Only you can make that decision, it was never up to him."

He stroked her cheek. "I don't deserve you some days."

"Of course you do." She shrugged. "You show me all of the time that you do."

His face softened as he lifted himself up, his hand never leaving her cheek as she leaned up and sealed his lips with hers. They weren't full of hunger or desire, but kindness and love. They moved against hers slowly, as if he was trying to remember every moment, every small detail. She supported the back of his neck with her hand, taking her time and savoring every bit, the smoky taste of whiskey against her tongue, the plush feeling of his full lips, and the careful way that he held her close.

She never wanted to forget, not one moment, joyful or painful, that they would spend together for the rest of their lives.

Chapter Seventeen

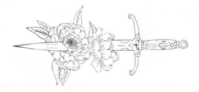

IT WASN'T EASY FOR THE ROYAL HALLWAY TO
go back to normal, tension filling the long, ornate
expanse whenever Christiana roamed. The Queen
continued to postpone wedding planning, shocking Christiana since
she had been so adamant that they barely had time to get everything
planned by the beginning of spring. Not that she minded...it gave her
more time to focus on the pressing matter at hand: the killer haunting
the halls.

Christiana, Robert and Zander spent the evening in her room,
claiming to the world they were enjoying an evening nightcap before
heading out for the night. In reality, they were waiting for Marek to
sneak in to give them an update about what he learned during his first
week.

"So, what is Marek's story anyways?" Zander asked, a glass
dangling from his fingertips.

"Are you sure this is what you want to discuss while we wait for him?" Christiana sipped her brandy, savoring the flavors of Robert's favorite brand.

"He did say you could tell us," Zander leaned forward, "and I have a feeling he wouldn't have said that if he didn't want me to know."

"Fair." She pushed herself from her leaning position at the fireplace mantle, setting herself down on her chaise. "Just know it's much more complicated than what I'm about to tell you, because even I don't know all the details."

Robert nodded. "Fair enough."

Christiana took a deep breath. "Before he became an assassin, he was in the Virian military."

"Really?" Robert perked up.

Christiana nodded. "He was a Captain in the spy and espionage division and served there for about twelve years."

"Well, what happened to force him into assassination?" Zander asked.

"His old commander framed him for war profiteering, claiming that he stole and sold thousands of coins worth of secrets and artillery to enemy countries over the years." Christiana looked down at the floor, her heart aching. She may have met him after the fact, but even back then, she knew he didn't deserve that fate. "In reality, it was Marek who discovered the ugly truth that the man he followed blindly was committing treason for years."

Robert's hand covered his mouth. "My goodness."

"When the commander realized that Marek was on to him, he framed Marek for the crimes." Christiana looked back up at them. "Luckily, one friend of Marek's did believe him and helped him fake his death before he was hung for his crimes."

"Who framed him?" Zander questioned. "What kind of investigation occurred to prove his guilt?"

"I don't know any more details than that." Christiana gave a weary smile. "He doesn't like opening up about the specifics."

"Understandable." Zander murmured, staring off into the fire, his glass perched against his knee, though he had yet to take a sip.

A few silent minutes ticked by before they heard a window being pushed open, the three of them looking up to see Marek vaulting into her common room. Setting her glass down on the table, Christiana went over to greet him, and he pulled his hood down before embracing her.

"Are you alright?" Christiana asked, her face buried against his chest.

"Of course, dear one." He smiled down at her. "This is easy compared to some of my other jobs, no need to worry about me. Do I get one of those?" He gestured to the decanter and glasses sitting on the low table surrounded by navy furniture, the light from the fireplace dancing off every surface.

"Of course." She smiled back at him, and they walked to the couch to rejoin the others. Christiana sat down next to Zander, his arm falling gently around her shoulders as she settled back into the soft cushions. "So, did you find anything out?"

"A bit." He took a sip of the delicious liquor and savored it for just a moment. "A lot of the servants here aren't afraid of gossiping, it seems, even to people they just met. It's worked out to my advantage."

"What are people saying?" Zander asked, his fingers tracing a nonsense pattern on Christiana's shoulders, a bolt of pleasure raking down her arm with each light touch.

Refusing to look at the Prince, Marek continued, "Every young girl is terrified in this castle now that the truth has come out about the victims. Most of them are trying to refuse to work past a certain hour. Some are able to get away with it, others have employers that refuse to let them."

"That's terrible," Christiana breathed, her grip tensing around her glass.

"It's to be expected," Robert sighed. "Servants keep the castle running, which means staff working every hour of the day. If it's expected of them, of course their employer is going to make them do what they were hired for."

Christiana ground her teeth together. "It's a bit different when there is someone going around killing them."

"They're safe for now, Christiana," Zander consoled. "My parents already tracked his pattern. He waits two weeks between killings. We still have a week before he may strike again."

"I suppose," she grumbled, taking another sip of brandy, finding comfort in the tingling trail it left behind as she swallowed. "Does anyone have any guesses?"

"Most people are just accusing others in the castle they don't like." Marek leaned back in his chair, his eyes wandering to stare into the fire. "Wanting to throw people's good names through the mud for their own pleasure."

"Great." Christiana dropped her head back, her neck cradled by the dip of the couch.

"However, I did a bit more digging into the details of each of the victims," Marek said, already draining his glass and pouring himself another. "Most importantly, they have all been around the same age—in their early twenties with dark hair."

"We knew most of that already." Zander rubbed his forehead.

"Well, Prince, did you know that all of them were romantically uninvolved?"

"That sounds like Natalia." A shudder ran through Christiana's body, trying to banish the image of her Lady's Maid helpless and hurt by this person's hand.

Robert leaned forward, hand grasping her forearm. "I'll make sure to keep an eye on her, especially on the dangerous days."

"Promise?" She looked at him with wide, begging eyes. She couldn't let someone she cared about get hurt, not when she could have prevented it.

"Of course," he said, giving her arm one last squeeze before leaning back. "I'll even escort her back to her bedroom every night."

"Thank you, and I'll make sure to send her away early on those nights as well." Christiana nodded, the knots in her stomach loosening a fraction as she rolled the edge of her glass across her lips. "So the killer could be a man luring them for a romantic tryst?"

"That was my thought as well."

Zander tapped his fingers against the couch. "Technically, we can't rule out the nobility yet either."

"Why do you say that?" Marek challenged.

"Well, since we've established that the girls are being lured someplace and not ambushed in the halls to be killed, technically a noble person calling a servant to their rooms is the most convenient way." Zander shook his head. "I hate the idea of someone I trust doing this, but we can't deny that's a convenient opportunity."

"Looks like I've been underestimating you, Prince." Marek raised his glass to Zander, who blushed slightly.

Christiana stared at Zander, her mind wandering back to a conversation she'd overheard.

"What is it, My Lady?" Robert asked, his eyes quizzical.

"I'm not sure." Her stomach churned, unsure if this was the right time to bring this up. However, people's lives were at stake, so every piece of possible evidence needed to be discussed. "It's just...I overheard an odd conversation the other day."

Zander froze. "Oh?"

Christiana bit her lip, peeking up at him through her eyelashes. "It was Elaine."

"Oh, Ana, please," Zander dropped his head into his right hand, then ran his fingers through his hair. "You can't actually—?"

"Now, hold on a moment," Marek held up his hand to cut Zander off, his eyes turning back to her. "What's making you suspicious?"

"I only caught a bit of the conversation, but Elaine's father was accusing her of dubious activities." Christiana tapped her finger against her lips. "Staying out late, refusing to talk about what she'd been up to, and even that she had come home one evening with her dress covered in blood." She looked between the three men, all of them giving her wary, unconvinced looks. "I'm not making this up!"

"I don't think you are." Zander shook his head. "But I spent enough time with Elaine over the years. She always seemed to be fairly open about the types of activities she enjoyed. Maybe she's just tired of answering to her father."

"What activity would involve a *bloody dress*?"

"I'm not sure," Zander said, rubbing a circle on her tense shoulder.

"I do agree it sounds suspicious," Marek nodded. "However, we've established Crimson Fire was the cause of death, and although a little bleeding can seep through from broken skin, it's nothing dire enough to soak a whole dress in blood."

Christiana groaned, her head falling against the back of the couch again. "I suppose that's true."

"We can't rule anything out," Zander cautioned. "I just don't think that's enough to go on right now. Maybe when we learn more about the ladies who were killed..."

"I'll ask around more, see what specific households they were assigned to and what the jobs were," Marek said. "Maybe if any of them crossed paths with Elaine, we can move forward with that line of investigation."

"I'm surprised your parents haven't already done that," Christiana said to Zander.

He grunted. "Who knows, maybe they have and it's just

something else they are keeping from me."

Christiana wrapped their hands together. "Well, lucky for us, we have our own team working on catching this person. You're doing what's right for your people, just as you promised."

"Very true." He smiled before turning back to the other two men, discussing what to do next. Christiana settled back into the plush cushions, but it did nothing to calm her tightened muscles and swirling heart.

Something just wasn't right with Elaine.

Chapter Eighteen

THE BRISK AIR SETTLED AROUND CHRISTIANA AS
she flew through the thicket of trees back to the palace.
She had woken up after barely any sleep the night
before, desperate to escape the confines of the palace walls. She
decided to spend time with the one who never questioned her but
always kept great company: her mare, Willow.

She tried to forget what her life would be like in the coming hours
and soaked up the last few stretches of galloping, her body moving in
sync with her steed. Her vision tunneled, focusing on nothing but
herself, Willow, and the winter-filled nature surrounding them. Finally,
a fleeting moment of happiness without the constant reminder of the
stressors in her life.

Her breath sped up as she struggled to pull in air, but she couldn't
stop. She didn't want to stop. All she wanted to do was release
everything from her body, her frustration, her troubles, her
aggravations. Though it felt like being truly free of her pain was

impossible, she could pretend, even for just a moment, as bare branches and chilled wind brushed against her.

When the wide opening of the forest entrance finally came into view, Christiana sighed and slowed Willow down to a trot before crossing the threshold into the palace grounds. The heaving mare came to a walk and then a complete stop just a few feet from the stables. A stablehand waited patiently, an amused grin on his face as he looked up at Christiana.

"May I take your horse for you, My Lady?" Marek asked, his hair secured at the nape of his neck, his clothes dirt-coated and sweaty from a long morning of work.

Christiana dismounted, "Oh, why thank you."

"We need to talk soon, dear one," he whispered, taking Willow's reins and rubbing her sweaty neck with his gloved hand.

"About?"

His lips tightened into a thin line. "That other matter you asked me to consult on while I'm here."

"Oh, yes, that." She crossed her arms. "I'll stop by the cottage in the next few days."

"Very well, looking forward to seeing you there." He gave her a brisk smile before he turned away, clicking his tongue to urge Willow after him.

Christiana began her walk back to the palace, each step heavier and heavier. It had nothing to do with exhaustion from the ride, but the unwanted anticipation of what the rest of her day looked like. She glanced up to the partially-clouded sky, wisps of white speckled across a bright blue background, the sun shining bright despite the chilled winter air. It burned her nostrils as she pulled in a deep breath, but she didn't care; the biting sting cleansed her soul, a sense of peace washing over her. She could make it through, just one day at a time.

She was not broken.

The sound of heavy swords clashing against something, grunts and screams peppered between each strike, ruined her moment. Christiana's brow furrowed as she turned to catch a glimpse of the training yard, her feet stopping abruptly, mouth gaping as she took in Rowan with a young lady slashing at him in a sparring match.

Dorina's voice rang out, attempting to growl in intimidation as she raised the sword above her head, but it sounded more like a feral cat then a ferocious beast. She kept hitting the sword downward, making contact with Rowan's weapon every time. However, her technique was rudimentary at best. Rowan shouted instructions with each blow, his own technique perfected, but she held the sword with both hands and struck haphazardly; in no way was she purposefully attempting to hit him. Her frustration creased across her face, but Rowan's gaze was trained on her, laughter escaping his lips, relaxation settling across his face even though he was in the middle of sparring.

Christiana had promised to give him space, and going over there could be construed as breaking that promise. Yet her best friend was obviously in distress, and she wasn't one to walk away from a friend in need.

She kept that reasoning in her head as she crossed the last few steps to drape her arms over the side of the training ring.

The pair continued their fight for a few more moments, Christiana attempting to contain her laughter when Dorina tried to kick Rowan's shins, almost tripping over her footwork in the process. Rowan disarmed her and then grabbed her wrist, pulling her sharply around and trapping her in a big hug. Dorina squirmed, kicking her legs forward, her melodic laughter drowning out her desperate pleas for Rowan to let go.

When the pair finally looked up, they froze, Rowan releasing Dorina at once, his shoulders stiffening. Dorina didn't seem affected, stepping quickly toward the edge of the ring.

"Do you want to talk about it?" Christiana asked as Dorina approached.

"Talk about what?" A layer of sweat coated Dorina's face, her biceps trembling. Rowan hesitated a few feet away, his sword-bearing hand tightening around the hilt as he shot a hard glare at her.

"Whatever is causing you to attempt murder?" she laughed, ignoring the pressure snaking up her spine from his weighted gaze.

"It's nothing." Dorina dropped the sword and hopped over the side of the ring next to Christiana. She ran her sweaty hands down the length of her black pants as she walked to the circle of stumps nearby.

"Obviously it's not nothing." Christiana took a seat next to her friend. "What is it? You can talk to me."

"Maybe she doesn't want to talk to you about it," Rowan mumbled, his hand methodically cleaning his practice sword as he joined them as well.

Christiana stifled a grunt. "Then she doesn't have to tell me, but that isn't going to stop me from offering."

Rowan scoffed, mumbling unintelligible words under his breath as he shoved the cloth back in his pocket and sheathed his sword.

"Rowan," Dorina scolded, squirting a bit of water from the tip of her waterskin, the flow hitting him across his tunic. "Don't be rude. Why don't you go back inside? I'll meet you for breakfast in a bit once I clean up."

"Alright." He nodded, squeezing her shoulder gently before picking up his satchel. "I'll see you soon." He didn't give Christiana one more glance as he stalked off toward the front door.

"On behalf of Rowan, I apologize." Dorina's eyes softened as she turned to Christiana, their knees knocking together.

Christiana held up her hand. "No need, it's not undeserved. I'm just happy to see mine and Zander's actions didn't affect your relationship with him."

She shrugged. "He tried to let it, but I showed him how idiotic that was. I didn't do anything and it was obvious he needed a friend to make living here bearable while he heals. I may not have been his *best* friend, but we were close enough. I figured I could be a support."

"I'm surprised they aren't trying to put you in the middle."

"Neither of them is stupid enough to try that." Dorina fiddled with the ends of her cranberry tunic. "We don't talk about you and Zander, mostly we just enjoy each other's company a few days a week. Finding normalcy is the best way to move on, and he can't do that if he's constantly talking and thinking about what happened."

"That's fair." Christiana nodded, her heart warming. She wished she could be there for Rowan, but that was impossible. If she couldn't, Dorina was the best person for the job. No one could be upset when in her effervescent presence.

"Enough about that." Christiana waved her hand over her shoulder. "What's troubling you?"

A few seconds passed as Dorina took a sip from her waterskin. "Well, Mother and Father decided to have an interesting talk with me at breakfast yesterday. Apparently, since you and Zander were otherwise engaged, they took it upon themselves to discuss what they consider to be an important topic."

A chill ran through her spine. "Oh, no..."

"Oh, yes," She leaned forward. "Did you know royal weddings are an excellent place to meet and mingle with potential suitors?"

"You know, I have heard that rumor before." Christiana gave a lighthearted chuckle that she promptly smothered when Dorina stared at her flatly.

"They just kept going on and on about how it's my duty and they want to make sure I am all settled and safe as soon as possible." Her heel kicked the stump underneath her. "I blame you and Zander for making me have to sit through that whole morning. If you two had been there, they never would have brought it up."

"Did they give you anyone specific they had in mind?"

"No," Dorina admitted, her bouncy curls shaking around her face. "But mother mentioned that there were plenty of potentials that they were inviting, both Virian nobility and foreign alliances. Edgar's name even came up briefly in the conversation."

"Oh no," Christiana shook her head, waving her hands between them. "Your parents would have to kill me *and* Zander before we let that happen."

Edgar had been a thorn in her side for years, but last summer he had proved to be an even bigger pain than she realized. He had attempted to trick her into marriage, wanting to take back all of the lands he had sold to her over the years to bail him out of debt. He was a snake of a man who didn't deserve any woman in this court, let alone Dorina.

Dorina laughed. "Don't worry, Father was actually the one to take his name off the list. Something about debts and not needing to incur any more."

Christiana snorted. "Well, that's good. Besides, last I checked the guest list, he had declined the wedding invitation because of...business needs that could not be put off." Christiana was happy that he wasn't going to disturb her wedding day. She didn't need that detestable man trying to ruin any part of it. Although his decision may have been swayed to stay away when Christiana had sent over a scathing letter during the fall months, requesting his absence and adding in a few hints about what she would do if he decided to try and show up. He had threatened her with revenge for embarrassing him, but she made sure to end that possibility before it could even begin.

"At least you're safe from that heathen," Christiana nudged Dorina's shoulder with hers.

"I suppose." Tears threatened to escape Dorina's round, russet eyes as she looked down at the ground.

Christiana's heart panged for her friend. "I'm so sorry." She grasped Dorina's limp hands. "We thought we had more time. I know that's what Zander thought."

She pouted. "So did I."

"Maybe you don't need to give up complete hope. Your secret admirer could be one of the men your parents are so keen to introduce you to."

"Maybe," Dorina sniffed, concern whispering across her face. "Although I am no closer to figuring out who that is as every attempt we've made has been fruitless."

"Well, if you're willing to get your hands dirty," she patted Dorina's knee. "I may have a few ideas on how we can figure it out."

Dorina wiggled her eyebrows. "What did you have in mind?"

***

"I'm back!" Christiana said as she burst through her apartment door, startling a yelp from Natalia's lips and a stack of linens from her hands as she whipped around, clutching her chest. "I'm sorry, did I frighten you?"

"Just a bit, My Lady." Natalia said, her hands trembling as she outstretched them for Christiana's soiled riding coat and gloves. "I have your tea ready, and I even had some chocolate tartlets sent up. I thought they would be a delightful pick-me-up before your midmorning meeting."

"Thank you." Christiana slowly walked to her dining room table, her eyes never leaving Natalia as she scurried around the apartment fluffing pillows and tidying up areas that looked perfectly clean to Christiana. "Natalia, are you alright?"

She looked over the edge of the couch as she beat her fists against the pillow to make it stand upright. "Of course, My Lady. Why? Am I doing something wrong?"

"Of course not! But would you mind sitting down with me for a moment?"

"Oh, um..." Natalia fiddled with the end of her black braid, gnawing at her full, bottom lip. "Of course, My Lady."

"Wonderful." Christiana pulled her chair out and brought the tea set closer, pouring two cups. Natalia gave it a wary gaze before pulling the chair out, slowly sinking into it.

She pulled her cup into her hands, taking a tentative sip before looking up at Christiana. "Thank you, My Lady."

"Of course," she said. "I wanted to check in. I know the minute we got here, things started spiraling out of control."

"A bit," Natalia mumbled, tracing the silver painted pattern on the saucer.

"I know rumors about the serial killer have been spreading." Christiana wanted to reach across the table and hold Natalia's twitching hand, but she kept it glued to her side. "I just wanted to see if there was something I could do for you."

Natalia blinked rapidly. "For...for me, My Lady? But why?"

"This is your home too, Natalia." Christiana leaned forward a bit, her forearms resting on the table. "You deserve to feel safe here. Please tell me if there is anything I can do to help ease your fears."

"Oh, My Lady..." she stuttered, squirming in the chair. "Truly, I feel fine, I promise...this is just...I don't..."

"Natalia," Christiana soothed, finally sliding her hand across and grasping Natalia's. "It's alright, I'm offering."

Natalia took a few deep breaths before looking back up at Christiana. "My Lady, that is very generous of you, but I feel perfectly safe here. I trust the King and the guards will keep it that way."

Christiana tensed for a moment, suspicion crawling into her thoughts. Natalia had always been a kind and bubbly person throughout their years together; never had Christiana seen her so uncomfortable. She wondered what would cause it...then again, her logical side told her it must just be a habit. She was used to giving, never receiving. Christiana's heart splintered just a bit at that thought.

"Alright," she nodded slowly. "Well, please, promise me you'll tell me if you start to feel unsafe so I can do something to help you feel better."

"I promise, My Lady," Natalia nodded emphatically, her braid bobbing over her shoulder.

Christiana smiled. "Wonderful. Just one more thing."

"Yes?"

"First off, I'm sorry I didn't do this sooner, I just got a bit caught up with the transition. But I did want to officially ask you if you would consider taking on the position of continuing on as my Lady's Maid when I become a Princess, and then eventually when I'm coronated as Queen."

Natalia clutched at the neckline of her dress, the dark blue fabric bunching between her fingers. "Oh, My Lady...I don't...I don't deserve this."

"Of course you do! You have served me faithfully for five years now! Do you really think I would want anyone else by my side?"

"Some days, I can't help but wonder what I did to deserve your kindness, My Lady," Natalia said sheepishly, blushing as she peeked up through her long eyelashes. "Some days I don't feel worthy."

"You are worthy, Natalia." Christiana stood up and walked around the table, her fingers trailing along the top until she was next to Natalia's chair, pulling her up into a hug. "Don't let anyone make you believe you aren't."

Natalia tensed, her back muscles rigid under Christiana's touch for a few seconds before she relaxed into the embrace, wrapping her arms around Christiana. "Thank you, My Lady. I would never want to be in service to anyone else."

Chapter Nineteen

HER STOMACH UNSETTLED, CHRISTIANA rode through the woods with Robert, an early-morning snow flurry floating around them as Willow and Arrow's hooves clomped against the frozen earth. They broke through the trees surrounding her cottage, a billow of smoke rising from the chimney as they slowed to a trot and dismounted. After a quick rubdown of the horses, the pair hurried to the house, knocking a handful of times before they pushed inside, the warm air welcoming them.

Marek looked up from his book, his feet reclined on the table in front of the couch. "Hello, dear one. What are you doing here?"

"Am I not allowed to come to my own house to visit a friend?" she teased, unclasping her cloak and throwing it on the kitchen counter before walking over to him.

He laughed, standing up and pulling her into a hug. "Of course you are, but I know you well enough to know you are here for a reason."

"Fair." She pulled away, the tension in her muscles easing a bit.

"Robert, come on in." Marek sat back down on the couch, Christiana settling in beside him. "You don't need to be on guard duty here, of all places."

"Forgive me." Robert pulled his gloves off, grabbing one of the kitchen table chairs and dragging it to the sparse sitting area. "Call it soldier habits."

"I understand," Marek nodded, leaning back to prop his long legs on the table. "So, does this mean you're ready to have the discussion you've obviously been avoiding?"

"That being—?" Christiana prompted, and Robert's brow creased as he leaned forward.

"Your Battled Brain," Marek said, tenderness filling the words as he leaned in toward her.

Christiana tensed. Even though she knew it needed to be said, she did not want to talk about that.

"You told me about your nightmares and the repercussions of it, along with your hand tremor." Marek reached out, taking a hold of one of her hands and rubbing circles with his thumb against her palm. "But is there anything else we should know about?"

"Yes, My Lady, please." Robert moved closer, shoving the table back a few inches so he could sit on it comfortably in front of the couch. "Tell us how we can help you."

Their looming presence should've felt suffocating as they towered over her even sitting down. But not with Marek and Robert, the two men who would protect her to the end of time. Their strength wrapped around her like a cocoon, defending her until she was ready to emerge.

So, she did something she very rarely did: she opened up and spoke the truth. She told them about the new, scream-inducing nightmares of heat-smothering woods and wicked, grinning men. The constant buzzing need to defend herself, even when no one was around. Finally, she admitted to the truth of her last case and what really happened when she took out a seemingly-harmless mark.

"My Lady..." Robert breathed, his eyes wide. "You should have told me. I should have gone with you."

"I know, but I didn't want to risk you," she mumbled, her chest heavy like Willow was sitting on top of her. "I couldn't put that on you. But even when I think about it, that wicked way her eyes gleamed when I mentioned her son...and the words she used, I just...I couldn't..." Her breathing staggered, her vision blurring around the edges as she dropped her head in her hands. Even the memory set her off, her mind and body spinning. Her condition was desperate to take over, clawing its way into every part of her life, determined to control her.

She would not let that happen.

A set of arms curled around her, pulling her against a firm chest. "Ana..."

Christiana tugged free and held her hand up to them, halting their voices as she hunched forward, blurry eyes trained on the floor while she tried to pull herself back to reality. She noticed the scuff of mud caked around the edges of her boots. She felt the sweat beading along her hairline. She smelled the savory scent of eggs and bacon still lingering in the air from Marek's breakfast.

She focused on anything that could ground her, the sensations of reality helping the air flow through her nose and from her mouth. Her thundering heartbeat slowed, and the tension in her muscles and mind eased.

She sat back up, and Robert and Marek looked at her, faces laced with concern. They stood by her even when she felt like she was about to crumble, when she was about to break.

But she was not broken.

"Better?" Robert asked, rubbing gentle strokes up and down her forearm.

"Much," she nodded. "But what am I going to do? I can't live like this any longer, especially in the palace. The King would never let me leave if he found out."

"Then we train again." Marek squeezed her shoulder. "Just as we did five years ago."

Once Marek discovered her Battled Brain back then, he'd started to incorporate training her body and mind to work together as one. He taught her how to cope and take control back. She didn't want to argue; all she wanted to do was feel like herself again.

"Alright," she said. "You should teach Robert, too. That way I can train with him at the palace as well."

"Good idea," Marek said, and Robert nodded. "And...maybe we should teach your Prince as well?"

Her breath hitched. "No, I don't think I'm ready for that."

"Ana." Marek shook his head. "I don't agree with this. You need the people who care about you most right now, and although I don't know him too well, I can already see that he fits into that category."

"I'm not ready." Christiana rubbed her face, her numb cheeks pecked with pins and needles. "He's going through so much right now, he's already felt betrayed by a few people, I don't need to put more pressure on him. Not when he needs to focus on himself."

That was part of her motivation to keep her secret intact, yet it wasn't the only one. She wasn't ready to admit the truth: that she didn't want Zander to pity her or love her any less. She was letting the darkness control that part of her thoughts, and it seemed she wasn't any closer to taking it back, not when her Battled Brain symptoms were raging inside her.

"My Lady..." Robert spoke up. "He would do anything for you, and the longer you wait to tell him, the harder it will be for him to hear."

"Let's start the training, at least," Christiana said. "That way when I do tell him, he can see we already have a treatment plan in place, so to speak."

"But you will tell him?" Marek's eyes narrowed.

Christiana nodded. "When the time is right, I'll tell him, I promise."

"Alright," Marek sighed. "Just let us know how we can help in the interim."

She crumbled into his embrace, her foggy muscles and mind dragging her down into the comforts of his arms.

***

The afternoon came quickly for Christiana, one of the few wedding meetings she was looking forward to finally upon her.

"Lorraine, you have outdone yourself this time!" Dorina gushed, her hands skimming over the dozens of sketches littered across Christiana's dining table. Awestruck, Christiana sifted through each wedding dress design perfectly detailed for her to pick from. She had never dreamed much about her wedding over the years, never finding a time or reason to do so. However, she loved picking out new dresses, so when she got engaged, this was one task she knew she would be up for.

"I went along with the colors Lady Christiana requested, but I wanted to give you a variety of options that would work." Lorraine fiddled around the table, pulling out different swatches of fabric, the finest Christiana had ever seen. From smooth, shining silk to soft, gauzy tulle and durable, regal damask, she had her pick. Whatever her dream dress was, she would find it with Lorraine. Christiana had met the young designer last year, when Dorina brought in Alda, the royal designer and Lorraine's mother, to help Christiana pick out a dress for the Masquerade Ball. However, Christiana had been drawn to Lorraine's design instead. She knew right away she was the perfect designer to help with such an important dress choice this time around.

137

Christiana studied each sketch thoroughly, the shapes, cuts, and embroidery all different and unique. She could choose a large, regal ballgown with applique jewels and beads, or a simple yet stunning A-line made completely of delicate, handwoven lace. Each one entranced her in a different way, giving her a reason to pick it, making it even harder for her to come to a decision. She stared at each one, hoping it would spark an answer.

A soft knock interrupted her thoughts, Natalia opening the door to reveal the Queen on the other side, her steps timid as she crossed the threshold. Christiana's shoulders stiffened, her pulse beating quickly against her throat.

"Mother!" Dorina clasped hands with Penelope, pulling her closer to the table. "Look how gorgeous these are!"

"In a moment, dearest." She kissed Dorina's cheek. "I was wondering if I could talk to you alone for a moment, Christiana?"

Christiana looked up, eyes wide. "Oh, of course, Penelope."

They walked silently to her bedroom, Christiana clicking the door behind them and turning to face the Queen. Penelope fiddled with her fingers, twisting the delicate ruby ring and band on her left hand. "I just wanted..." she took a deep breath. "I wanted to make sure you were doing alright, after what you discovered. I know it must have been hard to hear, but you deserved the truth after all of this time."

Christiana hadn't been sure how she would react when Penelope ultimately brought the subject up again, but she had a few guesses. She thought she would be angry, desperate to get her out of her apartment, or heartbroken, forcing herself to conceal tears threatening to escape. Instead, she felt grief, a twinge of heartache spreading through her chest.

Penelope took a step forward. "I just want you to know that I counted down the days until you and Maria would return to us for the summer every year until he passed. There was so much I wish I could have done for the both of you, and little Isabelle as well."

"How old was I?" Christiana asked. "When my mother told you?"

"Thirteen." Penelope's chin quivered. "I couldn't believe that a man we trusted so much was hurting you at such a young age. That anyone could be capable of...beating their own wife and child is just...the most horrific thing I think I've ever heard."

Christiana's chest caved in, her breath catching. Thirteen was the first summer back to the palace after her father's abuse started. Which meant her mother had stayed silent for years; she had taken the beating silently. Yet, when Christiana's safety was at stake, she spoke up.

For her, Maria had risked it all.

So much about her mother's decisions and past didn't connect in Christiana's mind and heart. She wanted to know the truth, the motivations and the reason why they were forced to stay in that house for so long. She wanted to hear the story from her mother's lips. Maybe one day, Maria would be ready.

"I want you to know," Penelope let a tear slip free, "if I'd had the power, I would have scoured the entire continent to catch your father and give you and your mother the justice you deserved. I would have kept you safe."

Penelope had been put in an awful situation, one that very few people would have expected to find themselves in. She did what she had to do to protect herself, her family, and the life she had built over the years. Helping Christiana and Maria threatened that. Lucian threatened that. Christiana couldn't be angry at Penelope for having to make that choice.

No, she was angry at Lucian for even forcing his wife to make it in the first place.

She couldn't think about that man now; she wouldn't let him ruin the whole day. She took a step forward, gently grasping Penelope's hand. The Queen squeezed back. "Who knows. If I had pushed harder, if I had brought you three to live here safely like I wanted, you and Zander might already be married."

"We can't change the decisions either of us made in the past," Christiana said, capturing Penelope's gaze in her own. "The best thing we can do now is move forward. If not for ourselves, then for Zander. I know how important family is to him, and I want to be a part of yours even if there was hurt and ugly feelings in the past."

Penelope's smile spread smoothly upward, the gold sheen of dust spread on her cheekbones reflecting in the firelight from the hearth. She tugged Christiana forward into a hug. "That's all I want as well." She whispered in Christiana's ear. "Now, shall we go and find your wedding dress?"

Christiana pulled away, laughter on her lips. "Yes, lets."

They walked back out into the common room where Lorraine and Dorina made pleasant conversation. Penelope went right to work, her brow creased as she studied each design. Christiana returned to her own observations, her mind falling deeper and deeper into indecision with each sketch she held.

"I don't see any gold on these designs." Penelope observed, two sheets of parchment grasped in her hands. "It's traditional for the next Queen of Viri to wear a gold and crème wedding dress."

"Oh, well, Lady Christiana requested gray and silver," Lorraine said, her complexion paling.

"I'm not much of a gold person." Christiana stood tall on the opposite side of the table.

"Is that going to be a problem, Mother?" Dorina's russet eyes darted between Christiana and Penelope, her teeth gnawing at her upper lip.

"Of course not," Penelope said, smirking at Christiana before picking up a new design. "Christiana is the bride, and if she wants a silver dress, then she will have a silver dress."

Christiana's heart warmed, the heat spreading across her chest and up her clavicles. They were taking steps forward. She didn't know how she would accomplish this with Lucian, but at least she was making progress with Penelope.

She tuned out the giggles and conversations around her, focusing on what was in front of her. Minutes ticked by, each sketch feeling beautiful but not quite right. That was, until she saw the one buried under the rest, her heart skipping a beat the moment her hand crinkled the edges of the parchment between her fingertips.

Her eyes misted, tears biting on the outer edges. "This is it. This is the one I want," she whispered, flipping the parchment to show the rest of them.

Dorina gasped, her hands covering her gaping mouth. "It's perfect."

"You'll look beautiful, my dear." Penelope wiped a tear of her own away before it could crawl down her cheek.

Christiana looked down at the sketch one more time, a shaky breath escaping her lips. This was her wedding dress, and she could not wait for the day she got to wear it.

Chapter Twenty

"TRY AND FOCUS ON THE TARGET," Marek instructed. "Don't focus on your hand, it will only make it worse."

They were spending the early morning at Christiana's cottage, their breath forming frosty puffs in the air as they began the lessons they agreed would be helpful. They had been working for almost an hour, the midmorning sun shimmering through the dusty gray clouds that littered the winter sky. Even with the cool breeze whistling through the branches and across her face, a slight sheen of sweat covered Christiana as she lined herself up for another shot.

She held up her knife, the rest of her arsenal secured to her leg for the practice. After a week of this training, her skills were still inconsistent, sometimes hitting the target perfectly and others missing it entirely. She kept trying to line the knives up for a good hit, but her hands would shake the minute she pulled back to throw. She was about ready to pitch a fit every few misses, but Marek was doing what he did best: calming her down.

"It's no use," she whined. She wasn't sure how much more her patience could take.

"Liar. This isn't about practicing, it's about retraining your brain." He gave her a slight smirk, his arms crossed as he leaned against the outer edge of the training ring a few feet away from the target area. "We did it once, we can do it again. And you know the best way to do that?"

"To keep repeating the movements," she deadpanned, glowering at him. She hated this method of retraining a Battled Brain, but it worked. It had taken her months last time to stop herself from shaking while holding a bow. Although she still hated using the weapon, avoiding it whenever possible, she had stopped her hand from shaking after months and months of practice. She hoped since the cause this time around was a fleeting moment compared to the years of abuse, it wouldn't take as long to control.

"Look, I know you're nervous about tonight." He walked over to her, the clamminess of his palm seeping through her tunic when he gripped her shoulder. "But we can't focus on what's going to happen in the future. Focus on training yourself, it will only be beneficial to both you and the case if you do."

Christiana's groan rattled through her body, her fingers tightening around her dagger. Tonight was the due date for the next attack if the elusive killer was keeping to the schedule of the past four victims. Lucian and Zander had already set a stronger rotation of guards throughout the servant halls so anyone who didn't know the patterns would easily be caught. It was a sound plan, and the most obvious way to help people feel safer.

Christiana knew she should have faith in Zander and the plan he devised with his father, yet her stomach still rolled, nausea making her dizzy each time she watched the sun crawl higher into the sky. She needed to get her mind off of it, not only for her sanity but for the impact it was having on her training.

She closed her eyes, pulling in a few deep breaths of chilly air through her nostrils and blowing gently through her lips, calm washing through her veins with each movement.

There was nothing she could do about it. What she could do was focus on herself and take care of what she needed for her own sanity.

She opened her eyes and peeked up at Marek, giving him a sharp nod. He nodded back, giving one final squeeze before he backed away. "So, let's keep going."

Another hour went by before they heard the sound of hooves barreling up the dirt path to the cottage. Turning around to see the intruder, Christiana's heart dropped at the sight of Zander and she shoved her dagger back in its sheath. Although she would typically be elated to see him, she didn't want him to see her struggle to hold a knife steady.

"What are you doing here?" she asked, trying for a lighthearted tone.

"Robert told me you were spending time here training. I wanted to come and watch," he smiled, planting a kiss on her sweaty cheek, rubbing warmth into her upper arms with his gloved hands.

"How romantic of you," Marek muttered.

"Marek." She twisted at her hips to look behind her, shooting him a glare.

"Well, Christiana and I have done a little sparring in the past." Zander's eyes glimmered. "I always enjoy watching her fight."

Marek's brow twitched. "You know your way with a sword?"

"I've been training with the guards for many years now."

"That is good to hear, but we aren't talking about fighting like soldiers." Marek sauntered over, his boots crunching against the dead leaves and twigs littering the lawn. "We're talking about the delicate art of assassination."

"There's a difference?" Zander asked, his face pinching. This had been the first lesson Marek taught her; he spent years retraining her proper fighting etiquette into that of an assassin.

"Certainly, they may have the same training, but their motives are completely different." Marek stood behind Christiana, once again trapping her between them. "Soldiers fight with honor, assassins fight for survival."

"It can't be that hard. I'm sure I could hold my own against an assassin."

"I'm sure you could," Marek stifled a laugh as he turned away and headed back toward the cottage. Christiana looked up at her fiancé, his face reddening at Marek's dismissal.

"I've been very successful in mock fighting matches against other soldiers," Zander said, striding after Marek. Christiana weakly turned and walked with him, her head starting to ache.

"I don't doubt that, Prince," Marek said, pulling some of Christiana's knives out of the tattered front of the target. "But tell me, have you ever gone up against an assassin before?"

"Yes," Zander puffed out his chest, a smirk on his lips. "As I said, Ana and I have sparred a few times."

Marek looked over his shoulder. "Any that aren't in love with you?"

Zander stopped in his tracks. "No."

"Well then, why don't you put your claim to the test?" Marek picked up a practice sword from the ground, his shoulder brushing past Zander's as he jumped over the ring's edge.

"Fine," Zander agreed quickly, swinging himself over the side and landing gracefully.

"Marek, stop it," Christiana interjected sharply.

"Why?" Marek leaned his arms over the top, his forearms resting across the thin wood as he stared down at her.

"Because I don't want you to hurt him," she said without thinking.

"You don't think I can handle myself?" Zander pushed himself against the fence beside Marek, shock hanging from his features.

Her stomach twisted, her eyes darting between Zander's frustrated expression and Marek's amused one. "That's not what I meant..."

"It's what you said."

"Zander." She turned to him, leaning forward to feel the rough wood against her chin. "Marek has years of experience over you. I know you're an amazing fighter, but he is an expert."

"It's just a bit of fun." He leaned over and kissed her cheek before backing up. "Besides, it might be good for me to test my limits."

She banged her head gently against the slats, the wood rough against her forehead as she heard metal clanging. Zander had thrown the first few blows, attempting to gain the upper hand and take the offensive stance. His movements were fast and precise, brows wrinkled in concentration as he attempted to penetrate Marek's defenses.

Yet none of that slowed Marek down, his face completely at ease as he watched Zander's footwork and sword. Where Zander held his blade like a deadly weapon he must control, Marek held his like an extension of his own arm, fluid and natural. It was clear by the gleam in Marek's eye he was just humoring Zander, allowing him to take the upper hand so he could observe his weaknesses to exploit at a moment's notice. Christiana knew this because it was her favorite trick, too, one of the best instincts Marek ever taught her during training—and now he was using it against Zander.

Stifling a plethora of groans, she watched their fight unfold.

After the first minute of fighting, everything changed. Marek moved in on Zander, throwing a few fast and well-aimed jabs; Zander tried his best to parry, his sword movements barely fast enough to block Marek's blade from hitting his face. In seconds, red splotches mottled his cheeks, his chest heaving. He was trying his best to keep up, but Christiana's heart fell as his once-perfect movements began to falter, his parries slowing and his footwork becoming slightly sluggish and sloppy.

With Zander distracted trying to keep up with the attacks, Marek took an open opportunity to lunge forward, side-stepping into Zander's footwork, making him stumble and lose focus. Marek rammed his shoulder into Zander's chest, knocking the Prince to the ground in a heap. Marek kicked his sword out of his grasp to win the match.

"Those were dirty moves!" Zander scrambled to his feet, wiping dirt from his cheek.

"Told you," Marek smirked, the tip of his dull sword poking Zander a few times in the arm. Zander swatted it away like a pesky bug.

"Alright, that's enough," Christiana yelled, hopping over the side to approach the two men. "You proved your point, Marek."

"Would you teach me?" Zander said—not as a question but more of a demand.

"Excuse me?" Marek asked.

"You just showed off that I can't handle myself against a well-trained assassin." Zander took a step forward, his chest puffed out as he stared at Marek. "It's a skill I would really love to learn. I think I need your training more than I realized until recently."

"You asked me to come here to help with your serial killer." Marek turned away, the hilt of his sword dangling from his hand as he headed to the edge of the ring. "This was not a part of our original agreement."

"I know, but I need to learn this. I need to do what is right for the safety of my kingdom, Christiana, and myself."

Marek halted in his tracks, then turned back to face them, a grin spreading across his face. "Alright, I can teach you."

"What?" Christiana gaped at them. Zander's stubbornness would not mix well with Marek's hatred against the crown; she did not need to see two of the most important people in her life try to beat each other up for the next few months, especially since she needed Marek to help train her as well.

"Now, now, Christiana, if the Prince wants to learn, who am I to stop him from that?" Marek teased.

"Wonderful," Zander said, turning back to Christiana.

"Zander..." she shook her head. "What are you doing?"

"I want to learn from the man who taught you."

"But...why? You're already a proficient fighter and there are plenty of people an assassin would have to get through to actually kill you."

"I know, I know," He placed his hands on her shoulders, the pressure soothing. "But it isn't just about the fighting. It's about learning how to...believe in myself again."

"Oh, Zander." Christiana touched his cheek. "Are you really concerned about that?"

"I know these secrets about my father now, secrets I was barely able to accept." He rubbed the back of his neck, peeking up toward the sky. "I sit in meetings with him, and every single thing he says, I doubt its validity. I wonder what is truth and what is covered in lies. Yet I still just sit there in silence, listening as if nothing has changed even though there is a part of me brewing inside to fight back with him."

"Then why don't you?"

"I don't know!" He threw his arms up in the air. "I really wish I did, but I don't. I know training with Marek helped you find your voice in some way. It helped you believe in yourself again."

Christiana looked down at her feet. "Yes, it certainly did."

"I just thought maybe it could do that for me as well." He shrugged. "I just need to be trained by someone I know will teach me something useful, even if I do just walk away with more refined fighting skills."

Christiana wrapped her arms around his waist, resting her cheek against his chest. "Alright, but I'll warn you now, he is a brutal tutor."

"She's not lying, Prince." Marek laughed, leaning against the side of the ring. "I can help you find your voice if you want, but the only way to make that happen is to push you to the edge of your boundaries and beyond, so you fight without proper decorum getting in the way. The only way I can do that is to poke every little annoyance of yours until you crack."

Zander wrapped his arm around Christiana's shoulders, his muscles tense. "If that's what it takes, then I'll do it."

"Wonderful." Marek saluted his waterskin in the air before taking a big gulp, a gleeful smirk still resting on his lips.

Christiana shoulders slumped. "Yes, just wonderful."

***

When nighttime fell, it was not kind to Christiana. Yet this time, it was not filled with nightmares and restless sleep, but tossing and turning, her mind and body refusing to settle down. All she could think about was what could be happening at that moment to one of the young ladies living within the palace walls. Did he pick another victim? Was he hurting her right now? Was she trapped inside his room, screaming for release from the pain and torture? Or was she already gone from this world?

She couldn't wait for someone else to discover if the killer had struck again. Her jittering nerves couldn't take it.

She shoved the covers off, shivering at the chilled air barely warmed by the dying embers inside of her fireplace. She had only gotten an hour or two of sleep, and already the moon was starting to descend below the horizon, a streak of pale-yellow lining the path for it to disappear.

She scurried across the cold stone floor on her tiptoes to her walk-in closet, the carpeted floor a reprieve for her poor feet. She pulled out the simplest front-laced dress she could find and shoved her feet into a flat pair of shoes, not even looking in the mirror to see the disaster that was her hair, before running out the door and through the closest entrance to the servant halls.

It was eerily quiet as she roamed in the odd moment between when the night ended for some servants and the day began for others. Her footsteps echoed off the narrow stone passage, the dark walls and floors barely visible even with the burning sconces that lined them. Her heart pounded, her fingers tightly wound in the gauzy fabric of her skirt, each step timid. She had no idea where she was supposed to look; the bodies were never dropped in the same place. She just kept pushing forward, keeping her eyes downcast but face visible for any of the passing guards. None of them bothered her, all of them nodding, smiling, as if they weren't patrolling the halls because of a loose killer.

She needed this night to be over.

It took almost an hour of wandering, sunlight starting to filter through the few windows, before her eyes caught sight of someone slumped and shoved in a corner. She rushed forward, coming face to face with a young lady strewn across the floor, her eyes frozen open in terror from the last moments of her life. Gagging overtook Christiana from the putrid stench of burned, sweaty flesh and soiled clothes, tears burning the corners of her eyes—tears of pain and heartache shed for the young lady that had lost her life too quickly.

A clanging jolted Christiana, her head whipping to the left just in time to see a shadow disappearing down the hall. She didn't even realize she was chasing after it until her feet almost slipped rounding the corner, her delicate silk shoes not meant for heavy running.

She pushed through, following the echoes of disappearing feet. For all she knew, it was a guard or another servant scared of the body, but it didn't matter. Adrenaline coursed through her veins, her mind screaming at her to chase, to find the person so desperate to put distance between themselves and the fifth victim.

Christiana's stomach dropped when she heard a slam, her movements quickening to the dead-end hallway and the only door that sat at the end. She couldn't get there fast enough, not even thinking about the possibility that she could burst into someone's private residence if she wasn't careful. Without hesitation, she pushed through the entryway, tripping into the long, ornately-decorated hall, not a soul in sight. She bent over, chest burning, breath ragged as she took in the surroundings her escapee led her to.

She knew exactly where she was: in the hall of the resident nobility. The hall where Elaine resided.

Chapter Twenty-One

OURS PASSED, FILLED WITH QUICK PEEKS at the scene before physicians and soldiers ushered them away, claiming they needed to keep everything as preserved as possible, although somehow Lucian and Penelope were perfectly welcomed to stay. It didn't bother Christiana because this time, she and Zander were one step ahead. They had made a contingency plan in case a new victim appeared today; a plan that would finally get them the answers they lacked.

The Court Physician's office was exactly how Christiana expected it to be: clinical, well-cleaned and eerily organized. A row of a half a dozen cots sat against one wall in the long room, the door perched open at the end. Even with the fireplace taking up half of the wall opposite the patient beds, the room still felt frozen, the cold creeping through Christiana's fingers as a reminder that death resided in this room. But it seemed they were alone, the prone form of the fifth victim lying on the cot in the corner, a crisp, snow-white cloth covering the entire body.

Zander paced, his boots clicking against the stone floor, the only sound echoing off the barren, unadorned walls. Christiana grabbed his wrist at his next pass of her, tugging him to the side. His cerulean eyes swirling like a hurricane, he hunched over, grasping the low footboard of one of the beds, shoulders heaving with each deep breath he took.

"Stop fretting." Christiana smoothed her hand along Zander's back, his muscles quaking under her touch. "It won't make waiting any easier."

She wanted to syphon off all his anxiety into her body. She was constantly used to it, at least she could give Zander relief. His pained expression creased inward as he peeked over his shoulder at her. "What if he doesn't come?"

"He will." Christiana squeezed his shoulder. "He's loyal to the betterment of the country. He wouldn't walk away if he could be helpful."

Zander nodded, releasing the bed, a pinkish color returning to his fingers with the blood flowing to the stressed ligaments. A click came from behind them, the pair whipping around to see Rowan entering the room, his posture rigid as he closed the door behind him.

"Thank you, Ro, for agreeing to help us." Zander strode forward, his hand outstretched to clasp with Rowan's.

Rowan just stared at it, his fingers tightening around the brown leather bag clutched between them. "I'm here to help the investigation. To help get this disgusting killer out of our hallways."

Zander's shoulders slumped, his hand falling back to his side. "Of course, we could use all of the help we can get."

This was the first time Christiana had seen these two interact in weeks, and it splintered her heart. Their friendship had once been the rock each of them needed: solid and stable and always there. Yet one decision of Zander's had crushed it into pebbles, barely recognizable from what it once was.

"We only have an hour before the Court Physician comes back," Christiana chimed in, both men taking their attention off each other to stare at her. "We shouldn't waste any more time."

Rowan's face settled, his steps determined as he crossed the room and set his bag down on the side table next to the victim. He pilfered through it for a few moments, pulling out a pair of gloves and a few medical instruments Christiana couldn't identify. He rolled up his sleeves, his simple evergreen tunic pushed past his elbows to keep them clean; then he stopped fiddling, picking up an envelope left on the table as well. He ripped into it, his face deep in concentration as he read.

He peeked over the parchment. "Do you know what this says?"

"The Court Physician said that was for your eyes only," Zander admitted.

Nodding, Rowan took a few more moments to scan the document before returning it to its place on the table. He reached for the top of the linen, looking up at Christiana and Zander standing on the opposite side of the bed. "Are you two ready to see this?"

"Yes." Christiana nodded.

"I am," Zander replied.

Rowan pulled the sheet free, revealing the body beneath. Zander sucked in a breath, both of them staring. The young woman was completely naked, every inch of her once-alabaster skin red and mottled, even black and crispy in a few places. Fresh bubbles welled up along her arms, legs, and torso, her face disfigured with terror and pain.

Christiana had brewed poison like this with her own hands. She knew the effects and could list them off and break each of them down in the most scientific manner. She had watched it take lives—lives she had rationalized deserved to be taken—yet this time she saw it for what it really was.

Dangerous. Murderous. Torturous.

She shook the thoughts from her head. She already knew she was a killer, but she killed for a purpose. That is what made her different. That is what separated her from the disgusting killer who stalked her home.

Rowan didn't waste a moment, hunched over as his eyes examined every inch, marking, and bubble on the victim's body. His gloved hands touched, prodded, and examined anything he could. "It's obviously death by poison, administered through the blood." He gripped the young lady's chin, tilting her head up to get a better look at her neck. "I am having a hard time finding any type of injection site, although with the disfigurement of the skin, that is to be expected."

"That we already knew." Zander nodded.

"I figured. She is consistent with the other victims."

"You mean by her age?" Christiana asked.

"And her hair color." Rowan smoothed a few strands away from her face. "The letter the physician left was a quick overview of the other victims. Apparently, they have all been dark brunettes."

"He told you that?" Zander's eyes were wide, fists balling at his sides. Christiana reached over, hand settling over his knuckles until he released and grasped her hand.

"He said he didn't feel right letting another physician examine the body without all the known facts. It goes against his moral code." Rowan went back to examining the body, taking a flat, metal instrument from the side to pry her lips open and look inside of her mouth. "Lesions along her lips, and her tongue looks bruised. Classic signs that she was gagged."

Icy chills infected Christiana's limbs. "Which means they aren't quick kills."

"Like my parents wanted us to believe," Zander rumbled.

Rowan shook his head. "No, because her wrists also have signs of bruising. It's hard to see through the lesions caused by the poison, but note the difference in color." He put his hands under the body, rolling her over and gently resting her on her stomach. Her back was just as bubbled as the front. "Here is what he was doing while he had her bound and gagged." Rowan's fingers traced along her spine, his fingers moving in a crisscrossed pattern. "He was carving into her."

"What?" Zander and Christiana said together, bending over to get a better look at the poor girl's back.

"See these markings? They've been cleaned, but they are fresh cuts."

"Couldn't the poison have caused it?" Zander questioned. "Since it affects the skin so violently."

"Possibly, but then we would have seen signs of skin breakage on other parts of her body." Rowan took a measuring tape, running it along one of the wounds. "This is the only part of the body I've seen it. Also, they are clean cuts. If it was caused by pressure against the skin, it would look more like a tear, not a clean line."

"They're being tortured," Christiana whispered, blood draining from her fingers and cheeks. This had been horrific enough with just the killings, but to know they went through hours of pain before succumbing...it made her stomach roll. "Can you tell us how long he was torturing her?"

"I can't be precise due to the damage the poison caused." He straightened, looking at both of them. "But if I had to take an educated guess, it all happened in one night. The wounds don't show any sign of having healed, even with the poison also marking the skin. Nothing looks like it reopened when she was fatally drugged."

"Alright, so the victims are young, unattached females in their early twenties, with dark brunette hair and pale skin." Zander shook his head. "How are we supposed to keep the rest of the servants that match that description safe?"

"Well, most of your examination is correct," Rowan jotted down a few notes on a pad next to his bag. "But this young lady wasn't unattached. She was engaged."

"How do you know that?" Christiana crossed her arms, her chest quivering.

"She told me," Rowan said, removing his gloves and wrapping them in a piece of clean linen. "She was one of the scullery maids who lit my fires at night. Plus, she came to me for medical advice three weeks ago and mentioned that she was leaving the palace to marry. I guess her fiancé took up a new post working on a private estate and she was going to follow in a few weeks."

Zander rubbed his forehead. "We'll have to send word to him as soon as possible."

"You've been taking patients?" Christiana asked. "Have many people have been coming to you?"

"Some." Rowan nodded. "But I can't discuss who or for what, it would go against the oath of privacy. It's the whole reason they come to me and not the Court Physician."

"Well, thank you so much for your help, Rowan," Christiana said. "You have no idea how helpful you have been."

"It's my job." He shrugged, snapping his case shut. "I can write up a full report of my findings for both of you and have it sent over by the end of the day."

"That would be extremely helpful, thank you." Zander took a step around the bed, attempting to get closer to Rowan, but he dodged, giving a curt nod before swiftly leaving the room.

Christiana sighed, striding over to Zander and wrapping her arm around the back of his waist, his arm gliding over her shoulder in turn to pull him close. "At least we've learned some new facts."

"Yes, but it came with even more questions," he grunted. "Why is he torturing them beforehand? How are they being tortured without anyone hearing them? How do they last so long without dying from their injuries?"

"And now we also know it isn't a romantic luring that's getting them into the killer's clutches." Christiana whispered, and Zander's body tensed under her cheek. "Which means the possibility of it being a noble is getting higher."

"Christiana," Zander groaned. "Please don't say it."

"You have to admit, some of these coincidences are just too suspicious to ignore!" She pulled away a bit, his face strained. "Now that we know the victims are bleeding with the cuts, it could explain why she came home with a bloody dress. And I swear Zander, I saw a shadow running away from the crime scene this morning. It ran right to the nobility hallway!"

"I just...Elaine has never seemed like a violent person."

"Sometimes it takes only one catalytic moment to make someone change forever." A fact she knew from experience. "I just don't think we should ignore it."

Zander sighed. "You're right. We can't accuse or question her with such circumstantial evidence, but maybe we try and find a way to keep an eye on her during the night of the next suspected kill."

"Good idea," She leaned her chin on his chest, staring into his glassy eyes. "We can ask Marek and Robert for advice. Maybe one of them could surveil Elaine that night."

"Maybe," He looked down at her. "At least I got an answer to one question."

"What answer was that?"

His gaze looked above her, staring out into nothingness. "That my parents have been keeping secrets from me."

Chapter Twenty-Two

"*S*TOP HOLDING BACK!" MAREK YELLED AT Zander as the two men sparred.

Frustrated grunts rang out from the pits of the fight as Christiana and Robert watched from the sidelines. Christiana worried Zander would soon regret asking Marek to train him; it was only their first lesson and Marek wasn't holding back, treating Zander more like an enemy than a fellow soldier or the Prince of his country as he pushed each match to the brink.

Pulling her thick cloak around her, Christiana tried her best to block out the chilling wind that brushed through the air. It was a beautiful day with the sun shining high above their heads, glistening against the dusting of snow that still coated the ground from the overnight flurries.

"Hm," Robert exclaimed, his arms crossed.

"What?"

"Just interesting to see your mentor finally in action," he

murmured, brow furrowed as his gaze fixed on the tight match. "You told me he was a soldier, but I didn't realize how accomplished until now."

"He's certainly a force to be reckoned with," Christiana grumbled.

The match was coming to an end as Marek cornered Zander. With one final blow of his broadsword, he forced Zander's sword out of his grasp, shoving the Prince to kneel before him.

"And that is how you get yourself decapitated," Marek explained, the point of his sword resting against Zander's jugular. "Stop fighting pretty and teach yourself to survive."

Zander shoved the training sword away and scrambled to his feet. "I'm not holding back. I don't know what you mean when you keep yelling that."

"It means you care more about your honor than your actual life. If an assassin snuck up on you, you would be dead." Marek walked away to grab a drink of water. Zander followed, his shoulders slumped as he dragged his feet. "You want to learn how to speak up for yourself, but it's obvious that some doubt is holding you back. Push past it, forget being proper, and do what feels right!"

"Good job." Christiana handed Zander his waterskin, trying her best to bring his spirits back up.

"Don't lie to him," Marek laughed, shoving her shoulder playfully. She shoved right back. "I'm not!"

"Keep telling yourself that." He winked at her. She couldn't help but smile, and Zander frowned.

"I think I could take some assassins." He leaned against the side of the ring, his elbows braced behind him. "Maybe not you, but I would be able to defend myself enough to survive."

Marek's laughter stopped, a frown falling on his face. "You haven't proven that fact so far."

"Well, maybe if I fought someone else."

"Unfortunately for you, there is no one else."

"I can fight him," Christiana chimed in.

"Are you sure that's a good idea, My Lady?" Robert's arms flexed as fists formed against his folded arms.

"I agree with Robert, you should stay on the sidelines," Marek replied, his stance wide and posture straight, as if he would tackle her if she tried to run from him.

She shrugged off their concern. "I'll be fine, it's just Zander."

"Of course she'll be fine. Do you both really think I would try and hurt her?" Zander wrapped an arm around Christiana, his eyes darting between the three of them. He didn't even know about the real reason why both men wanted to keep her out of the ring—and Christiana didn't care. An airy feeling spread deep inside her at the idea of sparring with Zander, whispers of memories in the training ring back at the palace making her feel almost normal again.

"Let's go." Christiana smirked at Zander, pushing him forward lightly as he walked into the center of the ring to prepare. When she pulled her practice sword from its sheath, Marek grabbed her arm.

"This is a bad idea," he rumbled in her ear.

"No, it's not," she seethed through gritted teeth. "Stop overreacting. I've been doing better."

She had, she knew she had. They had been training for almost three weeks, and her throwing daggers were almost back up to par. Marek had even started doing light ring sparring with her a few days ago. Although she wasn't perfect, her hand still shaking and giving out after some time, she wanted to keep pushing forward. She wanted to keep improving. She wanted to spar with Zander. Even though she knew she would likely lose when her hand gave out, she could easily disguise it and just enjoy the moment with him while it lasted.

"I know, but you're risking exposure right now, and you told me you didn't want him to know the truth."

"Well, I need to start reintegrating myself into fighting again. I might as well start with someone I trust completely."

He yanked her closer, his grip tightening. "You aren't ready for that!"

"Well, I think I am. Now let me go."

Staring her down for a few more seconds, he released her arm with disapproval darkening his eyes. Without a second thought, she walked toward Zander. "Ready?"

"Absolutely."

"Begin," Robert shouted from the sidelines.

Zander came in strong, trying his best to use his height and weight to his advantage. He attacked from above, attempting to push Christiana down into a difficult position, but he underestimated her abilities already, not realizing this was a trick easily thwarted. As he shoved her down, she allowed him to feel his strength against her until she was lowered to the perfect position. Then, when he lifted his sword back up, preparing to strike again, she kicked forward, hitting him directly in the knees. He stumbled, giving Christiana the advantage to escape.

"In over your head?" she teased, the two circling each other with goofy grins.

"Not a chance."

Taking control, Christiana went in for the offensive, hitting him with a flurry of strikes to try and throw him off.

The pair continued, enjoying every moment of the fight. Christiana finally felt like herself again at the joy in her practice and bonding with Zander. She couldn't help but giggle, her happiness bleeding through every movement and strike. Her strength and abilities had eluded her after everything she went through, but it seemed like her Battled Brain was finally starting to disappear once again.

They teased each other with stolen winks and flirtatious smirks, but they were both giving it their all—until Zander found the perfect moment to take an advantage. He pushed forward, determination in his eyes as his swipes became swift and aggressive. She tried her best to defend herself, but her arm started to give out, exhaustion prickling her overworked muscles.

Her heart sped up, not from excitement but fear. The aggression across Zander's face was terrifying, all too reminiscent of that pitch-black summer night in the woods. She tried to take in deep breaths, to calm herself and take the advantage back, but it was too late. Anxiety rose to the surface, spreading through her body.

She was not broken...

Zander descended upon her, forcing her to cower against the side of the training ring. Her hand spasmed, the sword shaking uncontrollably. Usually perfectly-weighted, it now felt like an anvil, and her weakened wrists wanted to let go. Trying her best to push forward and be strong for both of them, she forced herself to move her arm and block all of Zander's blows; but it didn't take long for her wrists to finally give out, Zander disarming her.

She was not broken...

"Well, seems there is an assassin I can defeat," he teased, lowering his sword to move closer. Not caring that Robert and Marek were still watching, he pushed himself against her. "Do I get a prize?"

Her head spun, tears threatening to escape her eyes. She chanted to herself she was not broken, but it all started to crumble around her, the cracks in her mind flowing to the surface and pushing against every inch of her. The force was deafening, painful shards striking against her chest, her throat, her head. Her breathing staggered as he leaned in to steal a kiss.

"Don't worry," he whispered, a teasing smirk on his lips. "I'm a kind winner, all I want is a little kiss."

Don't worry, My Lady, I'll be kind....

She screamed and recoiled, closing her eyes to hide.

"Christiana?" she heard Zander ask, but she couldn't respond. "What's wrong, did I hurt you?"

The screams kept coming, her throat raw from the pressure. Her skin crawled along her entire body, the feeling of small bugs moving right under her skin. She was surrounded by blackened clouds, suffocating her and pushing her back in time, forcing her back to the woods where the darkness and silence overcame her. She wanted to fight. She wanted to defend herself, thrashing about to get free, doing everything she could to break away.

A distant voice tried to break through. "Ana please, let me help you! Tell me what's wrong!"

There were hands on her, trying to contain her, to force her into the bondage of the ropes against the carriage, but she wouldn't go back. She wouldn't let someone put her back.

"Get away from me!" she screeched. "Untie me!"

Hands brushed against her cheek, her body cowering away from that touch. "Ana, love, please..."

"Get off of her!"

The hands were ripped away, releasing her from her bondage, but she couldn't stop screaming. She couldn't stop thrashing, trying to run away from the danger. New hands encircled her from behind, forcing her to her knees and trapping her arms from moving anywhere.

"Christiana it's me, you're safe!" Marek whispered in her ear—but no, he wasn't really there. No one had saved her that night. No one came to her rescue.

"What's happening to her?" Zander's voice cracked.

"She's having an attack. We need to calm her down." Marek's lips were back at her ear. "Dear one, you are home with people who care about you. Come back to us."

Christiana wanted to believe they were really there, that she was really in a safe space with the people she trusted, but she couldn't bring her mind back to reality. She felt every moment of that night: the warm air whispering through the trees, the stillness and sounds of crickets ringing through the forest. The biting scratch of rough ropes around her wrists. The pure fear of the inevitable spreading through her body.

She wanted it to stop. She wanted everything to stop. She couldn't handle this, not again. She tried her best to thrash again, weakening the bonds around her, but they were too strong. Not sure how else to escape, she began to bang her head forward, making contact with whatever was in front of her. The hard surface crashed against her forehead, snaking pain down through her face. But she didn't care; she wanted it to stop. She kept banging, trying to chase the fear away.

"Robert!" Marek bellowed. A moment later, her head made contact with something softer, now held in place against the warm surface.

"It's me, My Lady. You are safe." Robert whispered. She wanted to trust him, but the darkness whispered horrendous thoughts, feeding her with doubt and agony. She could no longer discern what was truth and what was a lie. It blurred together like ink polluted by water.

"Christiana, you are safe. He's dead, you survived, you are alive." Marek muttered. She wanted to go toward him; she wanted to find peace with him like she had in the past, but he wasn't here. There was no way he could be. "Make yourself useful, Prince. Run inside and grab the small leather pouch next to the bed."

"Why?"

"Just do it!"

Footsteps ran away, drowned out by Christiana's screams and cries for help. Robert was trying his best to contain them, muffled by the thick wool and fur of her cloak.

Many moments passed before the footsteps returned, coming

closer and closer. He was coming back. Julian wanted to take everything from her again.

Hot tears ran down her face, his smirk haunting her mind as he enjoyed every moment of her pain. His searing touch was branded on her body, committed to every memory flooding her. The flush of her skin as he ran his hands over her. Her body's reactions to his skin even though her mind and stomach were repulsed. Why had her body betrayed her?

"What do I need to do?"

"Open it up and pull out a dart and the milky white liquid. Dip the dart and hand it to me..."

The voices drifted farther and farther away as Julian continued to explore her pain.

"No!" Zander protested. "We aren't going to poison her!"

Marek grunted, trying to contain her writhing. "It isn't poison, it's an anesthetic. It will just knock her out for a bit."

"No, I won't do it."

"If you don't, then she's going to hurt herself even more! Do it!"

"Your Highness," Robert interjected. "Trust him, he knows what he is doing. He's trying to help."

Silence fell between them. They were disappearing, leaving her alone with the monster. Julian's grin twisted in front of her, his ghost trying to pull her into the pits of darkness with him.

A pinch pierced her neck, and warm fluid rushed through her body. The anesthetic passed through her blood, pushing Julian's ghost away from her. He disappeared, floating far away, his grin still heavy with promises to return. Then calm washed over her, allowing her to finally catch her breath and feel at ease. She relaxed, melting into the many arms holding onto her. She no longer felt them as bondage, but the protective comfort they were meant to provide.

"I'm so tired," she whispered, her head lolling back and forth.

"Sleep, Christiana," Marek murmured. "We will protect you."

Wanting to feel peace, she allowed the drug to take her, her mind whispering the truth she had refused to see for weeks: she had broken already.

Chapter Twenty-Three

HE DISTANT SOUND OF SHOUTING VOICES attempted to break through the fog of her past, too far away for her to distinguish who they were or what they were saying. She wanted to get closer, to find help. She kept pushing herself to the edge to find sanctuary away from the overwhelming haze. The voices grew closer, the words becoming clear.

"You didn't...help..." a male shouted.

"You...talking...she is..." someone retorted, their words making absolutely no sense.

"Calm..." came a third, and Christiana finally recognized Robert's voice. She struggled to rise and run; she wanted to find her way back to the safety of his presence.

Her eyes fluttered open, her consciousness finally realizing the fog was only a dream. She was lying on the bed in her cottage, her head propped up by a few pillows, her body wrapped in a thick-knitted blanket to help her shaking. Her head pounded as if an axe had been thrust inside. Touching her hand to the tender skin, she felt the soft fabric of a bandage protecting the gash along her brow. Groaning, she remembered what happened, the memories of her panic attack rushing back. She'd banged her head against the side of the fighting ring.

She hadn't lost control like that in years, let alone so violently. In the past, her attacks had always rendered her unable to move or control herself. It terrified her, losing control over every part so quickly. This time was different. She had lost control completely, her body flailing and fighting so much she barely recognized her own strength. She never expected her reactions to develop in such a way, but this trauma had awoken a different part of her.

Unlike her father, Julian was pulling her violence out of her. She wanted nothing more than to shove it back inside and forget it even existed.

More shouting echoed from the other room, and she let out a deep groan, yearning to get out of bed and learn why the three men were fighting so loudly. Her feet felt like they weighed twice their size as she dragged herself into the common area, finally able to understand what was being spoken.

"I deserve to know what is going on with her! She is my future wife!" Zander yelled.

Marek leaned against the wall, arms crossed. "It's not my secret to tell. She'll tell you when she is ready."

"Robert?" Zander turned, staring at Robert who reclined against the distillery counter, his fingers curled around the edges as if he was trying to break a piece off.

"Marek is right, Your Highness." Robert shook his head, his shoulders slumped. "I'm sorry, but he is. She'll tell you when the time is right."

"And only I know when that is," Christiana said, entering the circle of men.

"You're awake." Zander rushed to her side and she wrapped her arms around him. She let her weight fall on him as he helped her sit gingerly down on the faded brown couch that took up the common area.

"How are you feeling?" Marek asked, his voice laced with concern as he knelt to be eye level with her.

"Exhausted. In pain. Several other things that I can't quite pinpoint, to be honest." She tried to laugh it off, but all of them stared at her with an intensity she couldn't quite match on her own.

"What happened?" Zander whispered, his eyes desperate for answers.

She stared up at him, wanting so badly to keep a hold of the secret she had kept. She wanted him to believe she was still strong, to still see her as the perfect person to marry. She wanted nothing more than to just be normal for him.

"You don't have to tell him anything, Christiana," Marek said, his hand heavy on her knotted shoulder. "But he deserves the truth after what he just witnessed."

"I know." Keeping this secret any longer would be a stain on their marriage, which was the last thing Christiana wanted.

"What's going on?" Zander asked again, settling down next to her on the couch, the weak cushions bowing around him as he settled in.

"What I'm about to tell you isn't easy for me, but please just be patient, alright?"

"Alright," Zander nodded, grabbing her hands.

"Remember the panic attack I had last summer?" He nodded slowly before she continued. "It was like that, but much worse, and more violent. They're symptoms of something I have."

"What is it?"

Her mind screamed at her to stifle the words, but she forced them through her lips. "It's a rare condition called Battled Brain."

"Battled Brain?" Zander's brow creased, his thumb rubbing circles against the back of her hand. "Like the ailment soldiers have after their time in war?"

She explained everything to him, just as Marek had explained it to her all those years ago. She told him about the effect her father had on her, even after his death. How Marek had caught the symptoms and taught her how to control them.

He sat there, his face soft and eyes glassy with the whisper of tears, as he took in every word she spoke. Robert and Marek stood behind her, their strength supporting her as she let her secret flow out. The words were hard to say, like lead on her tongue right before they escaped, but her heart lightened with each one spoken.

This horrific secret was finally free between them. She just hoped that he wouldn't leave her the moment she finished talking.

"So, that is what I live with," she finished, her teeth tugging at her bottom lip as she waited for him to say something.

Zander didn't move, his body completely rigid, his eyes wide. Christiana stared at him, hoping he would say something or react to anything she had just admitted, but he just stared at her. Christiana couldn't decipher what was going through his mind.

"Oh, love." He leaned forward at last, his hand hovering in between them as if he was unsure if he could touch her or not. "I'm so sorry, I had no idea what you were going through."

She looked down at her lap. "I didn't want you to know."

"When did it start happening again?"

"A few months ago, after I killed Julian."

"Is his death significant? Did it do something to you?"

"It wasn't his death that did it." Her stomach rolled, an invisible vise enclosing her throat. "It's what happened when I fought him."

"What are you talking about?" Zander leaned back, his eyes narrowing. "You said everything went exactly how you expected it to."

She clutched her hands tighter, fighting against every inch of herself. "That's because it did, but I didn't tell you back then what I expected to happen."

She allowed the details of that night to flow out, admitting what Julian really did to her that night. How he beat her in battle. How he tied her up. How he touched her in ways that no other man besides Zander should be allowed to touch. Tears streamed down her face as she tried her best to keep herself together while the memories came back to the forefront of her mind.

"Love...I don't...you didn't deserve that, I'm so sorry," Zander whispered. "Why didn't you tell me sooner? I could have helped."

"I know," She wiped a tear from her face. "But I was never ready to."

"Why? Have I given you a reason to not trust me? Is it because of my father? Is it because I haven't stood up to him yet? Please, tell me so I can fix it."

"I ca—that has nothing to do with this." Christiana dropped her head into her hands, shaking it back and forth, the darkness snaking back into her mind and slowing down her thoughts. "It's difficult to understand...I just...didn't want you to look at me differently."

Zander stood, his face pale. "How could you think that?"

"Zander, this isn't helping." Marek strode forward, cornering him. "You are asking all of the wrong questions."

He blinked rapidly. "But they're the ones that I have."

"It doesn't matter!" Marek shoved him against the nearby wall, and Christiana's head jerked up to watch them. "You want to learn something besides fighting from me? Well, here is your first lesson. This isn't about you or how you feel about what happened to her!" Marek's fingers curled into Zander's sweat-stained tunic, their noses grazing as he stared into Zander's wide-eyed face. "You want to prove that you aren't your father, that you have more integrity and heart than he does? Well, it's time to prove it. She needs you to put her and her feelings first. She is in love with you and she wants you in her life, now show her that you deserve to be there!"

"Please, Marek, let him go," she pleaded quietly, unable to raise her voice. Releasing him from the wall, Marek walked to the opposite side of the room, taking a place next to Robert, who watched in silent shock.

Taking a few moments to compose himself, Zander sat back down next to Christiana, his chest heaving as he looked down at her, concern creasing his face. "Are you alright?"

"I don't know," she admitted, tears still staining her cheeks. "I want to be. I want to feel whole again. But after what he did...what he said..."

"You don't..." Zander took a deep breath, closing his eyes briefly before turning back to her. "You don't have to tell me any more, not until you're ready."

"I don't want to feel broken anymore. I just want to feel like myself again," she cried, dropping her head into her hands to hide her pain from all of them.

It wasn't ideal, having an audience at her breakdown, but she was too weak to care. All she could do was cry as she realized just how torn apart she felt. Ignoring the problem was never the answer but she didn't realize how bad it had gotten until everything finally caught up to her. She felt like she was dying, her insides twisted and mangled, her entire self at war with what she wanted to be and what the trauma was trying to make her.

"You are not broken, Christiana," Marek interjected, sitting on the table in front of her, lifting her chin gently to look at him. "I thought I already taught you that."

Hot tears kept falling, her mind and body weighed down. "Apparently, I need to relearn."

"You are not broken. You survived," Marek repeated the mantra. "Now you say it. Like you mean it. Say the truth."

She sniffled, the words hurting her chest as she croaked, "I am not broken. I survived."

"Again."

"I am not broken. I survived," she repeated, air finally filling her lungs as her breath started to even out.

"He's right, love," Zander murmured. "You are one of the strongest people I have ever met. You are kind and giving and will fight for everyone you care about, and I still believe that."

"You do?" she asked, her chest heaving as she caught up on breathing.

"Of course." He leaned forward, brushing away a strand of hair that had plastered itself to her wet face. "Nothing could stop me from seeing you that way, because it's the truth of who you are. No one, not Julian or your father, can ever take that away from you."

"I agree with the Prince." Marek nodded. "You control who you are. Don't ever let yourself believe that those two had a part in it."

"Thank you," she said to Zander, giving him a quick kiss on the cheek. "All of you. I don't think I would be able to get through this fight without you."

"We are here to support you, My Lady. Always," Robert reached over the seatback and squeezed her shoulder lightly.

All three men surrounded her, protecting her in a cocoon until she was ready to emerge. They would never let her feel alone, no matter how much she tried to convince herself she was. Her mind might be trying to lie to her, but the people who cared about her most would make sure she didn't listen.

She didn't have to go through this battle alone.

Chapter Twenty-Four

A FEW DAYS PASSED, AND CHRISTIANA'S bruised head was finally dulling down and easy to cover up with cosmetics. She had avoided the suspicious looks and whispers with a decent lie: that Willow had bucked her off after getting spooked during a ride. No one seemed to question her after that.

Her mind wasn't as foggy and her body settled with a more manageable amount of tension that allowed her to push through the days. She sat at her dining room table, a dinner for two untouched in front of her as she twirled the stem of her wine glass between her fingertips, rolling the base against the wooden surface, trying to distract herself from the fact that Zander was already twenty minutes late to their meal. Bile rose in her throat as she thought about all the possibilities why he wasn't here, the worst always coming to the forefront. Maybe he didn't want to talk to her. Maybe he was angrier at her then she originally thought.

Maybe he didn't love her anymore.

She tried to remove that last thought from her mind, her Battled Brain's sensitivity to darkened thoughts trying to get the best of her. She forced her rationality and logic to take over, reminding herself that finding out her most vulnerable secret wouldn't stop Zander from loving her. Yet she couldn't stop the idea from creeping back in and clouding her logic, the fog trying to consume her. She took another gulp of wine, trying to silence her screaming thoughts.

She couldn't take it any longer. Shoving her chair away and stalking from her room and down the hall, she pounded on Zander's door.

It promptly swung open, Jay's smiling face and bright eyes welcoming her. "Hello, My Lady, is there anything I can help you with?"

"Yes, I hope you can." Christiana relaxed her shoulders. "Do you happen to know where the Prince is? He's late for dinner."

"Oh, that's odd." He shook his head. "He must have lost track of time while working on his newest project."

Christiana's brow furrowed. "New project? And what would that be?"

***

Christiana's heels clicked against the marble floor, her chest tightening, breath shallowing as she moved closer to a place she never thought she would find herself again. She had been to this part of the palace once before, to investigate Julian. She never wanted to go back to someplace he frequented, but she didn't have any other option if she wanted to find Zander.

She knocked lightly on the door before pushing on the handle, the latch giving away easily. The room looked much different when she wasn't so focused on a target. It was spacious, two desks sitting opposite each other, one carved and ornate with glossy designs, the other simple and plain, shoved in the corner; the desk she had found Tobias at all those months ago. A fire burned warmly in the fireplace, either side of the stone structure flanked by windows, the sunset reflecting in the panes of glass.

Zander sat at the imposing desk, the one Christiana assumed was Julian's during his tenure as Chancellor. His head was bowed, lips muttering unintelligible words to himself as he read and sifted through stacks of papers that littered the surface.

"Zander?" Christiana shut the door behind her, and he flinched at the sound.

"Ana?" He lifted his head up, "What are you doing here? What time is it?"

She crossed her arms, head tilting to the left. "I'd say it's about dinnertime."

"Oh my goodness," his head collapsed onto the desk, his hair falling around him. "I'm late, aren't I?"

"By about thirty minutes." She joined him at the desk. "What are you doing?"

He sat back up, his body limp in the leather wingback chair, shuffling a handful of papers. "I'm...researching."

"Researching what?"

"My father's decisions and my involvement in them." Zander's fists curled around the papers, a loose curl falling into his eyes. "Did you know I was apparently at Marek's sentencing?"

Christiana dropped her palms on the desk. "No, I didn't. He never mentioned anything."

"I was young, only thirteen, but according to the court records I looked up about it, I was standing next to my father." He shook his head. "I stood there, proud to be my father's son, and watched him condemn an innocent man to death."

Christiana's heart panged. "It's not your fault."

"There was barely an investigation because the actual man responsible was on my father's council. So, when he came forward with the accusation, Father just accepted it and sentenced Marek." He lightly pounded his fist on the desk. "Now that man, General Wallick, is retired and lives comfortably on a large estate in Astary. He got away with everything, and there is not a shred of evidence to prove otherwise."

"Zander," Christiana whispered, circling around the imposing desk to stand beside him.

He stared off into the room, eyes glazed over. "How many times did I stand by and watch my father punish the innocent and exonerate the guilty?"

"You can't keep torturing yourself with this." Christiana perched herself on the edge of the desk, her feet dangling off the side. "The more you keep questioning it, the more tangled your mind and emotions will get."

"I know." Zander threw down a stack of parchment, leaning back in his chair. "I just want answers without actually having to talk to my father about it."

"Why not?"

"Well, first off, part of the story isn't mine, it's yours," he peeked up at her, his hand brushing hers. "Besides, I don't even know if I could believe any of his words if I didn't have evidence to back it up. So I'm sifting through all of this to see if I can find any for his treachery."

"Why here?" Christiana looked around the room, everything still perfectly preserved as if Julian would enter at any moment. "I'm surprised your father hasn't cleaned out some of this."

"He's taken all of the pertinent documents, but items from the past he hasn't touched." Zander shrugged. "I figured if anyone knew the truth about my father's actions, it was Julian. Seeing as he most likely agreed with all the decisions."

"That is a fair assumption."

"The amount of lies he has been feeding me over the years is...incredible." He shook his head. "With the country, our people, even his marriage."

"Alright, now I am very lost."

"When I finally calmed down and made up with my mother, she told me how much had truly changed about their relationship." He shook his head. "When she received the answer, she moved out of their bedroom."

"What?" Christiana's eyes widened.

"They share an apartment, but they don't share a bedroom anymore. She had the servants move her out while my father was still on the battlefront eleven years ago."

"Oh," was all she could let escape. The King and Queen always put up a proudly loving face in public; it never occurred to Christiana that it might be different behind closed doors. After years of fighting abusers, she still let society's masks cloud her judgment and surprise her when they were taken away.

"They have been lying to Dorina and me for years!" he said. "I knew I never wanted their idea of marriage, but that didn't mean I didn't admire it. I thought they loved each other, I thought they were dedicated to each other, and now I know that was all a façade."

"I understand that," Christiana sighed, "I thought for a very long time that my parents loved each other, too. I didn't realize the truth until I was too deeply within my father's clutches."

"I don't want our marriage to ever get to that point."

"Neither do I," She shifted over, her leg knocking against his. "I don't think we'll ever find ourselves in that place, though."

"That's true," he nodded. "If I ever tried to tell you what to do, I'm concerned you would poison me."

Christiana threw her head back with laughter, her cheeks

warming. "I don't know if I should be upset or proud that you are just the slightest bit scared of me."

"I don't think you'd ever kill me," he teased. "But I'm sure you have some kind of poison in that arsenal of yours that would cause me a few hours of pain."

"I can think of a few."

"I can't wait to marry you." His fingers drew circles on the back of her hand. "I can't wait until this whole wedding is over and it is just you and me."

A jolt of tingles ran through her body. "Me, too."

"Ana..." he tugged on her hand. "I would like it if you and Marek started educating me on your condition."

"You would?" Warmth spread from her chest throughout her limbs, a whisper of tears welling at the corner of her eyes. "It's not an easy subject to learn about. It's even harder to try and help a loved one through their symptoms. Are you ready for that?"

Zander stood, his chair scraping against the wooden floor. "I'm ready to be the partner you need me to be."

Christiana wrapped her arm around his neck, pulling him close so she could breathe in her favorite comfort of cedarwood and clove, their foreheads resting against each other. "You already are."

Chapter Twenty-Five

FTER MANY DAYS OF CHAOS, CHRISTIANA found herself back in a daily routine. Although they weren't ready for weekly breakfast with Lucian and Penelope again, Christiana, Zander and Dorina kept their time together, enjoying the sunny winter morning over steaming, fluffy eggs, dark chocolate cherry scones, and fresh ginger-and-mint tea.

Christiana paused from the tenant letter she was reading to grab a second scone and another helping of eggs, ravenous after a few days of her anxious stomach restricting how much she could eat with waves of nausea. The first meal after unwittingly starving herself was always a pleasant one, and she tended to overindulge to make up for it.

She caught sight of Zander, his face creased as he read a few papers in front of him. "What's wrong?"

He pulled himself out of his thoughts with wide, blinking eyes, shaking his head as he smiled back at her, "Nothing. Just some more...research I was able to get my hands on."

"Alright," she narrowed her eyes at him, a sly smile on her lips as he tried to stifle a laugh.

"Wow, you two already know how to read each other's minds." Dorina peered over the top of her book, a fresh scone in her hand. "Impressive."

"Just shows we actually talk to each other," Christiana laughed until a knock interrupted their conversation.

Jay pulled the door open, and a rigid guard entered with a bow, his tanned skin glistening with sweat. "Your Highnesses, I am so sorry to interrupt your meal."

"What's wrong, Hayes?" Zander pulled himself from his chair to meet the King's Head Guard.

"Your father asked me to collect you and Lady Christiana. He says it's urgent." Worry filled his eyes, his hand twitching at his side.

Christiana's veins ran cold. This must have to do with the castle killer.

"What about me?" Dorina slammed her book shut, frowning.

Hayes bit his lip. "I'm sorry, Your Highness, but the King only requested your brother and the Marchioness."

Her lips pursed out. "Fine." She stood, storming past Hayes and out the door, book in hand. Christiana's heart ached for her; her friend hated being left out of important things.

Zander reached out for Christiana's hand, his grasp firm as they followed Hayes quickly from the Royal Wing to the King's war room. Christiana had never seen the inside, and she wasn't expecting to until she was closer to her own reign. But Hayes pushed the door open, and they entered the large, intimidating room.

There were no windows, the entire space illuminated with dozens of candles and three hearths. Maps of Viri and the entire continent covered the dark stone walls. A long table took up most of the space, strewn with more papers and plans, the King and Queen standing at the head.

"Father," Zander quickened his pace, Christiana reluctantly following until they stood in front of Lucian. "What happened?"

Lucian and Penelope's stern faces betrayed no emotion. He said, "We've been researching further into the killer's habits. Trying to see if we could connect them to any other cases outside the castle."

Christiana's pulse sped up. A sick feeling churned in her stomach. "Any luck?"

"I can't believe I didn't notice it before." Lucian shook his head, handing a piece of paper over to Zander. "It seems this is the exact way Julian died all those months ago."

Christiana looked over Zander's shoulder, trying to peek at the document. This was the first time she was seeing the death certificate of one of her victims besides her father. All his symptoms were listed out, but his official cause of death was poison.

Her palms sweated as she wrapped them around Zander's arm. "And you still haven't found his killer yet?"

There was no reason she would be suspected, either of her personalities. She hadn't used her signature poison, she had used Marek's—with his permission. There was nothing connecting the Marchioness or the Maiden to the night, but it didn't stop her anxious heart from beating hard against her chest.

"We hadn't." Lucian began rustling with his many papers again. "Whoever completed the job was a professional, to be sure. But we finally figured out who that signature belongs to."

He pulled out a large wanted poster without a picture, handing it over.

Wanted for Murder and Assassination

The Crimson Knight

Reward from the Crown if caught alive

"Oh my." Christiana hoped her face didn't betray her, every muscle tight as she bit the inside of her cheek until she tasted blood. She handed the sheet to Zander, his jaw tense as well when he took it, his other arm wrapping around her waist and pulling her close.

"He must be behind the murders in the castle," Penelope interjected, arms crossed. "We have dozens of death reports here that are all linked to that assassin."

Marek had worked as an assassin for over fifteen years; it was no surprise that he had accumulated quite the kill list. Although, it really didn't help him in the current predicament. "That doesn't really make sense. If he's an assassin, why would he start murdering servants in the palace?"

Lucian tilted his head, his eyebrows furrowed as he stared at Christiana, the back of her neck prickling when she held his stare. "Maybe he wasn't getting enough jobs to feed his desires to kill," Lucian said. Christiana's grip on Zander's arm tightened, her knuckles white. "It's the only lead we have. Besides, this is a very specific type of poison and after twenty-five years as a King, I think I know more about hunting assassins. They do not tend to give out their poison recipes easily."

Christiana's cheek twitched. He did have a point there.

"That's a fair point, Father." Zander echoed her thoughts,

dropping the wanted poster on the table. "However, it isn't just the poison that is part of these ladies deaths, now, is it?"

Christiana stifled a laugh as Lucian's face drained of color, his jaw going slack. His gaze flickered to Penelope, who walked around the table's edge. "What are you talking about?"

"Don't keep trying to hide facts from me." Zander strode forward, putting himself in between his parent's gazes. "The markings on the back, the consistency in the victims' hair color, and that they are tortured for hours before the fatal poison is administered. Any of this sound familiar?"

"Son, we just wanted to keep the more terrifying aspects of the killings as secret as possible," Lucian said, docile and soft.

"How did you even find out?" Penelope whispered.

"I'm not a child anymore who just accepts what you tell him." Zander's fists balled at his sides. "I knew you were keeping secrets, so instead of waiting for you to tell me, I went ahead and found them out myself."

Lucian glowered, his glare flicking to Christiana before returning to Zander. "Those details are highly classified. If anyone else outside of this room knows about them..."

"Then you should have told me when you had the chance." Zander stalked toward his father, the two coming chest-to-chest, their noses only inches apart as they donned matching scowls. "I have earned my place as the next King, and I am sick of the two of you treating me as if I haven't. It's time for you to realize that very soon, Viri will be under my rule, with Christiana by my side. Accept it so we can do what's best for our country, especially now when there is an imminent threat to our people."

Christiana beamed as Zander stood up for himself, for them and their future reign. This was the man she had fallen in love with. This was the man she wanted to rule beside. This was the King Viri needed and would one day have. She could not wait to see what he would do for this country when it was his time to be in control.

"Granted," Lucian cleared his throat, his hand flat against Zander's chest to push him a few steps away. "That doesn't help us now."

"Nothing you've been doing these weeks has been helping." Zander shook his head. "All you've done is kept secrets and glossed over everything with talks of the wedding. It's time for someone to take action, which is why I believe Christiana and I should lead the investigation from now on."

Lucian scoffed. "Oh really? You may want respect, but you aren't King yet, you can't get everything you want."

"Give us until the wedding," Christiana suggested, stepping forward. "Give us a chance to prove what kind of rulers we will be."

"That's ten weeks." Lucian side-eyed her, her skin tingling under the pressure of his gaze. "Five more young ladies could die in that time."

"Five young ladies already have!" Zander's voice rose, echoing off the ceiling. "Yet you sit here saying you're going after an assassin who does not fit the actual profile of the killer because it is the easier option. It's a wild chase and you know it, you just want something to say to people to make it look like you are working."

"Hold your tongue!" Lucian yelled, his face contorting, his eyes swirling like a hurricane. "What gives you the right to judge me and my decisions? You never used to argue with me until *she* walked into your life."

It took all Christiana's strength to stay standing tall and not cower under his menacing glare. After weeks of pretending, she was finally seeing the man who had chosen to let abusers walk free in Viri. A ruler, not for the people, but for his own need for power. Her stomach rolled at the thought, acid-tasting bile rising in her throat.

"Don't you *dare* talk about Christiana like that!" Zander snarled. "Just because this is the first time I have spoken out against you doesn't mean I've always agreed with you. It just means I'm no longer afraid to say what I believe in."

"Alekzander..." Lucian growled, his posture menacing as he stepped toward Zander.

"Let them, Lucian." Penelope pulled her husband back, her eyes gleaming as she stared at her son. "He's earned the responsibility, both of them have."

Lucian gazed at all three of them, fury radiating from his rigid posture, his fists shaking at his sides. Christiana held her breath, her lungs screaming for release. She needed to hear his answer.

"Fine," Lucian grumbled at last, his teeth grinding together, cheeks mottled. "Make sure I don't regret this decision, because I will make sure you pay for it if you fail."

Chapter Twenty-Six

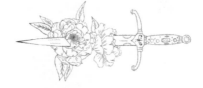

*S*TRESS ALREADY PULLED AT CHRISTIANA'S neck and shoulders as she and Zander walked back to his apartment in silence.

"Should we warn him?" Zander finally said when he closed the door behind him, his feet bringing him straight to his liquor cabinet. "I know we did a good job at convincing them it isn't him, but just in case."

Christiana rubbed her temples as she sat down on the evergreen velvet couch. "Yes, we probably should, just to be safe. We have no idea if your parents will continue the hunt for him without us."

"True." Zander's hand appeared in front of her face, a crystal glass swirling with her favorite whiskey dangling from his fingertips. She grasped it and took her first calming sip.

"He's going to be fine." She let his hand trail up her arm, his fingers freely twirling a lock of her hair. She hoped if she kept saying it, she would start to believe it herself. "I'll tell him next time I see him."

"You never had any links to him, did you?"

"You mean as Maiden?" He nodded, his face grim. "No, never. The only times we went on jobs together was before I was even active. Maiden didn't exist then."

"Good." He took another large sip from his own glass.

She took a few more sips of her own. "You should be proud of yourself."

"I am actually. I didn't know I was going to get so...passionate about it, but it was obvious my father wasn't going to do the necessary investigations to find this person. Somehow, that helped me find my voice."

"I'm proud of you. You did what was right, you did what was best for your people and not for you."

He clinked his glass with hers. "Thank you, love."

"I must say, seeing you so commanding, was very..." She ducked her chin, her cheeks tingling. "Attractive."

His eyebrows peaked, a dangerous smirk playing on his lips. "Oh, was it?"

Christiana hid her face behind a curtain of her dark hair. "Yes."

"Why so bashful?" he laughed deeply. "Are you trying to hide from me?"

"No!" She tried to deny it, but her hands rushed to cover her face, heat crawling over every inch of her body.

He hesitantly reached out to her, gently pushing her hair away from her face. "You just don't realize how captivating you truly are, do you?"

"Oh, please," she giggled, cheek leaning into his palm. "I am not that special."

"To me you are. You are the most breathtaking woman of my dreams."

Her body tensed as his hand skimmed away from her cheek and

toward her back, his featherlight touch seeping through her dress. It was only a thin layer of damask that separated him from her destroyed skin; her ugliness that lurked underneath the beauty of well-designed fabric.

She cringed away from his touch, her breath speeding up.

"Christiana?" He released her, leaning backward. "Love, are you alright?"

She pulled in a few breaths. "Just give me a moment."

She focused on what was around her, on the reality. The crackling of the fire. The soft, plush fabric of the couch under her palms. The lingering taste of honey on her tongue. She was safe, she was here.

She was not broken. She was a survivor.

She pressed her hand against her forehead, trying her best not to streak her cosmetics with beads of sweat. "I'm so sorry."

"Don't ever apologize for that." He shook his head. "Were you starting to have a panic attack again?"

She nodded. "Yes."

"Would you like to talk about what caused it?"

"No."

"I know we haven't had our lesson with Marek yet," his fingers tapped against his leg, "but my guess is, keeping this secret inside isn't helping, it's only making it worse."

"You're not wrong." She leaned forward, rubbing her temples with two fingers. Her insides crawled, dreading the idea of talking about something so intimate. But secrets had never been helpful in the past. She needed to speak them, she needed to talk about her fears to get past them, especially when they involved Zander. "Alright," she shifted to face him, his sapphire eyes intently focused on her, his forehead creased. "I've been...concerned recently about the idea of how...attractive I'll be to you."

He nodded slowly, confusion fluttering through his eyes. "I have always found you to be one of the most beautiful women I've ever met. I would tell you about some of my dreams to prove it, but I worry they are far from proper until we're married."

She shook her head, scratching at her legs through her skirt. "No, that's not what I mean."

"I'm sorry, I didn't mean to misinterpret. Can you explain it to me, then? Help me understand your fears?"

She whimpered, rocking back and forth. "I know I look beautiful now, but underneath the expensive clothes...it probably isn't what you are imagining."

"Um..." he shifted next to her. "Can you...elaborate?"

"My father ruined my body with his punishments." She wrapped her arms around her torso, bile rising in her throat. "My back specifically. It's destroyed with scars."

"And you're scared that I won't be attracted to you because of them?"

"Yes," she whispered, peeking at him through her curtain of hair.

His hands twisted in his lap, but his eyes were soft as they looked at her. "Just as anyone who comes out of a war with battle scars, I will see nothing but honor in them."

"It isn't the same."

"Perhaps not completely, but they are similar," he said. "I'm sure I will find them beautiful, just as I find every other part of you absolutely enthralling."

"You can't guarantee that, though." A tear slipped from her eye, her fingertips wiping it away. "We'll never know how you actually feel about them until you see them on our wedding night."

"That's true," he said. "However, what I can guarantee is that, no matter what my reaction to your scars is, I will still love every part of you: heart, body, mind, and soul. Even if my reaction is the worst-case scenario in your mind, just know that they could never change what I want in my life, and that is you by my side. You are all there is for me, Christiana, and nothing, not even your father's treachery, can change that."

She wanted to believe him, and the warmth spreading through her chest told her that a part of her did; the logical part. Yet it didn't stop the darkness controlling a piece of her, telling her that it was easy for him to say pretty words now, but he could change his mind when he actually saw her scarred body.

The pressure in her gut eased a little, but it didn't disappear completely. She had a feeling it wouldn't completely dissipate until the day finally came for Zander to see them. On their wedding night, the happiest day of her life that she was supposed to remember forever. It all could be ruined in one moment if she wasn't careful.

She let out a deep breath, turning to him. "Thank you for saying all of that. I know you believe every single word."

"But you don't?"

"It's...complicated to explain." She gripped his twitching hand. "A part of me does, I promise. However, words aren't enough to make these anxious thoughts just disappear. They will always linger when a *what if* is in the way."

He nodded. "So what do you need from me to help, then?"

She let out a chuckle. "When I figure it out myself, I'll let you know."

"Fair enough."

She leaned her head on his shoulder. "Even without a lesson, your instincts did a fairly good job at helping me this time."

"Well, I'm glad." He kissed her forehead, then rested his cheek on top of her head. "I want to do everything I can for you. I want you to feel safe with me."

"I do," she whispered, lacing their hands together.

They sat there for many silent minutes, needing nothing but each other and the peace of what this moment brought, until the rattle of the door opening brought them back to reality.

"Oh, Your Highness, I'm sorry to interrupt," Jay sputtered, the tray in his hand shaking as he set it down on the kitchen table. "I didn't realize you would be back so soon."

"It's quite alright, Jay," Zander straightened out his doublet, Christiana sliding away to a more appropriate distance.

"I thought you might want some more tea after what seemed like a...pressure-filled summons," Jay laughed. "But it seems you needed something stronger."

Zander held up his glass to his valet. "It wasn't easy, but it was productive. I'll warn you now, my life is about to get chaotic, so I apologize in advance for too many late-night requests."

"How so, Your Highness?"

"Christiana and I have taken over the investigations."

"Good." Jay nodded, taking up the whiskey decanter and topping off both of their glasses. "We need strong leaders like you two protecting us. I know you'll get the job done swiftly."

"Thank you, Jay, that is too kind of you." Christiana squeezed his arm lightly before he straightened. "How are you handling all of this, by the way? I know it must not be easy to live in those halls right now."

"I know it's terrible to say, but it's easy for me." Jay moved over to the dining table, a cleaning cloth in hand as he polished the varnished surface. "I'm not a target, so I don't feel the fear others do. My heart goes out to them, though. When you come to work at the palace, you feel an extra sense of security, with all the extra guards and safety provisions. Whoever this treacherous person is, they are taking that safety away from everyone."

"I never thought about that." Zander groaned, his head falling backwards.

"Don't worry too much Your Highness. I know both of you will do whatever it takes to protect everyone in this castle."

Christiana shifted her hips, resting her arm on the back of the couch to stroke Zander's hair. She knew the distance she was willing to go to protect people, but were they prepared for just how far this killer might take them?

Chapter Twenty-Seven

DORINA'S HANDS SHOOK AROUND THE LETTER, crumpling the envelope. Christiana stood with her outside the nobility wing, the two staring at the decorative vase for the past ten minutes.

"Just drop it in there," Christiana coaxed.

Dorina took a step forward, her hand hesitating over the flared mouth. "Is it too forward? Maybe I should rewrite it."

"Dorina," Christiana sighed. "There is nothing forward about asking the man who wants to court you who he is. Most people would probably say knowing his identity is a crucial part of a successful courtship."

"Technically we aren't courting yet."

"Which is even more reason to ask for a meeting. You should know the answer before you decide to."

Dorina tapped the edge of the envelope against the vase. "I suppose you're right..."

"Besides, it's just a precaution in case catching the person right now doesn't work."

"Alright, alright," Dorina shook her head, her gold-and-pearl-drop earrings almost catching on her curls. With one final breath, she dropped the letter in.

"Wonderful, now let's go." Christiana grabbed Dorina's wrist, dragging her to the end of the hall and back into the claustrophobic hiding spot behind a tapestry.

"I still can't believe you convinced me to do this." Dorina grumbled as she squirmed inside.

Christiana pressed her back against one of the walls, the darkened, cold stone seeping through her indigo taffeta dress. She was used to standing and hiding in shadowed, small spaces, although this was the first time she found herself with a companion.

"Just settle in." Christiana peeked through the slit of the tapestry, the creaking of wind pressing against the windows the only sound in the long expanse ahead of them. "We have no idea how long we'll be here for."

"I can't believe I am doing this!" Dorina covered her face, shaking her head. "How did I even find myself here?"

"You decided to correspond with an anonymous person," Christiana teased.

Dorina's russet eyes dulled. "Thank you for the observation."

Christiana smirked. "Anytime."

"I guess I just didn't picture it playing out this way when it all started." Dorina sighed, her back thumping against the wall opposite Christiana.

"What do you mean?"

"When the letters started arriving, I just loved the thrill of knowing that there was someone out there who...desired me." Dorina twirled a lock of hair, the tight coil looping around her fingertip.

Christiana's head fell to the side, "You have so many different men fawning over you."

"No, I have men fawning over my title and the idea of marrying a princess," she scoffed, her face pulling in disgust. "But Zander listens to your every word and he values it. It's what I always wanted."

Christiana played with her opal engagement ring. "Oh. I see."

"These letters aren't just about my beauty or how *intoxicating* this man finds me. We talk about our dreams, our fears, our desires for the future, what we hold dear in our hearts. We talk about ourselves past my title, and his...even though I don't know what it is."

"I understand." Christiana nodded.

"When I write to this man, I don't worry about having the perfect hair or smile or being concerned about my words. I'm just...myself. The way I am with you or Zander or Rowan." She shook her head. "So few people get to see this side of me, but I want my future partner to know all of me, not just what I could be useful for."

"You deserve to be noticed for more than just your title." Christiana gripped Dorina's hand. "You are worth so much more than what you were born into."

"Try telling that to my father." Dorina's eyes glistened in the dim light filtering through the cracks around the tapestry.

Christiana's stomach tightened. "What do you mean?"

"The pressure hasn't stopped. If anything, it's gotten worse since the first talk a few weeks ago. Father's made his stance perfectly clear: he wants me to marry a foreign dignitary to make an alliance."

Christiana shook her head, her heart racing. If Dorina married for a foreign alliance, she would be whisked away to a different country and they would rarely see each other. She would be ripped from the life she had always known and away from the people she had come to cherish, even if it made her miserable in the process.

"That is not happening." Christiana shook her head, her fingertips quivering. "I won't let it. Zander would never, unless it's what you wanted."

"We might not have that option anymore." Dorina scuffed the toe of her shoe across the floor. "I caught a peek at a list of potential princes and royalty across the continent he was compiling. Apparently, I have quite a few to choose from. Or at least, he does."

"We should tell Zander about this. Tell him what your parents are saying, he'll try and make them stop."

"No, not yet." Dorina said. "I know how stressed he's been, with the wedding and preparing to become King. Plus, with the whole killer running loose in the castle debacle, I just don't need to add even more to his burden."

Christiana bit the inside of her cheek, her muscles twitching. She was yet another burden added onto Zander's life, now that he was aware of her condition and the steps she needed to take to get it back in equilibrium. He had been a loving partner since finding out, trying his best to support her, encourage her, and console her when needed. He was there when she needed him, even if his time was already spread thin.

She tried not to overthink it, her stomach twisting at the idea of him doing so much for her when she did nothing in return. That wasn't normal for her, she wasn't used to letting others put her first. She just hoped that one day soon she would be able to repay the favor.

Lucky for her, she had a lifetime with him.

"Alright, fair enough," Christiana brought her attention back to the problem at hand.

"I'm hoping that once we find out who this man is, he will be my savior from my parents." Dorina let out a deep breath. "If he is at least a comparable nobleman from Viri, I may be able to convince my parents it's a smart match, even if it isn't exactly what they wanted."

"Plus, you'll have Zander and me to fight beside you if you choose to move forward with your mystery admirer," Christiana said. "We both believe you have the right to choose your future."

Dorina's cheeks reddened. "Thank you."

Shuffling feet from beyond the tapestry interrupted them. They peeked out through the tapestry on either side, Christiana squinting to get the best view through the narrow opening.

A twenty-something serving girl, with chestnut skin and dark, glossy black hair secured in a bun at the nape of her neck, moved slowly down the hall. Her gaze roamed idly as she stopped at each piece of artwork lining the walls to dust and clean.

"False hope," Dorina whispered, slumping back against the wall.

"Just a moment," Christiana muttered, watching the serving girl's every move until she got to the vase.

She glanced both ways before she snuck her hand inside the vase, as if she was going to dust it; yet it came out with Dorina's envelope, disappearing quickly into the pocket of her apron.

"Found her," Christiana said, flinging aside the tapestry.

Dorina stood up straight, rushing from the alcove. "Excuse me!" she called after the servant girl. "Please stop for a moment."

The girl halted in her steps, rigid as she turned back around to face them. "M—may I help you, Your Highness?"

"What is your name?" Dorina asked gently, stopping a few feet away from the timid girl, Christiana right next to her.

"Lilah," she said, her voice mousy and high-pitched.

"Can I ask what you were doing with the letter that you found in that vase, Lilah?"

Her shaking hands went back into her apron, the letter reappearing. "Oh...well...um...you see..."

"It's alright, Lilah." Christiana soothed. "We aren't angry, we just want to know the truth is all."

Lilah nodded. "Well, a young noble gentleman asked me to help pass letters between himself and the Princess. He has me check the vase every day on my cleaning rounds to see if you've left one, and then I mail it off to his residence."

"So you know who it is?" Dorina's shoulders perked up.

"I do," Lilah's lip quivered. "But he paid me quite a large sum to assist him along with ensuring no one ever knows his identity."

"The Princess would really like to know who she's been writing," Christiana coaxed. "Do you think you could help her?"

"I'm so sorry, My Lady, Your Highness. But I promised. Besides, I already had to spend the money on health expenses for my father and I'm scared if he finds out I told you, he'll demand I give it back."

"Well, we can make sure that doesn't happen."

Dorina put her hand up. "No, Christiana, it's alright. She doesn't need to reveal his identity if she doesn't want to."

Lilah's shoulders relaxed. "Thank you, Your Highness."

"Just make sure that letter gets sent off to him as quickly as possible."

"Of course, Your Highness." Lilah nodded emphatically, her legs shaking as she dropped into a curtsy before scurrying away.

"Are you sure?" Christiana whispered. "I'm sure we could have gotten an answer from her."

"I know," Dorina sighed. "But it shouldn't be her responsibility to tell me. If this man wants to be a part of my life, his answer to that letter will prove if he is worth my time or not."

Christiana linked arms with Dorina. "Good point."

"Besides," Dorina shrugged, the two strolling back toward their apartments, "where is the romance in the messenger telling me? I want to hear it from his lips when I meet him for the first time. It's the least I deserve after the mystery he's put me through."

Christiana threw her head back, laughter bubbling in her chest. "You deserve a lot for the patience you've had with him. Let's just hope he follows through and agrees to your request of finally meeting."

"Yes," Dorina's gaze flicked back over her shoulder before the vase disappeared from sight. "Let's hope."

Chapter Twenty-Eight

THAT NIGHT, CHRISTIANA TRIED HER BEST TO find a distraction. After another twelve days of fruitless investigations, she and Zander were nowhere closer to finding the elusive killer or protecting the people they would one day lead. It made her nerves sizzle, her mind spiral into darkness, and her muscles ache with exhaustion. She had spent the past five years dedicated to protecting those who needed her help, all in the secrets of the shadows. Yet when she was given the opportunity to do it in public, she felt like a failure. She was letting lives be taken and people live in fear.

She had a long way to go before she was ready to be their Queen.

"Would you like another serving, My Lady?" Jay graciously offered a tray of chocolate tartlets with caramel mousse for her to choose from.

Christiana looked up with a weary smile. "No, Jay, I'm all set, thank you."

Zander reached across the table, his fingers warm around hers. "What can I do to help?"

"Find this terrible man?" She rubbed her temple with her free hand. "My anxiety won't calm down until we stop him."

"I know," he leaned back, undoing the top two buttons of his doublet, the thick fabric folding over. "It was for the best that we took over the investigation, but having my father breathing down my neck every day is just making it worse."

"Two days." Christiana twirled her wine glass by the stem. "How are we supposed to face the castle staff when another body shows up?"

"It won't be easy, but we have to." His bright cerulean eyes softened. "As their leaders, they look to us for strength, even when we feel completely depleted of it. The only thing we can give them right now is the prospect of hope that we will bring them through this safely."

"How long did it take you to learn to do that?"

"Some days, I still feel like I'm learning." He rubbed his thumb just below his lower lip. "But you'll learn it, too, it will just take experience to understand how to handle the pressure of an entire country."

"I hope so," Christiana sank back into her chair, her bun catching in the carvings etched into the back. She didn't know if it was a lesson she was ready to learn, not when she was already so splintered and cracked within herself. Was she ready to learn how to put on a gracious face when everything felt so hopeless?

A loud, quick knock came at the front door, sending Christiana jumping a bit in her seat. Another thing she hated about her uncontrollable Battled Brain: she was an anxious, jumpy mess even when she was attempting to relax.

Jay opened the door swiftly, and Robert burst through the door, panting.

"Robert?" Christiana stood, crossing the room. "What are you doing here? I thought you went home already?"

"I did, however, I received a...letter that I think you should read." Robert straightened, his breathing ragged. His eyes flicked to Jay before catching Zander's gaze.

Zander nodded. "Jay, you are dismissed for now. Come back in two hours."

"Oh, um, are you sure, Your Highness?" Jay stared at them, already holding their finished dinner plates. "I haven't even finished cleaning up yet."

"I am, you can do all of that later." Zander walked around the table, his hand firm on Jay's shoulder. "We'll be fine with a little mess in here for an hour or two."

"Alright, Your Highness." He nodded, dropping the plates on the cleaning tray in the corner, picking it up only half-full and taking his leave.

"What is it, Robert?" Zander hurried back to join them, the three of them huddling as if they were not alone and had to keep a dastardly secret between them.

"I had a few Maiden correspondences that I was looking through tonight." He pulled open his bag, rummaging through it. "Just as you asked me to, I was looking to find other assassins to take the jobs while you were out of commission, and I came upon this letter."

His fingers shook as he held it out to her, the plain, black seal already snapped open, the parchment haphazardly shoved back inside. Christiana grabbed it from him, pulling out the contents. "I can't take a job right now."

"I know. This isn't about a job."

Christiana leaned against the dining table, her cheeks numbing as she began to read the mysterious letter:

Dearest Maiden,

I am coming to you for help as I am desperate, alone, and scared. I hold a secret I shouldn't, one full of shame I wish I could give back.

If you have yet to hear, there is a killer taking the lives of women within the Palace walls. He tortures them with deep bleeding slices on their back, he poisons them with a painful, burning death, then stands over them staring into their eyes as he watches the life leave their body. Once they are of no use to him, he discards them like old, dirty sheets for someone else to deal with.

If you are wondering how I know so many details about this terrible person, it is because I know who it is. When I was destitute, ruined, and alone, he gave me hope, he promised to help. Never in that promise did he mention murdering the innocent, but I was already too far deep into his plans to escape. I wish I had never been part of his desperate need for revenge, but I fear I am too far gone now.

I cannot tell you who this man is. Even though he is hurting others, there is still a deep-seeded part of me that is very loyal to him. However, I cannot allow him to take another innocent life, even if his twisted, deranged mind believes it is all for the better. I know who he is planning to kill next. Her name is Margret Pastelti and she is a kitchen maid. Please, Maiden, I know this isn't a typical job for you, but I have no one else. You talk of helping the innocent, those in need. Please come to the castle in a fortnight and save Margret. I fear you are the only one who can help her now, as there is no one to turn to in my own home.

I beg you, please help, or else Margret will lose her life.
Sincerely,
A Shamed Woman

The letter fluttered from Christiana's hands, her stomach gurgling, gags escaping up her throat. Dizziness overtook her, the room spinning as she rushed over to the edge of the room, to the only thing she could find before her stomach heaved: the small metal wastebin that sat next to Zander's desk. She knelt on the floor, a cold-sweat breaking out across her face as she retched up her dinner. A warm hand soothed her back, combing pieces of hair that stuck to her face, while soothing words rumbled in her ear.

The gagging finally relinquished, her breath rough and shallow as she sat up on her haunches.

"Ana, love?" Zander whispered next to her. "What can I do?"

"Help me up." She held her hand out to him, his grip tight as he assisted pulling her back onto her wobbling, numb legs. She wiped her forehead, a smear of cosmetics trailing on her palm. He propped her up against the edge of the desk, and she motioned to the letter discarded on the floor. "Read it."

Zander's brows creased, his hand tightening on her waist.

"I'll help her to the table, Your Highness," Robert came up beside them, wrapping his arm around Ana and guiding her back to sit down. Zander picked up the paper, silently reading as he walked to join them, finally dropping into the seat next to her.

"Oh, my...what?" Zander hunched over, the letter firmly in one hand while the other scratched his scalp and pulled at his curly hair. "Do you think this is real?"

"I don't know." Christiana collapsed into the seat next to him, Robert standing across from them. "Do you think someone else knows my secret?"

"I already thought of that, My Lady, and I would have to guess not." He shook her head, taking the letter's discarded envelope. "Whoever this is, they sent it through your Stroisia contact, which means they were lucky it even made it to you in time to get Margret to safety."

"He has a point, love," Zander tapped his fingers on the table. "Why risk sending the letter halfway across the country and not arriving to you on time if they knew you were in the castle? They could have sent it directly to you or through your channel with Robert to have it to you in a matter of days, particularly if they are as desperate to see Margret safe as they sound. They would have done anything to make sure this letter made it in time."

Christiana rocked herself back and forth, pulling in deep, biting breaths through her nose and holding them there, allowing their logic to settle in. She was safe, both of her identities were still secret. This person did not know who she was or what she was capable of. "That's a fair point. So let's focus on what's important: do we think this is real?"

"There is no way to prove if it is or isn't." Zander stared down at the letter again, smoothing the edges of the parchment. "The only thing this gives us is the possibility that the killer has been working with an accomplice this whole time."

Christiana's mind ticked, her spine tingling. "Do you recognize the handwriting?"

Zander shook his head. "No, and the letter clearly says that the killer is *him*."

"So, it's not Elaine and we are back to having no suspects to look out for." She groaned leaning forward to take the note from him. "The killer is set to take a life tomorrow night, and if it is this woman, we need to help her."

"I agree." Zander stood, going right to his desk and pulling out a piece of parchment and quill set. "Robert, we need you to find this girl tomorrow and bring her to us right after breakfast."

Christiana nodded. "Bring her to my room ten minutes after you typically arrive. I will make sure to dismiss Natalia before you get there."

"Of course, My Lady." Robert nodded.

Zander slid a slip of parchment over to Robert. "Make sure as few people as possible know you are looking, and don't tell her what it is about. We will explain all of that."

"Yes, Your Highness." He stored the note safely in the front pocket of his bag before rising. "I will bring her to you safely, you have my word."

"Thank you." Zander sighed.

"Robert?" Christiana reached out to him, his dark brown eyes staring down at her. "Can you do me one more favor?"

"Anything, My Lady."

"Can you ride out to Marek and update him tonight? I know it is a lot to ask, but he needs to know what is happening."

"I'll leave now." He slung his bag over his shoulder, rounding the table to her, her legs pushing up to meet him. "I won't let either of you down."

"I know," she said, and even though it wasn't the proper thing to do, she reached out and wrapped her arms around his torso, pulling him into a hug. His body tensed underneath her for a moment before his arms wrapped around her shoulders in turn, his chin resting on the top of her head. "Thank you for always keeping me safe, like the brother I never knew I needed."

He chuckled, the rumble tickling Christiana's cheek. "For the sister I always wanted? I would go through many battles with you if it meant keeping you safe."

Her cheeks warmed, and she gave him one final squeeze before releasing him. He bowed hastily and departed, the fate of this young serving girl resting in his hands.

Chapter Twenty-Nine

THE NEXT MORNING WAS SO RUSHED, Christiana barely paid attention to the dress she picked to wear or the way Natalia styled her hair or cosmetics. She barely tasted her breakfast before dismissing her Lady's Maid in a rush.

None of that mattered; what mattered was keeping Margret safe.

Only a few moments after Natalia left, Zander knocked and slipped into the room, his warm embrace and spicy scent comforting the twists in her chest and the weakness in her arms.

"We will get through this," he whispered in her ear. "We will save her."

She barely had time to nod before Robert joined them, a terrified young lady following him inside, her dark russet braid falling over her hunched shoulders and eyes downcast.

"Yo—you asked to see me Your Highness? My Lady?" She curtsied to both of them.

"Yes, please come sit down, Margret." Zander pulled a chair out for her.

Her gray eyes went wide. "Is there something wrong, Your Highness? Did I do something?"

"No, no, not at all." Zander gestured for her to sit, her petite frame perched on the edge of the chair. "We just wanted to talk to you about something."

Christiana and Zander sat across from her, Robert standing behind them. Christiana leaned her forearms on the table. "How much have you heard about the castle killer?"

"Just what everyone else has." She shook her head, fingers twisting on top of the table. "I don't know anything else, I promise!"

"We know." Christiana patted the backs of her hands. "Some recent information has come to our attention, and I'm very sorry to have to tell you this, but we have a strong suspicion that you may be his next intended victim."

"What?" Margret's lips quivered, her chest heaving for a few seconds as tears slid from her eyes. "No, that can't...why?"

She rocked back and forth in the chair, her head falling into her hands as her sobs grew louder. Christiana rushed around the table, taking up the chair next to Margret and rubbing gentle circles on her back. She rocked with her, soothing her.

"I wish I could answer that question, Margret, but I can't," Christiana whispered, keeping her voice sweet and comforting. "What I can tell you is that we are going to do everything we can to keep you safe. We won't let them get to you."

She peeked up from her hands, sniffling. "You promise?"

"I promise that the three of us will do everything in our power to keep you safe."

"Th-thank you, My Lady." She wiped away her tears with the back of her hand, collapsing against the chair.

Christiana leaned away, but stayed seated next to her. "Do you mind if we ask you a few questions?"

"I suppose, although I don't know how much help I can be." Her eyes were red-rimmed, her arms still trembling.

"That's perfectly fine, it just can't hurt to ask. Did you have any plans tonight? Were you going to be seeing anyone?"

"No," her voice leveled out a bit, "I was taking the precautions the royal family has suggested since the killings began. Every time he is suspected, I retire to my room the moment the cooks say I can. They've been nice enough to always let us retire early on those nights."

"Good." Christiana nodded.

Zander leaned forward. "Did anyone offer to keep you safe tonight? Or promise you a better hiding spot with them?"

Margret shook her head again. "No, no one did."

"Have you been assigned to any new nobility recently?" Christiana asked, heat crawling up her neck from Zander's sideways glance. "Or have any nobles asked you for help with something?"

"No," Margret wrinkled her brow. "None of the nobles talk to me, My Lady."

"Have you been courting with anyone?" Zander asked. "Or made any new friends?"

Margret scoffed. "I spend most of my time baking pastries and making sure the hearths don't go out. No one notices me that doesn't have a need to come into the kitchens."

Christiana leaned back in her chair. Margret's answers were the truth, she could tell by her candid words and relaxed posture. So, if there was no one new in her life, how was this person luring her away? The extra mystery layered into the already-tangled web of their investigation made Christiana's temples throb.

"Alright, thank you, Margret," she sighed. "Although you've been doing an excellent job at keeping yourself safe, we want you to sleep outside the castle tonight."

"I don't have anywhere to go," she admitted.

"You can stay with me tonight," Robert stepped forward. "I live in a house plenty big enough in Cittadina. I will make sure you feel safe all night."

"Oh...well..." she twisted her skirts in her hand. "I'm not sure if that is proper."

"It would just be for tonight, and I have a spare room for you to sleep in." Robert smiled gently.

"We just want to make sure you're safe, Margret." Christiana encouraged. "And I can personally attest to Robert's honor. He only means to protect you."

"Right now, the safest place for you is away from the palace and away from the killer," Zander added.

"Alright, if you think it's for the best." She let out a deep breath. "Where should I meet you?"

"I'll come by your room after you retire to sneak you out of the palace. Make sure there is no time in between now and then that you are alone," Robert instructed. "And do not breathe a word about this. We can't have anyone spreading rumors and the killer getting wind of this. We need them to think that you are still available for him to take tonight."

"What?" Her voice pitched upward. "But why?"

"We don't want him to have time to pick out another victim," Christiana explained.

"I'll try my best." Eyes flashing with fear, Margret stood. "Is there anything else you need from me?"

"No." Christiana patted her shoulder. "You can leave whenever you're ready."

"I'll escort you back downstairs." Robert offered, gesturing with an open arm toward the doorway. Margret gave a shaky curtsy before following him out of the room.

"Do you think we helped?" Zander wondered aloud.

Christiana let her shoulders fall. "We won't know until tomorrow."

***

Somehow, Christiana made it through the night, sunlight barely peeking through her window when she rushed out of bed to dress herself before Natalia arrived. Once again, she didn't have the patience to wait for someone else to tell her if they had succeeded or if the killer decided to go after someone else.

Once she was presentable enough, she rushed from her apartment to Zander's, knocking until he opened the door himself. His hair was still mussed and eyes were rimmed red, his plumb doublet and black pants the same ones he wore yesterday.

"You didn't sleep either?" She hugged him, his head resting heavily against hers.

"I couldn't." He brought her further into his room, dropping them into two of the dining chairs. "It's just a matter of waiting to see if anyone finds something."

"You don't think he could have gone to Robert's, do you?" Her fingers twisted into her black skirts, her palms sweating. Robert had offered to be Margret's protector, just as he was hers, but she would never forgive herself if he was injured because of this. She was meant to protect him just as much as he protected her.

"No, I don't," Zander stroked her cheek. "There was very little connecting the two of them."

They tried to distract each other for the next hour, until that cursory knock brought them to their feet, rushing to the door. A guard stood outside, his forehead rimmed with sweat, back straight at attention. "Your Highnesses, you need to come with me. We found something."

"Another body?" Christiana clutched at the bodice of her dress.

"No, My Lady." The guard shook his head. "But there was something in its place. You should really come with me, no one wants to touch it without you there."

He led them right through the servant halls, twisting through the maze until they came to a particular stretch of hallway—no corpse in sight, only a half a dozen guards surrounding a window.

"What is this?" Zander demanded.

All the guards turned, bowing and saluting. "We are not sure, Your Highness, but it has your name on it."

They parted, opening their circle for Christiana and Zander to enter. Her steps faltered when she saw what they did: an envelope with Zander's name scrawled across the front.

She clutched his arm, peering up at his quivering jaw, his eyes completely focused on the letter. Her skin crawled, that burrowing feeling deep under her arms and in her stomach, poking and prodding. This wasn't right, this wasn't supposed to happen. Saving Margret was supposed to be simple, but it seems the killer had a different idea now that they'd ruined his plans.

Zander pulled the letter from the ledge and whipped around, shoving it into his pocket. "All of you, get back to your rotations, now. If I hear a word of this filtering through the halls, you will all be punished severely. Understood?"

"Yes, Your Highness," they all murmured, scurrying away.

Zander grasped Christiana's hand and dragged her back through the halls, her vision tunneling. She put her trust in him that he would get her back to a safe space where they could deal with the ominous letter together.

He sat her down on his plush couch the moment they walked through the door and settled next to her, his weight compressing the cushions underneath them. He peeked over at her. "Ready?"

She couldn't speak, her words too jumbled in her mind and caught in her throat. She only nodded, watching his long fingers break the seal and pull the contents out, unfolding a tri-folded letter. She leaned over his shoulder to read it with him:

Dearest Prince Alekzander,

I'm sure you think you've bested me tonight. I'm sure you think you finally won.

Think. Again.

This palace, the people who live in it, and their safety now belong to me. You can hide one serving girl, but you can't hide them all. You've tried and you've failed and you will fail again.

I will continue to use this palace for my needs how I like. I feel no need to change my plans when you are too weak to even catch me. You do not scare me, and you never will.

Until I get what I want, until I get who I want, this palace will never be safe.

Sincerely, your humble servant,
The Castle Killer

Christiana didn't know when she had started to cry, but after reading the last line, steaks of moisture lined her face, the tiny specks of droplets staining her bodice. They may have succeeded once, but this person wanted so much more than just the freedom to kill their victims—they apparently wanted someone to pay.

His intended victim had yet to die.

"What have we done?" Zander whispered.

"It seems," Christiana stared at the paper, her mouth dry, "we've made him angry. There's no telling what we've unleashed now."

Chapter Thirty

A WEEK PASSED BY IN A FLURRY BEFORE calm settled back in the castle and within Christiana's mind. The muffled steps of Zander's pacing mingled with the cracking of the blazing fire were the only things filling the air as she waited in his apartment for Marek to arrive for Zander's first lesson about Battled Brain.

"When will he get here?" Zander's voice shook.

"Soon, he said he would." She followed his every step with her hooded gaze. "He took a lot of time over the years to make sure I understood everything. I know he wants to do the same with you."

Marek had always been the most consistent person to not only help her out of Battled Brain attacks, but to make sure she was trying to make herself better. His lessons had been more than just ways to physically protect herself; she learned how to protect her mind as well.

A rapping on the window took their attention as Marek opened it up, pulling himself through. He'd forgone his assassin outfit, the dangers of wearing it around the castle now not worth the risk. He was wrapped in dark clothing, enough to mask him in the night as he crept into the Prince's room. Christiana stood to greet him, and he wrapped her in a hug. She breathed in his musky scent before pulling away, a scowling Zander now by her side.

"Ready to learn, Prince?" he smirked, rubbing his hands together.

"Of course." Zander kept his arms crossed as they walked to the sitting area.

"Then sit." Zander and Christiana returned to the couch, Marek pushing the table backwards so he could perch on the edge in front of them. "First off, we need to explain that she has developed new symptoms because of this new trauma."

Zander's eyebrows rose. "Really?"

"Yes," Christiana sighed. "New trauma brings new symptoms, unfortunately. They correlate to the type of trauma you went through. My hands shaking is a similar one, but it seems my panic attacks are more violent now. I want to fight more."

"It also means there could be plenty of symptoms we have yet to find," Marek's gaze flitted between Christiana and Zander. "Particularly because this is a...different type of trauma, and Christiana is about to have some new experiences."

Christiana squirmed, a pained groan escaping her lips. "Marek, stop it."

"It's something you need to think about, dear one." Marek shrugged. "There isn't time for modesty right now."

Zander shifted towards her. "Does this have to do with your back?"

Marek sat up straight. "What about her back?"

"No!" Christiana swiped her hands between them. "That is not what he meant."

"Then what did you mean?" Zander turned back to Marek.

Marek leaned forward. "Well, because—"

"Can you please stop talking about me like I'm not here!" Christiana threw her arms in the air, slapping Marek across the bicep.

"Sorry," Marek smirked to her.

She rolled her eyes. "What he means is," she pulled Zander's hand, his attention turning back to her, face lined in concentration, "my father's abuse was purely physical punishments where Julian's attack was...sexual."

Zander sucked in a sharp breath, his eyes widening. "Oh, I see."

"It's alright," Marek jumped in. "Nothing may happen, I just wanted both of you to be prepared for the possibility."

"Thank you for the warning." Christiana gritted her teeth. "Can we please move on?"

"Alright!" Marek held his hands up in defeat, his dark hair skimming along his shoulders. "Now, what other advice do you have for him?"

Christiana's gut twisted, her skin crawling. She hated talking about herself, she hated being the center of attention, even if it was only for two people. This whole situation made her uncomfortable, but she had to push past it. This conversation was necessary, for her benefit as well as Zander's. She needed to do this for them, for their bond.

"Well," she cleared her throat, pushing past the jitters rumbling in her chest, "if I ever am triggered, be careful with touching. Unless I get overly violent and you need to protect me."

"Why?" Zander asked.

"It hurts. It can feel like your touch...burns? If that makes sense. Lighter touches are alright if you are trying to help calm me down, but anything overly familiar can sometimes make it worse."

Zander nodded. "Alright."

"Here is a piece of advice I know she won't tell you: after an attack, try and get her to talk about it." Marek glared at Christiana. "She despises it, but talking about the catalyst can help her understand and face it later on."

Zander ducked his head. "I already figured that one out."

"You did?"

"Yes," Christiana nodded. "It was uncomfortable for both of us, but we talked it through."

Marek shot her an unamused look. "And you feel better about it now, don't you?"

She huffed. "A bit."

"I was just concerned I was saying the wrong thing the whole time," Zander admitted, his cheeks reddening.

"You didn't." She turned to him, her fingers skimming along his temple to brush his hair back. "You actually did a wonderful job at staying patient and letting me talk in my own time."

"I'm glad to hear that, but I didn't feel like it in the moment." He looked up at her. "I didn't want to hurt you or disappoint you. I wanted to be supportive, but..."

"Alekzander," Marek leaned forward, patting him on the back, "it's going to take time for you to feel completely comfortable. You'll second guess yourself, and sometimes you will say the wrong thing. What's important is that you learn from those mistakes and try to understand. That's really all she needs."

Christiana's chest warmed. "He's right. I don't expect you to be completely perfect right away. We'll learn together as we grow as partners."

Zander ran his fingers through his hair, scratching at his scalp for a fleeting moment. "Can you teach me how to help you through one of those panic attacks? Like the one you had the other day."

Marek frowned. "Her attacks have evolved. It wasn't easy the other day."

"I know," Zander rubbed his palms against his thighs, "but I need to at least try and learn how, if I am going to be closest to her the most often."

"The first thing you have to know about them," Christiana said, "is that I can't think logically once it's started. You need to focus your words on the now, not on trying to make me feel better."

Zander tilted his head. "What do you mean?"

"Make me focus on myself, on coming back to equilibrium." Christiana thought of all the ways Marek and Robert had helped her over the years. "Counting backward, doing math equations, matching my breathing to your heartbeat, or naming sensations around me. All of those have worked in the past."

"But that didn't help last time," Marek pointed out.

"That's because it got too far before you tried to pull me out of it, so I was lost at that point." She crossed her arms, pulling her spine up straight. "If you can get to me earlier, you should be able to calm me down before the violence starts."

She wasn't sure if this was true, but she thought back to the sword fight. The symptoms had started while they were still fighting, and she'd tried to push herself through them unsuccessfully. She wondered, if she had dropped her sword, had been more forthcoming with what was really happening at that moment, perhaps they could have gotten her back without the drugs.

"A fair assumption," Marek said, staring at the floor.

"It's worth a try." Christiana shrugged. "I don't want to be drugged every time. Besides, if something happens during a social event, you can't just knock me unconscious and expect people to accept my disappearance. We need a long-term solution."

"Let me teach you what to do."

The next half an hour went by quickly, with Marek teaching Zander the proper ways to restrain her, comfort her, and force her mind back to her body. It wasn't easy on Christiana, but it was the right step to take; Zander was her forever, and she needed him to see all sides of her. She had been stupid to think she could keep this from him. She wouldn't survive without this support.

Chapter Thirty-One

T HE DAYS STARTED BLENDING TOGETHER. Christiana found any excuse to be in a ring, working on her Battled Brain symptoms. Between Marek, Zander and Robert, she had constant support, pushing her where she needed it and comforting her when frustrations got the best of her. They were her rocks, her pillars of strength.

Her body was already abuzz, fingers itching to be wrapped around the hilt of her daggers and sword, as she slowed Willow down to a trot to approach her cottage, Robert right behind her on Arrow.

"I thought you said Zander was meeting us here later?" Robert slowed next to her.

"He is." She looked over at him. "At least, he said he would meet us here."

"Then why is his horse already here?"

Christiana squinted. Zander's black-and-white spotted stallion, Atticus, was already relaxing in the tiny stable stall, happily chomping on a trough of hay.

Christiana dismounted Willow, her fingers flying to remove her saddle. "That's odd."

They quickly rubbed down their horses, hooking them to the side of the stable with feed and plenty of water to enjoy before rushing inside. Christiana's body tingled from the biting chill and anticipation; she pushed the door open to find Zander and Marek sitting at the two-person dining table, a slew of parchment spread across it, the two of them deep in conversation.

"Hello?" Christiana called.

Zander shot from his chair, eyes wide. "Christiana, you're early."

"I was going to say the same thing to you." She took a few tentative steps forward, watching as he quickly gathered up his papers.

He chuckled nervously. "All I said was that I would meet you here, and I did."

"What are you two up to?" She stopped in front of them, Zander shoving everything into his saddlebag while Marek leaned back in his chair, concealing a laugh.

"I thought you wanted us to get along, dear one?" Marek teased.

"Get along, yes," she gave him a pointed stare. "Not keep secrets."

Zander moved toward her. "It's not a secret, more of a...surprise."

"For me?"

"Yes," a coy smile played on his lips. "Marek was just giving me advice on a few things. I needed someone's opinion I could trust."

She narrowed her eyes at him. "Is this a surprise I'll like?"

"I hope so." Zander's eyes gleamed, the sapphire blues darker in the low lighting and overcast sky reflecting through the windows.

"Marek?" She peered over at him.

He nodded. "I think you'll be quite pleased. Just let him have his secrets a bit longer."

She huffed. "Fine, fine, keep your little secrets. I'll figure it out soon enough."

"Thank you." He planted a firm kiss on her cheek. "Would you like to practice now?"

She bit her lip, the balls of her feet bouncing slightly. "Absolutely."

***

They finally moved to the ring, the clang of metal swords and daggers filling the air for the next two hours as they paired off: Marek once again teaching Zander, and Robert helping Christiana.

"You're getting better." Robert patted her shoulder as he leaned over to pick up her fallen weapon while she rubbed her sore wrist. "We went for fifteen minutes."

"Slowly," she pointed out.

"Yes, but that was after you spent an hour on dagger target practice." He shook her shoulder, placing her sword back in her hand. "Where you didn't miss the target once. Not once, Christiana, remember that."

Her chest warmed, her fingers tingling. Her hand had been steady the entire time, ready and strong as it shot knives like an extension of herself. Her body had been buzzing all afternoon as they worked, her muscles tingling and sore with reforged strength. She was starting to believe the words she kept telling herself: she was strong, and she had power deep inside that was hers for the taking. Slowly, but it was there, and she was ready to pull more of it to the surface.

After they all reached their exhaustion points, they crowded into the cozy common area of the cottage, Christiana and Zander on the couch and Marek and Robert in the two kitchen chairs they dragged over. She pulled a blanket around her arms and leaned into Zander a bit, the back of her neck prickling at the tension in his muscles.

"What's wrong, love?" Christiana moved her hand to latch with his, their fingers twisting together.

"Just a bit on my mind." His free hand twitched at his side, tapping mindlessly at the armrest. Christiana stared at him, her gaze unwavering, until he sighed. "The killer will most likely be striking again in two days."

Christiana sat up straighter, her spine tingling. "It's been two weeks already?"

He nodded. "Yes. I changed up the heavier guard rotation in the servants halls to trap the person in case they've memorized the previous movements, but if our theory about the killer luring their victims to their death is correct, I don't know how much good it can do."

"I've been doing my own rounds as well every night." Marek sighed, rubbing his forehead. "I've caught nothing."

"The note said he wasn't planning to change his kill pattern though," Christiana said.

Marek snorted. "Like I trusted that."

Her stomach twisted, bile threatening to crawl up her throat. How had the days blended together so much? "I can't believe I didn't notice."

"You've had plenty on your mind, Christiana." Marek leaned forward, his elbows braced on his knees. "It's alright that you put your own health first."

"No." She shook her head violently, her hair escaping its leather strap at the nape of her neck. "I promised to help protect these people, to figure out what was happening in the castle, and I completely forgot about them. How could I do that?"

Her voice was higher with each word, the strain thick against her vocal cords as her mind raced. She didn't want to panic, not now, but she felt it crawling through her, starting in her gut and slowly snaking through her blood like poison.

"Christiana..." Zander murmured, but she just held up her hand, closing her eyes to block out the distractions around her so she could focus within. She pulled in deep, cool air through her nose and held it for a few seconds before forcing it back through her parted lips, the bite of it mixing together with the smokey scent of the fireplace. Her sizzling nerves calmed bit by bit.

She was present once again, stopping her panic from taking over.

She looked back up, her eyes wandering between the three men. "Sorry, I didn't..."

"Never apologize, My Lady," Robert said, gaze steady. "Never apologize to us about that."

She nodded slowly, taking in a few more breaths. "This is terrible timing. All of it."

"How so?" Marek's brows crinkled.

"Our engagement party is in a week," Zander said, his arm snaking around Christiana's shoulders to pull her close to his side. "People have already started to arrive."

"My family is going to be here tomorrow," Christiana grumbled. She had been dreading it ever since Penelope mentioned the pre-wedding celebration they just had to have for tradition's sake. She hadn't written to her mother for weeks, refusing to talk to her ever since their last fight. "But that doesn't matter." She shook her head, removing thoughts of the upcoming party. "The nobles aren't the ones in danger, the servants are. We need to try and catch him."

"I told you, we've been trying," Zander sighed. "The guards and Marek patrolling the hallways are constant and somehow he still sneaks through to dump the bodies without being noticed."

Christiana's pulse hitched, an idea sparking in her mind. "Well, then maybe you need a second assassin in the halls."

All three men's eyes went wide, their posture stiff in their seats.

"Christiana...no," Zander grumbled.

"It's the smart decision, Zander." She looked up at him. "Marek and I can keep an eye on the halls, our movements won't be trackable, not like soldiers set on a particular course. You can give us their movements so we can avoid them, that way we can focus on finding this monster."

"Your logic is sound, dear one, and I agree with it." Marek dragged his chair closer, his hand reaching out for hers. "But maybe I should go alone."

"No!" She almost screeched through her teeth, her vocal cords scratched from the harsh sound. "Two people are better than one, we can cover more ground together and watch each other's backs. I'm getting stronger, I can throw my knives again."

"Christiana, I don't think you'll get any of us to agree to this," Zander said, his hand rubbing up and down her upper arm.

Her heart burned, her body crawling with need. She had to do this; it was the code she lived by for the past five years. The safety of others came before hers, and that wasn't going to change. She turned to Marek, her gaze unwavering. "If you don't take me with you, I'll go myself."

"You wouldn't dare." The words rumbled out of Marek's chest, his eyes dark, lips curling as he stared at her.

"I think you all know that I would if it meant enough to me."

"You stubborn girl."

She let out a deep breath, rubbing the bridge of her nose with her fingers. "Look, I promise not to engage directly, I'll leave all of that to you. But you shouldn't go alone, and now that I have my throwing knives back in commission, I can be useful."

"Ana..." Zander squeezed her shoulder.

"I have to do this." She looked up at him, keeping her voice firm. "I have to do what's right for everyone. I can't just sit around feeling useless when I know I can help."

Silence fell as all three men stared at each other. Tension slowly built in Christiana's muscles, her neck clenching as she waited for them to say something, anything that would break the unbearable, suffocating quiet.

"You will not leave my side," Marek said, his grip tight on her hand. "You will only use your throwing daggers, and you will not engage unless directly given permission to. You follow every direction I give you, understood?"

Christiana smirked. "Understood."

Chapter Thirty-Two

"**IT WORKED!**" *DORINA BURST THROUGH* Christiana's bedroom door, Natalia close behind with an apologetic smile on her face. "Your plan worked!"

Christiana chuckled, rubbing lotion into her hands as she sat in front of her vanity. "Well, I'm glad I could be helpful. So, he agreed to meet you?"

"Yes! Look!" Dorina collapsed onto the bench next to her, waving the open piece of parchment in her face.

Christiana rolled her eyes as she snatched it from Dorina's grasp, scanning the page:

My Dearest Dorina,

Once again, you have brought a light to my day, your letter spreading joy within my heart and allowing me to make it through yet another sunrise and sunset away from you.

It hurts me to know that your parents have been pressuring you with thoughts of an arranged marriage. A smart, spectacular woman like yourself should not be treated so poorly, especially by your parents. You deserve the same respect your brother was given. I hope they come to learn that, just as the rest of the country will one day...that, I am sure of.

With that, I understand your desire to finally meet in person, and of course I will happily oblige to see you face-to-face instead of hiding behind our written words. Although, I must say, it is bittersweet to know that the thrill of our secret is about to come to a close.

I am back at the palace for your brother and Christiana's engagement ball. Let us meet in your favorite place to paint at sunrise the day after tomorrow. I cannot wait to finally be with you in person.

Until then, forever yours,
Your Loving, Secret Admirer

"Where is your favorite place to paint?" Christiana folded the letter and handed it back.

Dorina frowned. "You should know, we painted there together before."

"Ah, the rose grove," Christiana laughed. "Forgive me, I try to block out the truly dreadful painting I created that day."

Dorina giggled. "I'm sure."

"You need to be careful," Christiana hooked a simple pair of diamond studs in her ears. "The castle killer is likely to try hurting someone again tomorrow night. He wants you to meet the morning after that."

"Don't worry so much." Dorina waved her hand. "From what I've heard, he dumps the bodies overnight and he doesn't want to meet until the sun is up."

"Yes but…"

"And he only goes after servants." Dorina held up one of Christiana's necklaces to her decolletage.

"That doesn't give you an excuse to be reckless." Christiana sighed, her chest tightening.

"I won't." Dorina looked at her unamused. "You need to relax and trust people more. I don't think this man would have suggested it if he didn't think it was safe."

"I suppose that's true." Christiana sighed, her blackberry dress rustling against Dorina's. "Just promise me you'll be safe."

"Of course! You know I will." Dorina laughed, throwing her arms around Christiana's neck, her hair fluffing into Christiana's face, the scent of lavender and citrus enveloping her. Christiana hugged her back, melting into her almost-sister's embrace, although it wasn't enough to completely calm the itch of apprehension that crawled along her skin.

***

As the sun set, Christiana found herself outside the palace, a thick fur-lined cloak wrapped around her as she waited for her family to arrive. The last time she had welcomed them, she had been eager to spend time with them. Now, after her heated argument with Maria, her insides twisted at the idea of seeing her again. She would have to put on a smile and fake her way through it, pretending that she was very excited to be celebrating her engagement with her mother.

"It's going to be alright," Zander whispered into her ear, his arm firmly wrapped around her shoulder, his gloved hand rubbing up and down to create more heat through her bundle of thick clothing.

"If you say so," she mumbled back, her gaze drifting down the path as the distant clomp of hooves sounded against frozen earth.

Her stomach lurched when the carriage came into view from the trees, her body swaying back and forth. She was lucky Zander had such a firm grip on her, or else she might've fallen to her knees from lightheadedness.

Agonizing seconds passed before the carriage finally stopped in front of them. Servants leaped to action, grabbing trunks and cases strapped to the back of the rolling caravan. Robert took the lead and stepped forward, brushing off the footman's help to open the door and offering a welcoming hand to Maria and Isabelle as they exited the carriage.

Christiana took a deep breath and a step forward, pasting a smile on her face. "Hello, little one, welcome back!"

"I can't believe I'm here again!" Isabelle jumped a few times before launching herself into Christiana's embrace. "And to celebrate your wedding! I can't wait for all of the parties and events to start!"

"Just a few more days until the first one," Christiana said, wrapping her arm around Isabelle's shoulder before looking up at her mother's hard-set eyes. "Welcome back, Mother."

"Thank you, darling." She patted Christiana stiffly on the shoulder.

"Welcome back, Maria." Zander took a step forward, his face soft and inviting as he kept his head high.

She turned to him with a curtsy. "Your Highness."

"Mother! He doesn't want us to call him that!" Isabelle chided, her plump lips set in a deep frown. "He's our family now, so he's just Zander."

"It's alright, Belle, Mother can call Zander whatever she is comfortable with." Christiana squeezed her shoulder one last time before taking a step away. "Right, Zander?"

"Of course." His smile wavered, the corner of his lips twitching.

"It's just a habit from the years," Maria said, rubbing her hands together, the friction of her leather gloves uncomfortably loud. "I'll find a way to get used to it soon, I promise."

"Take your time, there is never any pressure," Zander said.

Christiana's heart twisted, her muscles aching with tension as silence settled around them. She moved over and grasped Zander's hand, giving it a few quick pulses to remind him she was there next to him. He had been giving her his strength for weeks now, letting her syphon it whenever her Battled Brain tried to overtake her. She wanted to remind him that she would always be there for him when he was hurting, too.

Christiana turned back to Maria, her mother's jaw tight and eyes staring at their clasped hands. "The servants will show you to your new apartment. It's in a different wing this time, a more permanent residence for your comfort."

"Can't you show us?" Isabelle looked up to Christiana, her bright eyes wide with begging.

"Not right now, little one, Zander and I have a meeting to get to," Christiana said, her fingers itching to wrap around a sword and practice again, the anxious energy coursing through her veins begging for release. Isabelle's shoulders slumped. "But I think Dorina and I might be stopping by later, if you're up for some company."

Her eyes sparkled. "Really? Of course!"

"Let's go inside, Belle." Maria wrapped an arm around her. "It's freezing out here and my weary body is ready for a nap."

"See you soon, Ana!" Isabelle waved as Maria led them inside.

"See?" Zander looked down at her, wrapping his arms around her shoulders and pulling her tightly against his chest. "It went perfectly fine."

"You're right," she mumbled, her lips muffled by the thick fabric of his cloak. She rubbed her cheek against the velvet, her stomach slowly settling with each deep, cold-stinging breath, the faint after-scent of cedarwood mingling. They'd survived the welcome, now they just had to make it to the wedding with both of their families under one roof.

Chapter Thirty-Three

THE LATE-NIGHT CHILL RAN THROUGH THE darkened hallways as Christiana and Marek made their patrol. The flicker of small candles lined the way with just enough light for the servants to pass through or soldiers to patrol, but for the most part, the area was abandoned and dark—perfect for two assassins to sneak around and investigate.

They halted every now and again to listen to their surroundings, making sure not to run into any soldiers. Christiana had taken the time to learn these twisted hallways over the summer, aiding in the investigation against Julian. With Marek now working in the palace and having a good excuse to roam them even during the daylight, he had clearly become an expert in them. He led the way with ease, each move purposeful, knowing exactly which spaces to avoid.

"What do you think?" he whispered. "Will everything stay still for the rest of the night?"

"Maybe," Christiana said hesitantly. They had been at it for four hours, and no one suspicious had crossed their path. "Just another hour?"

"Very well," Marek sighed, rubbing his brow under his hood, a yawn escaping his lips.

"Not as strong as you once were, soldier?" Although they both wore their face masks and hoods securely, Christiana caught a peek at his eyes a few times in the candlelight. They were filled with weariness as the night wore on.

"I am plenty strong, dear one," he replied, giving her a playful jab in the side. "It's the late nights I don't miss."

They kept moving, the minutes ticking by, Christiana growing more restless with each one that passed. Although she didn't wish for anyone else to be harmed by the castle killer, she also wanted to catch him; she didn't want their efforts tonight to be wasted, especially after all the persuasion it had taken just to let her go out.

"Did you hear something?" Marek whispered suddenly, straightening as he strained to listen. Christiana didn't answer, craning to catch whatever Marek was trying to pick up. It took a few seconds, but soon she realized he was right; she heard muffled movements off in the distance.

"This way," she urged.

They pushed through the corridors, the sounds becoming louder and more distinct with each turn—the scuffle of feet, the sound of a suffocated voice trying to break free, and the rhythmic growls of a man shushing someone. Christiana's heart sped up as they hunted for the culprit, almost tasting the excitement that they might be about to find the man they were looking for.

This could come to an end tonight.

Finally, she halted; they were close enough, the two people just around the corner. Ducking down low so Marek could see over her, they peered around the corner.

Christiana focused on the tall, stalking figure holding a helpless girl against a wall. He was covered head to toe in black, a mask and hood across his face, just like Christiana and Marek. She could barely see any details in the darkness, only that the long jacket keeping him warm grazed the floor.

The second thing she noticed, her stomach heaving at the sight, was a body lying on the stone floor just inches away from their feet. It was completely still, like a heap of used rags and sheets piled in a dark corner waiting to go to the laundry. Christiana could only assume it was a young girl, her life taken far too early, body abused and mangled in her final moments of living.

He had already taken his victim for the night. So, who was this other girl? Someone who caught the man in the act?

The man had a dagger in his hand, pinning the girl against the wall, whispering something to her in a hushed tone Christiana couldn't make out. She didn't want to see her get hurt, but she had made a promise that she wouldn't attack unless absolutely necessary. Pinching her eyes to focus, she strained to get a better look at the girl. After a few seconds, her face came into view, the killer dropping one of his raised arms to finally show off his victim. Christiana's heart dropped, shock running through her as she noticed who was trembling against the killer. Her petite form, curly hair, and soft features were unmistakable.

It was Dorina.

Christiana's blood boiled, as she reached for one of her daggers.

"Don't," Marek urged, grabbing her wrist and crouching down to be eye level with her, trying to pin her in place.

"We have to help her. It's Dorina!" Christiana hissed.

"Yes, but we have to do it right," he tried to reason with her, but she wasn't listening. All she could see was her best friend, her future sister, trembling and scared for her life. She didn't care what Marek had to say. Her fury was building so intensely and quickly, it would soon become unstoppable.

"You're right, I do."

Pushing Marek off, she darted around the corner and pulled out a dagger, throwing it, trying to make any contact with the man in front of her. It grazed his left arm, the one that covered Dorina's mouth.

"Get away from her!" Christiana snarled, Dorina's weeping growing louder with each step she took.

The slice of the dagger seemed to have shocked the killer, taking him off guard and giving Christiana the perfect opening to charge at him. She barreled into him, but her strength was not enough to push him away from Dorina, one arm tightly gripping her against the wall, the other reaching out and grabbing Christiana's arm.

"You bitch!" he growled in Christiana's ear, throwing her away from him like a piece of parchment. She stumbled backward, tripping over the body in the corner, her shoulder smacking into the opposite wall with a *crack*. She grunted, biting her cheek as the pain radiated around her shoulder and down her arm, numbing her fingers.

"Maiden, watch yourself!" Marek said, running toward them, but he wasn't fast enough.

It only took a few seconds for the man to slash at Dorina with his dagger, an angry red gash opening across her collarbone as he bashed her head against the stones behind her.

"No!" Christiana screeched, her vision tunneling, fingers scratching at the wall as she watched her best friend crumble to the ground just in time for Marek to charge the killer.

The fight burst out the moment Marek tried to knock him over, the killer side-stepping him and throwing a left hook into his chest. Marek stumbled backward, recovering quickly, drawing one of his daggers, the tip gleaming in the low candlelight that emanated from the sconces.

Christiana watched the fight for a fleeting moment, the two men well-matched as they fought hand-to-hand for a few seconds, dodging with impressive speed and agility. Then, trusting that Marek would catch this man, that he would do what needed to be done, she skimmed against the wall, keeping her pained arm clutched to her torso for stabilization and avoiding the two men as best she could, rushing to Dorina's side where she fell to her knees.

Dorina lay completely still, half-propped against the wall, the bodice of her magenta dress already half-saturated with blood. Christiana didn't have time to panic, letting her survival instincts kick in so she could do what her friend needed, trying her best to block out the sounds of the fight and focus. She pressed one hand against the wound and checked Dorina's pulse with the other, pushing through the throbbing pain still in her shoulder. She let out a breath when she felt Dorina's heartbeat tap against her fingertip, still relatively strong.

Pulling back Dorina's skirt to reveal the muslin underskirt, she yanked out her dagger and tore at the fabric, creating wide strips. She pressed them into Dorina's wound, putting as much pressure as she could with a weakened arm to try and staunch the bleeding.

Christiana's heartbeat was banging against her chest, her head light and spinning, but she didn't let herself give in. She used the last of her strength to stay in the moment, to stay there with Dorina.

A crack echoed off the walls, pulling Christiana's attention back to the fight, her jaw dropping as she saw Marek on the floor, coughing and wheezing while he scrambled to get back up. But he wasn't fast enough; the killer darted down the hall and around the corner.

"It won't be that easy," Marek grunted, rushing after him.

Christiana forced herself to breathe, hoping with all she had left that he would return with the killer in his grasp. She had promised to keep this palace safe, to find this murderer; he had been inches away from her, she had felt his bloodlust radiating off of him and his cruelty saturating the air. He was a monster, and she was never afraid to cut a monster down.

Yet it seemed her resolve wasn't enough to stop him from inflicting pain.

She tried not to think about it, looking back down at Dorina, her chest rising slowly with each shallow breath. She had a guess as to why the princess was in the hall—the meeting with her secret admirer was just an hour and a half away. If Christiana had to guess, Dorina wanted to get there early so she could hide and catch who the admirer was before they met. But she'd promised she would be safe, that she wouldn't be reckless. So why would she go through the servant halls when she knew the killer was on the loose?

Footsteps approached down the hall, setting Christiana's fingertips tingling, hoping that it wasn't a guard on rotation.

Her luck was still intact. Marek turned the corner—alone.

"Where is he?" Christiana hissed as Marek dropped on Dorina's other side.

"He got away. Disappeared out a window. I knew if I tried to follow, he would be gone by the time I reached the ground."

"Damnit," Christiana muttered. He had been right there. How had they failed so miserably?

"How is she?" Marek stared down at Christiana's hands, the torn piece of fabric already saturated with Dorina's blood.

"I don't know." Christiana shook her head. "She's still breathing, but she hasn't moved once, not a twitch or a groan. I think he drugged her."

"We need to get her help." Marek scooped Dorina's still form into his arms, Christiana rose next to him, keeping pressure on the wound.

"Let's go back to my room," she said. "Zander and Robert are there, they can help."

"Alright, lead the way."

Chapter Thirty-Four

SOMEHOW, THEY MADE IT THROUGH THE HALLS
without incident, stumbling through Christiana's door,
the crash of their entry bringing Zander and Robert to
attention in the common area.

"Hurry, help me get her to the bed!" Christiana urged. Marek
rushed through the parlor, kicking the door to Christiana's bedroom
open.

"What happened?" Zander ran right to the bed, where Marek
gently placed Dorina without Christiana letting go of the wound. The
princess didn't even flinch, her face peaceful, chest still rising with
each breath.

"We caught her in the halls with the killer," Christiana explained,
using her free hand to pull her hood and mask down. "She must have
been sneaking around and caught him by mistake."

"Why was she even out there?" Zander's words came out in a
hurried mess as he knelt on the bed next to his sister.

"I don't know. But that doesn't matter right now, what matters is getting her help."

"Let me see, My Lady." Robert took over the compression on Dorina, kneeling down at the bedside to get a closer look at the wound.

Christiana let out a deep breath, her still-aching shoulder releasing a bit of tension. "Can you help her?"

"I'm afraid this is beyond my skills. She's bleeding heavily even though I don't see any major arteries torn. Only a trained physician can help get this put together properly."

Marek emerged from Christiana's closet, three of her nightgowns in his hand, holding them out to Robert. "Here, use these."

"This is only a temporary fix," Robert shook his head, pressing the first nightgown against Dorina's chest.

Zander looked up sharply, eyes bloodshot with panic. "You know what we have to do, Ana. He's the only one who can help."

The adrenaline in Christiana's system was slowly starting to wean off, her stomach rolling as she realized what Zander meant. Her fingers twitched, her forearms seizing. "I know. We need to bring in someone who we can trust, depending on how the rest of the night goes."

"Who are you talking about?" Marek asked, grabbing another piece of cloth and handing it off to Robert.

"Zander's best friend is a trained physician."

Marek straightened. "Do you trust him?"

"Yes, I do." And despite everything, that was still true.

Zander walked quickly around the bed, giving her a brush of a kiss on her sweaty forehead. "I'll be back as soon as I can."

"Good luck," she said. Zander nodded sharply, disappearing through the door.

"You two need to leave before Rowan gets here," Christiana added, opening the trunk at the foot of her bed, unlatching her weapon belt and placing it back into the false top. "Marek, help me unlace this."

"We can stay if you need us," he murmured, pulling the lacings free and maneuvering if off without hurting her arm too much more, leaving her in just her black pants and black undershirt.

"No, there's no need to risk incriminating you as well." She sat on the edge of her bed, unlacing her boots one at a time and throwing them into the top. "Let me just change and then you can leave before Zander gets back."

They both nodded, and she walked into her closet, focusing on what was happening in that moment: removing her pants as quickly as possible, the ache in her shoulder as she pulled her shirt over her head, the soft graze of her cotton nightgown against her skin, and the warmth that slightly soothed her shaking hands as she wrapped a thick robe around her.

She had to be strong, to be the friend Dorina needed. She would not let her own struggle stop her from being that friend.

She was not broken. She was a survivor.

"I'll take over," Christiana whispered to Robert, using her uninjured arm to press another nightgown against the bleeding.

"Send a messenger to my house if you need me to come back." Robert kissed her forehead.

She nodded. "I will."

"Be safe, dear one," Marek gave her a sideways hug before the two men left, the room quieting to nothing more than the crackling of the fire and the ticks of the mantle clock.

***

Christiana tried not to worry that Zander was taking too long or why the minutes seemed to be passing quicker than normal. She kept her eyes trained on what was in front of her, on the wound she needed to keep compressed until help arrived.

"You're going to be alright," Christiana murmured, rocking back and forth slightly. "Rowan is going to make this right and you're going to be just fine. Don't worry, I've got you."

She repeated the words to Dorina as much as to herself, seeking anything to soothe her until the front door to the apartment clicked open.

"It's almost four o'clock in the morning, Zander." Rowan's voice filtered through the cracks in the door. "Just tell me what's going on."

"Well, it's a good thing you were still awake, then, for whatever reason."

The door burst open, and Christiana looked over without leaving her place next to Dorina. Rowan stopped in his tracks, his mouth gaping, the color draining from his face. "What happened to her?"

"A servant brought her here," Christiana said, keeping her words as steady as possible. "They found her injured in the hallway next to a dead body. We think the killer saw her. The back of her head is hurt, too, but her chest is bleeding badly."

Rowan rushed to Dorina's side, dropping his bag on Christiana's bedside table and taking the compress from her hands. He sat down on the bed, removing Dorina's bandages to start his examination. Seconds passed as he traced the lines of the wound with his fingers, ripping the bodice of her dress even more.

"I need to disinfect this as quickly as possible." His voice was completely professional, his movements precise as he opened his bag and withdrew an array of equipment. "The wound has been open too long, we need to close it before she loses any more blood. Has she been unconscious the whole time?"

Christiana nodded, stepping back toward Zander to give Rowan space. "Yes, she's barely moved. Do you think she's been drugged?"

"It's possible." He pulled vials of clear liquid, fresh bandages, and fresh gloves from his bag. "I'll know once I examine everything fully."

Silence fell, Christiana standing off to the side with Zander, her fingers curling into her side as she steadied her injured arm. She tried to distract herself from worrying about Dorina by focusing her attention on Rowan, watching him move and prep what he needed. He reminded her of herself; his face, though set with concentration, had a twitch of excitement. Everything he was doing, the movement of his hands, the concentration of his mind, was second nature. This was what he was meant to do in life, and he was loving every minute of it, even in the crazy situation they had unexpectedly placed him in.

"We need to talk," Zander whispered to Christiana.

"About what?"

They looked over to Rowan, his brow already glistening with sweat as he leaned over Dorina's prone form, methodically cleaning her wound. Zander grasped her hand, pulling her out into the common area and over in front of the fireplace.

"I need you to be honest with me about something," Zander said, his fingers squeezing hers. "Did she see you?"

Christiana let out a shaky breath, clutching her sore arm against her body. "I don't know. I don't think so, but I wasn't worried about that in the moment, I was just trying to help her."

Zander nodded, his forehead creasing.

"Although..." she bit her lip, looking up at him through her eyelashes, "Marek did call me Maiden while we were out there."

Zander's eyes went wide. "What?"

"What was he supposed to call me? Ana?"

Zander rubbed his brow. "Before or after she was knocked unconscious?"

The memories were already blending together, a flurry of rapid events she struggled to piece together in proper order. It felt as if it had happened long ago, not a mere hour, with the rush of adrenaline and survival instincts carrying her through most of it. "I don't remember," she admitted, dread snaking through her system.

"Wonderful." Zander raked his fingers through his hair, his gaze wandering down to the fire.

"What am I supposed to do?" Christiana leaned herself against the side of the mantle, her legs shaking.

"I don't know," he shook his head, a deep frown settling on his lips. "It's your secret, so it's your decision what you want to tell her."

Christiana groaned. She didn't want to lie to Dorina if she had recognized her in some way. It was already hard enough keeping this dangerous secret from those closest to her sometimes, but to outright lie to Dorina, to try and convince her that what she had witnessed was false or a hallucination, seemed cruel and unnecessary.

She would not be that person, not to anyone—especially her best friend.

She let out a breath. "If she recognized me and asks for the truth, I'll give it to her."

"Alright," Zander nodded, placing a light kiss on her forehead. "I wish you didn't have to, but if I was in your place, I would do the same. She doesn't deserve to have her memories manipulated because of our fears."

Christiana dropped her head against Zander's chest, a tear slipping down her cheek. "What will Dorina think of me if she finds out the truth of what I do?"

"What you do is noble Christiana, she'll understand that," Zander soothed, rubbing circles on her back.

"I wouldn't say killing people is noble," she laughed brokenly, rubbing her forehead. "It's more of a necessary evil."

"Alright, fair."

"I'm sorry," a voice came from behind them. "what did you just say you do?"

Chapter Thirty-Five

C *HRISTIANA FROZE, THE ROOM SPINNING AROUND* her, nausea rolling through her stomach. This couldn't be happening...she couldn't have allowed herself to be so reckless with people in the other room. She knew better; even in the most unexpected circumstances, she was trained better than this.

Curbing her internal chastisement and letting out a deep breath, she turned to Rowan, his body still half-concealed by the door, his jaw slack and bright green eyes wide.

"What do you mean?" Christiana tried to smile, but her muscles weren't strong enough.

"You know what I mean!" he hissed, stepping inside and closing the door behind him. "I just heard you say you kill people."

"Oh...well, you see..." Christiana stumbled over every word as she tried to come up with an excuse. She had been so focused on what she would say to Dorina, she never even considered what would happen if Rowan found out, too.

"Maybe this isn't the best time to discuss this," Zander suggested, "with Dorina in the other room."

"Do you two really think I am that much of an idiot?" Rowan stormed toward them.

Christiana's skin crawled. "No, of course not."

"Then why are you avoiding my question? I know what I heard!"

"Rowan..." Christiana took a step forward, and Rowan flinched away.

"I know you were more involved with Dorina's injury than you're saying," he accused. "You've been clutching your left arm the entire time I've been here. You're injured too, aren't you?"

Christiana tried to lower her arm to her side, the muscle aching when she did. "It's my secret to keep, you can't force me to tell it to you if I don't want to. Please, just try and forget what you heard."

"Stop lying, or I won't tell you what I learned from treating Dorina!"

Christiana stiffened. "Excuse me?"

"You have no right to withhold information about my sister's health!" Zander snapped, stalking to meet Rowan by the dining area.

"Actually, as her physician, I do if I believe it is for the safety of my patient...but that's not what I meant. I learned something else, something pertaining to the castle killer I think may be particularly useful."

Christiana halted, her heart skipping a beat. "You know something?"

"Yes, I do." Rowan crossed his arms, his eyes darting between them. "And if you want to know, you'll tell me the truth!"

"You would obstruct an investigation over this?" Zander gaped. "People's lives are at stake!"

"And based on what I just heard from Ana's lips, they already are! How am I supposed to know she can be trusted with information like this?" Rowan threw up his arms. "Right now the only thing I can think of is that maybe *she's* the castle killer."

Christiana clutched at her robe, her mind spinning. He was right; after what he overheard, he deserved to hear the actual truth. If she was in his position, she would be thinking the same thing. And they needed the information that Rowan was holding onto; they needed any detail they could to help catch the killer.

She had said earlier that she trusted Rowan; it was time to find out just how far that trust went.

"I'm not the castle killer." Her skin crawled, her mind begging her not to say the truth, but she pushed through. "But I am an assassin."

"What?" Rowan stumbled back, catching himself against a wall. "That...how...what?"

"I know it's a lot to process, but I was the one who brought her back here because I was the one who caught her struggling against the killer." She reached for him gingerly, his hand flinching away at her touch. "Trust me, that was the last way I wanted you to find out..."

"I'm sure you didn't want me finding out at all," he snapped.

"You're right, I didn't," She held her hands up in front of her. "I promise, you can ask me anything after, but please, just tell us what you know! Is Dorina alright?"

Rowan took a few deep breaths before pushing away from the wall. "There's something I noticed when I was treating and stitching the wound." He sat across from them, pouring wine into one of the glasses left on the table. "Dorina didn't move the entire time. That's not normal for someone who is forced into an unconscious state. It confirmed your suspicion that she's been drugged somehow."

"What?" Zander seethed, dropping into the chair beside him.

"Could it have been an anesthetic of some kind?" Christiana asked.

"That's what I thought at first," Rowan said, "But when I tested her reflexes, she didn't respond to any stimulation. Besides, her wound was bleeding excessively for how deep it was."

"So?" Zander rolled his hands in front of him, urging Rowan to speak faster.

Rowan sighed. "I think she's been given Body Lock."

"That's impossible!" Zander seethed. "The recipe for that drug is a Virian secret!"

"Actually," Christiana bit her bottom lip, "it's not as secret as you may think. I know how to make it."

Body Lock was one of the few non-lethal poisons in her arsenal. The Virian military designed it to help treat soldiers in the field by numbing the injured area while they carried the wounded back to safety. However, when they realized just how strong the paralytic was, they began to put it to a different use: torturing their enemies and war prisoners for information.

It became the quickest way to get them to give up even their darkest secrets, hurting not only their body, but their mind. First they terrified them by making them lose control; then they forced them to watch as someone marked their bodies with cuts and burns they couldn't even feel. Until the poison wore off, that was—then they felt it all at once.

It was a poison she kept stocked, but never used. The idea of it, the pain and mental torture it could inflict, was too much. The only reason she carried it around was because Marek insisted on it. Always a soldier, always prepared.

Zander shook his head, his chest heaving with each ragged breath. "That's how he's torturing the girls. If I had to wager a guess, he numbs their bodies so he can mark them quietly, and then kills them once it wears off."

Christiana wasn't a betting woman, but she would have bet her entire fortune on Zander's guess, too. Something in her soul churned, whispering to her that her instinct was right; this wasn't just about killing for this person, it was about taking pleasure in the entire process that ended his victims' lives.

Her skin crawled at just the idea, like burrowing bugs creeping along every inch of her.

"That's what I thought, too, when I realized what the drug was," Rowan agreed. "She's been through enough tonight, and that drug can have some mentally painful repercussions. So, I made the decision to give her an anesthetic to help her sleep through the effects. Hopefully it will help her cope with the trauma."

"Good," Zander nodded, running his fingers through his hair. "I think that was the right decision."

"Will the anesthetic last long enough for Body Lock to wear off?" Christiana asked.

"I'll test her reflexes as the night goes on in case I have to give her a second dose," Rowan said. "Once they start reacting, I'll stop administering it so she can wake up naturally."

"Alright," Christiana nodded. "Do you think either of the drugs could cause memory loss?"

"Why?" Rowan narrowed his eyes.

"Ro, we need to ask her if she remembers anything," Zander said calmly.

"After what she's just been through?" Rowan blinked at him. "Are you kidding me?"

"Rowan, trust me, we wish we didn't have to, but she's the only victim who's alive to talk about it." Christiana explained, leaving out the other reason she wanted to talk to Dorina; the selfish reason. "If she wasn't Dorina, and just some servant we brought to you, would you object this much to us trying to get answers about the killer?"

Rowan dragged his hand across his face, his cheeks red. "I wish the answer was yes, but it isn't."

"You can be in the room if you want," Zander offered.

Rowan perked up. "Really?"

"Unless she objects, but I know she trusts you. Besides, you've given us a lot of answers with this case. Your help is welcome."

Rowan smiled gently. "Thank you, Zander."

Zander nodded, and Christiana's heart warmed at the brief exchange—until Rowan looked away, crossing his arms.

"I'm going to sit with her for a while," Zander mumbled. "I don't want her to be alone."

"Alright," Christiana said.

Zander clutched her shoulder briefly, but she flinched away, pulling a sharp breath through her teeth, and he dropped his hand at once. "Sorry, love."

"It's fine." She shook her head, securing her arm against her torso again to try and stop the throbbing.

"No, it's not," Rowan sighed. "You're injured, let me take a look."

"But—"

"No buts. You sit. I'll just grab my bag and be out in a moment."

Christiana's heart squeezed, her stomach dropping as she walked to the table—wondering what other mind-bending turns this night could take before the day broke.

Chapter Thirty-Six

ROWAN DIDN'T TALK AT FIRST, TAKING HIS TIME pulling out all the medical equipment he would need for the exam. Christiana allowed the tense silence to wash over them, untying her robe enough so she could gingerly lower the collar of her nightgown to reveal her injured shoulder. He stood next to her chair, face serious as he concentrated on the job. Minutes went by, and still he wouldn't look up at her once.

"So, we're just going to sit here in silence then?" she asked, forced sarcasm lacing every word.

"I'm working," he said flatly, delicately pressing into different spots along her upper arm and shoulder.

"I can see that, but with physicians I have met in the past, they usually learn how to talk and work at the same time." She stared at him, glad to find his cheek twitching at her words. "Helps pass the time and keep uncomfortable moments to a minimum."

"What would you like me to say, Christiana?" he asked, his

emerald eyes filled with so many emotions Christiana could not decipher a single one.

"I just want to know if you're alright."

"Alright? I'm doing great." He rolled his eyes. "I've recently learned that my past potential suitor is also an assassin, that my best friend knew about it, and to top it off, I'm currently monitoring one of my closest friends because she ended up getting caught by the castle killer and was lucky enough to escape with her life!"

"Ow," she shuddered. His grip on her wounded shoulder had tightened, shooting a dull pain from the injury.

"Sorry," he grumbled, taking his hands off her for a moment.

"I know it's a lot to process." She shifted in her chair to look up at him.

He scoffed, reaching into his bag and pulling out a jar of pale green salve. He scooped a generous helping out and rubbed it on her shoulder, her body tensing for a moment until a cooling sensation washed over her.

"But now that you do know..." She hesitated for a moment. "You can ask me anything. You deserve answers now that the truth is out."

His hands stopped their gentle circles on her shoulder. "I can ask you anything?"

"If you want to."

He cleared his throat, pulling a bandage from his bag and loosely tying it under her armpit and around her shoulder. Christiana sat there in silence, letting him take his time. He pulled her nightgown back over her shoulder before moving to stand in front of her, wiping his hands with a towel as he sat down in the chair next to her. "Do you have a name?"

Her chest tightened at the first question. "I go by Midnight Maiden."

"How many jobs have you done?" he asked, shifting his chair so the two faced each other.

She bit her lip, squeezing her eyes shut. "I lost count after the first year."

He sighed her name, shaking his head with a gaping mouth, his gaze never leaving his work. "I didn't realize it was so easy for you. Killing people."

"I never said it was easy." She curled her fingers into the top of her robe, squeezing it against her chest. "But when you count how many lives have ended because of you...it makes the guilt unbearable. I had to separate myself from them as much as possible."

"Then stop."

"It's not that easy."

"Stopping assassination isn't easy? That's really your defense?" he shot back, face red and voice trembling slightly.

"I don't take just any jobs, Rowan, I only help those who need help." She let out a sharp breath, her shoulder throbbing under his ministrations. "Victims of abuse or rape. People who need to move on from what haunts them every day."

He leaned forward, his arm snaking across the table until his hand was on top of hers, his eyes softening. "What made you want to do that?"

She didn't want to say the words out loud, but there was no other explanation. She never expected for this moment to happen, but something about Rowan's concerned gaze and gentle hand on hers settled her rolling stomach. "Because I was a victim of abuse as well."

His chin fell to his chest. "Oh...oh, Ana. Who could do that to you?"

"My father," she twisted her hands into the dark fabric of her robe. "I don't want to get into details, but he hurt my mother and me in unimaginable ways for too many years before he died."

She looked at the shock now spread across Rowan's face, his jaw set with so much tension, it looked as if he was trying to bite his own tongue off. "I didn't know."

"No one did, Rowan. No one was supposed to know. It was shameful and wrong...things nobles aren't supposed to be."

"So, you help others...like yourself?" She nodded. "But the King and Queen..." Rowan started, then stopped when Christiana shook her head.

"There isn't much help for victims, and the laws that are in place favor the abuser, not the abused. There are so many loopholes for them to get out of punishment. That's if they even get arrested for it. Since it becomes a whole case of one person's word against another's, the cases are easily dismissed." She twisted the end of her ponytail between her fingers. "This was the only way I could think to help."

Rowan leaned forward. "How did Zander find out?"

"That isn't my story to tell," she said, not sure how much information Zander wanted Rowan to know. "You need to ask him."

Silence fell between them again, a pensive look forming on Rowan's face as he stared off into space. Minutes ticked by, neither of them moving to leave; clearly there was one more thing he wanted to ask, but was holding himself back.

"Is there something else you want to know?" she prompted at length.

"Why would you say that?"

"You're biting your bottom lip. Usually means you want to say something but are trying to stop yourself."

He looked at her a few seconds longer. "If I had known the truth, before you chose Zander, would you have chosen me?"

She softened at his question. She understood where it was coming from, but she knew the truth, and it was time for him to know it as well. It was the only way both of them would get closure on their failed relationship.

"No, Rowan, I wouldn't have."

His eyes shut as he took in her answer. She wanted to reach out to him, to comfort him, but all she could do was sit there, her hands crossed limply in her lap. "I see."

"I won't say that Zander knowing the truth wasn't a wonderful part of our relationship," she began, "but it wasn't the real reason I chose him. What Zander and I have, the feelings and the connection we share, is something you and I never had."

"I did love you," he admitted in a whisper.

"I know you did, but be honest, were you drawn to me because you felt passion, or did you see me as a good match? A person you could care for?" Rowan fell silent and stayed that way, which was all the confirmation Christiana needed. "We were too blinded by our duty to realize that something was missing between us."

"Most people wouldn't agree with that. Marriage for nobles isn't always about passionate love."

"I used to believe that too, but we can take control of our own lives more than we like to believe." She finally found the courage to reach out and pat his knee. "You just need to be willing to work for it instead of taking the easy way out."

"You're right," he replied, a smile spreading across his face as he grabbed her hand. "I've come to learn just how right you are." Hope broke through her at that grin. Their relationship was never going to be like it was before, but with the truth finally out, maybe they could start moving on and repairing the broken pieces into something new. "Your shoulder looks fine. It's going to be bruised and stiff for about a week, but my salve should help keep the swelling down so it can heal faster."

"Yes, sir," she laughed.

"I'll make sure to come and check on it and give you some more salve when I come and check on Dorina."

"You could always just leave a jar here, you know. That way you don't have to come back every day," she offered, not wanting him to feel forced into taking care of her.

"I know, but I want to," he admitted, heading back toward her bedroom.

"Really?"

"Of course. What else are friends for?" he grinned, closing the door behind him.

Chapter Thirty-Seven

*T*HE SUN WAS JUST ABOVE THE HORIZON BY THE
time Dorina's reflexes finally started to react again, the
first sign that the Body Lock poison had drained from
her system.

"Thank goodness," Zander let out a deep breath, his weary eyes
rimmed red, his body hunched over where he sat in the chaise in
Christiana's bedroom.

Rowan held Dorina's wrist, taking her pulse. "She'll start coming
out of her sleep soon."

Christiana shifted to look at Dorina, her eyes heavy, head propped
against the headboard of her bed as she lay next to her friend. The
adrenaline from the past few hours had disappeared, her heavy, aching
muscles and foggy brain hard to ignore. But she'd pushed through the
exhaustion, refusing to sleep until she knew Dorina was alright.

Until she knew if Dorina held her secret now as well.

She tried not to think about it, she tried not to let her mind spin out of control, even though it was her first instinct to jump to the worst conclusion. What if her best friend hated her after this? What if she became scared of her? What if she turned her in?

She knew there was no use worrying about it until Dorina woke up, but that never stopped her from thinking the worst. It was a habit that would be stuck with her the rest of her life; all she could do was try and cope with the terrible feelings it bred.

Rowan dropped into the dining chair he had pulled into the bedroom. "All we can do now is wait."

"Do you even know why she was in the hallways in the middle of the night?" Zander asked Christiana.

She rubbed her forehead. "Technically, no."

"An educated guess, then?"

She pulled her knees up, propping her chin on them. "I don't think I should say."

Rowan leaned forward. "Ana...what do you think it was?"

Christiana's pulse raced, her hands trembling. Her gut told her that her guess was correct, but these men had no idea that Dorina had begged her to keep the admirer a secret, especially from Zander. However, Christiana saw the questions in their faces, the concern for Dorina's safety clearly written in the creases in their foreheads. They needed answers, and if she didn't tell them, Zander would try anything to get Dorina to admit the truth. At least if she told him before Dorina woke up, he might have time to calm down.

She took a few deep breaths to calm her pulse, praying Dorina would forgive her for what she was about to say. "Dorina has been writing to a secret admirer for a few months now. I think she was on her way to meet with him for the first time."

Zander stood abruptly from his seat. "Excuse me?"

Rowan just stared at her, rubbing his chin slowly. Christiana turned back to Zander, his eyes begging her for more information. "He started writing her a few weeks before I arrived back at the palace. I'd been helping her try to track down who he was since she told me about him."

Zander frowned. "Why was she trying to track him down? Why not just wait for him to come forward?"

"Well, you see..." Christiana bit at the edge of her lip. "Time was running out."

"Why?"

"Um...well..." Christiana's guts twisted, her body squirming. "Your father has been trying to set up a marriage alliance for her the past few weeks."

A few beats passed, Zander's eyes darkening. "No. No, he couldn't have been. She would have told me."

"She didn't want to burden you." Christiana shifted, facing toward Zander. "You've been going through so much with your father, she felt that this would just make it worse. She hoped that if she found the secret admirer, he would be good enough to satisfy your father's opinions and she could be happy. She wanted to try and fix it on her own."

"It doesn't matter, she's my sister and she could never be a burden to me." Zander rocked back on his heels. "I made her a promise that I would protect her from an arranged marriage. She should have come to me when Father started."

"Either way," Christiana moved on. "She must have cut through the servant halls to get to the rose grove. That's where she was going to meet him."

"That's not possible," Rowan whispered, his foot tapping against the floor.

"Why not?" Christiana asked, surprised he had something to say after being silent this whole time.

Rowan rocked back and forth. "Because she wasn't supposed to meet him until sunrise!"

Christiana's heart skipped a beat, her body frozen as she stared at Rowan.

Dorina had only told Christiana about the letters, and she'd been careful not to mention when they were supposed to meet. Rowan shouldn't know that information.

Unless...

Christiana covered her mouth, her eyes wide. "Oh my goodness!"

"What?" Zander rushed over, standing next to the bedside, looking Dorina over.

"Rowan...are you..." Christiana moved to the bottom edge of the bed, her eyes never leaving Rowan, whose gaze avoided hers. "Are you her secret admirer?"

Rowan groaned, dropping his head in his hands.

"What?" Zander leaned himself against a bedpost, gaping. "You've been writing love letters to my sister?"

"Excuse me, you don't really have a place to judge." Rowan gestured between Zander and Christiana.

Zander's shoulders sagged. "Fair point."

"Rowan...how? Why?" Christiana leaned forward, shock still rippling through her body. "How did this even start?"

Rowan shook his head a few times, mumbling under his breath before leaning back in his chair. "It started about two weeks after you left for the summer. I was avoiding everyone as best I could, wanting to keep my distance, but Dorina wouldn't have it."

Zander chuckled. "Sounds like her."

"She said that just because something happened between Zander and me didn't mean that I could just cut her out of my life as well." A smile whispered across his face, his eyes glassing over. "She insisted that we start spending more time together. So we did."

"She mentioned that to me," Christiana tilted her head.

"We'd go riding, take walks in the garden during the fall months, and even have dinner together at least twice a week," He took a deep breath, "The more time I spent with her, the less I saw her as Zander's little sister and more as the woman she has become. An intellectual, kind-hearted, intuitive woman who would give her soul up if it meant helping those she cared about."

"Then why keep it a secret? Why not just tell her?"

"I was still so confused over what happened with the three of us," he said. "My heart was still healing, and at the same time I was developing feelings for another woman? It just didn't make sense to me. I couldn't tell her, not when it would seem like I was just transferring my feelings for you. Besides, I wasn't ready to be told that my feelings weren't reciprocated. Not again."

"Rowan..." Christiana said.

"I just wanted to understand what I was feeling without hurting either of us in the process." He shook his head. "I figured writing letters would allow us to explore if there could be something romantic between us without our pasts in the way."

Warmth spread through Christiana's cheeks, still a bit stunned but happy to know that the man who was writing those letters couldn't have been a more honorable person. She had been worried for her friend, concerned that it could be someone old or mean or selfish. Instead, Dorina was falling for someone perfect for her, someone who could be a true partner. She'd read a few of the letters, the words eloquent and beautiful; exactly what Dorina deserved.

"Wait," Christiana held up her hands. "I've seen the letters. It's not your handwriting."

"I know," Rowan snorted a laugh. "I've been having my valet write them for me. I figured Dorina would recognize my handwriting, too."

"Oh, sneaky." She couldn't help being impressed with Rowan's prowess.

"My best friend and baby sister are writing love letters to each other," Zander groaned, knocking his forehead gently against the bedpost. "I have learned too much new information in one night!"

"Technically, she still doesn't know it was me." Rowan rubbed his forehead. "Obviously, our meeting today never happened. Which was probably for the best."

"Rowan, no, you have to tell her," Christiana walked over to him. "She hopes you're her savior from her father."

Rowan shot from his seat. "I can't tell her now! This is just a sign that this was all just a big mistake."

"How?"

He began to pace back and forth in front of the fireplace. "I'm no savior! To the King, I'm nothing!"

Zander stepped in Rowan's path, forcing him to a halt. "That is not true! You are not nothing, Ro."

"I am. Nothing but a Marquess with adequate landholdings with no plans to grow." Rowan crossed his arms, staring at Zander, their chests grazing each other. "I don't have Christiana's desires to be a businessperson. I have no political advancement or a way to help Viri. I don't even have exorbitant wealth to make me more appealing. I'm nothing more than a kind noble with a desire to practice medicine. Tell me, Zee, do you think that's a man your father would find worthy of his daughter?"

Zander poked Rowan's chest. "My father's opinion is worthless. You. Are not. Nothing. You are worthy."

Rowan scoffed, pushing past Zander. "After last summer, it hasn't been easy to remember."

Christiana's heart sank. She knew he was hurt, that he was struggling, but she had no idea how much since the summer. He didn't deserve to see himself this way, not when it was completely untrue.

"You can keep hating me, Ro, I deserve it." Zander threw his arms out, as if ready to take a punch. "But do not let my selfish decision determine your self-worth. You deserve anyone you fall in love with, including my sister. She couldn't find a better man than you!"

"That doesn't matter though!" Rowan argued. "Your father makes the decisions for her marriage right now, and according to her last letter, he is doing anything he can to marry her off before he loses the throne to you."

Zander growled, his jaw tense. "My father is a tyrant. When will it stop?"

"When we bring it to an end." Christiana said. "But I hate to admit Rowan is right; we may not have enough time to stop him before he marries Dorina to someone."

"Telling her now will just give her false hope and cause her more pain when she is forced to marry someone else." Rowan shook his head. "There's no point in putting her through that. The best thing is for me to write her a letter ending all of this. It was a mistake to even start it in the first place."

Christiana's emotions were a tangled mess after the night, her body aching and begging for relief. It was crushing her, knowing that two of the most important people in her life were falling in love with each other and they couldn't even say it. She wanted to help, she wanted to find a way to bring them together, but there was only defeat written across Rowan's face. He had already tried to find a way, but it was no use. Lucian was in control, and they couldn't take it away from him.

"She deserves to know the truth," Christiana said, leaning herself against Zander, his arm around her shoulder for support.

"You both have to promise me that you won't say anything to her." Rowan's cheeks were mottled red, his eyes pleading.

Christiana held her hands up. "Rowan...this whole thing hasn't been easy on her..."

"Both of you want me to trust you again, now is the time to prove it. Don't say anything to her."

Zander's entire body was tense, his spine rigid. "Fine, if that's what you want, I'll respect it."

"Fine," Christiana balled her fists at her side. "But I still—"

A loud groan cut her off, all three of them freezing and turning toward the bed.

Dorina was finally waking up.

Chapter Thirty-Eight

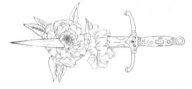

ORINA'S EYES FLUTTERED OPEN, HER BODY stirring, attempting to pull herself up. "Wha—where am I?"

"Shh, Dorina, you're safe," Christiana rushed over, leaning across the bed to grab her hand. "You're in my room."

"You were hurt," Zander added, standing next to Dorina. "Rowan has been taking care of you all night."

"I don—" she tried to sit herself up, letting out a cry of pain, clutching her arm to her chest, the other hand tenderly caressing her exposed collarbone and the bandage that now covered it.

"Take it slow," Rowan soothed, wrapping his arm around Dorina's shoulders to help prop her up on a pillow. Christiana forced herself not to smirk at the tender movements. This wasn't the time.

"Thank you," Dorina whimpered, pushing her hair out of her face. "How did I even get here?"

"You don't remember?" Christiana sat back down next to her, her heart leaping.

Dorina shook her head, looking around the room at all three of them. "The last thing I remember...I...um..."

"It's alright, little sister," Zander said.

"Zander, you don't understand." A few tears rolled down her cheeks, her body trembling. "I did something so reckless and stupid...you'd be so ashamed."

"Excuse me," he lifted her chin until she looked at him. "I could never be ashamed of you."

She nodded, her sobs calming down a bit. "I just don't know how to begin to explain."

Christiana touched Dorina's uninjured arm. Her fingers were numb, her mouth dry. It was now or never to come clean, to tell Dorina that she'd exposed her secrets. "Dorina, I'm sorry, but I already told them why you were out so late at night. I told them about your admirer and why you wanted to meet him."

Dorina blinked rapidly a few times. "You did?"

"I'm so sorry, but they were worried about why you were out there," Christiana's words rushed out. "I just wanted to put their minds at ease."

Silence fell for a few moments, Dorina's face pensive as she stared down at her lap, her fingers twisting in the blankets. Then she sighed, offering a reassuring smile to Christiana. "After this, it was going to come out anyway. How else was I going to explain why I was in the servant halls?"

A bit of the weight on Christiana's chest lifted. "I'm still sorry."

"I promised you I would be safe. So, I guess we're even."

Christiana scooched herself closer, touching her temple to Dorina's. Her first concern with Dorina was over; all she had to do now was answer the biggest question: did Dorina see her?

"I wish you would have told me sooner," Zander said. "I could have helped you with Father pressuring you."

"I know you would have." She looked up at him. "I just...this man seemed so wonderful. I had hoped he would be the answer. Although now, seeing as he probably thinks I abandoned him this morning, I'm just hoping he still wants to talk to me."

"Trust me, if he's a smart man, he will," Zander smiled, Rowan stiffening next to him. Christiana stifled a laugh at his expression. "I will fight with you against Father to make sure you are completely content with who you marry. This is your decision just as it was mine."

"Thank you, Brother," she whispered.

"Since we know what happened last night, we have a guess as to how you were injured." Christiana changed the subject, all three of them turning to her. "Did you run into the killer?"

She already knew the answer, but she waited for Dorina to slowly nod.

Zander sighed. "I'm so sorry, but we need to ask you a few questions about what happened. You're technically a witness in the investigation now."

"I understand." Dorina's shoulders sagged. "Although I don't think I'll be much help. Everything seems to blur together."

"Well, what do you remember?"

Dorina shifted in her seat, Christiana's quilt falling around her waist. "I remember walking through the halls to the entrance to the garden. I heard a big thump as I rounded the corner and saw a man standing over someone." She shook her head, her hands starting to tremble as she folded them into the blankets. "I must have made a sound, because he looked right at me. Then he attacked. He pinned me against the wall."

"Take your time," Zander said, Rowan hovering right next to him, his face pale, arms laced behind him.

"I heard someone yelling down the hall...and then a blinding pain and everything went black." Her breath hitched. "Next thing I know, I was waking up here. I'm so sorry, I'm useless!"

"It's alright," Rowan soothed.

"How about we try something different?" Christiana suggested. "Help you focus on specifics instead of the big picture." Marek had taught her this technique of questioning. Focusing on the senses allowed the person to find clarity in what had happened while also leading an investigation closer to catching a culprit.

Dorina sighed. "I guess it's worth a try."

"Hold my hand and close your eyes," Christiana said quietly. "Remember that I am right next to you, my hand in yours, keeping you safe. Now, you said he pushed you up against the wall. Do you remember what his hands felt like while holding you?"

Dorina shook her head. "Just strong."

"Alright." Christiana rubbed a circle with her thumb along the back of Dorina's hand. "When he was close to you, do you remember noticing any specific smells? Like a cologne?"

"Um," Dorina's eyebrows pinched inward. "I remember it smelling...chemical, not like a cologne at all. Kind of how my room smells after my lady's maid polishes the silver."

"That's good. Now, you said he had a hood. When you looked up, did you get a peek underneath?"

Dorina bit at her upper lip. "It was mostly dark...his hood kept most of his face covered."

"That's alright." Christiana patted her hand.

"Well...actually..." Dorina's head perked up. "I do remember catching a glimpse of his eyes. We were standing next to a sconce and I noticed that they glowed like amber honey when reflecting the candlelight."

"That's good, Dorina." She couldn't put the final question off any longer. "You mentioned that someone yelled from down the hall. Did you catch sight of the other person?"

Her heart pounded loudly in her ears. The few seconds Dorina took to think were absolutely agonizing, leaving Christiana convinced she was about to have a heart attack from waiting.

Finally, Dorina shook her head. "No. It was all just a blur, I only remember seeing the hooded man."

"Alright," Christiana let out a deep breath. She was safe, Dorina didn't see her. Nothing would change between them. "You can open your eyes now."

Her eyes fluttered open. "Did I help?"

"Absolutely," Christiana smiled. "If this man smelled like silver polish, it likely means he's a servant of some kind."

"And a specific kind, too," Zander added. "We can rule out stable workers, landscapers, and about half the kitchen staff. None of them would have a need to use that specific kind of polish."

Dorina sank lower into the bed. "Good, at least I could be useful for something."

"You're always useful," Christiana encouraged. A weary smile pressed against Dorina's lips.

"Now that you're awake, we should probably tell Mother and Father," Zander said. "We decided to wait until you were awake. Give you time to process."

"They're having breakfast with Christiana's mother and sister," Dorina groaned. "Do we really have to tell them?"

Zander gave her an unamused look. "I think it will be hard to hide the fact that you're injured."

"Oh my goodness, what am I going to tell them?" She covered her face with her hands.

"We'll figure it out." He kissed her forehead. "We can keep things as vague as possible, but we do need to tell them something."

"Ugh, fine!" Dorina rubbed her forehead. "Might as well let Maria and Isabelle come, too. They're basically family, and they'll find out eventually anyways. No need to keep them in suspense."

"I'll be right back." He slipped from the apartment.

"I'm going to go as well," Rowan hesitated by the bedside, both hands clutching tightly at his bag.

"Rowan." Dorina reached out to him, her hand begging him to grasp it. He faltered for a moment before grasping hers, his glassy eyes even more vibrant emerald than usual. "Thank you so much for all of your help."

"I'd do anything for you," he whispered, bending forward, placing a lingering kiss on her hand. Christiana's chest ached at the sight.

Dorina smiled, giving his hand one last squeeze before he walked out the door.

Christiana shifted closer to Dorina. "Let's get you out of that dress and into a nightgown before your parents arrive."

Dorina silently nodded, the two of them slowly moving out of bed. Christiana took her time unlacing Dorina's shredded dress, making sure to be as careful as possible to not put pressure on her wound.

"Are you mad at me?" Dorina whispered, her head hanging low as she held onto the bedpost for support.

Christiana's fingers stopped. She leaned over to try and see Dorina's face. "Of course not."

"But I promised you that I would be safe. Instead, I was reckless."

"You made a mistake," Christiana finished unlacing the dress, pulling each arm out of the sleeves before dropping it to the floor and helping her step out of it. She went right to work on her underskirts, untying each layer. "I was terrified and confused, but I wasn't mad. All I cared about was that you're safe now."

"I just..." Dorina shook her head. "I figured there were plenty of hallways the killer could be in, and he wasn't after nobles anyway. I was scared someone would see me sneaking around and I didn't need anyone asking questions, so I decided to take a shortcut."

Christiana lifted one of her nightgowns over Dorina's head, helping her into the soft fabric. "It was a mistake. You know that now, so you'll be safer from now on."

Dorina nodded emphatically, her lip trembling. "I was so scared, Ana."

She fell into Christiana's arms, the tears finally spilling from her eyes, her sobs echoing off every wall. Christiana held on tight, moving them to sit on the edge of the bed to help Dorina's shaking. She rocked her gently, whispering soothing words as Dorina let out the pent-up adrenaline and fear that had been coursing through her for hours.

"It's alright, you're safe now." Christiana whispered. "Nothing will ever happen to you. I will make sure of it."

Dorina sniffled. "You promise?"

"Of course." Christiana smiled down at her.

"You'll protect me? Even against my parents?"

Christiana snorted, kissing the top of her head. "I'll try my best."

Chapter Thirty-Nine

THE YELLING WAS DEAFENING THE MOMENT both families crossed the threshold of Christiana's bedroom.

Lucian bellowed above everyone, his voice booming against the walls as he demanded to know what happened. Penelope was beside herself, clutching at a pale Maria as ,they both rushed to Dorina's bedside, while Isabelle jumped right into bed with her.

"Would you all please be quiet for one moment?" Zander roared so loudly their parents closed their mouths instantly.

Everyone except Lucian. "The three of you best explain what happened, *immediately.*"

All eyes looked over to Dorina, her body shrinking down into the folds of blankets. "Um...well...you see..."

"It was my fault, Lucian," Christiana said, grabbing Dorina's hand as she stood next to her.

Lucian's cold gaze turned to her. "Excuse me?"

Christiana's mind stitched together an excuse as quickly as possible—something that could appear plausible. Her best friend had been through enough the past few hours, she didn't need to deal with her parents' ire as well. "I wanted to go out sparring last night, and since Zander wasn't available, I asked Dorina to go."

"Dorina went out and sparred with you?" Penelope's eyebrows creased inward, her arms crossed.

"I've seen her practicing with Rowan, so I thought she might enjoy time with me," Christiana shrugged, biting her cheek to stifle a groan from the dull ache in her shoulder.

"I—I was bored and it sounded like fun," Dorina looked up at Christiana, nodding. "I figured it would be a good way to pass the time."

"We weren't able to find a second practice sword, so I brought my own short sword." Christiana pulled in a shaky breath. "I told Dorina to follow all my movements and listen to my commands, but she side-stepped a bit too far. By the time I realized, my sword was already slicing through her tunic."

"Then how did she hit her head?" Lucian narrowed his eyes.

"The pain made me stumble and trip over myself," Dorina said. "I fell into the wooden slats of the training ring."

"How could you two be so reckless?" Penelope demanded.

Christiana lowered her gaze. "It was an accident. I would never put Dorina in unnecessary danger, I promise."

"I found a stablehand to help me carry her up here," Christiana added. "Once we got her into my bed, I rushed and got Zander so we could take care of her."

"Why are you just telling us now?" Maria asked.

"Dorina needed rest." Zander said. "She was tired and scared and the adrenaline from the injury was wearing off. She just wanted a few hours of sleep before telling all of you."

"I see," Penelope nodded, her thumb rubbing her daughter's

tearstained cheek.

"You put my daughter in danger," Lucian glowered at Christiana. Her throat closed at that look. "You reckless…"

"Father!" Zander snapped. "Watch what words you use next."

The men stared at each other across the bed, an invisible tether pulling taut between them in a battle of stubborn strength. All five women were still, eyes darting between them, waiting for someone to crack. Christiana swallowed the lump in her throat, her fingertips tingling, begging silently for this to stop.

Lucian let out a low grunt, breaking eye contact first and turning back to Dorina. "Well, I think the first thing we need to do is get the Court Physician up here to make sure your shoulder and head are alright." His eyes were stormy, swirling like a raging blizzard.

"No need, Father." Dorina attempted to sit up straight. "We already had Rowan take a look and stitch the injury. He said it is just a flesh wound that should heal within the next two weeks."

Lucian's eyebrow quirked upward. "The Court Physician will be displeased that you didn't go to him. He is here to attend to all of us."

"It was the middle of the night and she was unconscious," Christiana said through gritted teeth. "We figured Dorina would be more comfortable waking up to Rowan treating her."

"What matters is she was looked at and taken care of." Penelope glared at Lucian from across the bed, patting Christiana's shoulder, the heat from her palm dripping through her robe since she had yet to change out of her nightclothes.

"Of course, dear." He smiled back at her. "But we now need to discuss the Engagement Ball in two days. Will you even be able to attend?"

"Rowan said I should limit strenuous activities for at least a week," Dorina said.

"We can postpone it a week, can we not?" Maria chided, her palms sliding against the smooth fabric of her blueberry damask dress.

"I suppose," Lucian sighed. "Although it will be quite an inconvenience for the guests to extend their trips."

"If it is such an inconvenience, they can go home and return in nine days when we actually hold the ball." Penelope's chin jutted out, her nut-brown eyes blazing with heat as if daring Lucian to challenge her. "Besides, I think many of them will find it in their schedule to extend their stay for an extra week, which we are more than able to accommodate."

Lucian's face softened as he stared at his wife. "Of course, you are right, my dear. What would I do without you?"

"Be a fool most days." Penelope linked her arm with Maria's. Christiana stifled a laugh, her insides quivering to release the cacophony of giggles building up in her chest. She had never seen the Queen be so defiant against the King, in public or more recently in private. She wondered what had spurred her into action this time.

"Either way, we shouldn't tell them you're injured." Lucian wrapped his hand around one of the bedposts. "That is not the image we want to put out to the nobles. We will just say that you are sick and we need to postpone until you are in better health."

"I'm fine with that," Dorina nodded. "As long as Zander and Ana are alright with the excuse. It is their party after all, they should get a say."

"It's absolutely fine." Zander patted Dorina's leg.

"Of course it is," Christiana agreed. "Now, I believe rest and peace are what Dorina needs today. So, if you wouldn't mind, I think she could use a little privacy."

"Of course, darling." Penelope bent over, settling a chaste kiss on Dorina's forehead. Her eyes sparkled faintly in the rays of morning sunlight filtering through the window before she straightened and walked out, Maria and Lucian right behind her.

"Can I stay here for a bit longer?" Dorina looked up at Christiana. "I'm not ready to move back to my room yet."

"Of course." Christiana smiled down at her.

"Isabelle," Dorina turned to her other side. "Would you mind staying with me as well?"

"Can I?" Isabelle clung to Dorina's arm. "I want to help make you feel better."

Dorina leaned over, kissing the top of Isabelle's wispy blonde hair. "It would be the most welcomed cheering-up." Dorina fiddled with the lace trim at the edges of her long sleeves. "Are you staying too Zander?"

"I, unfortunately, have some meetings I'm sure Father won't let me get out of." Zander rubbed his temples.

Christiana took a few steps forward, a tentative smile tugging at the edges of her lips. "Well, then I guess it's up to Isabelle and me to make sure she has everything she needs."

Dorina perked up. "Perfect."

Zander gave Christiana a quick peck on the cheek. "Send word if you need anything," he whispered in her ear, a shiver running down her spine as his breath tickled the delicate skin behind her earlobe.

"I will." She smiled, his hand giving hers one last squeeze before he disappeared from the room.

***

"Am I really a natural talent at drawing, or was Princess Dorina just being nice?" Isabelle looked down at the sketchpad in her hand, the page still open to the vase she had been drawing all afternoon. Christiana kept her arm securely linked to her sister's, making sure she didn't run into anyone or anything as they walked back to Isabelle and Maria's apartment.

"I think so," Christiana said, peeking at the picture. To pass the time in bed, Dorina had decided to give Isabelle her first sketching lesson, the two of them spending hours with paper and graphite in their hands. Christiana had read a book and watched. "Trust me, you're already ten times the artist I am."

"Really?" Isabelle giggled.

"Yes," Christiana snorted, memories of the few art lessons she'd had buried in the back of her mind like a bad dream.

The sisters finally made it to the apartment, Isabelle bursting through the door. "I'm back!"

"Just in time for dinner," Maria smiled as she rose from the couch, dropping the book she was reading on the cushion next to her. "It should be here soon."

"Look what I did, Mother!" Isabelle held out her sketchpad.

"Beautiful, darling," Maria said, halting in front of her daughters. Christiana's spine tingled and she bit her bottom lip.

"She did a wonderful job with her first lesson," Christiana smiled, a few awkward seconds passing after her statement. "Well, I should probably leave."

"Why don't you have dinner with us?" Maria touched Christiana's hand. Her heart leaped at the contact; their encounters recently had all been so rigid and distant.

"I really should be getting back to Dorina," Christiana said.

"Oh, please stay, Ana!" Isabelle smiled from the dining table. "Rowan said he would be with Dorina a while anyway!"

"Please," Maria added, her lip quivering. "I'd really like to talk to you about something important afterward."

"Mother..." Christiana's eyes wandered to the door.

"Answers, Ana," Maria said, Christiana's body going rigid. "It's time I finally gave you the answers you've been seeking for a long time."

Christiana didn't have a response, all she could do was walk to the table and take a seat, already counting down the seconds until dinner was over.

Chapter Forty

HE LONGER DINNER WENT ON AND THE MORE idle conversation the three of them made, the more energy that built up in Christiana's chest. Isabelle had been carrying most of the conversation, barely noticing with her infectious energy bringing up new topics to discuss over the four courses. Christiana was thankful in that moment that her sister was much more personable than her; it was the only thing keeping this dinner moving at a decent pace.

Maria finally cleared her throat as two ladies maids walked out the door with the stacks of dirty plates. "Isabelle, why don't you start getting ready for bed? I need to talk to your sister."

"Why can't I stay?" Isabelle's shoulders slumped.

"We'll tell you when you're older."

Isabelle huffed, kicking her chair away as she stood. "I'm getting quite sick of that excuse."

She half-stomped to her bedroom, slamming the door behind her, awkwardness settling in her wake as Christiana stared at her mother across the table. A zip of anxiety raced through her, setting her skin tingling. She loved her mother, but something still gnawed inside her soul to keep her at arm's length. She was done with face-value; when her mother was ready to tell the truth, she would be ready to let her back in.

"So?" Christiana prompted at last. "You said something about answers?"

"Yes, it's time we finally talked." Maria moved around the table, her fingers trailing along the top as she moved to sit in the seat beside Christiana.

Christiana's leg twitched, numbness snaking upward. "About?"

"Exactly what you wanted to talk about your last night at home." Maria's gaze faltered, her fingers tracing patterns on the tabletop. "I want to tell you about your father."

Blood rushed in Christiana's ears, muffling Maria's words. "Why now?"

"Penelope told me you found out some truths about the King." Maria's eyes glazed over. "She mentioned how...confused you seemed about the whole ordeal. It made me realize how much of your past I've kept a secret from you."

"That hasn't been a secret, Mother." Christiana took a sip of her wine, the warmth spreading down into her chest. "You've just chosen to ignore it until now."

"I know, I know." Maria patted her hand, her fingers cool. "Still, you deserve peace of mind. I'm sorry I let my own fears and doubts get in the way of giving that to you."

Christiana's face twitched as she tried hard to keep tears from spilling over the edge of her eyelids, but it was useless. The wetness slipped down her cheek. She had wanted to know, begged and fought for her mother's truths. Yet, faced with them now, her entire body felt frozen, her mind trying to bind her to keep her from walking down this path.

"How could you let it happen?" Christiana's whisper was barely audible through her tears. "To me? To you?"

"To be honest, the reason changed over the years." Maria fiddled with her skirt. "I know you don't remember, but I did love your father once. Even though it was an arranged marriage, he was incredible to me at the beginning. And once we had you, he was so intoxicated with you; he loved to spoil you."

"I remember a little." Christiana's fingers twitched, desperately wishing they were doing something else. "But it's hard to think about the good when there was just so much bad. When did it change?"

"With the miscarriages. I had three within a year of each other. It was after the third one that he hit me for the first time." Maria touched her own cheek, her fingers barely grazing the flushed skin. "Each time my courses came, it would happen again. But it didn't matter what was happening to me, because you were still happy. You had your parents. I couldn't take that away from you."

Christiana scratched her chin. "But then you did get pregnant."

"The minute I did, my loving husband came back to me. Until the baby was born and it was another girl. The day Isabelle was born was the day I realized I had lost the man I loved forever." Maria stared at Christiana, her eyes welling up. "Then one day, I came downstairs for breakfast and saw the bruising on your face. You looked so confused and hurt, but I knew exactly what happened."

"Why didn't you leave him? Even after Penelope wasn't able to do anything?"

Maria clutched her chest. "How much did she tell you?"

"She said you told her when I was thirteen. You wanted to help us, but you stopped after the first try. Why?"

"I couldn't take you and run. We would have lost everything."

Maria wiped the tears from her eyes, her peppered hair sticking to the side of her face. "Or worse, he could claim you and Isabelle, take you away, and leave me in disgrace. You two were all I had left, and I couldn't risk losing you, so I stayed quiet."

"Oh, Mother..." Christiana wiped away a few tears.

"After Penelope sent word that Lucian refused to do anything..." Maria whimpered. "They were the only people who could help us without losing everything in the process. When the King said no, I knew that all hope was lost to bring peace to our lives."

"You knew Lucian refused?"

Maria nodded. "Penelope wrote to me as soon as possible, begging for my forgiveness for her husband's close-minded views and treatment of us. She was appalled by him, but she also knew there was nothing she could do to change his mind."

"Why did she tell you all of that?"

"She said she wanted me to know there was another person willing to cause me harm." Maria dabbed at her face with a handkerchief. "She didn't want me to live in ignorance anymore when it came to the man who was leading our country."

Christiana rubbed her hands across her face, massaging feeling back into her numb cheeks. Her mother had been aware of the country's issues for so much longer than she knew. She had known the truth about Lucian, about his neglectfulness and facades of strength. It made her head spin, questioning so many of their past conversations and arguments. "Was that the real reason you didn't want me courting with Zander? Because of his father?"

"Yes," Maria said. "I knew I couldn't tell you the real reason, I was too scared you would do something that would ruin all of the hard work you've done these past years as a leader. You deserve that credit, and I didn't want the King to take it all away."

Christiana scoffed. "Fair enough."

"However, the idea of you marrying into the family, it was a hard one for me to agree with when I knew the truth about the man who raised Alekzander." Maria inched forward, her shoulders hunching as she caught Christiana's gaze. "I was scared he agreed too much with his father's values, but over your engagement, between the way I see him treat you and the letters you send Belle, I realize now that Alekzander is not his or your father."

"I know that," Christiana said, but her heart contracted as she spoke each word. "I tried so hard to tell you that."

"I know, and I should have listened, but I was blinded by my own fears," Maria whispered, her knuckles gently grazing against Christiana's cheek to wipe away her tears. "All a parent ever wishes is for their children to have more than they ever did."

"I'm...I'm sorry for what happened to you." Christiana's head fell forward, her forehead gently touching her mother's fingers.

"No. Don't you dare apologize for what your father put me through. It was horrific and unhappy, but it gave me you and Isabelle." Maria shook her head. "I know this doesn't erase everything that we've been through in the past, but I at least hope you might be ready to start trying to keep the past behind us and move forward together."

"I can't say I'm completely ready to forget. You've kept plenty of secrets from me these past years that have caused me a lot of heartache. But I understand why you made your decisions, and now that I understand, I can start to forgive, I can start to move on...something I should have done long ago."

Maria let out a shaky breath. "I love you, my sweet girl."

"I love you, too, Mother," Christiana cried, embracing Maria like a small child. The two wept in each other's arms, the walls built around their hearts beginning to crumble.

"Be happy, Christiana," Maria whispered. And Christiana intended to do just that.

Chapter Forty-One

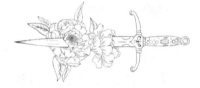

AFTER AN AGITATING FIVE DAYS OF RESTING her shoulder, Rowan finally cleared Christiana to start doing light sparring with Robert again. It had been less than a week, and already she had the itch for a sword in her hand, that deep-seeded desire to train and move forced down until her shoulder was ready.

She hadn't wasted any time for the hour of training that mid-afternoon, her chest tight and muscles sore from the workout. Her mood was lighter, a buzz in her veins that she had missed due to all the stress since Dorina was hurt. It was nice to feel relief again.

"Your arm moved quite well today," Robert encouraged as they walked back to her apartment from the training yard.

"Thank goodness." Christiana grumbled, rotating her shoulder a bit to try and stretch out some stiffness. "I was not going to be happy if I had to put off my training any longer."

"We'll go again tomorrow," Robert nudged her. "Make sure

you're back in fighting shape as soon as possible."

"It will have to be in the morning," she said, her eyes adjusting from the sunlight as they crossed the threshold into the palace. "I have an event tomorrow night."

"The ball is in three days, though."

"I know, but it seems we're having a family dinner before it with some visiting dignitaries from Atharia who are in for the wedding. Zander says they came a few weeks early to possibly negotiate for war assistance from our military."

"Hm," Robert said. "Sounds like fun."

"Zander's met some of their Royals and Generals in the past, he says they are kind and enjoyable to talk to."

"Am I required to work that night, My Lady?" Robert asked as the pair walked through the stretch of hallway that led to work offices for the Royals and Council Members, taking a shortcut.

"No, there will be plenty of guards at the dinner to protect me, you don't need to change any plans you might have." Christiana patted his arm. "Which reminds me, now that you work for me in a more official capacity, does this mean I finally get to meet your elusive partner?"

Robert chuckled, rubbing his fingers across his forehead. "I wondered if you were going to bring up Gerard again."

Christiana had known about Robert's partner for about two years, although the pair had been romantically involved for well over five. However, since Robert and Christiana technically hadn't known each other outside of Maiden work, there was never an excuse to meet him. "I'm just wondering if he is coming to the engagement ball with you."

"Yes, he is," Robert nodded. "Although, I won't lie, he still doesn't completely understand why I would go back into the military for you."

"I suppose I understand. It does seem odd, since to most, we only just met last summer."

"He figured it would take a much more...personal reason to reenlist." Robert sighed. "Which of course, we have, he just doesn't know."

Christiana tightened her grip on Robert's arm. Robert had left the military very soon after she assassinated his abusive older brother, Kerrick. Too much pain and heartache had been connected to his time there, Kerrick's jealousy over Robert's success turning dangerous. Robert left to heal from his own Battled Brain traumas. "Do you regret coming back for me?"

"Of course not, My Lady! This opportunity has given me a safe space to return to a life that I loved, that was almost destroyed by my brother. I would make the same decision today as I did many months ago."

"Alright, good." Christiana nodded, her heart settling.

"Gerard is just concerned, he saw me back then and he helped me through my own healing," Robert sighed. "He's overprotective."

"He's a good partner who loves you, I can't fault him for that." She nudged his side. "Maybe if he met me, he would feel more comfortable."

"Well, I suppose that's true." Robert patted her hand.

Sudden scuffling voices reached Christiana's ears, and she turned her head sharply. "Did you hear something?"

A light, female voice rang around the corner, distress lacing the tone even though Christiana couldn't make out the words. She tugged on Robert's arm, his brow crinkling as he scanned the area. They walked closer, turning the corner to see who was causing such a public disagreement.

"Natalia?" Christiana's eyes went wide when she spotted her Lady's Maid, back pressed against the stone wall, her face bright red, her full lower lip trembling. "What's wrong?"

"No-nothing, My Lady."

Christiana's gaze turned to Natalia's companion, his grip tight on her shaking wrist as she twisted to free herself. Christiana's hold tightened on Robert, her body leaning into him. This was an unexpected moment to walk in on.

"Jay." Christiana stepped forward, frowning at Zander's valet. "May I ask why your hands are on my Lady's Maid? Particularly when it looks like she is trying to make you let go."

Jay dropped Natalia's wrist as if she'd bitten him, his eyes wide as he turned to Christiana. "My Lady, we were just talking."

"Then why does Natalia look distressed?"

"I'm not, My Lady!" Natalia shook her hands in front of her chest. "I promise."

"It's my fault." Jay straightened, his gaze downcast, unable to look Christiana in the eye even though his body was tilted in her direction. "I was concerned for Natalia's safety and I've been trying to convince her for weeks that she needs to talk to you in letting her have the...particularly dangerous days off."

Christiana's spine stiffened, numbness trickling down each vertebra. She'd offered Natalia those days off for weeks now, even ordered Natalia a few days ago to take any future nights off when it came to the killer roaming the halls. Each time Natalia contended that she didn't need it, but now Christiana wondered if it was all a lie out of fear of getting fired.

"I keep telling him it's unnecessary." Natalia frowned, her arms crossing, fingers digging into her upper arm. "But it doesn't stop him."

"Well then, Jay." Christiana turned to the tall man, his hazel eyes wide as he stared at her. "If you must know, I have already ordered Natalia to take those nights off in the future, which I will make sure she does even though she insists she doesn't need them. Since that is all settled, I suggest you get back to work."

Jay's head hung low. "I'm so sorry, My Lady. I didn't mean for you to see us."

"Then may I suggest making sure the next time you two squabble, you keep it out of a public hallway?"

Jay gave her a slow nod before walking away, disappearing through an inconspicuous door leading to the servants halls.

"Natalia, is he harassing you?" Christiana grazed her hand along Natalia's upper arm, her maid flinching away. "Please, let me know and I can talk to Zander about having him reassigned or let go."

Natalia gnawed at her lip. "No, My Lady. It's nothing like that. He really is just concerned for me, especially with the dangers flying around."

"I meant what I said. You will be taking those nights off until this person is caught."

"I know, and I will, but I promise I do feel safe." She shook her head, a weak smile pushing at the edges of her lips. "Jay is just being protective. We've been getting to know each other since our households will be converging in a few weeks. We wanted to make sure the transition was smooth for both you and the Prince."

Christiana narrowed her eyes, a smirk playing on her lips. "Is he sweet on you?"

"Oh, goodness, no!" Natalia blanched, her mouth hanging open. "He's just a friend who wants me to be safe! Probably so he doesn't have to get to know a whole new Lady's Maid if my luck runs out on me."

Christiana's stomach churned, her mind trying to pick apart every detail Natalia and Jay were telling her. Everything seemed innocent enough, yet some part of her was still trying to find the lie in it all. She didn't know if it was her typical need to think everyone was hiding something, or if it was just concern for someone she considered important in her life. "Well, if he starts getting out of hand, you'll let me know?"

"Absolutely, My Lady." Natalia's shoulders drooped, her face falling in relief. "You have my word."

"Alright, then." Christiana gave her one final squeeze on the arm and let go. "Go on with the rest of your chores."

Natalia scurred away through the same door as Jay.

"Did that seem suspicious to you as well?" Christiana looked up at Robert.

His brow furrowed. "I don't know Jay well enough to say, but I promise you I will be keeping a closer eye on Natalia from now on. For her own safety."

"That would be for the best," Christiana murmured as they turned back to her apartment for the rest of the day.

Chapter Forty-Two

HE NEXT EVENING CAME QUICKLY FOR
Christiana, where she made her way downstairs to one
of the formal dining rooms with her mother and sister.
Isabelle looked radiant in her gold-and-sage gown, one of the new ones
Christiana had helped her pick out on the last visit. This would be her
first experience entertaining not only wedding guests, but visiting
dignitaries.

Christiana was a businesswoman, always comfortable talking and
negotiating. However, hosting was a completely different set of skills.
Although she was confident in herself, she wanted to prove that she
was meant to be Queen, and charming other royal families was a part
of that job.

Knots twisted in her stomach with each step. She continued to
remind herself the entire way that she was ready for this, that this was
what she was meant to be.

The dining room was already half-full once they arrived. Unlike past events, Zander and Dorina were there, chatting with two men Christiana didn't recognize, who she assumed were the visiting royals.

Isabelle went right to Dorina, the princess's eyes lighting up the moment Isabelle approached. She gave a quick goodbye before bringing Isabelle to the refreshment area, which a servant had already prepared with multiple types of beverages. Maria gave Christiana a quick pat on the shoulder before joining Isabelle. Christiana hurried to join Zander.

"Welcome, love," he greeted her with a kiss on the cheek before tucking her hand in his arm. "May I be the first to introduce you to Prince Stephan of Atharia. Your Highness, this is my fiancée, Christiana, Marchioness of Tagri."

Christiana turned to the visiting royal, his hand outstretched to accept hers. His tawny skin and deep brown eyes were offset by his obsidian hair and handsome features. She couldn't precisely place his age, but if she had to guess, he was in his mid-thirties, from the whisper of grays speckled in his hair.

"Wonderful to meet you, Your Highness." She curtsied.

"Pleasure is mine, My Lady." He kissed the top of her hand. "And of course, congratulations on your upcoming marriage. May I introduce you to my friend and travel companion, General Evander."

Christiana turned to the other man, his imposing height even taller than Robert's. His porcelain face was sternly set, an expression Christiana had seen on many of the soldiers who roamed the halls. His ashen brown hair was slicked back, the ends grazing the nape of his neck. He was also a handsome man, but what really captured Christiana were his blue eyes. Unlike Zander, whose deep sapphire irises constantly glimmered, General Evander's icy, bright gaze looked as if a snowstorm was just about to rage within them. They had a haunted quality to them, not unlike her own.

"General," Christiana nodded.

"My Lady." His voice rumbled from his chest as he bowed deeply.

The four fell into an easy conversation, the two men recounting the journey here and the sadness that they would miss their country's end-of-winter celebration, though it was worth it to attend such an important royal wedding.

The King and Queen arrived after nearly twenty minutes, inviting everyone to sit down for the first course of carrot-and-ginger puree soup. Christiana found herself in between Zander and General Evander, Dorina directly across from her next to Prince Stephan and Isabelle.

As Zander conversed with his father and Stephan, Christiana turned to the General. "So, do you travel often with Prince Stephan for formal negotiations?"

"No, it isn't typical to my job, but I did it as a favor to him." Evander shrugged. "He wanted more of a friend to go along for this special negotiation to help...calm any nerves."

"Do weddings make him nervous?" Christiana chuckled.

"When it possibly has to do with his own, it does."

Christiana almost dropped her spoon. "Excuse me?"

Evander's cheeks drained of color. "I'm sorry, I shouldn't have assumed it was known to everyone in the room."

"What isn't completely known, General?" Christiana's skin crawled, pins and needles jabbing up her arm. He refused to look at her, his eyes leading hers across the table to Dorina and Stephan.

He didn't have to say it, she understood perfectly well just by the way Lucian pulled Dorina into the conversations, which was not very typical of him. Stephan was staring at the Princess, his brown eyes sparkling each time she laughed or made a comment. She didn't even seem to notice the slightly-enamored man next to her.

Prince Stephan was here to gain Dorina's hand in marriage from Lucian.

"Zander," Christiana tapped his hand under the table. "Did you know about this?"

"About what?"

"That part of Prince Stephan's negotiations involves Dorina's hand?"

Zander's eyes went wide, his body leaning away from his father closer to Christiana and Evander. "Excuse me?"

"According to Stephan," Evander confirmed. "I'm sorry, Your Highness, I shouldn't have said anything, but we were under the impression that you knew."

"I'm not surprised by that." Zander leaned back upright, Lucian's eyes flickering over to him before returning to Stephan and Dorina.

"I apologize," Christiana cleared her throat. "It's a...sensitive topic for Zander and myself."

Evander's jaw loosened, eyes softening. "I understand. It is in Atharia, too."

Christiana kept her focus as best as she could in the different conversations. She talked about the wedding with Isabelle, Maria, and Penelope, learned more about Atharia's ongoing war with their neighboring country, Vilamor, and continued to make conversation with General Evander. By the time dessert was done and people began to mingle around the table once more in conversation, she couldn't pretend anymore; and by Zander's tired expression, neither could he.

She walked over to Dorina, who was still talking to Stephan. "Sorry to interrupt, but Alekzander and I are retiring for the evening. We wondered if you wanted to walk back with us?"

"Oh." Dorina's nose crinkled, her eyes narrowing. "I suppose."

"Oh, well, I hope we will meet again over the coming weeks, Your Highness." Stephan bowed, giving her a kiss on the hand in farewell.

"I'm sure we will." Dorina nodded with a warm smile.

They walked away with quick goodbyes to their parents, meeting

Zander, who was already in the hall.

"Let's go," he said, and the three of them scurried away, their steps as quick as possible with Dorina still mending from last week.

"What is with you two?" Dorina laughed, clutching at her torso to help with the pain.

"We have to tell you something." Christiana whispered as they turned down into the Royal Hallway.

Dorina's smile fell, her eyes full of concern as Zander opened his apartment door, Jay nowhere to be found. "What's wrong?" She followed them to the couch, Christiana sitting down, Dorina next to her, and Zander across from them in one of the matching evergreen chairs.

"I'm sorry this is how we have to tell you," Zander began, launching into the new pieces of information they had learned at dinner.

Dorina's lips quivered, her fingers clutching her chest. "But...but...I knew Father was looking, but I always assumed he would let me know before introducing us!"

Zander sighed. "I'm so sorry, Dorina. I'm going to try my best and fight him on this, I promise."

"What's even the point." Dorina sagged lower into the couch.

"The point is that it's your life and you should have a say in it," Christiana encouraged. "You've always believed in that."

"Yes, I suppose," Dorina mumbled, her eyes downcast.

"What about your admirer?" Zander asked, his eyes flicking to Christiana briefly before turning back to Dorina. "You're not just going to give up on him, are you?"

"I wasn't planning to, but it seems he beat me to it." Dorina twisted her hands together.

"What are you talking about?" Christiana shifted closer to her, Zander leaning forward on his knees.

"I received a letter from him yesterday," Dorina said, tears pricking at the edge of her eyes. "He said that when I didn't show up, he took it as a sign that this wasn't the right time for us to meet. That maybe we were daydreaming too much, believing we could be anything more when I'm a princess meant to marry someone worthy, and he believes he is far from that."

"Oh, Dorina," Christiana soothed, drawing gentle circles on Dorina's back.

"It's fine." She brushed away a tear, shrugging Christiana's hand off. "He's probably right. It was foolish of me to believe that I could have this control over my life. It's been father's all along."

"We can fight this," Zander urged. "We can still try and find this man!"

Christiana's heart lurched, the knowledge on the tip of her tongue begging her to tell the truth to Dorina. It took most of her self-control to shove it back; she had made a promise to Rowan, and she wasn't about to break it, even if it was crushing her heart to watch her best friend suffer.

"I'm not going to try and force someone to be with me when he's made it clear that's not what he wants anymore." Dorina shook her head.

Christiana's jaw stiffened. She knew that wasn't true, she saw it in Rowan's eyes only a few days ago. Even if he wasn't ready to admit it out loud, he wanted to be with Dorina. She deserved to know that truth at least, to know that even if they couldn't be together, at least he wanted to be.

Still, it wasn't her decision to make.

"Why does it sound like you're giving up?" Christiana asked.

"It's not giving up," Dorina said with a weary smile. "It's accepting reality. It was a wonderful fantasy to believe that this could work. But we all know Father too well. He was never going to let me go."

Christiana swallowed a lump in her throat. "Dorina..."

"You know what, I'm tired," Dorina stood slowly, smoothing her skirt. "I'm going to bed. I'll see you both tomorrow."

They each mumbled a goodbye as she let herself out, the door clicking shut behind her.

Christiana turned back to Zander. "We have to convince Rowan to tell her the truth."

"No, because he's right." Zander stood, crossing the room to sit beside her on the couch. "Even if he did say something to Dorina, father would end it immediately. Especially now with Stephan interested in marrying her. He wouldn't care about Dorina's desires when an entire alliance depends on it."

Christiana threw her hands in the air. "So, what? We just give up?"

"I never said that," Zander wrapped his arm around her shoulders. "We just need to convince my father to give up his claim on Dorina's marriage."

Christiana snorted. "Now *that* is a fantasy."

"Maybe," Zander smirked. "But some fantasies have been known to come true if you work hard enough for them." He winked at her, coaxing a laugh from her lips.

They spent the rest of the night trying to brainstorm ideas to help Dorina.

Chapter Forty-Three

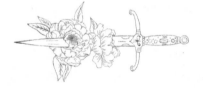

HE NIGHT WAS STILL YOUNG, A PEEK OF
moonlight breaking through the twilight sky, reflecting
off the ballroom windows. The décor was opulently
seasonal, with garlands strung around the whole room, the greenery
accented with silver and light blue ornaments. There were tables all
around, tall silver candelabras on every surface, their dusty-gray
candlesticks illuminating the room. Bite-sized appetizers and fizzing
drinks were passed around for everyone to enjoy, but Christiana could
not seem to find a free moment to enjoy any of it.

Christiana and Zander stood at the front of the room, talking with
guests as they arrived for the engagement ball and thanking them for
their support for their upcoming marriage. Her face was already
burning, her cheekbones stiff from only one hour of welcoming every
single person. She leaned on Zander for support, his upbringing in the
royal light making it easier for him to survive such a painful
experience. The only thing to bring a genuine smile to her face was

when Robert finally arrived.

"Welcome!" She had to keep herself from reaching out and hugging him. He was dressed handsomely in his formal officer's uniform, the midnight-blue knee-length jacket and matching doublet decorated with a few medals of honor along with his five-point star knighting metal for extraordinary service to Viri.

"There was no place else I would be tonight." He bowed, kissing her hand. "You look absolutely beautiful tonight, My Lady."

Christiana looked down at herself, heat crawling up her neck. The dress Lorraine had created for her was impeccable. The soft gray, ivory, and black full skirt cascaded in layers of different tulle. The bodice was tight against her torso, composed of the same gray tulle, but accented with intricate lace appliques crawling up toward her shoulders and down the long sleeves. "Thank you, Robert."

Robert gestured to his right. "May I introduce my partner, General Gerard Matlas."

Christiana turned to the man next to Robert, his imposing height almost matching Robert's broad build. His short, sandy hair complimented his tanned skin well, the vivid color of his jade eyes standing out against them. He also wore his officer uniform, the two of them matching perfectly and professionally.

"It's wonderful to finally meet you." Christiana curtsied, Gerard matching with his own bow. "Robert has told me so much about you since we started working together."

"And he's told me much about you," he said with a charming smile. "Prince Alekzander has certainly sung your praises a few times over the months in our different meetings as well."

Christiana turned to Zander, a playful smirk on her lips. "Oh, have you now?"

"Of course." He shrugged, lifting her hand and kissing it. "Can you blame me?"

Christiana laughed. "I suppose not."

"We should move on as to not stop the dozens of other people desperate to talk to you," Robert teased. "But we will talk more later?"

"Of course." Christiana nodded. "We'll find you after dinner."

"Wonderful." The two walked off after their goodbyes, hands clasped as they disappeared into the sea of people crowding the space.

Finally, after another half an hour of greetings, Zander and Christiana were relieved of their duties, able to actually join their party. They strolled around its edge together, Zander refusing to let go of Christiana's arm. Then they stood off to the side, taking a moment just the two of them to appreciate the event from a quiet corner.

"Wine, My Lady?" came a deep, familiar voice from beside her.

"What are you doing here?" Christiana asked, tilting her head as she took in the well-dressed Marek carrying a tray of wine.

"It seems with such a large crowd, they needed some extra help serving. I suppose my appearance was well enough to be in the main hall."

Christiana took him in, the black, gold, and maroon servant doublet and matching black pants and boots completely out of character for him. In the many years she had known him, she had never seen him dress so formally, especially in a uniform. The only thing that had come close was the many times he dressed as the Knight, but it certainly didn't carry the same professional quality as the server's livery.

"A stable hand was their first choice?" Christiana teased, her gut telling her there was something missing from this story.

"Well, maybe not their first, but when a few servants fell a bit ill, they had fewer options to choose from. Terrible what food poisoning can do to some people." He winked, and her smile spread.

Zander leaned forward, peeking around Christiana. "Are they going to be alright?"

"They will be perfectly fine, just a few stomach cramps. Nothing a little rest and hydration will not cure," Marek replied. "I wasn't going to miss tonight."

Christiana's glass hovered against her lips, her head tilting further. "Really?"

"Even if it's in a servant's outfit, I should be allowed to celebrate the engagement of my close friend." His hand twitched under the silver tray, the glasses on top quaking a bit without a drop spilling.

Christiana's heart warmed as he turned to leave, back to his duties of serving the nobles. She knew he wouldn't leave her alone for long, which gave her comfort, but he had to put up the appearance he was doing his job right. She hoped he would find a way to be a part of the wedding servant schedule, allowing him to be at least a small part of her wedding celebration.

Zander and Christiana enjoyed themselves with laughter, wine, and delicious food. Dinner had started promptly on time, the two of them taking their place with the rest of their families at the Royal Table raised on the dais at the front of the room while the guests sat at the long tables laid out in front of it. Course after course was served, stuffing Christiana to capacity. As trays of delectable desserts and finger pastries were being placed on all the tables, the string quartet began to play.

Lucian leaned over to them, his arm pressing against Zander's. "The two of you need to open dancing."

"Oh, um..." Christiana stuttered, her palms sweating.

"Something the matter, dear?" Lucian raised an eyebrow.

"I'm just...a bit nervous to dance in front of everyone," Christiana admitted. "Could we possibly do an opening dance with the whole family instead?"

"No," Lucian said flatly. "It's tradition that the couple opens the dancing. Alone."

"Father." Zander rubbed the bridge of his nose as if nursing a headache. "I don't see the harm if we have a few more couples on the dance floor. It's not going to ruin anything."

In truth, Christiana loved to dance, to let Zander twirl her around the floor. It was always one of her favorite parts of balls, the freeing feeling of the music influencing every move, the connection between the melody, the steps, and her partner. She just didn't want to be the only one on the dance floor, all eyes watching her every move and step. Though it was a part of the life she was agreeing to, she wasn't completely ready to shine for everyone around her.

"I understand the two of you are having your fun rebelling against my decisions," Lucian growled, his cheeks blotching red. "However, we are in public and we have an image to maintain. As long as the throne is still mine, you will follow the image I choose to give this court and this country. Now, Zander, escort your fiancée out to the floor and begin the dancing before I drag her out there myself and force her to dance with me."

Christiana was not in the mood to fight, not when they had been enjoying themselves for the past few hours. This was their night, not Lucian's, and his stubbornness wasn't going to ruin it for her. Zander's resolved expression let her know he was thinking the same thing: they might as well dance and move on.

Zander pushed his chair out, his hand outstretched to her, her fingers curling around his as he led her to the dance floor. All chatter hushed until it was nothing but the music in the room, all eyes on them. Christiana's stomach knotted, her gaze darting around, the pressure of everyone's stares forcing against her and turning the air heavy.

"Don't look at them," Zander whispered, wrapping his free hand around her waist, pulling her close. "Just dance with me."

She focused on just him, his loving gaze, his enticing smile, the pressure of his hand on her body, the feeling of his satin jacket under her hand. Everyone else didn't matter; it was just them and the music and that was it. That was enough.

He floated her around the floor, the music coursing through her veins, flowing into her and inspiring her movements, her gracefulness taking over and pushing her feet forward. She didn't care about the people around her, she cared about the drifting of her mind and the lightness in her chest and stomach.

She felt free, she felt real. She felt like herself once again.

Chapter Forty-Four

ZANDER ESCORTED CHRISTIANA OFF THE dance floor the moment the song ended, claps still echoing around them as they blended back into the crowd. The feeling finally returned to Christiana's fingertips.

"I'm going to find my mother and dance with her," Zander said. "I promised her."

"Of course." Christiana stood on her toes, kissing his cheek. "I'll just...mingle for now."

He squeezed her hand and let go, heading toward the dais where his mother still sat next to his father. Christiana's eyes wandered for only a moment before catching sight of Dorina and Isabelle off to the side of the room.

"Hello, beautiful ladies," Christiana greeted them, placing a kiss on Isabelle's head.

"Oh, Ana, your dance with Zander was so romantic!" Isabelle squealed. "I can't wait to start dancing myself!"

"You won't have to wait long," Christiana teased. "I'm sure there are plenty of men in the room just waiting for the right opportunity to ask."

Isabelle giggled, her cheeks reddening. "I hope so."

"How are you feeling?" Christiana asked Dorina.

"My shoulder is fine." She waved her hand, taking the last sip of her wine before depositing the glass on a passing servant's tray. "Rowan said it was healing quickly."

"I wasn't just talking about the shoulder."

"I know." Dorina linked her arm through Christiana's. "But what's the point in discussing the other?"

"But—"

"Your Highness!" Stephan's deep voice broke through the crowd as he and Evander came to join them.

"Hello, Your Highness." Dorina curtsied, Christiana and Isabelle following suit. "General."

"Please, I told you at dinner the other day, you can call me Stephan."

"You started it by calling me Your Highness first," she teased.

"Dorina, then. Your father told me just now that you love to draw and paint," Stephan said, his eyes glimmering in the candlelight.

Dorina straightened a bit. "I do actually, I've been doing it since I was young."

"I have as well. Although my strength is with ink sketches."

"Really?" Dorina asked, leaning forward.

He nodded. "Art is very important in Atharia, we have all different forms and mediums. Painting, sculpting, body art..."

"I'm sorry," Christiana interrupted. "Body art?"

"It's called tattooing," Stephan explained. "The artist uses needles to infuse the ink into the skin. It's quite addictive, I've heard. Isn't that right, Evander?"

Evander chuckled, staring into his glass of whiskey. "I would certainly say so."

"Do you have some, General?" Isabelle asked, her brows crinkled. "Can we see?"

"Isabelle, that's rude." Christiana nudged her shoulder, but Isabelle didn't seem fazed, still staring up at Evander.

"No, it's quite alright," he said, handing his glass to Stephan before rolling up his left sleeve, revealing the cluster of designs underneath. Swirled patterns danced across his forearm, the dark black ink contrasting dramatically with his pale skin. Clearly they were some kind of symbolic designs, but Christiana didn't know what any of them meant.

"Woah!" Isabelle stared at his arm, wide-eyed.

Dorina reached out, her fingers hovering over Evander's skin, pretending to trace the pattern. "That is incredible."

"It looks painful!" Christiana couldn't help but blurt out.

"It is." Evander shrugged. "But I find it's worth the pain. Some of the best things are, in my opinion."

Christiana nodded. "I would agree with that."

"I'd love to learn more about your favorite subjects to draw," Stephan smiled coyly at Dorina. "Would you honor me with your next dance so we could discuss it further?"

"I would love to," she smiled, taking his outstretched arm and lacing hers with it.

"Do you dance, General?" Christiana turned to him.

Evander cleared his throat. "I do, although I'm not sure if I'm the best partner."

"Oh, don't listen to him, he's a splendid dancer." Prince Stephan laughed, slapping the back of Evander's shoulder with his free arm before disappearing onto the floor.

"Is that so?" Christiana teased. "Well, care to dance with me?"

"Is it proper for the guest of honor's second dance to be with a lowly military man?"

"Please," Isabelle scoffed. "My sister doesn't care about being proper."

"Isabelle!" Christiana chided.

Evander laughed deep from his chest. "Well, in that case, I would love to dance with you."

He led her to the dance floor, right by Dorina and Stephan. The prince was right, Evander was graceful, even with his towering, broad build. He spun her around to the quartet's jovial tune, leaning slightly forward. "It seems that maybe the two of them could make the best of the situation."

Christiana's heart lurched as Dorina threw her head back in laughter, Stephan's gaze trained on her. "Yes, maybe they could."

But her words felt like ashes on her tongue; she didn't believe any of them.

***

Dancing was in full swing, laughter and cheers filling the room almost as loud as the music itself. After her dance with Evander, she had found Zander again, and they made as many happy memories as they could possibly create in that one night.

"I need a break," Christiana laughed as their fourth consecutive dance came to an end. "My feet hurt."

He chuckled as well. "Fair enough."

They moved back towards the dais, her throat dry and in need of water. Marek had a glass already outstretched to her the moment they ascended; she took a few sips before a throat cleared behind them, pulling them both around.

"Hello, Zander." Rowan bowed, a strained smile on his face. "Christiana."

"Rowan." Christiana took the first step down, her second faltering when she caught sight of Rowan's companion.

"My Lady." Elaine curtsied, her smile not matching the exhaustion in her eyes. "Your Highness. Once again, congratulations on your engagement."

"Thank you, Elaine," Zander said, wrapping his arm around Christiana's waist and pulling her close. "We're happy you could join us. Both of you."

Rowan smiled at him. "I wouldn't miss it."

Silence fell, all the small talk taken up in a matter of sentences. Christiana's muscles tightened, her fingers clenching the glass tightly, her knuckles white. The tension was thick, the four of them stuck between wanting to have a conversation and not wanting to be rude by walking away.

Christiana's stomach churned. She couldn't take this much longer.

"Elaine, would you like to dance?" Zander asked, finally breaking the silence.

Christiana's eyes widened. It wasn't the exact way she thought of breaking the awkwardness, but it certainly did the job.

"Oh." Her jaw tightened as she stared down at Zander's offered hand. "Um...yes, alright, then."

She took his hand, Zander giving a wink to Christiana before escorting Elaine to the dance floor. Christiana turned back to Rowan, who gave a grin and an over-flourished bow, his hand outstretched. "May I have the next dance with the bride-to-be?"

"I suppose so," Christiana laughed, letting him lead her into the throng of dancers.

The song began, and they fell into the dance as they had many times in the past. The music built, the percussion shaking her nerves and building in her chest. She had questions for Rowan, and she didn't want to put them off any longer. She let the music flow around her, building up her strength.

"Do you think you'll talk to Zander again soon?" she blurted out. "With everything that happened the other day, it seemed like...maybe?"

"I'm not sure..." He trailed off for a moment, a pensive look shadowing over his sharp features. "Contrary to what you may think, I do miss him. It felt like losing a family member when I cut him out."

"He says the same thing about you."

"I want to. I want my brother back," he said wistfully, twirling her out before pulling her back into his arms. "It just feels like I don't know how to take the next step forward. Something is holding me back."

Tightness pulled in Christiana's limbs. "To be fair, you made a point to tell us both that you would approach when you were ready. I'm not speaking for him, but I think he's scared to make another move toward repair when he feels like it could do more harm than good. That he could push you too far."

"Yes, that's fair."

"Just wait until an opportunity arrives. Don't force it, but don't ignore it either."

"Probably a smart idea." He glanced at her, a smirk on his lips. "He's very lucky to have you. No matter how much I would have hated to admit this a while back, you two do balance each other quite well."

Christiana's chin fell to her chest, a giggle escaping her lips. "We certainly try." A few beats of silence passed, Christiana wondering if she should continue. "He needs you, too. He's going through a lot right now. I'm trying to be there for him, but I'm biased on a few accounts and he could really use his best friend to talk openly with. I know he's trying to stay strong, but honestly, he needs to let his pride go and admit he can't handle all of this alone."

"No offense, Ana, but you need to take your own advice," Rowan chuckled.

"Oh, stop it!" She smacked his arm, then shifted the subject. "Now that we're friends again, may I ask you a personal question?"

His brow furrowed as he spun her again. "I suppose."

"Do you know if something is wrong with Elaine?"

Rowan's gaze shot up to her, his emerald eyes wide. "Excuse me?"

She gnawed at the edge of her lip. "She's just been acting suspicious lately, and I may have...overheard one of her conversations with her father. I just want to make sure you're safe."

His grip tightened on her waist. "What did you hear?"

She told him everything, almost reciting it word for word as it had sifted through her mind many times over the weeks trying to break it down and figure out exactly what was happening, her obsessive behaviors getting the best of her. His face was drained of color by the time she finished speaking. "What did you think when you heard that?"

"You don't want to know."

"Now I have to." He narrowed his eyes. "Christiana."

"Fine! I thought she was the castle killer! Happy?" She said, her forehead falling to his shoulder to shield her burning face.

"Ana! Why would you think that?"

She groaned. "Because the conversation was odd and a few other small details that made my nerves suspect."

"Ana," he shook his head when she drew away. "She was keeping *me* a secret from her father, nothing as nefarious as you thought."

"And why is that?"

"I could tell that she needed a distraction after this summer. So did I. So, I began teaching her how to be a physician's assistant. Something her family certainly wouldn't approve of their cherished, noble daughter dabbling in."

Christiana tilted her head. "You really did that for her?"

"I had a lot of extra work over the past few months. The help was welcome."

"Why the extra work?"

"Well, after the summer, it didn't always feel like I belonged here anymore, not with my relationship with Zander so terribly at odds. I needed a distraction, too...something to keep me busy and happy. My work does that for me, so I started offering physician services to the servants."

Christiana's spine drooped, her eyes burning. "Oh."

"It's better now, especially since I started spending more time with Dorina. She's really helped make it feel like home again." He softened his smile, but his eyes were pained, his gaze drifting to the side.

Christiana caught a peek at Dorina dancing with Stephan again, and cleared her throat. "Rowan, maybe..."

"Stop, please," he begged. "I'm not ready to talk about that again."

"Alright, I'm sorry," she said over the final notes of the song.

"I'm going to find Elaine, I promised her a certain number of dances tonight." He pulled away, straightening his gray-and-plum jacket. Then he leaned over, his lips hovering by her ear. "All I will say is you might want to be easier on her. You two have more in common than you think."

He gave her a final weary smile before walking off the floor. Her mind and stomach twisted as she tried to decipher his final words.

Chapter Forty-Five

THREE DAYS PASSED BEFORE CHIRSTIANA AND Zander could sneak away from the palace, away from the prying eyes of family and the visiting nobles taking up all their time. Christiana took in the peaceful moment as she sat on one of the bales of hay on the outskirts of her training ring, observing another of Zander's fighting lessons with Marek. His movements were becoming sharper, his reactions quicker and more instinctual. Her chilled skin tingled as she watched him improve with each lesson and sparring match.

She took another swig from her waterskin, quenching her thirst after an hour of target practice with her daggers. She flexed her hand a few times, the muscles still a bit stiff, but her skills were back to being as sharp as they once were. She just had to continue pushing through her sword fighting training, and then she would be back to her typical fighting abilities.

She was counting down the days.

"My Lady!" Robert bolted toward them from the front of the house, his cheeks wind-chapped rosy, his day clothes rumpled.

"Robert?" Christiana hopped off her perch, walking over to the side of the ring. "What are you doing here? It's your day off."

He stopped in front of her, his hands pressing to the outside of the ring as he caught his breath. "This came for you. You need to read it."

She snatched the envelope from his outstretched hand, tearing into it. "Is it another letter about the killer?"

Robert fixed her with a grim stare. "No, not exactly."

Her brows creased, her stomach doing flips as she pulled the trifold letter open to reveal jaggedly-written words within. Her veins ran cold the moment she read the first sentence:

Dearest Marchioness,

I know who you are.

You are the masked beauty I fought in the servant halls only a few nights ago, the assassin known as Midnight Maiden. You not only interrupted my night, but you interrupted me taking care of a nosey princess who caught me doing something private. She deserved to be punished for that, a punishment I am itching to carry out.

Christiana was lucky she hadn't eaten anything recently, her stomach violently heaving, forcing her to gag and sputter on air. This could not be happening. Concerned, unintelligible whispers she couldn't make out surrounded her, yet her eyes and mind were too focused on the letter.

However, I am willing to give you a chance to fight for not only your friend's safety, but the safety of the rest of the castle.

You claim to be an assassin that helps those in need, to bring life back to those who have been violated. As our future Queen, you plan to take a similar vow for this country, to protect Viri's citizens. However, I have many doubts that you can do that for all of your people. If you want to fight for them, if you want to prove that you are actually willing to put your life before theirs, then I challenge you to a duel. You will fight for the safety of this castle, a safety that is currently firmly in my grasp.

One month from today, when the full moon is at the highest point of the sky, we will fight to the death. Meet me at your secret cottage, and bring absolutely no one with you. If I see even one guard, I will make sure everyone knows who you are. If you somehow arrest me, I have a very special friend who has compiled plenty of evidence proving you are a killer yourself. I have instructed them to release that evidence if I am captured during this fight. The only way to keep your secret from getting out is to kill me.

I hope you find the time to prepare for a fight I'm sure you are not ready for. Until then, I will not kill another person in the castle, you have my word.

I look forward to crossing blades with you once again.

Sincerely,
The Castle Killer

Christiana couldn't move, her legs locked in place, her insides quaking. "What is he doing to us?"

Marek grabbed her by the shoulders, forcing her to turn toward him. "Christiana! What is it?"

"This can't be happening, this can't be happening..." her voice shook.

"Ana...you need to..."

"I know! To breathe!" she snapped. "Just give me some space, please!"

The air around her cooled as the three of them backed away. She propped her hands against the sides of the ring, the letter still clutched in one; then she stared at the ground, digging her toes into the hard earth, feeling the biting sting of the cold air through her nostrils as she pulled in deep breaths. She focused on the sweat beading on her forehead, the crackling of the parchment between her hand and the wooden slat, and the warmth of the sun pressing against her back.

She focused. She breathed. She found herself again.

She exhaled loudly before pushing away from the side, looking up at the three men still staring at her. "I'm alright."

Zander stepped forward. "Can we talk about what happened?"

"Not here." She jumped over the ring. "Let's go inside for this."

***

Silence fell in the common room, her legs and arms numb as she sat and watched the three of them bend over the parchment, their faces contorting in different reactions as they scanned the page.

Zander was the first to look up, his sapphire eyes dark and stormy. "You can't do this."

"I have to." She leaned forward, cradling her head in her hands. "If I don't, he will go back to killing, and he will most likely expose Maiden in the process. Besides, fighting him means bringing safety back to the palace."

"Then we set a trap." Zander's words came out rushed, jumbled together. He collapsed next to her.

"Did you even read the letter?" Christiana threw the blanket off her lap, angling herself toward him. "The risks are too great. He will expose me if I do anything to put him in harm's way."

"Dear one, he was a strong match for me." Marek reminded her. "His skills are impeccable."

Zander peeked over at her. "You could die."

"I know." She grasped his hands and placed a kiss on his knuckles. "But I have no choice."

"He's going dark, Your Highness," Robert said. "Which is a blessing and a curse. It means the servants are safe again, but it also means we have lost the opportunity to track him."

"You agree with this dastardly idea?" Zander demanded.

"I wish I didn't have to." Robert sighed, his fingers combing through his cropped chestnut hair. "But with the threats laid out in this letter, it seems he has given her no choice. She either fights and risks her life, or doesn't, and he exposes her...ultimately leading to her death penalty."

Zander looked over to Marek. "Do you agree as well?"

Marek sighed, sinking to perch on the edge of the table. "I wish I didn't have to. I don't want to see her going into a fight so soon, but this man has the details in place. If we take the risk and try and trap him, or she doesn't show up, we still put her life at risk. If he exposes her as the Maiden, your father will not hesitate to execute her."

"I'm wanted for many deaths, Zander," she whispered. "I know we've never said that out loud, but you should know this. I was never hesitant to put calling cards on my victims, it marked them as abusers...but it also allowed the crown to pin the deaths on me. If my identity were revealed, I would hang and you would have to let me die."

"You're still retraining yourself to fight." Zander tugged at his neck, his slicked curls tangled in between his fingers. "It's too dangerous."

"We have a month. Every spare minute I have will be in a ring getting my tremor back under control."

Zander scoffed. "I hate this."

"So do I." Christiana whispered, swiping a tear from his cheek. "But we have no other choice. I either die fighting for what I believe in or die like a criminal. I think you know which path I would rather take."

"You know she's making the right decision." Marek patted him on the back. "You just don't want to admit it."

"No, I don't," Zander shook his head, his fists balled at his sides. "All three of you are giving into fear instead of taking a few days to try and figure out a better solution. One that doesn't put my fiancée in mortal danger."

"Look, Zander, we don't have time to start arguing about this!" Christiana said, her muscles tense. "I don't have a few days to try and figure out a new plan. I'm doing this, and you can either pout or you can help me train. Now, which is it going to be?"

Tension filled the room, Zander staring at her for a few moments before walking out the front door, slamming it behind him. Her heart fell, her lip trembling as she rose to follow him, but a hand grasped her arm.

"Let me, dear one," Marek said, striding out the door.

Christiana couldn't help herself, walking over to the window in the common room, peeking out to see Marek jogging after Zander, stopping him from reaching the stable. Christiana couldn't hear what they were saying, but Marek spoke first, his stance strong, his finger prodding Zander's chest. Zander's face turned red, his fist balling at his side before swinging forward, aiming at Marek's solar plexus. Marek caught it instead, his other hand clasping Zander's shoulder. Marek kept speaking, the tension in his face showing how passionately he was fighting for her.

With each word he spoke, Zander's color slowly returned to normal; she could see the pain and hurt written all across his face, her heart aching to go out there and fix the problem, to give him what he wanted...but she couldn't. She desperately wished she could make a different choice, but no matter how quickly her mind tried to come up with a plan, it only led to one answer: she had to fight.

Christiana scurried away from the window when the two men turned back toward the house. Robert touched her shoulder, giving it a tight squeeze just before Marek and Zander walked back through the front door. Zander was still frowning, his jaw so tense it made his sharp cheekbones protrude even more. Still, he walked over to her, taking her hand.

"Alright," he said. "I'll help you train."

Christiana let out a deep breath. "Zander, thank you."

"I still don't agree with this." His eyes brimmed with pain and confliction. "I don't want you fighting him, but I know I can't stop you. So I'm going to do everything I can to make sure you're as prepared as you can possibly be."

"I understand," she nodded. "But thank you anyway."

"Come here." He tugged her to his chest and wrapped his arms around her shoulders, her body melting into the embrace while her darkened thoughts tried to take control, feeding her lies that she was too weak to save herself, let alone the entire castle.

You are not a leader. You are not a protector. You are a slave to your darkness.

She pushed them away, forcing them back into the dredges of her mind. They had no place in her forethought, not when so many lives now sat on her shoulders. She lived by a code: the safety of others before her own.

It seemed she was about to put that code to the ultimate test.

Chapter Forty-Six

THE COLD AIR OF LATE WINTER BIT AT Christiana's flushed cheeks, sweat dripping down her hairline and grunts of frustration ringing from her lips. A week had gone by since she was fed the challenge from the castle killer. A week of constant anxiety reminding her that time was ticking away day by day.

She didn't know how she was going to survive the rest of the month.

She tried her best to focus not on the fight ahead, but the training in the moment. She found every excuse to get into a ring, mornings spent with Marek back at the cottage and any free time in between wedding planning and Marchioness duties she split with Zander and Robert.

The sun was slowly melting into the horizon, buttercup-yellow blending with the hazy blue of nighttime beginning to emerge. She and Zander had been training for an hour, pushing her tremor to the limits, attempting to extend her fight time more and more. It didn't stop her from punching the slats of the castle's training ring or throwing her sword clear across the grass when she was particularly frustrated, though.

"I'm not progressing fast enough." She clutched her knees, bending over, her chest heaving as the pressure to breathe deeper built in her sternum.

Zander's hand rested between her shoulder blades, drawing tight, soothing circles. "Don't focus on the *enough*, focus on the progress you've made. You are going two minutes longer than you were four days ago when we started this. That's crucial."

"I just wish it were easier."

"Wishing is easy, but this isn't an instant gratification situation. If you keep focusing on the progress you should be making, you're just going to hinder the progress you could be making."

Christiana straightened, lifting her chin to take in a biting, cool breath through her nostrils. "I hate when you're right."

"I know," Zander chuckled, wrapping his arm around her shoulders and pulling her close, sweaty musk mixing with his cedarwood scent. He placed a gentle kiss on her forehead. "I'm starving, I think we should call it a night. Have dinner with me?"

Christiana shook her head. "I can't. I already promised my mother and Isabelle I would spend the evening with them."

"Alright then, we should get you back so you can clean up." Zander walked her over to the edge of the ring, his hand in hers. "Let me just tidy up the ring a bit and then I'll walk you back."

Christiana wearily smiled and leaned over to place a kiss on his lips before jumping over the side of the ring. His cheeks burned a bit brighter at the contact as he turned around, picking up a few discarded swords, wiping them down and then returning them to the wall of practice weapons.

"I wish you two would have told me you were training," came a voice from behind Christiana; she turned just as Rowan leaned on the railing next to her. "I could have used the workout."

"Would you have actually come?" Christiana teased, gesturing to his riding boots and outfit. He must have been on his way to the stables when he saw them.

"Why not?" he shrugged. "You and I have been doing better."

"It isn't me that you need to do better with." She nodded to Zander, who was casting nervous glances their way as he finished cleaning.

"That's true..." Rowan trailed off, his eyes locked on Zander for a few moments before he pulled himself over the side and walked toward him. "Hey, Zee, how about a match?"

Zander's eyes went wide. "Really?"

"Yes." Rowan shrugged, pulling a sword off the wall. "Not like we haven't done it before."

Zander smiled. "Alright then. Do you mind, Ana?"

"Not at all!" she shouted back.

They fell into sparring without another word, throwing parries and jabs, trying to catch each other off-guard. It was nothing more than a typical noble sparring match; the movements were methodical, their brows furrowed with sweat dripping down the sides of their faces. Then Rowan's frown deepened, and he landed his next jab with extra force. Christiana's heart began to pulse faster as his movements intensified. Zander's eyes filled with worry as he tried his best to block them, refusing to strike back as fiercely as Rowan seemed to want; he was letting Rowan get out all his aggression without complaint. It was such a Zander thing to do, but it made him look helpless. It made him look like he was in trouble.

Just as Christiana had been so many months ago.

Shh, My Lady, I'll be kind...

The ground tilted and Christiana clung to the fence, her heart thundering in her ears. Whispered memories of summertime air and shallow cuts covering her arms assaulted her senses, pressing against her, attempting to drag her back.

Damnit, not here, not now...

She cursed under her breath, desperate to sprint from prying eyes as the pieces of her mind broke apart. She needed to get away from this.

She stumbled back from the ring, her clouded mind making her clumsier than usual. She gave out at the pressure, collapsing to the ground as she wrapped her arms around her torso. Her freshly-callused hands began to shake, her mind desperate to regain control as she tried to pull in air through her nose.

"Christiana?" An alarmed voice rang in the distance, the pounding of footsteps filling her dulled ears as she tried to focus. Her cheeks flushed in embarrassment as hands wrapped around her shoulders. "Love, what's wrong?"

She couldn't speak, her wheezing breath the only thing escaping her lips as she tried to calm herself down. She needed to stop it before it got any worse.

"Alright," Zander mumbled, his fingers lacing around her chin to force her face up. "Look at me, love."

She brought her eyes to his, his face full of concern as he knelt in front of her. A second set of hands pressed against her back, Rowan crouching on the other side as he supported her. She hated that yet another person saw her this way, but at least their bodies were blocking her from other people who might be passing by.

Zander smiled as she stared at him, his voice soothing. "What is twenty added to thirty-two?"

Her mind anchored to the numbers, her thoughts swimming through the thickness of her anxiety as they tried their best to solve the problem. "Fif...fifty-two." Her voice quaked, but she knew the answer was correct.

"And thirteen removed from forty-seven?"

Her mind moved more freely, the murkiness dissipating slightly as she answered, "Thirty-four."

"One hundred twenty-one added to seventy-five?"

Her breath evened back out, her lungs filling slowly inside her chest as her vision came back to focus, Zander's sapphire eyes the first thing she found. "One hundred and ninety-six."

The shaking slowed, exhaustion settling over her as she found the clarity she desperately needed. She fell back on her haunches, rubbing circulation back into her numb cheeks.

"Thank you," she smiled at him, the tips of her lips shaking slightly.

"I told you," he whispered, his forehead leaning against hers. "I'm here for you, no matter what."

"Are you alright?" Rowan asked, emerald eyes filled with concern as he moved himself next to Zander in her line of vision.

"I'm so sorry you had to see that." Heat spread down her neck as she lowered her gaze.

"Why?" Rowan shook her lightly, her gaze meeting his. "You shouldn't apologize for it."

"But you don't know..."

"I'm a physician, Christiana." His expression was gentle. "After what you admitted to me a few weeks ago, it's no surprise. You have Battled Brain, don't you?"

Christiana nodded weakly. "Yes, I do. But please don't tell anyone," she begged him, Zander's grip against her arm tightening at her quiet plea.

"Physicians don't betray their patients, just as I don't betray my friends." He smiled, and relief flooded her entire body at his kind words. "Wonderful job at helping her, Zee." He patted Zander on the back.

"Thanks," Zander looked between both of them. "It was my first attempt."

"He's right." Christiana smiled, her fingers tracing a mindless pattern in the dirt. "You helped."

"Thank goodness, I was scared I would choke." The three of them laughed together, something they hadn't done since the summer months. Her stomach fluttered with joy to see this wall finally crumbling at their feet.

Christiana peeked back to Rowan. "That's why we have been out here so constantly." She swallowed a lump in her throat. "My Battled Brain has been affecting my ability to fight and it has put me in danger a few times."

"That's why you were injured," Rowan whispered, understanding flushing across his face. Christiana nodded. "So you're trying to retrain your mind?"

"Yes."

"Let me help too, then, I can train with you as well. I used to with some of the soldiers when they had similar struggles." Rowan turned to Zander, his face soft, "If you need help learning other techniques or getting a better understanding of different symptoms, my door is always open for you, Zee."

Zander's smile reached his cheekbones as he wrapped his other arm around Rowan's shoulders, shaking him slightly. "I think I'll have to take you up on that, thanks, Ro."

"Me as well." Christiana pulled in one final breath before straggling to her feet, the two men following. "I have a bit of a...time-sensitive issue depending on it."

Rowan's eyebrows rose. "Oh?"

Christiana sighed, her soul settling. She needed as much help as she could get, and since Rowan was ready to mend the friendship between the three of them, it was time to accept a new set of helping hands. "Walk back to my apartment with us? If you want to help train me, it's probably best you know what you're actually training me for."

Chapter Forty-Seven

CHRISTIANA FOUND HERSELF ONE RAINY afternoon wandering the main entryway, her steps mindless as her eyes glazed over. Every inch of her vibrated with the need to move, desperate to get back into the ring and train for this fight that was looming only a few weeks away. She was counting the minutes until the rain stopped and she could find an excuse to get Marek, Robert, Zander, or Rowan back to training.

She hadn't realized that she'd wandered into the gallery, surrounded by dozens of portraits from royal family members over the decades. A shiver ran up her spine as she remembered the last time she had been here—when her investigation into Julian was starting. She could almost feel his tall specter looming next to her. She swallowed a large lump in her throat, the candlelight flickering around her as she pulled in deep, cleansing breaths to keep a panic attack at bay.

The sound of muffled sobs pulled her from her memories, Julian's ghost disappearing from her thoughts as she crossed the gallery. She walked on the balls of her feet, her toes aching as she kept her footsteps light and peered around a corner of the room. Her eyes went wide at the sight that greeted her, her stomach tightening into knots. Elaine sat on a velvet-covered bench, her dress spilling over the sides. Her hands covered her face, jagged fingernails scratching at her forehead, marking it with red lines. She rocked faintly back and forth, mumbles escaping her lips that Christiana couldn't make out.

Christiana had no idea what pulled her toward this woman she disliked for so long, except for Rowan's words and his kindness toward her. She halted before her, reaching for her shoulder. "Elaine?" The woman flinched at her touch, and Christiana hastily withdrew. "What's wrong? Are you alright?"

Elaine peeked up, sneering the minute she recognized Christiana. "Wonderful! Of course it had to be you who found me! Just leave me alone."

"No." Christiana sat next to Elaine, their skirts flowing together, a contrast of plum purple and sage green blending into one. "You are hurting, and no one should be alone when they are hurting. Not like this."

Elaine scoffed, gazing across the room, eyes still glazed with tears. "Like you have any understanding of what I'm going through. No one understands."

Christiana's shoulders fell as she leaned against the wall behind them, her eyes never leaving Elaine's. Her face was splotched, her tears glistening in the soft candlelight that illuminated her face. Something scratched along Christiana's skin, pinpricks running up and down her limbs. There was something about Elaine...something all too familiar. She didn't know if she should ask, or even prod, knowing how painful it could be; but Rowan's words from the ball kept ringing in her mind.

You two have more in common than you think.

Christiana's hand twitched at her side. She wrapped her skirts in her fingers, forcing them to stay still. "Elaine, are you in danger? Is someone...hurting you?"

Elaine was as still as a sculpture, her eyes falling flat. Every muscle in her face relaxed, as if she had slipped into a trance—retreating within the darkness in her mind.

"Elaine, please." Christiana slid closer, her shoulders hunched as she leaned over to whisper, "If someone is hurting you, let me help. Talk to me, please."

The silence was deafening as Elaine continued to stare. Christiana's mind swirled, trying to find any way to help this woman. Never mind their past difficulties or the fact that Christiana always thought she was an entitled brat. That didn't matter anymore; if Elaine was being abused, Christiana would do anything to help her.

Her heart clenched as she continued. "You can trust me, you can talk to me if someone is abusing you, because I understand. My father used to hurt me growing up."

Elaine's eyes went wide, her lip trembling. "Christiana..."

"I know it's hard to talk about," Christiana added, hoping the truth might allow Elaine to see she was not alone. "I know the pressure and the pain and the desperate need to keep such a disgraceful thing secret. I know the deep-seeded, gut wrenching shame that builds every time you hide the scars and the bruises that someone who says they love you marked you with. I had my own for many years, every time I disappointed my father. No matter how perfect we looked growing up, it was far from the truth. He was an abuser, and I was lucky to escape with my life."

"You really went through that?" Elaine sniffed, her glistening eyes turning to Christiana.

"Yes." Christiana rested a hand on Elaine's bony shoulder. This time the other woman didn't pull away. "Please, Elaine. Tell me, and I will make sure to get you to safety."

"No one is hurting me." The words barely escaped through her chapped lips. "Not anymore."

Christiana's brow creased, her mind racing to understand. She followed Elaine's entranced gaze, her body filling with dread as realization flooded into her. The portrait in front of them was not just a random person; it was Julian, his face full of smug arrogance as he stood tall, every feature proud.

Christiana knew many things about Julian, including his dirty and dark secrets. One of them had been the key to her success in killing him, it gave her the opportunity to ambush him on the road. She didn't want to believe it, but it didn't stop the words from slipping out. "Were you and Julian having an affair?"

Fresh tears fell from Elaine's eyes as she nodded. "I don't need your judgement."

"I'm not, I promise. I'm the last person to judge others for their decisions. But I do know that Julian wasn't the kindest man, even though many people believed him to be."

"I didn't want it," she whispered, her eyes finally flicking back to Christiana. "My father made me. Julian showed an interest, and he pushed me to do it."

Christiana's skin crawled. Not only was she abused by Julian, but her father as well. "But why?"

Elaine's eyes stared deep into Christiana's. "Because Julian promised him I would become Queen."

"I'm sorry," was all that Christiana could think to say. There were no words to describe the emotions that brewed in her heart, her insides a mess as she realized what her engagement to Zander actually did to Elaine. It was never about wanting Zander or being jealous of Christiana, it was about doing what her abusers wanted of her—and failing. Failure was always the reason for Christiana's punishments, and her gut told her the same rang true for Elaine.

"So am I." Elaine looked back at the portrait. "I'm sorry for what your father did to you. I only dealt with Julian's whippings for a few months, you are strong to have handled it for years."

"It doesn't matter if it was months or years, no one deserves to have their skin slashed at like that," Christiana mumbled, her words no longer filtered with this fellow survivor.

"Do you have scars as well?"

Christiana nodded. "All over my back for the most part. It's mangled."

"Me too. My body is so ugly now, how will any man want me?"

Christiana's vision tunneled as she absorbed Elaine's words. Zander insisted that she was beautiful, that he would find every piece of her beautiful. Yet doubt crept in. How would he react when he saw her naked on their wedding night? How would he find her beautiful once he saw just how disgusting her body actually was?

"You will find a man who will love you no matter what." She forced the words past her lips, desperately trying to believe them herself. "A good man, one you deserve, who will make sure you never feel ugly for the pain and torture you went through. All he will see is the survivor you are."

Elaine scoffed again. "What a dream that is."

Silence fell for a few fleeting minutes before Christiana's heart pulled her to speak again. "You can come to me whenever you need. If you are having a bad day or need to talk, I'll be there for you."

"What, you want to be friends now?" Elaine scoffed, her nose crinkling as she glared at Christiana.

"Hardly," Christiana rolled her eyes. "But we share something. We have a bond we can't ignore. I just want you to know that you can come to me and talk if you ever need someone to listen. Someone who understands."

"I don't need your pity," Elaine kicked the bench as she stood, a few raven curls escaping her ponytail as she looked down at Christiana. "I'm not...I'm not...one of those."

"People want to put the bad word on us. They want to call us victims so we see ourselves in some negative light." Christiana reached out, her hand grasping Elaine's, her fingers cold and shaking. "But you don't have to see yourself that way. Neither of us do. We both found ourselves in dangerous situations, and we lived through it. My father wasn't my fault, and Julian wasn't yours."

"It isn't the same." Her voice shook, silent tears falling down her cheek, streaking her cosmetics. "Your father was forced on you. I chose to let Julian in."

"But you didn't choose the relationship he forced on you." Christiana stood up, refusing to let go.

"I could have left. I could have told him to stop."

"At what risk?" The words she spoke months ago filled her mind as she continued. "Stop making excuses for him. You are not responsible for the decisions he made."

Elaine's fingers clutched tightly to Christiana's. "Sometimes it feels like I have to. My mind tells me it's the right thing to do."

"Don't listen to the darkness." Christiana brushed a piece of her hair aside. "Don't listen to the voice telling you that you're a helpless victim. See yourself as I see you. See the survivor you truly are."

"I don't want to keep feeling this way," Elaine whispered. "I want to be the person I was before."

Christiana lowered them back down, Elaine's face creased with exhaustion. "I know you do, I wanted that for so long. And I hate that I have to be the person to tell you this, but you won't be able to. We're changed by our experiences, we can't control that, but what we can control is if we are changed for the better or if we let it take control of us."

Elaine looked up, her sea-green eyes still glassy with tears. Christiana's heart wept as she looked into them, realizing for the first time that they were more alike than Christiana ever thought she would admit. Elaine was just like her five years before, when Marek showed her what her future would be like. She didn't have to go through it alone back then, and Elaine didn't have to go through it alone now.

"I can teach you ways to cope." Christiana gave her a weary smile. "And I can be there for you if you ever need someone to listen when you feel like the world is crumbling around you. Although, I'm guessing Rowan has been that person for you over the weeks?"

"He has been, thank goodness." Elaine sniffled. "Teaching me medical...techniques."

Christiana smiled slightly. "Are you enjoying it?"

"A bit, I suppose." She shrugged. "It's really not my favorite activity if I had to choose, but I had little options when I needed an excuse to get away from my father and keep busy with my hands."

"I understand. Staying busy helps me, too. I find ways to keep me focused."

Elaine swallowed. "You're truly willing to be there for me as well?"

"You don't have to feel alone ever again," Christiana assured her. "I'm here."

Chapter Forty-Eight

CHRISTIANA SLIPPED HER BOOTS ON BEFORE walking out into her common room, where Robert was already sitting at the dining table. She sat down across from him, taking a lavender-vanilla scone from the plate in the center of the table. She wanted to eat quickly before meeting Zander and Rowan for a training session.

She looked at Robert, staring at the table while one of his fingers traced a pattern, his face pensive. She hesitated. "What's wrong?"

"Is Miss Natalia here?" Robert whispered, leaning over the table.

Christiana shook her head, the back of her neck tingling. "She left to do laundry. Why?"

Robert leaned back, rubbing his temples. "I wasn't sure if I should tell you this, but I also know that I cannot keep this a secret. I think she's in danger."

Christiana's breath caught, her hands bracing on the table. "Tell me everything."

"It isn't much of anything. I could honestly be reading too much into it."

"Tell me, please." Christiana's throat was closing, the words choking from her lips.

Robert nodded grimly. "I came back here the other day when you were in a meeting. I must have startled her by just walking in, because the moment I did, she threw a silver candlestick she'd been polishing at the door."

"Alright..." Christiana nodded.

"When I asked her what was wrong, she kept avoiding the subject," Robert went on. "But her hands were shaking and when she walked away, I heard her...muttering to herself. Something about keeping it together."

Christiana's heart sank. "Oh, no..."

"I wouldn't think much of it normally," Robert leaned back in his chair. "But after what we saw in the hall the other day and our knowledge of these types of symptoms, they seem very reminiscent of Battled Brain to me."

Not Natalia; not the one who had been with her for the past five years, with the sweetest nature Christiana had ever met. She had been a constant companion, a pillar in her life. Even though Natalia was unaware of Christiana's mental struggles, she always seemed to know exactly what she needed. Natalia was one of the most giving, selfless people Christiana knew. She would rip anyone apart who would try and hurt her.

"I had noticed she'd been jumpy and nervous lately, but it just seems to be getting worse." Christiana looked up at Robert. "Do you think Jay has something to do with it?"

"I'm not sure," Robert sighed. "I asked her if someone was causing her distress, and she said it was just the pressure of planning the household merging after the wedding."

"Did you believe her?"

"Debatable," Robert said. "And without her admitting anything or naming someone, I have no right to go and question Jay. It would be unethical to interrogate him on a gut feeling alone."

Christiana knocked her fist against the table. "Should I talk to her about it?"

"I fear if you do, she'll just alienate herself even more. She'll know I told you, and it might just make her cower away from our help."

Christiana groaned. "You're probably right." Approaching someone who was possibly being abused was a difficult situation. If handled incorrectly, or approached too bluntly, it could make the person run away, pushing them even closer to their abuser and away from helping hands. Christiana needed to handle this delicately if she was going to bring Natalia to safety. "I'll wait for a time when it can come up more naturally so I can make her comfortable to open up."

Robert nodded. "That's a wise choice."

***

A flurry of snow floated around Christiana, speckling her plain tunic with moisture. The grounds were quiet and the frost had yet to melt as the sun rose above the trees, thin rays desperately trying to peek through the cast of gray clouds across the sky.

Each day that passed by, she felt a little extra sliver of confidence start to creep back in as she pushed farther and farther with her limits. She fought, struggled, and tested herself with every sparring match, switching off between Zander and Rowan whenever her hand gave out.

"You know," Rowan heaved, his sword dangling, "even with your hand, you still challenge me with every fight."

"Stop flattering me, it won't help any," Christiana grinned, rubbing her thumb against her shaking palm, working the tired, quaking muscles until they calmed down so she could fight again.

"It's not flattery if it's true." Zander came over from the ringside, taking the practice sword Rowan offered. "Your skills are the same. Really, we're just working your stamina."

Christiana shrugged. She had never thought of it like that before. "I suppose that's true. Ready to go again?"

Zander nodded sharply, Rowan backing away to the edge of the ring. The minutes ticked by, their routine continuing with each of her failed attempts at controlling her own hand. After a few more rounds, Zander suggested it was time to take a break and handed her the waterskin to drink from. As the cool water soothed her parched throat, she heard the crunch of feet heading towards them.

"Looks like we have a visitor," Zander muttered.

Christiana smirked as Dorina, dressed in one of her many winter riding outfits, stomped toward them, determination spread across her face.

Rowan let out a low whistle. "That is not a happy face. Do you know what she's upset about?"

"No, but I'm dying to find out," Christiana laughed, hanging her hands over the edge of the ring, Dorina's steps getting faster and faster as she approached.

"Hide me!" she seethed, throwing herself over the side of the ring, barricading herself behind Rowan.

"What's wrong?" Christiana asked, glancing around the open space, down the path that led to the stables.

"I'm evading!" She peeked around Rowan, her eyes darting around. "I just caught sight of Stephan and Evander."

Rowan stood stiff, refusing to move away from his post hiding Dorina, his head tilted over his shoulder to gaze at her. "What?"

"Why are you avoiding him?" Christiana asked, earning a scowl in return. "I thought you were making the best of the situation."

"Well, I started second-guessing that decision, alright?" Dorina glared at her. "I don't know, I'm just...confused."

"Arranged marriage can do that to a person," Zander grumbled.

Rowan straightened, his eyes going wide. "I'm sorry, an arranged *what?*"

Christiana's heart dropped, watching Rowan's attempt to hide the panic in his voice and the stress etched into the lines of his face. Dorina threw up her arms. "The three of you are very lucky. None of you had to deal with intrusive parents trying to force a marriage on you!"

"Excuse me!" Zander shot back. "Just because I ultimately chose my partner, that didn't stop Father from throwing women at me like he was bribing a child with candy."

Dorina stuck her tongue out at him. "At least you were able to get out of it. As of right now, if Father tells me I have to marry Stephan, there is nothing stopping him from dragging me down the aisle and away from Viri."

Rowan glowered. "That's not going to happen."

Dorina's lip quivered as she stepped out from behind him and turned to Christiana. "If only that were true."

"I thought you liked Stephan." Christiana said, though she knew her words were not helping. "You two were spending more time together, drawing and whatnot."

"Yes, and it's been lovely." Dorina rocked back and forth on her heels. "But with each date, he gets more and more intense. You can tell he's already decided that this is going to happen, and I don't think I'm ready to make that kind of commitment to him."

"Dorina, I'm sorry." Christiana grabbed her hands, pulling her forward into a hug, her face buried in Dorina's curls. Her forehead fell on Christiana's shoulder, her breath shaky.

Rowan turned to Zander. "Why is your father so against his daughter's happiness?"

"I wish I knew." Zander turned to his friend, arms tightly crossed against his heaving chest. "I've been trying to find something, anything, to get Dorina out of it, but I haven't been able to come up with anything."

"That's not good enough!" Rowan seethed, his fingers curling around the edge of the training ring. "We need to figure out a way to stop this!"

Christiana and Zander stiffened at his outburst, shame written all over his face the moment the last word left his lips. His countenance drained of color, his body collapsing against the ring. Zander patted him on the back. Dorina pulled away from Christiana, looking over to Rowan and Zander. "I appreciate the concern, Rowan, but I know Zander is doing all that he can. That's all that matters."

"Your happiness matters, too," Rowan muttered, rubbing his forehead.

"I know, but that doesn't mean I get it right now." Dorina turned away, using her hair to curtain the blush crossing her cheeks. "I'm sorry, I didn't mean to interrupt you three. I'm just having a bad day. I'll feel better about Stephan come tomorrow, I'm sure."

"Dorina," Christiana wrapped her arm around her friend's shoulders. "You don't have to pretend with us."

"I'm not pretending, I promise," she said, pulling away and walking back to the ring's edge. "Just overwhelmed with all of the changes. I just need to get used to them."

"Well, you don't have to do it all in one day," Zander said. "Why don't I walk you back to the palace and we can have breakfast? That way if we run into Stephan, you have an excuse to avoid him today."

Dorina sniffed. "Thank you, Brother."

"Of course." He wrapped his arm around Dorina's shoulder. "Are you two alright to clean up here?"

Christiana nodded. "Yes, go on."

Zander smiled tightly at her before turning him and Dorina toward the castle, disappearing down the path. Christiana turned to look at Rowan, his forehead resting on top of the ring. She walked over, leaning next to him.

"Are you alright?" she murmured.

"No."

"Ro, you have to tell her." Christiana said. "It's crushing you both keeping it a secret."

He snorted, looking back up. "What good will that do? We have a few days of stolen romantic moments that we have to hide before she is promised to another man and taken away from me? No, Ana, I won't go through that."

"If she knew the truth, she would choose you," Christiana said. "You didn't hear her talk about those letters, how much hope she had in them."

"I can't go through another heartache." Rowan shook his head. "I just got over you, I'm not going to put my heart on the line again until I know that it isn't doomed from the start."

"Just let..."

"Let's go again," Rowan pushed away from the ring, walking back to the middle. "We still have twenty minutes of training left."

"Rowan..." Christiana sighed, her footsteps sluggish moving after him.

"My petty romantic problems are nothing compared to what you have to do in three weeks," Rowan said, readying his stance. "Now, are you going to keep getting distracted, or are you going to train?"

Christiana rolled her eyes, pushing the protests away and picking up her sword. She may be staying quiet for now, but that didn't mean she was giving up completely.

Chapter Forty-Nine

*C*HRISTIANA WASN'T SURE IF THIS WAS THE RIGHT thing to do, but after her conversation with Elaine, it was something she had to do for herself.

For the first time since she came back to the palace, she scaled the wall to Zander's bedroom, the midnight hour casting a moonlight glow along the dark stone that rubbed against her gloved hands. The chilled air made her fingers numb with each handhold she grasped, her arms screaming as she pulled herself through the window. He was already waiting for her, his smiling eyes welcoming her as he offered a hand, helping her down onto the floor.

"Thank you for letting me come." Her hands shivered in his grasp, his warm touch bringing a tingle to the tips.

"Of course." He leaned down, capturing her lips against his, dancing with them gently before pulling back. "You're always welcome here, you know that. Although, I am a bit confused why you came through the window this time."

Tension radiated in her cheeks, her temple aching with a pin-pricking pain. She came through the window for one particular reason: she needed to wear her Maiden outfit tonight. It would make what she needed to do easier.

This was the right thing to do; she only hoped he would understand.

"Can I have a drink?" Was the first thing to come to mind, her taste buds and her nerves begging for a smooth glass of whiskey.

His face pinched as he looked down at her. "Of course."

He kept their fingers laced together while he led her to his couch, the evergreen velvet welcoming her as she sank into the cushions. The decanter and two glasses were already set in front of them, poured for her arrival. She grasped the chilled crystal, the amber liquid dancing as she brought it to her lips. It was her favorite brand, imported from a neighboring country with full flavors. If her mind wasn't racing so quickly, she might have been able to enjoy it, but all she tasted was the bitter burn of the alcohol spreading warmth through her body as she took a few more sips.

"Are you alright?" Zander put his own glass back down, shifting to face her.

"I hope so," she mumbled against the glass still poised on her lips.

His brow creased. "You're starting to scare me. Is it your Battled Brain? My father?"

"No, it's not your father." She drained the last of her whiskey, forcing herself not to pour another serving. She needed the first one to calm her nerves, but she had to make sure her mind was clear with what she was about to propose. "But it does have to do with my Battled Brain...at least a concern I have for it."

Zander's voice was soothing, his hand stroking the top of her fingers. "Talk to me, Ana."

"I had a conversation with Elaine the other day." She thought carefully for her words, wanting to make sure that every one was perfectly in order so he would understand why she needed this. "One that really helped put a lot about her into perspective. It also helped me realize that she and I have a lot more in common that I originally thought."

"Why do you sound sad about that?"

"Something she said made my mind start spiraling, thinking about other moments where my condition could cause an issue." She took a deep breath. "Most of them I can handle, but I'm still not completely convinced of one."

"What is it?"

"Our wedding night," she whispered.

His eyes widened, and he bit his lip before saying, "I know it isn't easy for you to think about, but I promise, I am very confident I will find every bit of your scars beautiful."

"Zander, I've rarely shown this part of myself to others, and you'll be looking at me in such a different way than they ever did." She shook her head. "I just want you to be prepared, my body isn't as beautiful as my face. My father took it from me."

"Love..."

"I don't want our wedding day to end with you seeing such a repulsive side of me for the first time."

He settled forward, grasping her cheek, their eyes connecting deeply. "I would never be repulsed by any part of you."

"You don't know that. You haven't seen them." She held back tears; this wasn't easy for her to talk about, but she needed to do it. For herself and for Zander. "I want you to see them tonight. I want you to see them so you can prepare yourself."

He squirmed in his seat, his face pinched together. "I'm not sure if that's the best idea."

"Zander, please. I need this." She looked at him, silently begging him to see what was stirring deep in her mind and soul. "I need to know your reaction. If for some reason it's negative, I would be devastated if that was how we ended our wedding day. Please, don't do that to the happiest day of our life."

Silence fell between them, Zander's gaze dropping to the couch. Christiana's stomach twisted, bile rising in her throat as she waited for him to answer. He let out a deep breath, his eyes rising to hers at last. "Alright. I don't feel comfortable doing this here, though. Come with me."

He took her hand and pulled her from her seat, walking her to one of the doors she had yet to enter. It revealed his expansive bedroom with a giant four poster bed in the center, a maroon quilt with a swirled silver pattern resting across it and a handful of pillows strewn on top. Two brown leather chairs sat by the bay window, a small stack of books and papers on the table in between them. The black stone fireplace crackled as they entered into the room. If Christiana hadn't been so nervous, she would have been awed by the comfort of the space. She looked forward to spending lazy mornings with him here.

He closed the door behind them before pulling her close, his hands on either side of her face as his gaze never wavered from hers. "I love you. Never forget that."

She nodded, "I love you, too. Thank you for this."

He smiled and released her, and she strode to the bed so she could pull off her outfit. She unclasped the small sleeves, pulling them gently down her arms, the pinpricks of her anxiety spreading with her skin's exposure to the air. She threw the sleeves on the bed before moving to her corset lacing, her shaking fingers tugging them loose so she could pull the whole jacket and skirt over her head. She stood in nothing but her black, sleeveless undershirt and pants, having taken the risk to only come with one dagger tonight.

She peeked over her shoulder to find Zander standing a few feet away, his arm resting on the mantle of the fireplace. She smiled weakly. "Ready?"

His footsteps echoed in the silence as he came up behind her. "If you are."

She pulled in one more breath as she tugged up the back of her shirt to rest on the edge of her shoulders so he could see the entirety of her scarring without completely exposing herself. Her entire body shook, his gaze burning her as it moved slowly up and down. She winced as his fingertips grazed the numb, jagged skin wrapped around her entire back. She hated that her father had not only taken a piece of her mind, but a piece of her body too. He had to leave his mark everywhere, reminding her he would never truly be gone. Julian had made sure to do the exact same thing only a few months ago, their ghosts constantly haunting her waking and sleeping life. But she wouldn't let them have control over her.

Not anymore.

Seconds went by, her mind begging her to turn around and see his face, but she was stiff as a statue, just standing there for him to take in every inch. She didn't know if she should move or break the silence, but she had no idea what she would say.

At last, his arms snaked around her waist, pulling her close, his shirt scratching against her exposed back. He placed a gentle kiss on her bare shoulder, his fingers twisting in the extra fabric covering her stomach. "You are beautiful, no matter what marks your body."

Her weight collapsed against him, her shirt falling back into place as his body supported her, a rush of relief spreading through every muscle. She clutched at his arms, turning herself around to face him. His words were still written all over his face, eyes filled with desire and love. She raised her hand, gently grazing her cheek.

"Thank you," she whispered against his lips before planting a kiss on them.

"You can't scare me away, Ana," he mumbled, their lips still touching as he smirked against her. "So stop trying to."

She rested her forehead against his. "Alright."

A promise, she realized, she wouldn't have trouble keeping anymore.

Chapter Fifty

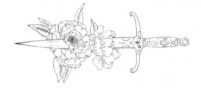

CHRISTIANA'S LIFE TURNED INTO A REPETITIVE style of training, meetings, and more training. It was all she could think about, all she could focus on: getting stronger, making herself ready for a duel she never expected to be part of. She refused to focus on the one question she couldn't help but ask herself: why her?

She had rushed to awaken that morning, Natalia barely able to keep up as they prepared her hair and daytime cosmetics before she expected Rowan, Dorina, and Zander to come by for breakfast. In the mirror, Christiana watched Natalia focus on the twisted updo she was creating.

"I need more pins," her maid grumbled.

"Here, let me get it." Christiana reached forward, her hand colliding with Natalia's as she grabbed for them as well. Natalia recoiled, her sharp pull knocking Christiana's lipsticks and a jar of perfume onto the floor, the bottle smashing against the stone.

"Oh, My Lady! I'm so sorry!" Natalia yelped as she knelt down, a cloth already in her hand to wipe up the spilled liquid.

"Natalia?" Christiana turned in her seat, looking down. "Are you alright?"

"Yes, I'm fine." A nervous chuckle escaped her lips. "I have no idea how you've kept me employed for so long, I can be such a clumsy soul some days."

"You don't seem it." Christiana stood, closing the gap between them. "Let me help you."

"I'm fine!" Natalia snapped, dropping the rag and standing up to look at Christiana. "I promise, My Lady, there is no need to concern yourself."

"Natalia." Christiana kept her voice calm, resting her hand on Natalia's upper arm. "I am concerned because I care about you. Please, I just want to help."

Natalia's face creased, her head hanging, tears beginning to well up in the corners of her jade eyes. "No one can help me. I'm too far gone."

"Alright, now you're scaring me." Christiana turned Natalia around, gently pressing on her shoulders to lower her to the dressing table bench. "Please, talk to me."

"It's so shameful," Natalia shook her head, her shoulders hunching over, shaking with each sob.

"I know it seems that way now, I know it seems easier to just let it keep happening," Christiana kneeled in front of her, grasping Natalia's cold fingers. "But you've seen my back, you must know what I went through growing up. You aren't alone in this, I can help you."

"But it isn't like that," Natalia stared at the ground, barely blinking. "I can—I don't know—it isn't easily explained!"

"Alright, alright," Christiana soothed, attempting to rub some warmth into her maid's long fingers. "Let me ask you this, then: does it have to do with Jay?"

A flash of fear grazed Natalia's eyes. She stiffened for a fleeting second before shaking her head furiously. "No."

"Are you sure?"

"Yes. It has nothing to do with him."

Christiana sighed, her gut twisting. She could tell Natalia was lying, there were just too many connections and concerns with Jay for him not to be involved. Christiana had believed her when she said they weren't romantically inclined, but there was something going on with them and she was determined to find out what it was so she could get Natalia to safety. "I just want to help you."

"No!" Natalia yelled, her hands yanking away from Christiana's to clutch her head. "You shouldn't want to help me! You shouldn't be kind to me!"

"Of course I should." Christiana's mind struggled to keep up, spiraling with each word Natalia spoke. "You have been my constant companion for five years now, why wouldn't I want to help you?"

"Because I've betrayed you!"

Christiana leaned back, frost snaking through her veins. "Excuse me?"

"I know who you are," Natalia blubbered, her face splotchy from crying. "You are the masked beauty he fought in the servant halls only a few nights ago, the assassin known as Midnight Maiden."

Christiana scurried away, her legs and skirts dragging against the floor as she recoiled from Natalia. She had heard those words before, she had seen them written on a piece of parchment meant to taunt her. "How do you know those words?"

Natalia looked up, her eyes brighter from the film of tears encasing them. "Because I was with him when he wrote the letter."

Christiana stood, her chest pounding, breath barely able to fill her lungs. The sensations pummeled her, crawling, itching, swirling, and dizzying, trying to take over. But she couldn't let them, not when answers were finally so close. She needed to push through.

With all her strength, she focused on the woman in front of her, trying her best not to collapse. "You know who the castle killer is?" Natalia nodded. Christiana took another step forward. "Who?"

"It's so much more complicated than any of you know." Natalia whimpered. "He won't stop until he gets what he wants."

"Who is it, Natalia?" Christiana urged, no longer thinking about how she could know about this or how she got involved. She just needed Natalia to say his name; she wanted to arrest the murderous man that haunted the palace.

"I can't tell you! He's too dangerous for anyone to stop. I've taken enough risks to try and stop him, but it hasn't worked. I can only imagine what he would do if he found out I told you the truth."

Christiana tried not to grunt in frustration. She knew who the person must be, her gut telling her Jay was somehow involved. Yet, there was no way she could arrest him without evidence or a formal accusation from Natalia's lips. Until she gave his name, Jay would be free to roam the halls.

The halls he had most likely been hunting for months now.

Christiana took a deep breath, lowering her voice. "We can keep you safe."

"I will never be safe!" Natalia screamed. "Don't you understand? The only way for you to keep me safe is to go to that duel and kill him before he can hurt anyone else!"

Christiana just stared at Natalia, who began muttering under her breath, her fingers tapping against her legs, eyes still wide, staring at the floor. Christiana couldn't understand what she was saying, but she did understand what Natalia was struggling to control. She had her own darkness lurking, a darkness that only came from years of abuse. It was deep-seeded, controlling her in ways Natalia didn't seem to understand. However, Christiana did, which is why she knew this was fruitless. There was no getting anything out of her while she was still so desperate to protect her abuser.

"Robert." Christiana called, her fists clutched to her sides, fingernails biting into the soft flesh of her palms in hopes of keeping her shaking legs from collapsing.

"Yes, My Lady?" He peeked in through the door, concern written on his face; he'd clearly overheard Natalia's last scream, at least.

"Please escort Natalia down to the dungeons." She turned to find his mouth gaping. "She is under arrest for treason and accessory to the murder of six women. And the attack on the Princess."

Robert hesitated for a moment, his brows furrowed, before moving into the room. "Y-yes, My Lady."

Her heart broke, her limbs numbing as she watched Robert yank Natalia up from the bench, his large hand grasping her upper arm as he walked her from the bedroom and through the common room. Natalia didn't even struggle, her steps matching Robert's, mutters still escaping her lips.

Christiana pushed against the fog, opening the front door for Robert; the pair walking out and down the hall, leaving Christiana half out of her doorway, staring at them.

She watched the past five years of companionship drift away with Robert and Natalia, her mind struggling to figure out what was truth and what had been deception.

Chapter Fifty-One

*C*HRISTIANA HAD NEVER FOUND A NEED TO GO deep into the palace dungeons until today. She walked down the dimly-lit stairs, the strong scent of mildew and stale air filling her senses. Her nose wrinkled as they made their way down the row of cells, only one occupied. The guard stopped them, handing over a lamp before leaving them alone with the cowering prisoner.

Natalia curled up in the corner, sweat clinging her raven-black hair to her face. Her cheeks were flushed with tear stains as they fell from her eyes onto the dirty stone floor. Christiana's chest tightened at the sight. She wanted to grab the key and release this woman she had known for five years—someone who had been a constant in her new life, who she planned to have next to her when she was Queen. But it seemed that might not come to pass like she once thought.

Christiana clutched the bars, anchoring herself to stand tall and look the regal part like she was supposed to. Zander stood next to her, bringing her the strength she needed to make it through the interrogation. Natalia pulled herself up on shaking legs to meet them, taking a few steps forward, her hands trembling as she reached for the bars. "I can't say anything else."

"Why not?" Christiana forced her voice to stay steady, full of power as she looked down on the trembling girl.

Natalia's jaw tensed slightly. "He will come for me."

"We can keep you safe." Zander's deep voice rumbled against the damp stone walls. "All we need is for you to give us his name. Confirm our suspicions and we will make sure he can't hurt you or anyone else."

"You don't get it!" Natalia shook her head, taking a few steps back from the door. "I'm never safe from him, no one is! He is a master at going unseen, at being the perfect servant and kindest person even though a beast lurks beneath the surface."

"Open the door," Christiana murmured to Zander.

"Are you sure?"

She didn't have time. She needed to get the real answers. "Yes."

Zander's eyes were grave as he nodded. He stuck the large key into the lock, twisting it with a loud groan and pulling the rusted metal gate open. Christiana walked in, determination surging within her as it clashed shut behind her.

"I get what you're feeling, you know I do." Christiana moved in front of the girl, eyes staring deeply into each other, noses barely grazing. "Just let me help you."

A moment passed before Natalia whispered back, "No."

She gripped Natalia's arms, her sleeves moist with sweat and water. "You know who I am, which means you know that the Maiden helps people like you. Like us."

"So what?" A fresh wave of tears escaped Natalia's eyes, every inch of her face full of pain as she tugged free of Christiana's grasp and collapsed to the floor.

"So, you know the lengths I'm willing to go to ensure people like him are stopped." Christiana crouched down, keeping herself eye level with her Lady's Maid. "I'll kill him for you, Natalia. Just tell me his name, and I'll make sure he pays for what he's done to you."

Darkness swept across Natalia's eyes, determination and desire swirling in the shadows. "You promise he won't survive your duel?"

"If we don't get him before that, I promise, I will make sure he doesn't live." She held out her hand. "My services are yours for free, if you just tell me his name."

Natalia stared at Christiana's outstretched hand, the silence thick between them. Christiana begged in her mind, pleaded that this would work. No matter what, this man wouldn't survive, she would make sure of it. If not for Natalia, then the six other women who perished at his hands. All Natalia had to do was give them the name Christiana already knew was the truth.

Natalia leaned forward, her clammy hand wrapping around Christiana's to seal their new deal.

"Who is it?" Christiana asked.

"It's Jay, but I know him as Joshua," she bit her lower lip. "Joshua Anders Yalaris."

Christiana's heart dropped. "Natalia Yalaris. Is he related to you?"

"Yes." She nodded, looking up with glassy eyes. "He's my older brother."

"We need to find him." Zander rushed out, his voice booming as he ordered guards to search every inch of the castle.

Christiana leaned forward, grabbing Natalia. "Is he after Zander? Is he going to kill him?"

"No." Natalia shook her head. "He's after you."

Christiana released her, staring at Natalia wide-eyed. "But why?"

"He wants revenge." Her fingers curled against the ground. "For what your father did to me."

"What are you talking about?" Christiana quaked as she slowly lifted herself up, the sound of Zander's footsteps echoing down the hall as he rejoined them.

"It was when I was just one of the house maids, before you promoted me." Her tale began, her eyes never leaving Christiana's. "I was sixteen years old and one of my jobs was dusting his office every night, usually after you went to sleep. Sometimes he would be there and make pleasant conversation. I always thought he was a kind master, until one night..."

"No," Christiana's stomach knotted, bile rising in her throat. She didn't want to hear this, to know the sins he committed against other people. She had enough proof of his crimes permanently marked across her back and mind. She imagined what happened to Natalia, and none of it was good.

"When he locked the door to his office and forced himself on me." She clutched at her body, trying to cover every inch of herself she could.

"No!" Christiana seethed. The door swung open, Zander barreling inside and pulling Christiana to his chest.

"My family disowned me after." Natalia pulled herself up again, leaning weakly against the wall. "Joshua came with me, to protect me, but he saw how much your father had hurt me, how deep the pain of my shame ran. I could barely function some days. He became so angry at your family, an anger that festered into desperation for revenge. He was determined to kill your father."

"But then the heart attack took him first," Christiana whispered, her hands still wrapped in Zander's doublet.

Natalia nodded. "He felt robbed, that your father deserved to suffer more."

"What does this have to do with Christiana?" Zander demanded.

"Joshua realized, if he couldn't kill my attacker for me, he could kill everything he worked so hard for in this life," She stared deep into Christiana's eyes. "You are his legacy, and Joshua is determined to end it."

"My father has been dead five years! Why now?" Christiana demanded.

"Joshua had me apply for your Lady's Maid position, so we would be close enough to kill you," she explained. "But soon into it, I found your poisons and your weapons. I quickly deduced that you must have been the one to kill your father. That you were training to become an assassin. There was no other reason to have all of those weapons and keep them hidden."

Christiana's veins filled with ice, paling as she realized just how long her secret had been exposed. She thought she had excelled at hiding herself, but it seemed she could have done better. Her head spun, face numb as she tried to swallow all of this new information.

"I told him he needed to stop. That you were too dangerous to go up against." Natalia shook her head. "But he wouldn't listen. He said if you were getting strong, he would get stronger. So, he started learning how to fight, too."

"This is insanity," Zander said.

"I know!" Natalia took a few steps forward. "My Lady, I soon realized how undeserving you were of his wrath. I looked into who you became, what the Maiden does. When I saw your scars for the first time, I realized you weren't protected from your father any more than I was. You felt his sins for so much longer than me. I tried hard after that to stop him, but he wouldn't listen."

"But why come here?" Zander questioned. "I hired him two weeks before Christiana even arrived at the palace for the summer!"

"He always wanted to be close to her, in case an opportunity to attack you came available, so he used some connections to find a job and that was the only one available." Her eyes were full of regret, her body shaking. "I did everything to keep him away from you. I lied, I locked your doors and pretended you had the key, I even gave him food poisoning sometimes to keep him from getting close. Please believe me, I started in this job to help him, but I stayed to protect you!"

"And you think that makes this alright?" Christiana snapped.

"Of course not!" she cried, "But it was all I could do! When you accepted the Prince's proposal, he became obsessed over it. Ranting and raving about how you didn't deserve to rule over people you could never protect since you couldn't even protect me. I would get barely-legible letters about how nothing you could ever do would be good enough, and he was going to prove it."

"That's why he started killing? All because he thinks I'm not going to be a good enough Queen?"

"I suppose. I barely understand it myself." She wiped her hand across her face. "I didn't even realize he had started killing until I got back here and heard the rumors. When I confronted him about it, he said that he was going to use all of his abilities to show you that you aren't the person you think you are. That you can't protect people from the evil of the world."

Christiana tried to piece it all together, her father's evil smile clouding her judgment. Would his specter ever stop tormenting her life?

"There's just one more thing that doesn't make sense. The killings started after you and I left to pack up my life and move it here." She narrowed her eyes at Natalia, "So how did he get access to Crimson Fire when you weren't here?"

"He needed a weapon, something to make you suffer." She lowered her chin to her chest, eyes squeezed shut. "While we were here over the summer, he forced me to give him answers, so I told him to check your cabin. I knew you still owned it after going through your papers."

"Oh, no," Christiana mumbled.

"What?" Zander whispered in her ear.

"Last summer, when I was frustrated with Julian's case, I needed to keep my hands busy. So, I brewed an extra vial and kept it stored there as backup." She wished she could punch something or break an object, but nothing was in sight. "I can't believe this! Your brother is the one who broke into my cabin last summer?"

"Yes." Natalia nodded.

She would never forget that day; she had been so desperate and upset about the purgatory poison being ruined, she hadn't even thought to double check her arsenal, to make sure her vials were all in place.

"And Body Lock?" Zander growled. "How did he get his hands on a Virian weapon?"

"He stole it from a soldier after he heard a few guards talking about it."

"No wonder he had his daggers treated with it," Christiana whispered. "Unlike Crimson Fire, he had better access to use it more liberally."

"He became so angry after that night," Natalia said. "When he realized he was so close to ending you, until the other assassin got in the way. That's why he set the challenge, he realized how distracted he got with the other women."

"You betrayed me," Christiana whispered, staring at Natalia.

"I'm so sorry, My Lady!" she cried. "I never meant to hurt you. I promise."

Christiana bit back another sharp accusation. Natalia may have been a part of the assassination attempt, but she was a victim like Christiana, too. She couldn't let her anger out; she had suffered enough at the hands of her family, she wouldn't include herself in that list.

Christiana stood tall, clutching at Zander's arm for stability. "We made a deal, one that I promise to keep, but I cannot promise that we will be gracious on your fate. Many women have died because you refused to come forward and tell us about Jay."

"I know," Natalia nodded, sinking back down and curling herself up into a ball. "I don't deserve any kindness for the sins I've committed."

Christiana backed away to the cell entrance. "I will let you know when our bargain is complete. Until then, you will stay in this cell while you await trial."

Natalia nodded. "Yes, My Lady."

Christiana gave one last look to Natalia before slamming the cell door shut and rushing from the dungeon hall.

Chapter Fifty-Two

*T*HE WALK BACK TO HER APARTMENT BARELY
registered as Zander led her down every hallway, up
every staircase, and through her door. Every inch of her
was collapsing from the inside out, pieces falling as she tried to process
exactly what just happened.

Marek was there when they returned, rising when they entered.
"What is going on? Robert told me I should come by and check on you."

Christiana still clung to Zander as she faced him. "It's Natalia.
She's helping the killer."

"How? Why?" Marek rushed to her, his arms supporting her other
side as the two men led her to sit at one of her dining chairs.

"To help him get vengeance on his real victim...me." She looked
up. "It's her brother, and he wants to kill me."

"Did you take the life of someone he loves? A past victim?"

"Technically," Zander mumbled. Marek's brow furrowed.

Christiana took a deep breath and explained everything to Marek, down to every detail of Jay's intended vengeance on her family. The words tasted like acid on her tongue, her stomach retching at every syllable spoken. After everything Francis had put her through during his life, somehow, he still found a way to torture her in death. She thought she hated him before, but to know what he did to others outside of her family, she wished she could bring him back to life just to kill him again. As many deaths as it took to get revenge for all his victims.

Marek's face was as white as a sheet when she spoke the last detail, his body tense. "What now?"

"All the guards are searching for Jay," Zander began. "But I fear if they haven't found him now, he already got out somehow. I'm waiting for someone to confirm it."

"I had Robert go to check the cottage." Christiana rubbed her forehead, her hands shaking, her anxiety taking full control as she began to crumble under the pressure.

"Christiana, you're shaking." Zander touched her head.

"I just...I want..." Christiana stammered, trying to put words together. "I just want to lie down. I need to calm down."

The darkness crept into her mind and soul, trying to bury it under the rubble of what was once her life. Everything she had built over the last five years, everyone she had helped, could be taken from her in an instant. The strength of the Maiden—who not only saved her clients, but had saved Christiana—might not be able to save her this time.

She was in a haze as Zander offered his hand. She stood and walked with him to the bedroom, collapsing on top of her bed, fully clothed. She was shutting down and she didn't know how to bring herself back. She had been working so hard for months to regain control of her body, to take back what Julian had stolen, but she wasn't sure she had the strength to try anymore. All she wanted to do was give up.

"I'll be right back." Marek's voice sounded rushed, his footsteps fading away as a door slammed.

Zander looked down at her, brushing her hair away from her face. "What do you need? How can I help?"

"Lie with me," she whispered, her arms snaking around to clutch her pillow close to her body. "Just hold me, please."

She didn't always like having people touch her—in fact, she rarely did when she was having a panic attack—yet something about this moment, this betrayal and hurt, made her wonder if she needed help banishing the darkness. For all she knew, she would push Zander off her the moment he touched her, but she wanted to try. She wanted to see if it would help.

The bed sank down, his arms snaking around her body and pulling her into the warmth of his. "I'm right here, love, and I'm not letting go."

His nose nuzzled into her hair and gentle kisses trailed along her neck, his soothing presence enveloping every inch of her. She felt his strength, and he was trying to give it to her. She saw the light peek through the darkness, her mind gaining a thread of clarity as she pulled in deep breaths of cedarwood scent, her hands gripping Zander's arms around her.

After some time, Marek returned, a tray of tea in his hand as he put it down on her bedside table. "Drink." He handed her a cup.

She narrowed her eyes at it. "What's in there?"

"A wonderful combination of green tea and peppermint." He gave her a stern stare. "No drugs, I promise."

She sat up before taking the teacup, the cooling scent of the peppermint filling her nose. She took small sips, testing the liquid before finally allowing herself to consume it. Each warm swallow filled her chest, a deep breath following. Her mind was ridding itself of the clouds, not because she used a coping skill, but because she used the strength of the ones who loved her.

She hadn't realized how much she needed them.

A new set of footsteps came from the front room, heavy against the floor as her bedroom door opened and Robert arrived.

"Anything?" Christiana asked.

"He wasn't there." He shook his head, his face grim as he approached. "According to the guards I passed, he was able to escape on a caravan of kitchen workers going into town to pick up some extra supplies needed for the wedding."

"Damnit," Zander muttered. "I can't believe he was able to sneak away."

Robert looked down at Christiana. "I found this on the kitchen table at the cottage. I believe it was meant for you."

He held out an envelope, deep black ink scrawled on the front with the words *Midnight Maiden*. Christiana's stomach lurched at the sight. He had been in her house—invaded it. If he could get in there, where else in her life had he touched?

She took the letter, ripping it open and pulling out the piece of parchment. She took in a shaking breath as she read it out loud.

Dear Midnight Maiden,

I see you finally discovered the truth of who your father really was and what he did to destroy everyone in his path. He didn't deserve to live, which you seemed to agree with by taking his life before I could. But what we do disagree on, dear Maiden, is the way you killed him. That vile man deserved to suffer, and you chose to give him a peaceful death. Something I don't intend to give you.

Your father may have answered for the crimes he committed against you, but he never answered for the crime against my sister, a woman you claim as a friend. So, since he is no longer around to answer, it seems his heir must take his place. I plan to ruin everything he worked for by cutting it down from its roots so it can never grow back. The root of that legacy is you.

I still expect to see you at our duel next week. Natalia may be imprisoned, but I have plenty of evidence against you that I can release if I am captured. If you choose not to come, just know, the killings won't stop. I may not be able to get back into the castle, but there are plenty of villages in the area with young girls ripe for the taking. As their future Queen, only you hold the power to save their lives.

I look forward to meeting you face to face again soon. Until then, I hope you rest well. This will be a fight you will never forget.

Sincerely,

Joshua Anders Yalaris

"It's all starting to make sense now." A tear slipped from Christiana's eyes, dripping onto the crumbled paper in her hand and bleeding the black ink. "How he was able to avoid the guards when dumping victims, how he was able to compile evidence against me, and even why he chose his victims."

"How do you relate to them?" Marek kneeled in front of her.

"The markings on their backs." Zander looked at her, rubbing his wrinkled forehead. "He made them look like yours. He was fixated on you."

"He's gone insane. Had a psychotic break of some kind when you two got engaged and you were gaining more power," Robert murmured. "He's let his desire for vengeance twist him into something...horrific."

"You can't go." Zander shook his head. "Not when he is so desperate to kill you."

"Of course I'm still going." Christiana turned to him, her heart steady. "You heard him. If I don't show up, he'll keep killing. Besides, I made a promise to Natalia. I gave her the Maiden's services to kill him, and I intend to keep that promise."

"But we know his identity now!" Zander stood. "We can send out guards and search for him. He won't be able to hide forever."

"And how many women have to die before you find him?" She challenged, her hands crushing the letter. "He hid in literal plain sight inside the palace walls. How long do you think he'll survive in the freedom of the country?"

Zander's lips pulled into a thin line. "I can't lose you. I won't survive if I lose you."

"Then you need to trust I can survive the fight," she whispered, pulling his hands up to kiss his knuckles. "So many women have lost their lives because of me. I can't let any more die because I want to protect my own life. I'd never be able to live with myself."

"Then let us send guards to capture him," Robert offered. Clearly they were not going to let her go until they exhausted every possible option, but Christiana already knew the only option.

"Do you really think he doesn't have an escape plan?" She scanned all three of them. "Besides, the amount of incriminating evidence against me and Marek in that house, along with what he apparently has stashed away somewhere safe? We may get him, but we risk my exposure in the process."

"That's probably why he chose there," Marek grumbled. "He knew she would protect the secret."

"Exactly." She wasn't shaking anymore, her mind clear of all fog. She was sure of what she needed to do. She knew it was the only way. "I have to face him. I have to right this wrong."

"Why do you feel responsible for this?" Zander clutched her arms.

"Natalia was raped because of my father, and all those women killed at the hands of Joshua because of that one night." She grabbed Zander's face. "But he's right, my father didn't answer for the other crimes he committed. Natalia didn't get retribution like I did, and like you said before, she's a victim too."

"So, you're willing to die?"

"I'm willing to fight. My father wasn't her only abuser. Joshua has taken advantage of her for far too long and tortured her for years over his twisted vengeance. I need to put a stop to it. It's the only way to make up for what my father did to her."

Silence fell. The air shifted in the room; they were finally starting to understand. There was only one path forward, and that was through taking Joshua's life.

"We've known about this fight for a month," she added. "You've all worked hard to train me and get me as ready as I can be for this. Let's not put that effort to waste."

"Alright." Zander nodded, placing a kiss on her cheek. "We'll do it your way."

"But just because you are going to fight him," Marek stepped forward, "doesn't mean you go in without a plan."

"Oh, I can never forget the first rule you taught me." She smirked at him, his eyes lighting up briefly at her words.

"I promised to protect you with my life," Robert shifted closer, the three men surrounding her in a protective cocoon. "What can I do to assist?"

Christiana smiled. Thanks to them, she would never feel alone again.

Chapter Fifty-Three

*T*HE DAY FINALLY ARRIVED FOR CHRISTIANA TO face Jay. She woke as if it was any other day, as if she wouldn't be fighting for her life in a few hours, and got up to spend the early morning in a last training session with Zander and Robert—the two of them pushing her as far as possible without exhausting her. She would need all her energy tonight if she was to have a chance.

The walk back to her room afterward was quiet, her arm tightly secured in the crook of Zander's. She didn't know what to say, so she just let the comfort of their silence wash over every inch of her. She was still trying to decipher her flooding emotions, still deciding if she was prepared for all possible outcomes for tonight.

"I have something for you," Zander said as he stopped them in front of her door. He pulled an envelope from his bag, the contents thick, almost bursting at the seams. "I was planning to give this to you on our wedding day, but seeing what is going to happen tonight, I felt

I should give it to you now."

"What is it?"

He smiled at her. "The surprise I told you about all those weeks ago. The one Marek was helping me with."

Christiana took the package, ready to tear into it. "No not yet," Zander said, his hand stopping hers. "Open it an hour or two before you leave and read every detail."

She nodded. "Alright."

"I promise you that no matter what, the contents of that envelope will come to pass." He stared deep into her eyes, his resolve strong. Whatever was in her hand, it was something dear to his heart, she could tell. "Know that this never would have happened without you."

Christiana furrowed her brow. "I love you, Zander."

"I love you too, Ana." He kissed her once more, a gentle whisper on her lips as a reminder of what would always connect them. He smiled one last time before disappearing down the hall, leaving Christiana dazed as she pushed open her own door.

***

Christiana's entire body twitched, her insides scrambling as she walked to her family's apartment. In only a few hours, she would be astride Willow, rushing off to a fight that she was unsure she would survive. But she had determination in her mind and bravery laced through her heart. She had reasons to fight, people to fight for—though that didn't stop the darkness from attempting to taint her mind and bleed into her. She used every ounce of her strength to push it back, to keep it away from forethought. If she let it take control, she had no chance of winning, and she had to win.

Yet even with that in mind, she couldn't leave without saying goodbye, without seeing her family one last time. No matter how many times she told herself she could defeat Jay, there was still a piece of her that needed this, for her own peace of mind.

She rapped her knuckles against the door, internally pleading with herself to keep her composure during this.

"Ana!" Isabelle exclaimed as she yanked the door open, her eyes wide as she pulled Christiana into a hug. "I missed you!"

Christiana's heart tightened as she kissed her sister's forehead. "I saw you yesterday, Belle."

"I know." Isabelle dragged Christiana into the apartment. "Still, it's so odd to be in the same place as you and still not see you every day."

"I get it." Christiana squeezed Isabelle's hand, refusing to let it go. "Where is Mother?"

"She's with the dressmaker for her final fitting!" Isabelle jumped on the balls of her feet. "I just finished trying on mine and it's perfect!"

Christiana chuckled. "Even though it's navy?"

"Yes, even then." Isabelle stuck her tongue out, her face pinching inward. "For you and your wedding, I can suffer through looking like I'm at a funeral."

Christiana's neck tightened, her breath smothered in her chest as she dragged in air through her nostrils. She was trying not to think about the wedding, the happiest day of her life slated to arrive in two weeks. She couldn't focus on it, or else her heart would shatter and so would her resolve. All that mattered was tonight and what she would face at midnight. But her heart ached as she wondered if she would be walking down the aisle or if she would be carried in a casket.

"Hello, darling!" Maria said from the bedroom doorway, a bright smile spreading across her face as she strode through the room, adjusting the bodice of her turquoise silk dress. Christiana had no idea what came over her as she strode across the room to her mother and wrapped her arms around her torso and pulled her close, just as she used to when she was a little girl. Maria hesitated for a moment before circling her arms around her waist, hugging her tightly as Christiana dropped her cheek to her mother's shoulder.

"Ana," Maria mumbled into Christiana's hair. "Darling, what's wrong?"

"Nothing." Tears burned in her eyes as she forced them not to fall. She didn't want them to worry about her, or think that she was about to do something life-threateningly dangerous. She just wanted to hold them one more time, give them one more kiss and tell them how much she loved them. After everything they had been through over the past few years, it was the only thing she wanted to do. She had been through so much with her mother, years of pain and unanswered heartbreak finally revealed and open between them. They were rebuilding their relationship, refusing to let Francis have control over them anymore and keep a wall of pain between them.

And now Joshua was threatening to take it all away from her.

"Ana..."

"Nothing, really." Christiana straightened, a fake smile plastered across her face. "With the wedding in only two weeks, I was overwhelmed and just needed to see you."

Maria's face lit up, her eyes sparkling as she grazed Christiana's cheek. "Oh, Ana, everything is going to be just wonderful, you'll see. Zander will make sure of it."

Christiana's cheek twitched. "I know, I know."

"And we'll help, too!" Isabelle bounced over, linking her arm with Christiana's. "That's why we're here, after all."

"I know, little one." She squeezed her sister's arm. "I'm so lucky to have you both, no matter what."

Silence fell for a moment, Christiana's gaze falling to the floor as she felt Maria's eyes linger, grazing up and down her form. There was nothing more to say except one more thing.

"I love you, Mother." She looked up, collapsing internally as Maria's face softened. "Just please know that no matter what's happened in our past, I forgive you."

She couldn't leave with that kind of stain on her mind; it would be one of her biggest regrets. Her mother deserved forgiveness, even after the years of secrets. Maria had done what she thought was right in the moment, what she thought would keep them safe. Christiana couldn't fault her mother for trying to protect them.

"Thank you," Maria said, tears escaping down her cheek as she pulled her daughters to her. "We love you, Ana."

She relished in the moment for a brief second before turning to Isabelle. "I love you, too, little one."

Christiana wrapped her arms around them both, trying to forget that this could be the final time she ever did.

Chapter Fifty-Four

*C*HRISTIANA STARED AT THE LARGE ENVELOPE. She was already dressed, ready to leave for the cottage, yet she still had one more promise to keep before she did.

She didn't know why she was struggling to open it, but something about its overstuffed contents made her stomach flip one too many times. She forced her hands forward, pulling the heavy paper to her and ripping it open. She had expected a long, beautiful letter, but as she sifted through the dozen pieces of parchment, she realized it was far from that.

Her heart sped up as she absorbed the information. Zander's words were persuasive, every piece of research well-thought-out and detailed. Christiana had no idea how long he had been working on this, but she could feel the passion in every line. His love for her bled through the ink as if he had infused his own blood into it before letting it dry on the page. A tear slipped from her eye as she placed the final piece of parchment back on the stack.

She had many words to describe what was in front of her. A miracle, a lifesaver, or a beautiful tribute. Every inch of her coursed with love, her arms aching to wrap around Zander and show him just how elated this spectacular present made her.

***

Christiana should have headed right to the stables to gather Willow, the hour growing late as her time ticked by before she was expected to meet Joshua in the ring, but she couldn't leave without saying goodbye. This wasn't like her fight with Julian, when her heart and mind were fortified with strength. This fight was different; her strength was crumbling. Although she had come far over the past few months of healing, it might not be far enough for her to win in a fight.

She crept quickly and quietly through the palace gardens toward the back. She had asked him to meet her in the one place that would always be theirs, that no one could ever take away from them. The night sky shadowed the willow as Christiana approached it, the moonlight casting a halo glow around the protective branches that feathered down and around the trunk. She pushed them aside as she entered its protective embrace to find Zander already there, his back leaning against the trunk with his arms crossed.

Christiana and Zander just stared at each other for a moment, the envelope he had gifted her clutched against her chest.

"I see you've read it." He gave her a weak smile, sending her heart leaping. "So?"

"Zander..." was all she could say before throwing herself into his arms, the only place she wanted to be right now.

He pulled away slightly, the biggest smile plastered on his face. "You liked it, then?"

"I can't believe you did this." She handed the envelope back to him. "You're going to build shelters around Viri for the abused. You're going to give them somewhere safe to go."

"I haven't stopped thinking about what we could have done better to help you and your family when Maria came for help. It's time we show Viri we no longer stand for that behavior. We aren't on the side of the powerful, we are on the side of the victim, and we will stand by them to the end."

Christiana curled herself back into his arms, forgetting about everything that had happened this past week and what was about to happen. Thoughts of Jay, Natalia, Julian, and her father dissipated, releasing her for just a brief moment. For once, she wasn't thinking only days ahead, but years. Thinking about the possibilities of what she could do for this country made her shake.

She didn't want to go anymore.

"I'm scared," she whispered into his chest.

"I'm going to ask you one more time." He pulled away, clutching her face in his hands. "Don't go."

"I have to." She pressed their foreheads together. "Just...have a little faith."

"I do." He chuckled hoarsely. "Please don't doubt that. I believe in you, I have faith in you. I just don't want to lose you."

Christiana's chest swelled at his words. He had faith in her, believed in the strength that was hidden deep within her. She stared into his eyes and saw his fears swirling, the idea of losing her already hurting him. She didn't want to—she wished she didn't have to do this—but she had a responsibility. Too many people had perished at Jay's hands, all because of her family's secrets. She could live with the pain her past inflicted on her every day, but now that it was hurting others—she had to put a stop to it.

She took a deep breath as she leaned forward, trapping his lips with hers. She wrapped her arms around his torso and pulled him close, pressing herself against him as they stumbled backward, Zander flipping them around so her back was pressed against the trunk. His heat swept over her, the flames wrapping her in a comforting embrace as he kissed her back. She felt every bit of his love and adoration for her in that kiss, filling her heart to the brim with something to fight for.

She kissed back with just as much passion and love, showing him exactly what he meant to her, but she also gave him something else in that intimate moment. As their lips connected, as their bond burned brighter, she handed him a promise. A promise to fight with all her strength so she could return to the future they were destined to live together. They had plans for this country, and she would use every last bit of her strength to bring them to fruition.

She shivered as his tongue danced against her lips, a slight moan escaping her when she gave into the pleasure of his touch. She didn't want this moment to end, clutching his black linen shirt as she danced her tongue with his, tasting the smoky whiskey lingering on his tongue. Everything disappeared around her, the willow, their responsibilities, and the impending fight. There was only him, his love and the desire he brought to her. She was out of control in that moment, and for once she reveled in every second of it.

She finally released his lips, their foreheads touching as they breathed heavily. "If you wanted to make this goodbye memorable," he laughed, "you certainly succeeded."

"I needed to leave you wanting more," she teased, letting out a shaky breath. "Let you see just how wonderful our wedding night will be."

"I'm happy to see you still have hope." He brushed a piece of hair from her face, his featherlight touch dancing across her cheek.

She smiled at him. "I found something new to fight for...a new purpose. I'm not going to let a deranged man run mad with vengeance take it all away from me."

"Good." He rolled his forehead against hers, his teeth gently nipping her earlobe. "I will call you my wife one day, I know this with all I am."

"Just as I will call you husband."

She wrapped her hand behind his neck, her fingers tangled in his soft curls. She didn't want to let go, every inch of her begging her to stay in the safety of his embrace. He had spent the last few months giving her all his strength whenever she needed it, but it could only go so far. She needed to do this on her own; she needed to tap into her own strength buried somewhere inside her.

She was about to fight for her life, to face a man and answer for her father's sins. She might not survive, but if she didn't have reasons to live before, it seemed she did now. Her heart burned with a new fire, a wildfire, and it would take a monsoon to put out the last ember.

Chapter Fifty-Five

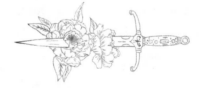

THE NIGHT AIR STILL HELD THE BITTER CHILL AS
the winter season began to bleed into spring. Silence
surrounded Christiana as she rode Willow up to her
stable. She had always felt her strongest at night, when the moonlight
reflected off her skin and the still air filled her lungs. She pulled it in
through her nose, calm flooding her body. She could do this, all she
had to do was find her strength.

She was not broken. She was a survivor.

She tied Willow up before walking slowly to the ring. Since it was
a duel, she didn't want to be weighed down by unnecessary things,
keeping it to her sword strapped across her back, her dagger sheathed
in her boot, and a few throwing knives strapped around her thigh. The
grass crunched under her as she approached, hopping over the side to
wait for her opponent to arrive. She looked up at the moon, sitting
silently at the highest point: the midnight hour was officially upon her.

"Glad to see you showed up," a deep tenor voice came from

behind her.

Christiana whipped around to face a tall figure standing just a few inches away. He was covered head to toe in black, his long coat reaching the ground and clasping up his chest with half a dozen buckles strapped tightly. His hood cast a shadow over his face, a long veil covering the bottom half just as hers did. She couldn't help but notice that his outfit looked like the male version of hers.

A shiver ran up her spine; this couldn't be a coincidence.

"You didn't give me much choice." Christiana kept her voice steady, refusing to lower it as she typically did when she was behind the mask. "So, are you ready?"

"First things first." He pulled out two rags, throwing one to her. "We watch each other wipe down every last blade we carry."

Christiana's stomach lurched. "Why?"

"I know your moves, Christiana, just as you felt mine." A smirk hung in his voice. "An honorable duel is completed with clean blades. No poison."

Christiana let out a low growl. There went her first backup plan. "The last word I would relate to a murderer is honor."

"I could say the same about an assassin."

She watched him with a hard gaze, his hands slowly rubbing the cloth up and down his long sword, down to the hilt and pommel. He was proving to her that no poison would be left behind. She let out a sigh as she pulled her own sword out, mimicking his actions.

Minutes passed as they cleaned each blade, her heart aching with each drop of Midnight that absorbed into the cloth. She sheathed her last knife and threw the soiled cloth over the side of the ring. "Now can we get this over with?" Her anxiety was crawling up her spine; she wanted this to end.

"Patience." He mocked, walking heavily toward her in the center. "I've been waiting for this moment for five years, I'm going to enjoy every single second."

They stared into each other's eyes, the only part exposed. His deep hazel irises swirled with hatred and bloodlust, every inch of him tense. He wasn't that much taller than her, but she hoped that his bulk was from his thick coat and not years of training.

"If you are so set on killing me," she said, refusing to back down as she balled her fists at her sides, "then why don't you stop being a coward and show me your face?"

His eyes narrowed. "You first," he growled, ripping her hood back. She let him, his grip tight as he yanked her veil down, exposing her.

"Your turn." She didn't give him a chance to answer, grasping the thick fabric and exposing his face. He looked like Natalia in some ways now that she knew to look for it—the sharp cheekbones and raven black hair—but his full, plump lips and hazel eyes set him apart.

She sneered at him, her blood already beginning to simmer. Her twitching fingers wanted to grip the hilt of a blade.

She was ready to fight this man.

"If you win today, you stop the killings." She knew she couldn't trust his words, but something deep in her stomach propelled her to remind him anyway. "That is the deal."

"Of course." He smirked down at her, every inch of his face twisted with a vile desire for blood. "You were the only person I ever wanted. Well, your father first, but you beat me to that, didn't you?"

"You have no idea why I killed my father." She pulled her sword from her back, the blade glinting in the moonlight as she began to circle the ring.

Joshua fell in step as he pulled his own blade. "Don't I? Natalia told me how he must have abused you, scarred your body into a mangled mess. Did you like the artwork I put on my victims? It was an ode to you."

"They didn't deserve to die," Christiana snarled, her knuckles turning white around the hilt. "None of them deserved the disgusting things you did to them."

Joshua shrugged. "No more than you deserve the titles you are about to receive. You are no protector, you are no Queen. You are nothing more than a weak woman whose thirst for power will be her doom."

"Be quiet." The words rumbled from deep within her chest.

He scowled at her. "I am prepared to protect our country from the truth I know about you: you are your father's daughter."

"Don't compare me to that man!" Fueled with fury, she threw the first blow, their swords clanging together in the empty night. He pushed her off with such force she stumbled back, catching her footing quickly.

"Why not?" He tilted his head to the side, face full of amusement. "You have a hunger for power and no shame in hurting people. When I look into those raging gray eyes, all I see is him."

"It's not my fault I have my father's eyes." She threw a few more strikes, but he blocked every one of her moves. "Stop acting like you knew him."

"But I did." His smile contorted cruelly. "You didn't know I worked on one of your landholdings as a farmhand? I met your father many times when he came for his collection visits."

Her face twitched; her father had always been ruthless when collecting debts. That, combined with what he did to Natalia...no wonder Joshua saw the monster hidden within Francis. "He doesn't matter anymore, he's dead."

"True, but I can take what he loved most, and that was his legacy." His eyes turned dark. "Which means taking away the person destined to carry it on."

He loosed a loud cry like a man running into war as he charged her. His anger pushed against her sword as she held him back, her footwork quicker than his so she kept him at a distance. She pushed forward, keeping Zander's smile in her mind, reminding her what she was fighting for.

She was fighting for a better future.

She pushed herself forward, using her speed as an advantage, forcing him to keep up with her attacks. She had hoped to tire him out quicker, but he seemed immune to the strain, his face never betraying him as he blocked each jab of her sword. She needed to find a weakness, but every inch of him was tense with muscle and determination.

It didn't matter, she wouldn't stop until he was dead and this whole ordeal was behind them. She wanted to win, and she had a better purpose than he did—but it snuffed out the minute he began laughing, a wicked grin of pleasure stretched across his lips while he watched her move. It was a flash, a brief one, but that was all it took. Just one small sight of his haunting face, and Julian's icy eyes filled her mind. She forced herself to forget, bringing Zander's last words back to her, repeating them over and over.

She wanted it to be enough, but it wasn't.

The trembling at the tips of her fingers begged to be released. She tightened her grip around the sword, trying her best to hold on as Joshua took the offensive. She didn't want it to end this way—for him to win not because he was a better fighter but because her symptoms took control—but it was too late. Her fingers ached, the muscles tensing in every inch of her hand.

She screamed in agony as her blade fell from her hands.

Joshua swung his blade above his head, giving her just enough time to pull out her dagger and block the sword. It felt as if the weight would break her blade like a twig, but it was enough to push him off. The dagger shook in her grip, but she forced herself to keep a hold of it. He swung at her a few more times, her quick feet keeping the sharp edges from making contact with her body. She blocked one more time, pushing his sword off to the side, giving her the perfect opening to punch him hard in the nose.

When he screamed in pain, she took the opportunity to slam her elbow into his wrist, knocking his sword from his grasp. He stumbled back, blood already pouring from his crooked nose, and drew his own dagger.

The fight was far from over, but at least she was able to bring the match back to an even playing field.

But it didn't matter, because as he resumed his attacks, her hand grew weaker with trembling. It didn't take long for him to send her dagger flying; she reached for one of her knives, but he was quicker, grasping her jacket tightly, pulling her toward him and slamming her down onto the ground, the wind escaping her lungs at the impact. He climbed on top of her, her eyes coming back into focus to find his dagger looming over her.

"Say hello to your father for me," he whispered, plunging the dagger downward.

Instinct kicked in, her hands wrapping around his wrists and pushing upward with all her strength, the dagger hovering inches above her chest. She wished she was strong enough to push him off, but this was inevitable. Her hands would give out soon enough, releasing the dagger to pierce her chest and stop her heart.

She wished she could have spent one more night with Zander, curled up on his couch drinking a glass of whiskey. She wished she could have told Dorina all her secrets. She wished she could have seen her mother and sister, given them one last kiss. She wished she could have seen all the people who made up her family, both chosen and unchosen. As she stared at the sharp tip of her murderer's weapon, she said goodbye to all of them, catching the reflection of Francis and Julian in the shining blade as they welcomed her to the afterlife.

I was not broken, I was a survivor...

Her final thought before her wrists collapsed.

Everything happened quickly: the piercing of the chest, the dripping of the blood, and the guttural cries of pain. It was exactly how Christiana had imagined it.

Almost.

But instead of her screams filling the air, Joshua howled like a wolf, the dagger in his hand falling next to her shaking body. She looked up to see the pointed end of an arrow peeking from the center of his chest, the shaft and fletching sticking proudly out of his back.

She gasped as she watched him choke, his own blood spilling from his lips, spewing across her face. He collapsed next to her, chest-down, bleeding out across the ring.

Christiana's entire body shook, unable to lift herself from the ground. She wanted to run, to get as far away as possible from the man who had been so set on killing her, but her strength was gone. Staying in the exact same spot, she listened to a new set of footsteps approaching.

"My Lady?" Robert's concerned face loomed over her as he knelt, lifting her body into his arms, resting her against his chest. "Are you alright?"

"Ro-Robert..." she stuttered, her mind reeling. "What are you...what are you doing here?"

"I made a vow to you. And I never break my promises."

She clutched herself against him, the adrenaline starting to wear off as hot tears fell from her eyes. "Thank you," she whispered against him, his hard leather armor rough against her sweaty cheek.

"Did you really expect us to just let you go into a fight without backup? Think again."

She let out a laugh through the waves of emotions crashing into her weakened body. "I'm glad for once the three of you decided to ignore my wishes."

"We figured." He brushed her tears from her face. "I'm so sorry I didn't get here sooner. I knew I had to give you a head start. I didn't want to risk Joshua seeing me before the fight began and running. I needed to make sure I arrived after the battle started."

"It doesn't matter, all that does is that you made it in time."

"We shouldn't linger." He stood up, reaching down toward her. She took a deep breath, sitting up and reaching back for his hand, to be pulled up and to go home. To start her new life.

"Christiana!" Robert yelled.

Searing pain attacked her whole body, engulfing her. She gasped for air, hunching forward toward the center of the pain, shaking as she turned to look beside her. Joshua half-leaned against her, his face caked in mud and blood, eyes gleaming with wicked delight.

"I—I win..." he breathed into her ear before slumping against her. She stared at him, mouth gaping, as the last bit of light left his eyes, leaving behind nothing but the dull hatred that would haunt his corpse forever.

Robert loomed behind him, a bloody dagger in his hand. Christiana didn't know what to do, what to feel or what to say. So she screamed.

She screamed until the world went black.

Chapter Fifty-Six

HRISTIANA WOKE UP AS THE SUN WAS RISING, her body and mind weighed down like lead that filled every inch of her. She let out a deep, painful groan as she tried to pull herself upright, her right side screaming with blinding, all-encompassing pain. The memories from the duel flooded her mind, sending her stomach lurching. She choked on air, her throat constricting around the dry-heaving gags.

"Ana? Are you alright?" Zander was at her side immediately, his presence startling her as she fought to control her empty stomach. His hair stuck up in different directions, his pants and doublet rumpled. He sat on the edge of the bed next to her, his hand rubbing soothing circles up and down her spine as she gasped for air.

After a few minutes, her stomach settled, her breathing labored as she gulped down air, her body collapsing back against her pillows. "Wha—what is going...where..."

Zander collapsed to his knees, his head falling to the edge of the bed. "Thank goodness you woke up."

"Zander, what is...what..." She stuttered over her words, trying to make sense of everything. She was in her room, in pain; the sun was in the sky and her fiancé was sobbing next to her. Her last memory, she was bleeding next to a dead body in the middle of the night with Robert's hand outstretched to take her home.

Nothing made sense, nothing was connected. Her memories and reality were jumbled, leaving her dizzy and desperate for answers.

"Zander what happened?" she croaked, her voice cracking over every syllable.

"You lost so much blood..." he lifted his head, his eyes red-rimmed and glassy, staring at her in awe. "You were so pale and barely breathing when Robert carried you into Rowan's room. We didn't... Ana, we didn't..."

"Joshua stabbed me." The memory flooded back to her. "I almost...Zander, I almost..." She couldn't say the word out loud, but she thought it over and over.

Died. She had almost died.

She had walked into that fight knowing it was a possibility, that Joshua was stronger than her and that her Battled Brain symptoms were still not completely under control; yet her mind and body still felt disconnected as she tried to swallow that truth. It didn't seem real, not after everything she had been through. How could a man already on the brink of death almost bring her down?

"So, what...what happened?" She tried to pull herself together, to focus on the facts. If she knew the facts, then she could absorb the shock better.

"Robert did field medicine before rushing you back here to Rowan," Zander reached for her hand, her fingers tingling as he gripped them. "He can tell you all the technical aspects of what he did to save your life."

She furrowed her brows, looking over at him. "I've been unconscious all night?"

"Ana, you've been unconscious for three days."

"What?" she whispered.

And then the sobbing took over.

She couldn't control the tears, her body shaking so much it ached all over from her injury. She let it all out, the reality that she had been on the brink of death. That the ones who loved her, who had stood by her for years, had to wait an agonizing three days for her to wake up. She could have died because of one man's frantic need for revenge and her desperate need to help people.

She could have *died*.

Minutes passed before she controlled the sobs, her breath shaking. "Have you been here the whole time?"

"Did you expect me to leave you?" His brow furrowed, his grip on her hand tightening. "I needed to be here when you woke up."

"But where did you sleep?" Her cheeks burned, wondering if she had just shared her bed for the first time with her future husband and didn't even remember it.

"The floor, love. I took some extra blankets and pillows from your closet."

"You could have at least slept on the couch in the common area," she mumbled, hiding her flaming face behind her bed-tousled hair. "It would have been more comfortable."

"I wasn't leaving your side." He wiped a few tears from his face. "Besides, Robert and Rowan took up too much space out there."

She shook her head, a slow throbbing settling behind her eyes as she wiped her hand over her face. She should be more surprised that they'd all refused to leave, but she knew them too well. She dropped her hand, her fuzzy eyes finally adjusting to the morning light. "Are they still out there?"

Zander chuckled, nodding. "Yes, of course. Marek would be here too if he could, but our families have been in and out the entire time, he didn't want to risk it. He's been coming to check on you overnight when it's just the three of us."

"Always the practical one."

Zander smiled at her, leaning back on his haunches as if to stand. "I should go get them. Rowan will want to examine you."

"Wait." Her shaking hand clutched his, tugging him back toward her. Her chest tightened as he leaned his head next to hers, their foreheads barely grazing. His eyes filmed over with tears, as she reached out to caress his cheek. "Oh, Zander. I'm so sorry." A tear of her own slipped from her eye. "I'm sorry for what I put you through."

"I know why you did it." He kissed at her palm, his words muffled. "I get it, Ana, I do."

"I made her a promise, Zander. What he did..." Christiana's mind flooded with the memory of Natalia's delicate, beautiful face twisted and contorted in fear, her jade eyes wide as tears pooled in them. Every inch of her body ached, not because of her injury. "I couldn't break that promise."

"I know, love, I do." His fingers raked up her arm, his knuckles gliding over the thin fabric of her nightgown. "But the truth is, you should never have been there in the first place."

"Zander..."

"Ana, listen," he said firmly, pulling himself up to sit on the edge of her bed. "You knew when you left that I still didn't want you to go. We can't change that fact. However, that's not what's important. What's important is that you woke up and that you're alive. What we focus on now is getting you better."

Her hand fell from his face, landing limply against his shoulder where he caught it in his own grasp. "I'm sorry. I was just sick of feeling useless and unnecessary."

"You aren't useless." He shifted toward her, one leg hanging off the bedside to support half of his weight. "But you weren't ready for that, you're still mentally healing."

"Physically now, too."

"Ana, please." He grabbed both her hands. "Please, promise me you'll be more careful from now on. I can't...these past three days have been almost unbearable for me, watching you struggle between life and death. I won't be able to survive with myself if something happens to you. I need you to be safe. Viri needs you to stay safe, it needs you as its Queen just as much as I do."

Her lips trembled as she looked up into his eyes, tears rolling down his cheeks. In the past, she would never care about her own safety, just the safety of others; but for the first time, she realized how much her safety affected Zander. Her own recklessness could have caused him so much agony, and she had barely given it a second thought.

"I promise." She leaned forward, grazing her lips against his. "I won't fight again, not until I'm actually ready."

His sigh of relief brushed across her skin. "Thank you, love. Thank you so much."

She kissed him again, his hand wrapping around to cradle her neck as she sealed her new promise.

***

Christiana lay in her bed while the three men surrounded her, Rowan checking her pulse, breathing, and wound, Zander lying next to her on top of her covers, and Robert standing at the foot of the bed, rigid and ready to intercept anyone who arrived.

"Now will someone tell me what I missed for three days?" Christiana moaned as Rowan helped her lean back after replacing the bandage that wrapped around her hips to cover the wound on the lower right side of her back, just above her pelvis.

"We were ready to leave, I thought my bolt had killed Joshua, but..." Robert cleared his throat, "apparently he had a few breaths left in him, because when we went to move away, he pulled one of his daggers and stabbed you in the back."

"Yes, that I vaguely remember. But what happened after you got me back here? Did anyone see me?"

Rowan shook his head. "No, Robert brought you straight to me and we were able to get you out of your clothes and into a riding jacket while I triaged the wound before moving you down to the infirmary to operate."

"Operate?" Christiana's heart sped up, her breath hitching.

"You had internal damage from the knife, we needed to go in and make sure none of your organs were damaged," Rowan said calmly, stroking her arm. "Luckily, he was so weak from his own mortal wound that the knife didn't make it deep enough, and his aim was too low. We were able to get the bleeding under control and stitch you up. You were in the infirmary for about a day before we moved you back here."

"So how long will my recovery be?" Christiana pulled herself up a bit. "I'll be strong enough for the wedding, right?"

"Ana, we already postponed that," Zander said, smoothing back her hair.

"No," she shook her head, more tears welling up. "No, we're getting married in two weeks."

He leaned forward, placing a kiss on her temple. "It's fine."

"No, it isn't." She hated how her voice cracked yet again, but she couldn't seem to stop. "I want to marry you."

"And you will," he smiled down at her. "When you are strong enough to enjoy every moment of it."

"It will take about two months for you to heal," Rowan said. "You'll be on bedrest for a time, but luckily the location of the wound won't hinder any major movements. As long as you follow my instructions, there's no reason why you can't dance at your wedding this summer."

Christiana took a few moments, closing her eyes and filtering through the mountain of information they had just given her. She was healing, she was safe, and if she followed physician orders, she would still be able to marry Zander. Her life was not over, just slowing down for the time being. Then it could go back to normal.

She opened her eyes again when the vise on her throat loosened, thinking of one last question to ask. "Where are all of my weapons and my jacket?" The three men looked between themselves, guilt written over their faces. "You kept them safe and away from everyone, right?"

"We hid your weapons in my room," Rowan said. "I've kept them safe, but we didn't have an opportunity to move them."

"And my jacket?"

"Ana, you were bleeding out when you got back here, we had to act quickly and get you ready to move to the infirmary." Rowan looked down, taking a deep breath. "But I didn't have the time to try and wrestle you out of the jacket and it was already soaked in blood and ripped from the stab wound. So..."

"So?"

"I had to cut you out of it." Rowan bit his lip. "I'm so sorry, it was shredded by the time I got it off you."

"It's ruined?"

"We needed to make sure the cover story we would feed people would be as solid as possible," Robert added. "Which meant tying up as many loose ends and destroying as much evidence as possible. We all agreed, Marek included...burning it was the best way to keep you safe."

She choked, the pressuring building in her chest, her skin flushing with heat. Her coat was burned, thrown on the flames before she could see it one last time, feel the lacings through her fingers and the surge of power that zipped through her every time she put it on.

"I'm so sorry, love," Zander whispered in her ear.

"Marek already sent out to the person he commissioned it from." Robert patted her quilt-covered foot. "It should be here in a matter of weeks and look exactly the same as the last one."

But that coat had been a gift from Marek years ago, when she was ready to become the Maiden. She had dressed in it for her first solo job, where she had met Robert. She had worn it countless times in front of Zander, where she finally allowed herself to be open to love. She had become herself with that jacket wrapped around her.

It had been her armor. It had been her strength. And it had been stripped away in a moment.

"It's fine." Christiana looked at them all, finally able to hold back the tears, trying to give them a weary smile. "It's all going to be fine."

She stared at the ceiling, knowing that the Maiden was still a part of her and would never leave her no matter what. But though she kept reminding herself that, a pang in her heart tried to tell her that it would never be the same again.

Chapter Fifty-Seven

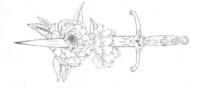

TWO WEEKS PASSED, THE PALACE STILL ABUZZ with the lies they had been fed. Everyone believed that Christiana and Robert had been on their way home from visiting one of her tenants when Jay ambushed them, catching her off guard and hurting her before Robert took him down. With his dying breath, he'd admitted that he had killed Julian, setting him off on a killing spree he couldn't stop. No one knew the truth, no one knew his real motives...exactly how they needed it to be. The gossip was spreading like wildfire, everyone talking about the relief that their lives were once again safe in the palace walls—as if nobles had been the victims, not the poor servants they forced to keep working during that terrible time.

Christiana tried to forget what happened, to remind herself that she was once again safe, but it didn't seem to work. The tremor was back with a vengeance, all the hard work over the past few months wasted after yet another brush with death. She couldn't help but wonder if her past would ever stop haunting her or if she was doomed to carry their ghosts for the rest of her life. She could just imagine the specters of Francis, Julian, and now Joshua constantly by her side, standing next to her as if they were rulers, too. She could only hope one day she would learn to ignore them.

She wasn't going to let that stop her, though; she wouldn't let it keep her from living her life. Not anymore.

Christiana and Zander had made decisions after her fight with Joshua that she knew were for the best. It had led them to answers and revelations they were eager to bring out in the open. At least, to one person in particular.

"Are you sure you're ready for this?" Zander asked as Christiana's temporary maid answered the knock at the front door.

"I am," she nodded, her back supported by pillows propped against her headboard. "We can't wait any longer."

They clasped hands, Zander standing tall next to her as her bedroom door burst open and Lucian stormed inside, stopping at the end of her bed. "Did you invite me to gloat about the fact that your valet was the one killing people, or that her maid was assisting him?" He looked at them, eyes dark, a smug smirk on his face. "I must say, very well done at hiring your staff."

"Be quiet, Father," Zander growled. "I don't think you have a leg to stand on when it comes to judging character."

Lucian glowered, bracing his hands on the footboard. "How dare you talk to me like that. I have always put this country and its people as my top priority."

Zander shook his head. "I've learned plenty over the past few weeks, a lot of pieces of information you have chosen to keep a secret. Our poverty levels, the amount of crimes that are received yet never see the light of day in a trial, and of course, let's not forget the excess taxes you've been applying to the population to help fund the *peace talks* you are so proud of."

"You don't know what you're talking about."

"Oh, you think so?" Zander took a few steps forward. "Tell me, Father, how would the people react if they learned the way you actually made so many countries stop trying to invade us was because you bribed them?"

Zander's research in Julian's office and his need to discover the truth about his father had been a fruitful endeavor. It seemed that when Lucian told the country that it was military strength and his diplomacy skills that stopped the wars, it was an outright lie. All the treaties he signed came with hefty amounts of money owed to the other countries, some debts Lucian was still paying off—and bankrupting Viri because of it.

Lucian's fingers curled, the color draining from his face. "How did you learn all of that?"

"Your precious Chancellor kept a record of everything," Zander said. "By the look on your face, I will take that as you didn't know about his many, many journals?"

"No." Lucian gritted his teeth. "He never mentioned those."

"Which leads me to assume a majority of the council is unaware of this as well?"

"You don't understand." Lucian shook his head. "When you are a King, you have to make the toughest decisions. Sometimes, you have to let go of things for the better of others."

"Is that what you told yourself when you found out about my family?" Christiana leaned forward, his head slowly turning toward her.

She hadn't been sure going into this if she would be ready to say the truth out loud to him. She knew he was aware, and the terrible decision he had made because of it, yet that didn't make it easier to talk about it with him. However, she and Zander had both agreed it was time. Lucian was able to get away with his ignorant treachery because no one had tried to fight back.

It was time to stop.

"That was none of my business," he muttered.

"It was completely your business!" Christiana yelled, the pressure pushing against her wound, forcing a grunt from her lips. "You are my King! You made a promise to protect every person in Viri, and that included me! So tell me the truth, why didn't you stop my father?"

"I don't see what the point of me telling you could be." He lowered his gaze, his cheek twitching.

Christiana balled her fists at her sides. "I have a right to know what my life was worth to you." She knew the answer, but she wanted to hear it from his mouth. She wanted him to confirm it. She needed it.

"Your father was one of the few nobles who helped to keep the balance of our wealth from breaking," He looked her up and down. "I could not risk all of that by taking away his power and giving it to an uneducated thirteen-year-old."

"And if I had been a boy?" Christiana challenged. "If I had been a thirteen-year-old boy, would you have made the same decision?"

Lucian just glowered at her, shaking slightly. Christiana snorted a laugh, not even a little disappointed, because it was the exact reaction she expected.

"The only reason I am not taking this evidence to the Council to force you to abdicate is because I know I am not ready to be King yet," Zander said. "Especially since Christiana isn't prepared to be Queen, thanks to you barring her from meetings. However, that stops today."

Lucian's face was hard as carved stone, his eyes dull as he turned to his son. "What exactly do you want?"

Zander smiled, Christiana linking their hands together, her stomach fluttering at his triumph. Not only had Zander found his voice, he had learned to use it for what he believed in.

Chapter Fifty-Eight

CHRISTIANA WAS SICK OF BEING STUCK IN BED, A whole month rushing past with minimal opportunities to move outside her room. Every muscle crawled, her body begging her to get out and move. Rowan told her she needed at least one more week before he would allow it, and it was taking every ounce of her self-control not to disobey him.

A soft knock came at her door late one restless night, Marek sneaking inside before anyone could see him. "Hello, dear one."

"Are you coming to say goodbye?" Christiana asked.

"Not quite," he smirked, sitting on the edge of her bed and pulling her into a hug. He was wearing a simple velvet black doublet, creme linen shirt and black pants with matching black boots; not the typical outfit for a stablehand. "Your dear fiancé gave me a gift."

He handed her a folded piece of parchment, her eyes narrow as she opened it to read the contents. She gasped. "He's promoted you to his new valet?"

"He had the opening, and he said after working with someone who turned out to be a traitor, he needed someone in the position he knew he could trust." Marek ran his fingers through his newly-cropped hair. "Besides, he wants his next valet to have my...particular background with espionage."

"Why would he need that?" Christiana collapsed back against her pillows.

"He said it could be useful." He leaned against the bedpost. "With all the truths he's learned about his father the past few months, he wants to make sure he surrounds himself with people who will help him always find the truth. Apparently, I'm one of them."

Christiana's mind was spinning. "This is insanity."

"Of course, we had to forge a few more documents to make it seem I am completely qualified for this job, along with making sure his father didn't recognize me at all now that I will be around him much more often," Marek said. "However, we did a quick test where I served lunch to the two of them, and the King barely even looked at me. We both think it's safe."

Christiana's heart swelled. Zander had outdone himself yet again. "Are you sure? After everything you've been through with the crown over the years?"

"It's going to be a little odd, coming back fully after fifteen years away. However, being back here, working on the case and with you, reminded me what I loved about my time in the military. Feeling like I have a greater purpose again made me feel a part of myself that died when I apparently did. It seems this may be a way to gain it back again."

"So, you're staying?"

"I am."

Christiana had never seen Marek smile so brightly, but she could hardly blame him—his life back to a familiar place Christiana always had wondered if he missed more than he let on. Apparently, he did.

She looked down at her hands, her fingers mindlessly twisting her engagement ring. "It's going to be so odd seeing you almost every day again."

"A good odd, I hope?"

"Oh, a wonderful one," Christiana chuckled. "I'm just going to have to get used to the fact that you'll be serving me some days."

"Well, Zander also guessed that I would be interested in staying around to be closer to you." He smiled. "Which brings me back to the fact that I came to check in on you."

Christiana frowned; she wasn't ready to start discussing it. "I'm fine."

"I know you're lying."

"My wound is healing!" She threw up her arms. "Ask Rowan."

"I'm not talking about your physical wound."

She shook her head, swallowing a lump in her throat. "I had worked so hard to banish Julian. But the duel put me right back to the beginning. I'm unsure if I will ever regain the control."

Marek pondered in silence for several moments before he said, "May I ask you something?"

"Of course."

"Why are you so determined to keep your life as the Maiden? You're about to take on so many new titles, first wife then Queen of Viri. Why is holding on to her so important when your life is obviously turning in a different direction?"

"You just don't get it," she whispered, her voice cracking. "Midnight Maiden isn't just some assassin who helps the abused. She saved me from myself when all I wanted to do was drown in my symptoms. If I gave her up, I would lose all of that."

"Do you really believe that?" his words were sharp, as if his tongue were the tip of a dagger.

Christiana nodded. "Yes, I do."

"If that's what you believe," he leaned forward, shaking his head, "then you have learned nothing since I started teaching you."

Christiana's eyes widened. "Excuse me?"

"I told you all of those years ago, the only person who can help you is yourself." He took hold of her arms and forced her to look at him. "The Maiden is not your savior, just as I wasn't five years ago. Your strength will always be inside you, you just need to find it again."

His words swirled in her mind, a thought she had refused to think. She had spent the past three years convinced that Maiden had given her the determination to overcome her Battled Brain. She had taught Christiana strength and gave her a confidence she never had as a child. She had given her so much; was she really willing to part with it, even if that strength Marek spoke of still lived within her?

"Just think on this," he took her attention back. "Your Battled Brain returned after a traumatic incident as the Maiden. Did you ever think that your progress gaining back your control may have been inhibited by your desperation to keep hold of her?"

Her veins ran cold at his words, wishing with every inch of her he hadn't spoken them out loud. It was a thought she didn't want in her head, festering in her beliefs and polluting them with such dangerous ideas. Maiden was her strength, so how could she be holding Christiana back from healing again?

Chapter Fifty-Nine

*C*HRISTIANA'S FOOT TAPPED AGAINST THE EDGE OF
the bed as she stared up at Rowan, his face pensive while
he continued with his examination.

"Just tell me!" She blurted out.

He chuckled. "You are the most exasperating patient I have ever
treated," He pressed a few more times against the swollen, red scar on
her back, an aching groan escaping her lips.

"I just want to know if I can finally get out of this bed! Please give
me some good news."

He stood up straight, crossing his arms, and stared down at her
with a worried look for a few seconds before dissolving in laughter.
"You're off bedrest."

"Yes!" Christiana threw her hands in the air, instantly regretting
it from the stretch on her wound.

"I said off bedrest, but you still need to keep strenuous activities
to a minimum," Rowan warned. "I'll check on you a day or two before

the wedding to clear you for dancing."

"Alright." Christiana watched him pack up his medical bag. "Now that I'm relatively better, can I finally talk to you about something besides my health?"

He looked over his shoulder, one eyebrow raised. "I suppose."

"Dorina," Christiana smiled sweetly, and Rowan dropped his head with a groan. "I'm sure Zander told you the good news."

"Yes." Rowan nodded, collapsing beside her on the bed. "He did, and I am unbelievably happy for her."

During the hours of negotiation about the plan for Lucian's final year of power, Zander had brought up Dorina—and how Lucian would no longer use her as a bargaining tool in negotiations. He had secured the rights to Dorina's marriage, and they had very eagerly given them back to her the moment Lucian signed a contract stating that fact. The excitement on Zander's face while he watched Dorina read the contract had been equal parts adorable and sweet.

"So?" she nudged his shoulder with hers. "Why haven't you told her how you feel yet?"

"Ana..." he groaned.

"Well, you said the reason you didn't was because of Lucian, and now that obstacle is gone!" She had been waiting weeks for Dorina to burst into her room with the news that her and Rowan decided to start courting. She felt like she was about to burst out of her skin each time she saw her friend and wasn't able to say anything.

Rowan and Dorina deserved their happiness together. She wanted to celebrate that.

"What do you remember about our courtship?" he said. "About the life we could have had."

She let out a deep breath, tilting her head. "A quiet, simple life following the paths we love. That's what you promised."

"Exactly. That's all I wanted. I don't want to give up medicine or living with my family on my estate, being a father and a partner. I don't know if I could have that as a Prince Consort."

Christiana grasped Rowan's hand. "Do you still love her?"

He chuckled. "Yes, I do."

"Then why are you holding back the truth from her?"

"Sometimes love isn't enough," Rowan whispered, staring at the ground. "I'm not saying that's what's happening here, but I suppose only time will tell."

"You sound scared."

"Maybe I am," Rowan looked over to her, smiling. "I think that just means I'm not ready to be the partner she deserves. Maybe one day I will be, but not now."

"I'm not giving up hope," Christiana teased.

"Neither am I," he winked, standing up. "I'm just going to give her time. She wants to find a purpose, and I already have mine. Maybe one day, those purposes will collide, but right now they are meant to stay apart. My soul is settled on that decision."

"Coward," she kicked him playfully with her bare foot.

He laughed, leaning forward to place a kiss on her forehead. "Maybe, but I can live with that. For now, at least."

He gave her one more smile before leaving the room—one full of hope.

***

Now that she was cleared to walk, Christiana had one more place to go that day, one more person to visit.

She turned down the hall parallel to the Royal Wing, the quiet space muffling her footsteps on the dark green carpet. Her back was aching, but she didn't care when she caught sight of Elaine's dark hair a few feet ahead of her, her pulse picking up as she approached.

"Thank you so much for meeting me," Christiana smiled. A part of her wanted to lean in for a hug, ready to pull closer to Elaine, yet she held back, her skin tingling. She wasn't sure what was shifting between them, but it was certainly new.

Elaine gave a weary smile in return. "You said you needed help with something?"

"I do," Christiana nodded, pulling a key from her dress pocket and opening the door in front of them. She pushed it wide, gesturing for Elaine to enter first.

The apartment was set up similar to her own, but with less customized touches. The furniture was the traditional maroon color, the walls bare of décor and half the furniture covered in a layer of dust from disuse. Elaine turned, her eyes narrowing. "Why are we here?"

"These apartments are for nobility who have joined the Royal Household. This specific apartment is for you."

"But I'm not a part of the Royal Household."

"That's the point," Christiana took a step forward, leaning against the table for support. "I want you to be. I want to make you my head Lady-In-Waiting."

Elaine's bright cornflower eyes widened, her posture stiffening. "You—what? Why? You barely know me."

"I barely know any woman at this court besides Dorina, and it isn't proper for me to ask her." Christiana pulled out one of the dining room chairs and let out a deep breath as she sat down, Elaine taking up the one across from her. "My Lady-In-Waiting is my key to the court, she is my right-hand woman who will help me through everything and anything when it comes to hosting and planning and being the Queen. She will need to be willing to help me make tough decisions and not afraid to tell people what to do when things need to get done. You seem like the perfect candidate for that."

Elaine tapped her fingers on the table, her eyes downcast. "Many people find me too abrasive for such a high-esteemed position."

"And I find many people intolerable to be around." Christiana shrugged. "I think that makes us well matched."

"Christiana, you don't have to do this," Elaine said. "I don't like being pitied."

"It's not pity, Elaine. I need someone like you, someone who is honest." Christiana leaned forward, her wound aching, but she pushed through it. "I don't need someone who will fluff my ego to stay on my good side. I need someone who isn't afraid to be blunt and candid when needed. We may have not always gotten along, but one thing I know about you is you're never afraid to speak your opinion."

Elaine chuckled. "My father tells me it's my worst trait."

"Well, I'm here to tell you that, like in many things, he is wrong." Christiana shook her head. "I need that, I want that, and that's why you're the perfect choice."

"He will never allow it." Elaine shook her head, her curls falling over her shoulder. "He wants me ready to marry when the highest bidder comes along."

"It isn't his decision to make," Christiana smiled, "and neither will your future marriage be, if you decide to take the position."

This was one of the many reasons Christiana wanted to offer this to Elaine. When members joined the Royal Household, they became loyal above all else to their job—making their marriage, if not already bound, the responsibility of the crown. After their talk with the King, keeping Elaine's marriage their responsibility wouldn't be difficult.

Her father was an obvious tyrant who saw his daughter not as a human but a game piece. She didn't deserve the treatment, she didn't deserve what he put her through, and Christiana was determined to give Elaine her life back. Just as she had done many times as the Maiden, she could now do as a Queen.

"You know mine and Zander's stance on arranged marriages." Christiana grasped Elaine's hands. "You know we would never make you marry anyone you didn't want. You could find someone you love and marry them. As long as you are happy, that is what we would support."

Elaine's lip quivered, her eyes glossing over. "You don't have to do that."

"I know you aren't used to accepting help. I know it feels like you should be able to do this on your own." Christiana swallowed a lump in her throat. "But don't let that stop you from doing what is right for you. What you need to feel better and be who you want to be."

Silence fell between them, Elaine's eyes not focusing on anything. Christiana hoped she wasn't pushing too far, that she wasn't being too much for what Elaine needed. However, she could never live with herself if she didn't make the offer, even push a little. She needed someone to push her all those years ago, when Marek gave her a reason to fight again.

Elaine deserved the courtesy. She had earned it tenfold.

Elaine tapped her fingers a few more times before sitting up straight, her old, smug smile returning to her lips. "I don't do politics, you can leave that with Zander."

Christiana chuckled. "Fair enough."

"But events..." she nodded mockingly, pondering the idea. "Events, I think you could use my help with."

"Well, then," Christiana stood, pushing the key across the table. "This is yours. Expect your contract in a few days for you to review. Do you need me to talk to your father?"

Christiana knew the fear that coursed through the veins at disappointing an abuser, at making them feel powerless. You never knew what reaction you would get, but you always assumed the worst. Standing up for yourself was the hardest part, and if Elaine wasn't ready, Christiana would be there to help.

However, a gleam reflected through Elaine's eyes at the challenge. "No, leave him to me."

Chapter Sixty

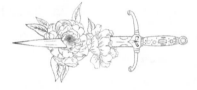

HE WEDDING WEEK WAS FINALLY UPON THEM, and yet Christiana still didn't settle. Marek's words ran on a constant loop in her mind, through welcoming guests back to the palace, her final dress fitting, and smiling with each gift that arrived at her apartment.

But she wasn't smiling on the inside. Deep in her soul, the struggle brewed and raged, forcing her to face facts she didn't want to. She tried to ignore it the day before as the final details were put into place, while both families enjoyed a big celebratory feast. As the night quieted down, she found herself in her common room with Dorina, the fire crackling while they indulged in cups of steaming tea and double chocolate tartlets. They were celebrating the end of Christiana's recovery, the final day before the wedding, and a moment for just the two of them.

"How are you feeling?" Dorina propped her arm on the back of the couch, her fingers curling into her hair to hold her head up.

"Nervous?"

"No, I don't think so." Christiana nuzzled deeper into the couch, her nightgown and robe already secured, a blanket wrapped around her lap. "I feel...settled? Eager? In awe? Honestly, I have no idea what this is."

"Happiness, Christiana." Dorina nudged her shoulder. "I think it all can be summed up with happiness."

She wasn't used to using that word when it came to her life, the idea of the unknown usually making her anxiety spike in terrible ways. And there were unknowns...there always would be. She didn't know what to do with her life, or what choices would be best for her to move forward. Yet when she thought of just Zander and the plans they had for their future together, as partners, as lovers, and as leaders, she could not stop herself from feeling it.

Peace. Happiness. Excitement.

"I think you're right." She took another sip of her tea, the rim of the glass hiding her smile.

"Thanks to you and Zander, maybe now I have a chance at feeling that as well, the night before my future wedding," Dorina teased. Christiana's heart warmed, her hopes still that Dorina and Rowan might one day find the happiness together that they deserved.

Dorina leaned forward, placing her cup on the table before standing up and walking over to the dining area. Christiana's eyes trailed her, watching her go for the tray that held an additional teapot, stopping a few feet shy of where it sat.

"What is this?" Dorina asked, staring at the dozens of papers Christiana had left haphazardly on the table.

"Oh." Christiana stood, keeping the blanket wrapped around her shoulders as she moved to stand next to Dorina. "It's a project Zander and I are working on. I should probably put it away for the next few days, but I had a few ideas I needed to put down first."

Zander had given the envelope back to Christiana while she was still on bedrest and told her to make as many notes as possible, go through all of his plans with a fine-toothed comb to make sure they were not only perfect to convince the council, but perfect to show the country how they planned to protect them going forward as well.

"You two plan to build shelters?" Dorina looked up at Christiana, awe glistening in her russet eyes.

"Yes." Christiana's cheeks warmed. "It was Zander's idea, but it's something I've wanted to figure out for a while."

"This..." Dorina shook her head, her fingers grazing over the scattering of parchment. "This is what I am jealous of. This is what I want."

"Hordes of work?" Christiana joked, pulling the blanket tighter around her. "Mountains of paperwork to read through?"

"No." Dorina laughed, looking up at Christiana. "Purpose. You know your purpose and you're going after it."

Christiana's breath caught in her throat, her mind stumbling for a moment for words. All she had strived for the past five years was to follow her purpose, and it had always been to help others. She had done that through the Maiden for so long, a way of bringing strength to a country that didn't always share it. She had found a piece of herself through it all. Yet it seemed her purpose was starting to shift in a new way.

"Do you think it will be enough?" she asked. "Do you think the people will feel protected with me as their Queen?"

Dorina wrapped her arms around Christiana's shoulders, their heads close together. "You make me feel protected every day. Why would you give any less to the people?"

"You're my best friend," Christiana sniffled. "Of course I want you to feel protected, you matter to me."

"Well, when you become Queen, will the people matter to you?"

Christiana nodded, her heartbeat settling. "Yes. More than anything, I want them to feel safe with me."

"That's how I know it will be enough." Dorina squeezed her tightly. "When you decide to care about someone, you protect them with a ferocity that rivals any foe. The people will see that, and my gut tells me they're going to love you for it."

A tear slipped from Christiana's eye. "Thank you."

"Of course." Dorina kissed her temple. "Now, I should probably leave so you can get some sleep."

Christiana snorted. "I'll certainly try my best."

Dorina gave her one last wave before she let herself out, the door clicking shut behind her, leaving Christiana alone with just her thoughts for the first time in what felt like days. She took a deep breath as she let them run free—a dangerous thing to do some days, but her gut told her it was what she needed to find an answer that would settle her heart.

Marek had been so insistent that her strength wasn't as connected to Maiden as she always believed. Maybe it was mere coincidence that the first time she felt the true surge of power, the control over who she was, just happened to be under that hood and mask. But Christiana didn't believe in coincidences, she believed in Marek's lessons. It was obvious he was trying to teach her a final one before she headed off to a new life. She just wondered if she could follow through on accepting it.

She stared at the papers, at the different yet still impactful way she could carry out her purpose. A new place to find resolve, to give strength. It was all in front of her; all she had to do was give herself over to it fully.

She looked up, noticing the tray of tea and pastries again. She stared at the contents, only a few tarts left and the teapot most likely cold from sitting out for so long. Looking at them, she found a spark of an idea buried deep in her mind, a crazy one that might be impossible to accomplish.

But if she could find a way, if she could bring it to reality, it might just be what she needed to move on from her life as the Midnight Maiden.

Chapter Sixty-One

I T WAS VERY EARLY IN THE MORNING, THE SKY still dark as Christiana peeked out her window from her seat at her dining table. It was officially her wedding day. In just a couple more hours, she would be walking down the aisle, binding herself to the man she loved. She expected to find herself struggling to sleep the night before, but she didn't expect it to be for this reason. She should be so elated, her body didn't want to go to sleep; instead, her mind was running rampant, her stomach in knots as she tried to figure out what she needed to do to help herself.

She had been brainstorming and writing all night, every little detail that she would need to make this work. It flooded out of her, a surge of inspiration propelling her hand as she watched every piece of the plan unfold in front of her. She dropped her quill, the ink still wet as she reread everything she'd just written. It was one of the best plans she had ever concocted. A smirk settled on her face as she looked up at the mantel clock to see it claiming the early hour.

Zander would still be asleep, but this couldn't wait.

She ran to her bedroom and picked up the first robe and slippers she found, wrapping the thick damask fabric around her as she rushed out the door. Her footsteps fell lightly, trying not to wake anyone else as she knocked on his door. A few minutes passed before it fell open, revealing his face.

"Christiana?" Zander's eyes were still half-asleep, his face etched with exhaustion as he squinted at her. "Are you alright?"

"I need to talk to you about something." She clutched her notebook to her chest, her thick robe keeping her warm as she moved inside, the large hearth unlit in the common area.

"Alright." He closed the door. "Come into my bedroom, the fire is lit in there."

She followed him in silence, concern etched on his face as he sat them down at the leather chairs situated in front of the window, the warm fire filling the room with comfort. "What's wrong, Ana?"

"I've been thinking a lot since...my incident with Jay." Christiana took a deep breath. She hoped Zander understood what she was about to say. "After talking to Marek, I realized something that I have to do, something that I think will help me overcome my Battled Brain symptoms and control them again."

"What is it?" Zander leaned forward, his hands grasping Christiana's.

"I need to give up being Maiden."

She couldn't believe those words had just left her lips, but the settling of her stomach showed her just how needed they really were. She needed to move on. She needed to heal.

She watched Zander's face, the many emotions passing across it. "Are you sure?"

"Marek made a point, something I couldn't stop thinking about." She furrowed her brow, thinking of the countless hours she had pored over those words in her head. "My Battled Brain symptoms returned because of a new trauma I experienced as the Maiden."

"I never thought about that," Zander whispered, his grip tightening around her fingers.

"I thought about it for a long time." She forced herself not to cry; this wasn't the time to mourn the Maiden. "I can't figure out a way to move forward with my healing if I'm so desperate to hold on to the thing that got me hurt in the first place. That's no way to live, especially when I'm trying to start a life with you."

He stroked her cheek lightly with his thumb. "I understand why you're doing it, and I can't say I'm not a little happy that you've decided to take yourself out of danger. I'll be here to support you throughout the whole transition. Whatever you need from me."

"I know you will." She bit her bottom lip. "But I need you to know that I'm not making this decision because you want me to retire. I'm making it for myself and no one else."

He smiled, squeezing her hand. "I know that."

"Alright, good." She took a deep breath, trying to find the right words to explain her new plan. "I still believe that Viri needs the Maiden, though. There are too many people out there depending on her for her to just disappear into oblivion."

His brow creased. "Then how are you going to do both?"

"I have an idea about that. I'm not sure if you're going to like it, but I think it's the best way for all of us to find a solution."

She detailed everything out to him, his eyes widening slowly as he listened, his mouth gaping when she suggested exactly what needed to be done. Once she finished, she felt winded, her heart pumping as she waited for him to break out of his shock.

He blinked a few times. "Are you sure?"

Christiana nodded. "We need someone who will believe in Maiden's code. Someone who will listen to me. Can you think of anyone better?"

"No," he sighed, leaning back in his chair. "Do you think she'll agree?"

"I'm not sure. But we won't know until we ask."

He sighed heavily, smiling as he shook his head. "What do you need me to do?"

She smiled back, giving him a deep kiss on the lips. As the sun rose to welcome their wedding day, Christiana and Zander began to plot their next plan.

***

This was the last place Christiana expected to spend time on her wedding day. She was unsure if this plan would succeed, but if they could convince her to say yes, it might just be the answer to the future she and Zander wanted.

Natalia was in the same cell where Christiana saw her last, her black prisoner dress ragged and caked with dirt from too many days of wear. She huddled in the fetal position in the back corner, her eyes half closed.

Christiana knocked against the bars to wake her up. "Good morning, Natalia."

"My Lady?" she groaned, her head rolling side to side as she came into consciousness. When her eyes finally opened, they locked with Christiana's, her head snapping upright as she stood on shaking legs. "What are you doing here?"

"I'm here to make a deal with you." Christiana laced her arms through the bars, hanging over into the cell as she stared Natalia down. She knew what she had to do. She knew it was best for all three of them.

"But isn't today your—?"

"Our wedding day?" Christiana's eyebrow rose. "It is."

"Then why are you here?" Natalia pulled herself forward, her shoulders hunched as she moved into the light.

Christiana smirked. "This couldn't wait. Zander and I have talked it over, and we have an offer for you."

"I don't deserve any mercy or your kindness." Natalia lowered her head, silent tears slipping down her cheeks. Clearly she had been crying for weeks, yet she still had tears to shed.

"I never said a kindness, I said an offer." Christiana's heart pounded; she desperately needed this plan to work.

Beside her, Zander interjected, "You have two choices: you can stay in prison and serve out a life sentence..."

"Or," Christiana interrupted, "you can agree to be the next Midnight Maiden."

"Become an assassin?" Natalia's brow furrowed as she approached the bars, her thin fingers curling around the thick metal pipes.

"Yes."

Natalia pushed herself against the bars, her acrid breath warm against Christiana's face. "You want me to help people like me?"

"People like *us*."

"Why me?"

Christiana sighed. "I took back the strength my father stole from me with the help of the Maiden. I think she can help you find the strength my father and your brother took from you."

"I'm not a fighter."

"But you can learn," Christiana cut her off. "I had a tutor teach me everything I know, and he's willing to teach you, too."

"I have the ability to...hide some of the evidence against you." Zander leaned against the bars. "Particularly the evidence that incriminates my almost-wife in the process. With that, and Christiana's plea to my parents, I think we can convince them that you were another of Joshua's victims."

"So, if I agree, what will happen to, me?" Natalia's eyes were filled with questions.

Christiana smirked. She had her hooked. "You'll come back into my employ under the pretenses that you're my Lady's Maid again. Along with those responsibilities, you'll train in the art of poison assassination and a few other weapons. You'll go on jobs with me or my tutor to get an understanding of what I do, until one day, you'll take over the jobs yourself while I keep control of the network and solicit the cases. I'll keep control of the business, you'll just be my new set of hands."

"And I'll only be sent after abusers? To help victims?"

"Yes. Maiden has a strict code, one I expect you to follow. But know this, Natalia, I don't trust you. The relationship we had, the woman you used to work for, is gone. You broke the bond we had, and it will take a lot to reform it."

Natalia's head hung low. "I know I did."

"So, if you come back to work for me, don't expect the kindhearted mistress you once had, because I can't promise that my feelings toward you won't show themselves most days."

Silence fell as Christiana waited for more questions, but Natalia's lips stayed sealed in a straight line. Her face was full of creases, her eyes downcast as she played with the ends of her knotted hair.

Christiana needed this just as much as Natalia did. She silently prayed as she watched, each second feeling like a lifetime as she waited for an answer.

"So." Christiana's patience wore out. "Do we have a deal?"

Natalia took a deep breath before looking straight into Christiana's eyes. "Yes."

Epilogue

*H*OURS PASSED, CHRISTIANA AND ZANDER had finalized all the details with Natalia about the new deal, promising she would be released from prison before they left on their honeymoon. They had destroyed evidence, making sure both Christiana and Natalia's names would stay spotless.

Everything was in place for the transition—for the new Midnight Maiden to start taking power.

With all of that behind her, Christiana let the matter escape her thoughts. She for once allowed herself to absorb the moment, to feel every second of the day as she prepared. Her afternoon was filled with laughter, love, and happiness; Isabelle, her mother, and Dorina keeping her company as she transformed from a beautiful Marchioness into a breathtaking bride.

Lorraine had outdone herself with Christiana's wedding gown, the soft tulle sleeves slipping over her arms as her maid fastened the many pearl buttons along her back. The misty gray bodice was decorated with delicate silver lace, the appliques spreading up along her chest and down each arm. The skirt was made of matching misty tulle, the layers falling perfectly with silver lace gently dissipating as it reached the bottom.

Her cheeks hurt from smiling, but she couldn't stop herself as the group of women gasped.

"You look stunning, my darling girl," Maria whispered, her eyes already hazy with tears.

"You look like a princess!" Isabelle giggled, her deep navy dress swishing at her feet. To celebrate Christiana's wedding, all three were wearing dark blue dresses in honor of the bride's mysterious color tones. Christiana wanted to laugh; all three of them preferred bright colors and looked a bit out of place in the dark gowns.

"No." Dorina shook her head, circling Christiana. "She looks like a Queen."

Christiana took a deep breath, her hands resting gently on her sternum as she stared at herself in the mirror. Every part of her was perfectly placed, down to the pearl-and-sapphire necklace and silvery gray highlight dusted on her cheeks. She held out her hand for her lipstick, gliding the dark burgundy tone across her lips to complete the look.

A gentle knock came from the open door. "I think there is one thing missing."

Penelope smiled at Christiana from the doorway, her delicate fingers wrapped around a mahogany box. She glided into the room, placing the box on the dressing table and removing its contents.

Christiana sucked in a breath as the Queen approached her. "I wore this tiara on my wedding day, and Lucian's mother wore it on hers. It is meant to be worn by the future Queen of Viri." Penelope placed the delicate crown on Christiana's head, the maid helping to secure it with pins into her twisted updo. It sat perfectly, the thin band peeking out from her dark reddish-brown hair. It was a delicate weave of silver handcrafted leaves with clusters of pearls and diamonds encrusting the entire length. It was the perfect size, pulling together Christiana's entire look without overwhelming it.

"Thank you, Penelope." Christiana whispered as the Queen folded her into a warm hug.

"I also came here to get you," Penelope pulled away, her hands still grasping Christiana's shoulders. "It's time for you to join my family."

An eruption of claps and laughter filled the room as Christiana's heart burst inside of her chest. She was ready for this moment, a moment that once seemed like a lifetime away. She was ready for this next step, her soul settled over the uncertainty of what her life would be from now on. She had been convinced for too long that she needed to make her life as the Maiden work with her future as a royal; she never realized that it was alright to take a step forward and leave something in the past, as long as she never forgot how it shaped her. She had accepted that, and she was ready to take what she had learned as the Midnight Maiden to become the Queen she was destined to be.

The walk to the Grand Ballroom was a blur, Christiana constantly surrounded by an outpouring of support as they took the path to her future. They arrived at the antechamber, Lucian the only one there standing with a proud smile on his face. Penelope gave Christiana's hand one last squeeze before she took her husband's outstretched hand.

Christiana stayed hidden in the corner as they made their entrance, the music of piano and lutes flowing through the doors as they opened and the King and Queen glided in with their heads held high.

"I love you, my dear." Maria gave her daughter one more tight squeeze and a kiss on the cheek before rushing to the door, her shoulders pulled back as she walked into the throng of guests.

Isabelle let go of Christiana's hand, practically floating as she took her place and entered. Dorina was the last to go, giving Christiana a quick wink before she made her graceful arrival. Christiana's heart swelled as she moved after them, the doors pulling open to reveal the crowd. Everyone stood in rows, their eyes descending on her. Usually she hated being the center of attention, but today she didn't care, because her eyes were focused ahead. She saw only him, his sapphire gaze pulling her forward.

Zander was a vision—Christiana's cheeks flushed at just the sight. His long, charcoal velvet coat hung to his knees, a dark silver filigree pattern decorating the entire length. His onyx vest and creme linen shirt hugged his body and melted into the matching black pants and boots. The entire look was completed by the small, silver circlet crown resting on his brow. He stood tall and proud, Rowan clapping him on the shoulder gently from his place next to his best friend.

Christiana would barely remember the ceremony and the pomp and circumstance that came with it. She wouldn't recall every word spoken, just the important ones. The moment that would be forever branded on her heart and soul was the moment she promised herself to Zander forever.

"Do you take his Highness, Prince Alekzander of Viri, to be your husband?" the officiant asked.

Christiana's smile had never beamed so brightly. "I do."

"And do you take the Most Honorable Marchioness Christiana of Tagri to be your wife?" the officiant went on.

Zander's grip tightened around her fingers, his sapphire eyes swirling. "I do."

An eruption of cheers and clapping vibrated off every surface of the room as Zander pulled Christiana toward him, sealing their vows with a kiss.

Acknowledgements

OW! I CANNOT BELIEVE WE ARE HERE ONCE again. Feels like only yesterday I was writing this section for Midnight Maiden. Well, here we go...

First, thank you to my amazing husband, Nathaniel. Who gives me strength and support when I need it. Who makes me laugh and smile when I'm particularly stressed. Who sends me music and random Reddit posts throughout the day just because. You are my partner, my Heart's Bond, and I love you for supporting me through these crazy dreams of mine. I love you always & forever.

To my wonderful family! My parents, Ellen and Mark, and my sister, Elizabeth (aka Dr. Liz). You celebrate every little moment with me. You push me to be my best and follow the passions that I have. You are the greatest family a girl could ask for.

To the best friends a girl could ask for, Alyson, Chelsea and Meaghan. All of you came into my life exactly when I needed it. Your support is unwavering and you make this journey so much more special than I ever knew possible. Thank you for always standing by my side when I needed it most.

To my wonderful and talented editors, Cassidy and Renee! Midnight Revenge and Christiana's journey would not be the same without you. I am not only lucky enough to have your support through the stressful journey that is editing, but to call you both my friends.

To the cover artist who makes me look good, Celin! I will forever feel lucky to have randomly come upon your Instagram profile because it changed my author journey forever. Your talent knows no bounds and I cannot wait for us to begin working on another project together.

To my spectacular beta team! To Alyson, Bailey, Brianne, Chloe, Gee, Jennifer, John, and Yasmine. You have all helped me develop Christiana's story to be the absolute best it can. I am forever grateful for the time you took to read her journey at such a rough stage and help me.

Special shoutout to my proofreaders! To Alyson, Kaysie, and Meaghan. Thank you for making sure that Christiana's story was as clean and ready for this day as possible!

To the indie author community, for making me feel welcome every day. You help me see that my dreams were possible. You have changed my life for the better. Special shout out to Brianne, Cassidy, Catherine, Dani, Leah, Lina, Renee, Miranda and Sydney.

Finally, to you wonderful readers. Thank you for spending time with Christiana. For listening to her story and watching her journey. Although it may not be over forever, this chapter of her story is over for now. She has grown, she has learned, and this part of her journey will always hold a special place in my heart. I hope that these two books have brought you hours of enjoyment. I hope you were able to escape through the pages and find yourself where you never thought possible.

Remember, you are in charge of your own strength, and no one can take it away from you.

Until next time, my dear readers!

*K*ATHRYN MARIE BEGAN WRITING AT THE young age of thirteen, when she was stuck in bed recovering from spinal surgery. Ever since then, she's loved creating stories and characters for others to enjoy. When she is not at work or busy writing in her home office, Kathryn can be found spending time with her wonderful husband or friends, experimenting with new makeup techniques, or watching reruns of her many beloved TV shows.

Follow Kathryn on social media for updates on all of her projects!

Website Newsletter: www.authorkathrynmarie.com
Instagram: @author_kathrynmarie
Facebook: @authorkathrynmarie
Twitter: @author_kathryn

CPSIA information can be obtained
at www.ICGtesting.com
Printed in the USA
BVHW072354160521
607527BV00001B/56

9 781734 832327